The Boy Who Hugs Trees

Dougie McHale

Azzie Bazzie
Books

Acknowledgments

Heartfelt thanks to Sheona, my wife, for her continued support, constant encouragement and proof reading. Thanks to Aaron McHale for his technical wizardry, formatting skills and design. Thanks to Tracy Watson, Angela Waddell, Stuart Mcainsh, and Kirstine Watson who gave me feedback on the novel. Thanks to Effrosyni Moschoudi for her guidance and advice from whom I have learnt so much and will always be grateful. Finally, I am indebted to Katrina Johnston for her editorial skills, advice and time.

Prologue

1994

Her movements are slow, but deliberate, as she places the teapot on the kitchen table. The low sun washes the room in an autumnal light. A soft illumination rejuvenates the floor tiles with a white shine that her years of monotonous cleaning have failed to produce. She moves a wisp of hair behind her ear; a weariness lodged in her chest escapes with a sigh.

As she positions the vase of flowers into the centre of the table, she touches the yellow petals between her forefinger and thumb, as an eruption of colour and perfumed scent declares its simplistic beauty before her pale and drawn face.

She stares out of the window. Unwashed weather-marks stain the glass. A creased smile curls the edge of her lips, as she feels a distinct urge to venture out and wade through the mounds of raked leaves, small mountain ranges, that wait by the shed to be collected.

Fallen leaves litter the hardened ground, a collage of brown and gold, crisp and undisturbed in the stillness. She looks at the trees that line the periphery of the garden. The air is motionless where a tapestry of leaves shimmer in a blaze of copper. In time, the light will fade and eventually soften and dull them. Birdsong reverberating in the garden is clouded by an ache in her forehead.

And then, as suddenly as it began, her reprieve is ended by a heaviness that is relentless.

Her eyes, set deep into hollow and blackened sockets, camouflaged by powder, are blind to the intense colour of this day.

She will arrive soon, she thinks.

She stretches her arm, retrieving teacups from a cupboard; it is an effort that affects every cell and bone. The crashing of china, disintegrating, like a nail bomb, drags her screaming from the dark cell she has crawled into. Panic creeps into the room. Cursing the small fragments, she frantically sweeps them into a cluster before they are disposed into a bin.

Placing a plucked cup on the table, she hears the inexorable crunch of footsteps on gravel.

'It's only me mum.' The voice moves through the house, like an intruder.

She is not ready for this. She clings to the cocoon she has inhabited. An anxious wave crashes into her, a foaming and riotous sea, as the invasive sounds from the hallway predict an imminent meeting. She slumps into a chair.

With a laborious effort, she hoists herself from the chair. A dignified posture erects itself, like a rejuvenated yet delicate flower. Standing, hands clasped, an anguished strain pulls at the lines that splay from her eyes. She tries to imagine an air of normalisation around her. She feels a dull sensation radiate from the nape of her neck. There is a panic to her breathing; the air is sucked from the room.

She is exhausted. She picks some fluff from her skirt and wonders why she feels self-conscious.

Her daughter's voice summons an urgency to compose herself. She runs her fingers through her hair and down her skirt; these adjustments are performed and driven by a need to gain an element of control and of self-preservation.

Georgia sweeps into the kitchen, cold air still wreathed around her, clinging to her clothes in defiance.

She kisses her mother. 'It's freezing out there. The traffic was awful. They've got it down to one lane again. They seem to dig up the road for fun. It makes you wonder who plans these things.'

'Would you like tea dear?'

'I'd love a cup,' Georgia says and smiles.

She gulps for air, steadies her hand and pours the steaming tea into a cup and then tentatively into another. It is a ritual she has repeated a thousand times but performed today as if it was her first. She has displayed an assortment of biscuits onto a floral plate.

'Would you like a biscuit?' she asks as an intoxicating clamour disturbs her thoughts. She must be in control, she tells herself. I will not allow this to beat me.

She sits down. A relief enters her, she assumes Georgia has not detected her unsteady demeanour, encouraging a short-lived smile that fades, rubbed out before maturity.

With a manicured finger, Georgia wipes a crumb from the corner of her polished lips and sips her tea.

'You're looking well, how are things at home?'

'Fine mum, Stephen gets home Saturday morning. He's been in London for a week this time.'

'How is the house coming on?' She plays with the handle of her teacup.

'Most of the work is finished, thank God. It's been like living on a building site. The decorators start on Monday. It'll be finished for Christmas. You must come and see the house once it's finished.'

She shifts in her chair. 'Yes, I'd like that.'

'In fact, mum, why don't you come for Christmas dinner?' Georgia says enthusiastically.

'That would be lovely.' She fiddles with her dress. She has not given Christmas a thought and is reluctant to pore over such a time.

'Are you sure mum? Don't tell me you've got other plans.' Georgia watches her interrogatively.

'No... not at all, I'd like that, really.' She forces a smile, appeasing the moment.

She notices a natural shine from her daughter's cheeks. Georgia has her father's eyes. It is more an observation than an attempt to study her. She takes a deep breath, she has rehearsed her words yet, in their moment of delivery, she feels vulnerable and scared. She must choose the appropriate time with caution.

She stares at her cup, the undrunk tea. Her throat is dry, uncomfortably tight.

'Mum, I've something to tell you.'

Georgia's voice pulls her back. 'Yes dear, what is it?'

'I've spoken to Stephen, and he doesn't mind if I tell you.' She is starting to smile. 'The thing is, well, as you already know, we've been trying for a baby... God, what I'm trying to say is I'm pregnant.'

There is an unexpected silence.

'Aren't you happy for me?' Georgia sounds like a wounded child. She gazes into her mother's eyes.

'Of course, I am. What wonderful news.'

She rises from her chair, scraping it over the floor and embraces her daughter.

'You are pleased for us... Aren't you?'

'Oh darling, of course, I am.'

The realisation that she will not see this child creeps upon her. She will not experience the transition from mother to grandmother. Tears well up in her eyes and cement the ache in the pit of her stomach. She is reluctant to release their embrace.

She remembers the courteous greetings, her nervous smile.

'How long?'

He moves in his chair, shifting his weight. His words enter her, like a hail of bullets. 'Between three... six months.'

'But I don't feel any pain...'

She cannot remember how she arrived home that day, yet, the numbness that inflicts her has remained ever since, taking root like a mature tree. There has been no release from its anaesthetizing presence, not even the revelation of a new life growing inside her daughter.

'Stephens convinced we're having a boy. He's already talking about taking him to watch Scotland play rugby and I'm only twelve weeks!'

'Your father was the same. It's a man thing.' She hesitates before running her fingers through her daughter's hair. It is unthinkable to neglect her joy.

'You will make a wonderful mother,' she says, retreating to her chair.

'I've had the best teacher,' Georgia says spontaneously. The words float over to her like feathers.

'Are you ok?' Georgia asks anxiously.

'Of course dear, just a little tired. I haven't been sleeping too well that's all. I'm happy for you both. It's not every day one becomes a grandmother.' She pauses before summoning a broad smile. In this instant, she knows the opportunity has escaped her, as she hastily pours another cup of dark tea, now watched by a contented Georgia.

She is shining with happiness, she tells herself.

'You must come to ours for Christmas mum,' Georgia insists.

'I will dear. Nothing could stop me.' She breathes deeply and gazes at the steam rising from her cup.

'Good, that's settled then,' Georgia says in an accomplished tone.

She composes herself. Most mothers would savour the news of a daughter's pregnancy with irrepressible excitement and expectation, yet there is a gulf between them. How can she tell Georgia now, today of all days? It has been a lifetime of waiting, her daughter's lifetime. Georgia has the right to know. She regrets the opportunities spurned, like today, another one slides from her, as does time, for now, her body is not her own. She has no influence over this foreign invader; it has entered her uninvited, spreading its destruction, like an oil slick.

She stands at the kitchen sink, looking at the trees, and it is as if she is seeing them for the first time. She scratches the palm of her hand, taming an irritable itch.

She notes that two wood pigeons sit side by side on a branch. She observes the way the light from the fading sun, throws changing and evolving shadows over skeletal branches and bark. She studies the way that thinner branches fan out from singular sturdy ones, like veins and capillaries. Long shadows shade grey slabs, grass, stones, and fallen plant pots, in projected patterns. As the light fades, she wills it to splay its luminance across her garden, so that she can witness, once more, the things she has spent a lifetime ignoring.

In this moment, she decides to open a box in her mind's eye, place her secret inside and tenderly close the lid and there it will remain, never to be released.

Chapter 1

2008

A Decision Made

Georgia awakes with the shrill of the alarm clock. Leaning over, she ends the incessant noise with a thud and sighs into the precipitous wall of silence.

She swings her legs from the sheets. The bedroom is warm, unlike the ice air around her shoulder, which pulls her to the surface during the night. The heating has been on for an hour, a reminder she has to change the timer on the boiler. She adjusted all the times on the clocks in the house when British summertime began, but reprogramming the timer on the heating system was a chore that never graduated to the top of her list or Stephens.

In the adjoining bathroom, she flicks a switch and dims the light, until it is soothing to her eye. She leans across the basin and yawns into the mirror, observing her reflection. Auburn hair falls around her shoulders, natural waves and curls that, as a teenager, she straightened each morning, frantic attempts that exasperated her fragile patience. Now thirty-five, she has called a truce long ago. She gently stretches the skin below her green eyes, where lines that have once been faint, now fan from the corners. Stephen says he hasn't noticed, but this does nothing to stem the surge of panic that grasps her.

Methodically, she massages her face and another involuntary yawn tests the acoustics of the room.

From the corner of her eye, she catches a dark object scurrying across the bathroom floor before coming to a sudden and motionless stop, as if contemplating a decision. Georgia recoils in horror, carefully stepping over it.

'Stephen, there's a spider in the bathroom, get up, get up.' She shakes his shoulder.

Stephen groans.

'Quickly get it before it disappears.' She shakes his shoulder more forcefully this time.

'Who's disappeared?'

'There's a spider in the bathroom.'

'Alright,' he mumbles.

Stephen shuffles unsteadily, a sleepy frown accompanying him to the bathroom. He tears a few sheets of toilet paper, crouches down, scoops up the spider and tosses it into the toilet.

Georgia flushes the toilet with a conspiratorial smile.

'Thank you.'

'And good morning to you too,' he grunts, disappearing into the bedroom.

She showers and changes into jeans and a red blouse. Before going downstairs, Georgia gently opens the door to her son's bedroom. Dylan is still sleeping, like an angel, she thinks.

She collects The Telegraph from the hall floor and begins the morning ritual of opening blinds, emptying the dishwasher and preparing breakfast - toast, corn flakes, coffee and orange juice, which she sets in their specific places on the kitchen table.

Next to the coffee maker, she notices two wine bottles, one empty and the other quarter full.

Stephen appears, freshly showered and shaved, wearing pin-striped trousers, a white shirt and gold tie. He sits down, heavily, takes a sip of coffee and scans the front page of the paper.

Georgia sits opposite him, cradling her cup.

'How many glasses did you have last night?'

'I don't know, three, four maybe, I wasn't counting.' He continues to look at the paper. 'It's not as if I'm driving. The taxi will be here at eight.' He checks his watch.

'What time did you come to bed?' she enquires.

'About one, I finished some paperwork and had a few glasses of wine, that's all. That reminds me, I may have to stay on in London, depending on how the meeting progresses. I'll stay at the flat. With luck, it should all be tied up within the week.'

Georgia sighs. 'Are you remembering Dylan's appointment today?'

'Of course honey, I'll phone you later, around five, if I get the chance.'

She sips her coffee and places the cup on the table, with a force that catches his attention.

'Look, I know I've been busy lately and neglected you both, but if this deal goes through…'

'God, Stephen.' She cuts him short. 'Your son's struggling at the school you insisted he attend because, how did you put it again… ah yes, its ethos would give him a solid grounding and prepare him for the realities of life. Well, the reality is, he's spent four years there and they still don't understand him and all you can think about is building bloody houses in Spain.'

'Look, within the next few days, I'll be able to spend quality time with you both,' he says insistently.

'You've always said there's nothing wrong with him, you keep making excuses for him. You're hiding from your own son, Stephen. You've always been in denial.' She turns her head coldly.

'This isn't the right time Georgia. We can discuss this when I get back.'

'Is there any point?'

He stands up abruptly. 'Apparently not. I need to get ready.'

Georgia frowns. 'That's your answer to everything, isn't it Stephen? Ignore it and hope it goes away. This isn't just going to go away. I'm taking him out of that school no matter what the outcome of this meeting is. I've made up my mind. I'm going to Corfu. We'll stay at the house while you do whatever it is you have to, to build your precious houses.'

Agitated, Georgia flicks a strand of hair from her face. Stephen sits down heavily.

'This isn't the right time Georgia, this project will take months. I've already told you that. My suite at the hotel has been blocked booked. We agreed I'd fly home at weekends and anyway I'll be in Palma, you'll be in Corfu, for God's sake.' Irritated, he scratches his chin.

'I've been thinking about this for days. Dylan knows the house and the area well; it's like a second home to him. We need a fresh perspective. I'm going to advertise for a home tutor,' she says firmly.

'Don't you think you're taking this just a bit too far?'

'I've already worked out the details and I'm quite capable of interviewing people Stephen, I have previous experience, remember.'

'I'm not saying you're not capable, but Christ Georgia, it's a big commitment moving to another country, even just for a short time, never mind taking on a complete stranger teaching Dylan. I'm surprised at you. There's the matter of where would this teacher stay? And what would you do?'

'The house is big enough. It hasn't been decorated for years, not since mum spent her summers there. I'm going to give it a makeover, it's long overdue.'

'Ok.' He nods in a weary resignation, sensing defeat. 'I can see you've given this a lot of thought. Look, if this is what you really want, then I won't try to change your mind, but remember this is not a holiday for me, I'll be working most days.'

'Nothing new there,' Georgia frowns, her tone fused with sarcasm.

'It's a major investment for the company. It's taken months of preparation; you know how hard I've worked on this. Most of the plots are sold. We're talking millions.'

'We're comfortable enough compared to most people. Why does it always come down to money with you?'

He is in the hallway now, collecting his suit jacket, his laptop bag and a small luggage bag. The doorbell rings, to Georgia's annoyance.

'That'll be the taxi,' Stephen calls. He strides towards the front door with an air of relief.

'Aren't you going to say goodbye to your son?'

She is in the hallway now. She catches her reflection in the mirror.

Stephen swings the door open in a purposeful manner.

'Ah, Miss Devlin,' he says deflated, placing his bag down. He scratches his chin; the sight of the old woman on the doorstep drains his urgency.

Georgia stands beside him, unable to repress a satisfied smile. 'Hello, Miss Devlin.'

'Oh, I'm sorry for calling at such an early hour,' Miss Devlin says apprehensively. 'The thing is, Fluffy has been out all night and I'm worried something terrible may have happened to her. You see, I let her out every evening at six; she does her business and is back in by ten past six. But, last night she didn't come home at all and I've been at my wit's end with worry.' She wipes a tear-stained eye with her handkerchief.

'At least it won't shit in our garden again,' Stephen whispers in Georgia's ear.

Georgia glares at him and the weight of her scorn makes him lean back.

'What was that dear?' Miss Devlin says, bending forward and turning her good ear to Stephen.

Georgia touches the old woman's arm. 'He says we haven't seen it sit in the garden.' She emphasises the word *'sit.'*

'I'm sure she'll turn up,' Georgia raises her voice. 'What do you think dear?' She turns to Stephen.

'Oh, I'm sure you're right. It'll probably turn up today.'

'You will call round if you see her?'

Georgia nods. 'Of course, try not to worry,' she says soothingly.

A black cab draws up.

'Ah, that's the taxi.'

Stephen retrieves his bags and kisses Georgia on the cheek. 'Kiss Dylan goodbye for me, I'll phone you later.'

Stephen waves from the taxi as it moves off. Georgia can hear movement from upstairs.

'I'd better see to Dylan.'

'Of course, dear. I'll check the garden one more time.'

Miss Devlin turns and shuffles down the path.

Chapter 2

The Interview

Adam Newman sits in a large room with high ceilings. His eyes run over the solid oak flooring, where sways and tails, around a large bay window, splay light onto its grain. The walls, coated in warm magnolia, blend with the stone hearth of the fireplace. He sits on one of two bespoke sofas, one cream and leather, the other striped fabric. A flat-screen TV sits perched above the fireplace, and opposite, a large gold-framed mirror magnifies the depths of the room. In front of him, flowers in a glass vase sit on top of an oak coffee table. His eyes pause on a framed photograph, taken in a studio, and professionally orchestrated. The family are sitting on the floor, relaxed poses, but staged.

Adam wonders if he has made the right decision. He puts this down to unaccustomed nerves, as he has not applied for a job in years and this does not feel like a typical job interview.

The highly polished door opens to reveal Georgia carrying a tray. With a composed smile, she places the tray on the table and sits opposite Adam. She pours dark brown coffee and invites him to take his own milk from a small white jug. He politely declines an offer of assorted biscuits.

Georgia's head bows slightly, self-contained in her thoughts; she consults the sheaves of paper that sit on her lap. He gazes at her and then looks out of the window.

'Shall we begin Mr Newman?'

'Please call me Adam.'

'I'd prefer to keep this formal.' Solidity cases her words, yet he senses an aura of vulnerability around her, that seems to leave an impression upon her skin.

When she opened the front door and welcomed him out of the rain, he trained his eye over her slender figure and the sweep of her hair, as she showed him to the front room, and then again, he could not help himself, when she left to fetch the coffee. Even now, sitting opposite her, his eyes pause upon her and he considers that image.

'Thank you for coming. As you know, I'm interviewing for a suitable candidate who'll tutor my son. To let you know the history that has led you here, school hasn't been a pleasant experience for Dylan. In the world of private education, there is no room for compromise, in his case anyway. His particular school didn't accommodate him well, nor was it compatible with his needs. This may seem a biased view, but it's one I'm afraid has developed through bitter experience. Dylan's wellbeing is my only concern,' Georgia insists.

Adam nods.

She continues business-like. 'As you're now aware Mr Newman, the post is quite unconventional, in that it involves the successful candidate moving to and living in Corfu. During the latter part of his time at school, Dylan was becoming increasingly anxious and stressed and moving to Corfu, I believe, will be a therapeutic experience for him. It's a place he knows well, filled with wonderful memories. He obviously needs to continue with his education, therefore I need to find a suitable and qualified tutor.' Georgia pauses before continuing. 'At present, Dylan doesn't know about this process. As you may appreciate, he associates the house with fun and happiness and certainly not school lessons, so it will be a time of uncertainty for us all. Change, at the best of times, can be a challenge for him. So, I need him to get used to the idea that while we're there, he'll be continuing his education and that a new person will come into his life facilitating this.'

Georgia glances at Adam. 'I'm aware that part of the motivation for most of the people who apply for this job, will be the attraction of working and living on a Greek island, I understand that, but the focus must be about educating Dylan. There are contractual obligations.' She delivers the words as the future employer she will be. She glances at the papers on her lap.

'I don't doubt your competence and capabilities, your references and colleagues at the university speak highly of you. Therefore, I'm interested in why a man of your standing, in your chosen profession, would apply for this kind of undertaking?' If the truth be told, Georgia is intrigued.

Adam's face does not register it, but her directness surprises him. He ponders the question.

'It's not a decision I've taken without giving it a lot of thought. To let you know, I'm weighing up my options. I'm aware of my responsibilities. I've gone over the contract and job description so, in that regard, I'm well informed and under no illusions concerning the demands that such a job will undoubtedly entail. My motives for applying are simple. I'm at a crossroad in my career. I need a change. I've deliberated on this for some time now and the timing just seemed right. I need a challenge, something new and at the end of the day I suppose I'd like to make a difference.'

'A difference.' Georgia studies him. 'What kind of difference?'

'To your son. As you've pointed out, it seems his educational experience has left much to be desired. I'd like to change that if given the opportunity.'

She consults her prearranged questions. 'Mr Newman, what qualifies you for this position?'

Adam trained as a teacher, then after a few years, he specialised in teaching children with special needs. By then, he developed an interest in autism and undertook further studies, a postgraduate diploma and then a Masters in autism. He moved to Manchester and took up a post at The Abbey School, a centre of excellence for pupils with autism and moderate learning disabilities. After several fulfilling years, he returned to Scotland and taught at a residential and day school. Eventually, he moved into research at Glasgow City University and lectured in autism. His speciality led him to be invited to join Glasgow's NHS autism diagnostic team.

'Don't you feel overqualified for this position Mr Newman?'

'You can never be overqualified. I might have a lot of experience working with children who have special needs, but I'd never say that learning stops just because there are letters after your name.'

Georgia smiles for the first time. 'What are your interests? Do you have any hobbies?'

'I do, I like to read, fiction mainly when I'm not reading about the Roman Empire. William Boyd is probably the author I most admire. When time allows, I like to travel. I love most things Italian and I've got a consuming interest in ancient Rome... books, films, documentaries, anything about the Roman Empire, really. I know it's sad, but there you are, it's out now. I believe that our knowledge and understanding of the past helps to create a better future. Well, that's how I justify my obsession with Rome.' Adam smiles.

'There's nothing wrong in being passionate about history.' She runs her fingers through her hair; it is an involuntary motion, a ritual within her conversation. 'This is a bit awkward, but as you know, I've stated on the application that I'd prefer those who applied were not married or in a relationship. I know it's not politically correct. I'm asking everyone the same question. I need someone who doesn't have the emotional ties that would force them prematurely back to the U.K. By asking such a question, and I believe I have to, I'm implying that it's obviously imperative that you're able to fulfil the contractual agreements. After all, I don't want to end up in the unpleasant situation where I'm left in Corfu with no one to provide for my son's education.'

For a moment he hesitates. 'I'm a safe bet there. I wouldn't be running back to Glasgow. I'm not married, although I've been told I'm married to my work.' He smiles confidently.

'But not anymore?' Georgia raises an eyebrow, creasing her forehead.

'I like to think of it as a period of separation.' He regrets his reference to work. 'It's not a permanent arrangement. As you know, I've been given a sabbatical year from the university.'

'The contract is for three months, but I reserve the right to terminate it without notice if need be. Is that agreeable to you?'

'Yes.'

She leafs through the papers on her lap.

'As I said, your references are exceptional. However, to be honest with you, when I first began this process, rightly or wrongly, I imagined the applicants to be female, it never occurred to me that a man would apply.'

Adam looks down at his cup, contemplating the sudden awkwardness, the silence. Again, she runs her fingers through her hair.

Her face is suddenly flushed. Finally, she begins to speak, 'The successful applicant will be spending a great deal of time with my son, in another country, so in that respect, the character of that person is of paramount importance to me. After all, they will only be offered the position if Dylan accepts them and after the necessary disclosures are verified.'

Adam nods.

'And for this reason, I'll initially be selecting two applicants. There will be a period for Dylan to meet with them and spend time together. The first meeting will be short, just an introduction really, and for each subsequent one, the length of time will increase. I suspect this will take a few weeks and then we'll be in a position to decide. Dylan's opinions will influence my choice.'

Georgia refers to a photograph of Adam clipped to his application. 'Dylan will need to know what the person looks like before they meet. It will be an anxious time for him.'

'And for you also, I suspect?'

'Yes,' she says softly.

For the second time, there remains a silence in between their exchanges.

'Do you have any questions, Mr Newman?'

'Can I ask about Dylan?'

'Of course.' She nods.

'You said that this process will be difficult for Dylan. As someone who doesn't know him, how would I know?'

Georgia pauses. Having to articulate Dylan's most intricate feelings to a stranger suddenly makes the process feel personal. For a moment she feels uneasy, no one else has enquired about this. No, one other had skirted the issue. Was that their failing or was it his? She decides on the former.

'You know there is something not right when Dylan is quiet and he's been in your company for a while. Usually, during such times, he will stare, his expression blank. I think he is trying to make sense of what's in his head or what he is feeling at that particular moment. At other times, he may become erratic and talk continually, never with you, but at you. Sometimes, he can become so distressed that it's as if he shuts down and blocks out the world around him, but that's rare. He's also very sensory and that can be difficult especially in social situations as you would expect.'

'You just mentioned Dylan being sensory. I often find that a child's sensory difficulties can be underestimated, especially in relation to behaviour. What is Dylan sensitive too?'

'He has difficulty with noise, especially a noise that is unexpected. He covers his ears because certain sounds hurt him. He tolerates sounds better when he has initiated them. Also, certain fabrics and textures irritate him to the extent that he won't wear certain clothes or eat certain foods. These were particular issues at school where he was perceived to be a bad child... a disruptive child.'

'From my experience, I've found that tactile and auditory sensitivity can limit classroom performance, and in some cases, contribute to academic underachievement. That's why it's crucial to have the appropriate strategies in place that cater to the individual's needs.'

Georgia nods in agreement. 'Unfortunately, his school didn't subscribe to your theory, hence the reason you're here and we are embarking on this course of action. I feel that, sometimes, Dylan's sensory sensitivities can be more of a problem, to Dylan anyway, than his difficulty with social communication and interaction. I'd be interested to know your thoughts?'

Adam hasn't anticipated this form of detailed questioning. 'Well, in the academic world, research has highlighted that up to eighty percent of people with autism may demonstrate behaviours that are related to impaired sensory modulation, things like rocking backwards and forwards and spinning. I've even witnessed children cover their ears in reaction to a level of noise that I hadn't even noticed. Some may not even respond to their name or environmental cues, so you can imagine how things like social activities, play, self-care skills and even learning can be compromised. So, in answering your question, I believe sensory processing difficulties can impact greatly upon an individual's social and emotional behaviours and this is pertinent, especially when considering the learning environment.'

'How would you approach Dylan's sensory issues?'

'I'd use known strategies that work for him. I'd be guided by a support plan or from yourself.'

Georgia leans forward, encouraged to talk more freely.

'I need to be flexible when considering family activities; this involves accommodating Dylan's needs. It's a lot easier at home, his sensory needs and routines are predictable so we know how they impact upon his behaviour. We create routines that Dylan knows will be predictable in various situations. We experience problems when we're out. As you know social environments are less predictable. So we try to plan in advance whenever possible. The order of the day is predictability and routine. When I'm out with Dylan, I need to be aware of the environment, it's a constant process, but you can't always predict when there's going to be a loud noise, a light that's too bright or lots of people around. In such situations what would you suggest Mr Newman?'

'That's when you need reactive strategies, so you're prepared as best you can be. You can't always legislate for what's about to happen but knowing how to react, when it does, may make it less of a stressful situation for Dylan.'

Georgia smiles, she is indeed impressed. Adam is the last to be interviewed, and he has proved his suitability during the interview. His qualifications and experience set him apart from the other candidates. However, he is a man, and this is a complication.

How would Stephen react to a man teaching Dylan? More importantly, Georgia speculates, how would he react to a man, a stranger, living in the house?

'Oh, I almost forgot.' She holds up an A4 document.

'This is Dylan's communication passport. I'm sure you're familiar with them, it details his likes, dislikes, what makes him upset, happy, that sort of thing. Only those chosen as the final two will get a copy.'

She stands and composes herself.

'Well Mr Newman, I think we've covered everything. I'll only contact you if you've been successful. Thank you for coming.'

Adam rises from the chair and extends his hand. She shakes it gently, as her fragrance moves across space between them. Her hand is warm to the touch.

'Thank you,' Adam says and then Georgia leads him to the front door.

Chapter 3

A New Rhythm

Georgia found the whole process of interviewing eight candidates exhausting and draining. During those four days, she often doubted her self-assurance. Was this the right thing to do? The reasoning she formed when embarking on this venture was built upon the realisation that Dylan's school could not be thought of as a permanent arrangement due to the anxiety it provoked in him; therefore, his educational needs would be best served elsewhere.

During the interviews, Georgia did not mean to be seen as formidable. She wanted to portray a business-like exterior, yet in the cold light of the last few days, she often felt swallowed in a quicksand of self-doubt. She felt vulnerable and at times uncomfortable. Was she making the right decision? There were moments when the conciliatory remarks of Dylan's guidance teacher, patronising and worthless, reverberated in her head, reinforcing her belief that by sending Dylan to that school they had set him up to fail. No, they failed him.

Would Dylan cope with the changes that would be enforced upon him? They had stayed in the house on family holidays. However, this would not be viewed by Dylan as a holiday when there would be daily lessons, with someone he would regard as a stranger. There would be so many changes. None of this was ordinary. She must prepare him, gradually, yes; it could be done with the correct preparation.

Stephen's initial reluctance to subscribe to her plans minimised his involvement to a grudged endorsement. Would she be feeling any different now if he had been more supportive, active and involved? His stubbornness to invest any of his time in the planning and organising of the interview process infuriated her and spurred her with the determination to give life to the idea and see it through to completion. Her focus in all of this was her son, not a preoccupation with property development. The opportunity had presented itself at a favourable time and Dylan's best interests stirred her into an unquestionable conviction, a crusade even, and Stephen's grudged blessing was incidental.

Was this about Georgia and her relationship with Stephen? Had it permeated their weaknesses as a couple and exposed that Georgia's sense of identity had deserted her. Georgia once had a rewarding career, she organised and managed, she made decisions that affected lives, that influenced outcomes. Was she trying to show to Stephen, and ultimately prove to herself, that the attributes and skills she once projected, on a day-to-day basis, were still as natural to her as breathing?

What of her motives, did she continue to view them with clarity? They were discernible to her because Dylan was at the centre of every decision she made, yet, as she poured over each detail, she became encouraged by the prospect of escaping another unfulfilled Scottish summer and absorbing herself in her project of giving the house a much-needed makeover. The thought of it and the practicalities stirred a nervous excitement and invigorated a sense of purpose she had not contemplated for years. Her scales of priority were maybe no longer weighed towards the concerns of Dylan's education. Her move to Corfu was now also a pretext to fulfil what had been missing in her life and by breathing life into the prospect of leaving behind her everyday existence, cracks in her contentedness had emerged from the shadows. She yearned for a new rhythm to her life.

And now it was time to reflect upon those she had interviewed. She had envisaged set criteria, professional and personal, that the successful candidate would need to fulfil, surpass even. However, such perfection did not reveal itself within the personal qualities of those she had seen. Academic qualifications and experience were only part of the jigsaw she had planned. Now she had disentangled Dylan from the education establishment and taken responsibility for his future education, her standards and virtues needed to be reflected in those who sat opposite her. At times, during the process, she felt she was the one having to prove and justify herself, but what had become tangible was the fact that she had started a process that invigorated her.

She had a purpose that served her instincts as a mother and as a woman. To her mind, there existed no conflict there. Such things were the building blocks she identified with, and, for that reason, she would continue what she had started.

Chapter 4

Passengers

Adam enters the block of flats, where the stench of urine clings to the air, like an affliction. He locates the appropriate door and knocks, willing it not to open. The door squeaks on its hinges, revealing a small but portly woman, underdressed in a nightgown, that has seen its natural colour fade to a dull grey, interspersed with islands of encrusted stains.

'Have those wee bastards been pissing on the walls again? It'll be the last thing they ever dae if I get ma hands on them,' she croaks, craning her head out of the door.

'Eh hello Mrs MacAndrew, I'm Adam. I've come about beginning the assessment of your son.'

He lifts his identity badge.

'Oh Aye, you're from the autism team. I forgot you were coming the day,' she says, without looking at the photograph. 'That wee psycho of a hamster is on the loose again, it's behind the fridge this time. If it wisnae for Liam being fond of the wee shite, the cat would be shitting hamster the night.'

'Look if it's a bad time I could come back when it's more convenient,' he says, almost apologising.

'No, you're fine. In you come. I was only watching the telly before psycho got oot the cage.'

Once in the dim hallway, Adam notices three layers of wallpaper flaking from the walls, like peeling skin. Small mountains of empty cardboard boxes sit against the wall.

Mrs MacAndrew gestures to the boxes. 'Sorry about the mess, the boxes are Liam's, he gets them from the Spar shop and makes things out of them. Would you like a tea or a coffee?' She disappears into the kitchen.

'Eh no thanks, I've been drinking coffee all morning,' he lies.

'Ah, the perks oh the job eh… well, you'll no mind if I have one then.'

'Go ahead, I'm fine.'

'Just take a seat in the living room. I'll no be long.'

He moves into the room. It is small and overcrowded with dark furniture. Stale cigarette smoke clings to the air, a stubborn smell, that he imagines infesting the fibres of his clothes. He moves aside a torn copy of The Sun newspaper, to make space, as both sofas are littered with empty crisp packets, discarded chocolate wrappers, empty cartons of juice, various magazines and a chipped plate that still has the remains of what he considers to be toast and beans. The dark thick pile carpet has evidently not seen the suction from a vacuum cleaner in some time and to his astonishment, he seems to be surrounded by dolls of every description.

A shelf runs the length of one wall, where he counts twenty dolls sitting in a row, staring through marble eyes at a 52' TV screen, their reflections eerily mirrored along with Jeremy Kyle.

Eventually, Mrs MacAndrew shuffles into the room, her slippers scrape the carpet as she carries her coffee. Adam drags his gaze from the dolls.

'Ah, you've seen ma collection then. It's a hobby o mine,' she proudly proclaims. 'There's more in the bedroom if you'd like to see them. I've collected them for years. Everyone has a name ye ken.'

She laboriously lowers herself into the sofa which creaks in protest under her weight. As she proceeds to light a cigarette, Adam notices an overflowing ashtray on a small side table, its surface dusted in small islands of ash. The only window in the room remains closed, as the oppressive air inhabits the room, like a third person. His stomach sinks and he shudders at the prospect of having to go through the assessment and, in retrospect, he wishes he had offered this woman an appointment in his clinic. However, he is eager to escape the small confines of his office and lecture rooms at least a few times in the week, and this offered the perfect opportunity.

'Did you need Liam to be here son? He'll no be home from school until four.'

'No that's ok. Today's just about asking you lots of questions about Liam that you've probably been asked a hundred times before, but I'm afraid it's essential for the assessment.'

'That's alright then. If he was here, we widnae get a minutes peace.'

The assessment lasts almost an hour, in which time, four more cigarettes are smoked and another coffee drank. Adam has collated a plethora of valuable information about Liam, due to the insatiable talent Mrs MacAndrew has for talking, which only ceases when she sucks on her cigarette, at short interspersed intervals.

Relieved, Adam says his farewell and leaves the flat, walking into a constant drizzle of rain. It's a relief to be outside and as he heads towards his car, the smell of stale smoke clings to his clothes, like an intrusive layer of damp skin. At least their next meeting will be in the confines of the diagnostic clinic and he wonders how Mrs MacAndrew will cope with not being able to smoke for three hours. He imagines her cumbersome frame heading for the exit at every available opportunity determined to gratify her craving.

***

He arrives late, apologising and blaming his sense of timing.

'We've ordered some starters to share,' Chloe says, touching his arm.

Two bottles of red and two of white wine sit waiting to be poured. A jug of water is passed around the table's occupants and only Chloe refuses.

'I've ordered a diet coke,' she says, smiling at Adam.

He explains that he has been browsing in Waterstones and hadn't realised the time.

The Italian restaurant serves as a favourite haunt for the university teaching staff, an established venue for birthday celebrations and staff leaving meals.

Adam gazes around the table and is met by the familiar faces which have defined his years of teaching at the university; Professor Bill Waters, engrossed in discussion with Charlotte Hays, whose skin, suffused in a pink complexion, seems to stain her face, no matter the weather or temperature of a room. Arthur Waters pours red wine into Jackie Galbraith's glass, overriding her gesture he has poured enough. Dr Sally Williams, fresh from a conference in London, where she presented a research paper on, *'Generalising the social skills of children and young people with autism.'* peers over her glasses and acknowledges Adam with a smile as the starters arrive. Two waiters hand out plates of Bruschetta with cherry tomatoes, roasted red peppers and sautéed mushrooms, Apulian sautéed mushrooms and spinach, Antipasto platter, meatballs, ravioli with balsamic brown butter and mixed olives.

'Just place them in the middle of the table,' Arthur instructs. 'We're all going to share,' and with a grandiose gesture of his hand, he booms, 'Tuck in everyone.'

'How did the interview go?' Chloe asks Adam, as she places a crisp white napkin on her lap. 'I must admit, your decision has taken everyone by surprise.'

'As far as I can tell, it went fine,' Adam offers.

'And it took place in a house, that must have been odd,' she says.

'No. Not really. It didn't feel like an interview. The husband wasn't there, he works in London, involved in property developing, something like that. He's building houses in Majorca I think, but that's not where I'll be going. The job advert stated that it involved going abroad, I didn't know where until the interview. They have a house in Corfu. That's where I'll go if I get the job.'

'Corfu, wow you lucky devil.' Chloe's eyes are wide with excitement.

'It's not as if I'm going on a holiday,' he says, almost apologetically.

Chloe sighs. 'Imagine wakening up to the sun every morning.'

'Is it too late to apply? I fancy a bit of the sun myself.' Sally smiles over her wine glass.

'I still can't believe that you're leaving us,' Chloe says.

'It's only for a year. You'll be surprised how quick that will go. The teaching job's for three months and anyway, I don't think I'm in the running.'

'What makes you say that?' Chloe leans her head towards him.

'She made it quite clear her preferred choice would be female.'

'Then why did she offer you an interview in the first place? That doesn't seem fair. Rather rude actually, making you go all the way to Edinburgh just to tell you you're the wrong sex.'

Chloe rants on and he listens half-heartedly, thinking of the day before, in Edinburgh, answering Georgia's questions, qualifying his interest in Dylan. She told him the absent husband would visit them in Corfu, he doesn't even know where in Corfu that will be; only the successful candidate would be told. This was all he knew, it was not much to go on, to base three months of living and teaching in another country.

Chloe is still talking. 'That's sex discrimination, Adam.'

He shakes his head and smiles. 'It wasn't like that.'

'Then how was it?' Sally inquires.

'There was a sense of apology about her. Anyway, I got the distinct impression she was more interested in why I applied.'

'So she was suspicious of your motives, given your position and background,' Chloe says, dabbing her mouth with a napkin. 'And what are your motives Adam?' she asks.

'I don't know, call it a midlife crisis.' He laughs.

'At thirty-three!' A cynical smile bares Chloe's brilliant white teeth.

'A few weeks ago, after a lecture, I noticed a job advert on one of the information boards to tutor a thirteen-year-old boy with Asperger's syndrome. It stipulated that, if interested, you needed to live abroad for three months. I phoned and was e-mailed the job application that evening.'

'She was keen,' Chloe says.

'That must have been weird, I mean, applying for a job like that out of the blue,' Jackie Galbraith says, attempting to defuse Arthur Waters' unwanted attention.

'I felt excitement and a sense of quietude all at the same time.' He contemplates that it has been some time since he has experienced similar feelings whilst lecturing.

The main courses arrive along with instantaneous sounds of approval.

'How did the visit go at the MacAndrews? Did you feel you were being watched?' Sally inquires, with a teasing smile.

'Ah, the dolls.' Adam shrugs and then smiles. 'It went well. The diagnostic assessment is next week.'

'This will be your last clinic. How does it feel?'

'Oh, I don't know ask me when it's over. I suppose I'll have mixed feelings. You know my work's important to me as is everyone around this table.'

'I should think so too,' Claire injects, draining her glass.

Sally looks at him suspiciously. 'So, why are you leaving us?'

'It's not just about teaching anymore, is it?' he says petulantly. 'That part of the job seems devalued now. I hate the politics, the budget constraints, policies, legislation and recommendations that offer the earth, but few are worth the paper they're written on. I used to be an idealist, but you can only be kicked so many times. I've lost that passion, you know, when you wake in the morning and it drives you forward. That has slowly drained from me.' He thought what that meant. 'I need another challenge.'

Adam was never one to lambast Monday mornings and the start of the working week. It was never just a job, it was a vocation, and it was all he had ever done. He felt privileged; he worked in an environment that inspired achievement and motivation. Adam was never one of those who felt they had wasted years in a job they hated. He did not get 'that Friday feeling' on the last working day of the week, work was not a shackle over his wakening hours. Adam cannot pinpoint with any accuracy when that changed.

'Do you think you'll find it teaching this young boy?' Sally scrutinises him, looking over her glass.

'I honestly don't know.' Adam shrugs. 'Look, we all know what needs to be achieved to gain real meaningful change and improve autism services. We need to empower families by consulting them on their views, they need to be an integral part of developing and planning services. We need to make access to resources easier, improve the quality of services and make families equal partners in creating services. I'm sick of the amount of reports and papers that are churned out by government, advocating this action plan and that recommendation, spat out like a production line and yes when implemented, some have had a real lasting impact on the lives of families, but too much of it is just a paper exercise. Well, I have been to that gym, bought the membership, but I won't be renewing it. You can have all the action plans and recommendations in the world, but in a climate where local authorities have to deal with the reality of reduced budgets, then that shifts their priorities.'

'But surely that's the challenge,' Sally says, trailing a finger over the rim of her glass. 'We all acknowledge the lack of money, and going by current trends, it will get worse, but I believe that we have an unprecedented opportunity to design services and support these families from a starting point that will need cooperation and effective partnership between the services and agencies involved with a child. It will provide the impetus, if it's grasped, to implement approaches that place the choice of control and funding at the centre of the families we work with. It should offer the prospect of early prevention and intervention for these families, ensuring that service delivery is well designed and cost-effective relative to the need of families and,' she leans forward as if to give more weight to her point. 'It should police that resources are being used more efficiently.'

'That's my point,' says Adam, waving his fork. 'There's enough evidence in journals and research papers that promote the effectiveness of early intervention, but due to the already limited and draining resources of current service provision, it's not provided in a proactive way. Then when families find themselves in crisis, the shit hits the fan, commissioners and managers climb down from their ivory towers and demand answers to why was it not prevented in the first place, who is supposed to be supporting the family? Who is responsible?'

'I understand that, but the challenge is to work with families with the limited resources we have and collect the evidence that identifies and strengthens our arguments and highlights the failings and the common themes. Services need to be responding to these families needs in a way that is flexible and coordinated.'

He nods in agreement, a simple gesture that acknowledges defeat, or his lack of enthusiasm for an argument.

'I can see I'm not going to win this one.'

'Then you will stay with us?' Sally tilts her head.

Adam laughs. 'It wasn't that convincing.'

'Well if you get the job, you must visit Professor Tzakis Konstantinos, at Ionian University in Corfu? He's a wonderful man and eminent academic. He studied here in Glasgow, we went to university together. It was his first time abroad and a few of us took him under our wings. We've been good friends ever since.'

The restaurant pulses to the dance of conversation and laughter. Another two bottles of wine arrive; a smiling waiter asks if everything is ok with their meals. The lights dim and a second waiter brings a cake, crowned with candles. A chorus of 'Happy Birthday' punctuates the air, an unmelodic crescendo that makes Jackie Galbraith flush with embarrassment as she becomes the centre of attention.

Once everyone says their goodbyes, Adam decides to walk home. He lives only a few streets away and the walk will clear his head. When he first moved to Glasgow, he found the grey buildings intimidating, unwelcoming even;

now they were just part of the landscape he moved through. A rain shower has just fallen and is in the throes of dying out when he crosses the street. The tarmac glistens in streetlights and headlamps as capacious light glows from the windows of shop fronts and bars. He is drawn to a small cafe bar and once inside orders an Americano (coffee.) He sits at a table next to the window, staring at his reflection and not for the first time, his solidity of purpose arouses a disconcerting thought that unsettles him. Ever since the interview, Adam has ruminated on the absence of Georgia's husband. If he had been in a similar situation, given the gravity of their endeavour, he would have interrogated each interviewee as if his life depended on it. There would have been no sense of resignation, that work commitments would restrict his involvement. Yet, this was precisely the impression he received, even though there was no intention on Georgia's part to convey this during their meeting. Also, Georgia's frankness, concerning her preferred gender, has embroidered doubt on the fabric of his optimism that seems to fade from him with each passing day.

Three young mothers huddle around a table, each with an infant strapped into a high chair, around them, their abandoned buggies sag with coats, shopping bags and toys, like desolate pack horses on a mountain trek. An old couple abandon their half-drunk cups of tea and walk towards the door with lethargic, arthritic movements. Leaning on a carved walking stick, the man holds the door open for his wife, who negotiates the step onto the pavement with slow deliberate motions.

Adam observes this spectrum of human life where joy, happiness, contentment, love, loss, heartache, even desolation will have shaped each milestone of each individual's journey and it occurs to him that we are all passengers moving through time from one thought, one emotion and one destination to another.

Chapter 5

It's all about the Money

Stephen sits behind a large desk in his London office, its opulent surroundings reflecting his success. Two Apple screens face him and from a silver-framed photograph, Georgia and Dylan smile at him. Chris Hastings reclines on a black leather sofa, immaculately dressed in a made to measure Savoy Row three-piece suit. A pallor crosses Stephen's face, he shakes his head.

'Look it's come as a bit of a shock, I can see that and I should've consulted you way before now, but remember Stephen, this deal is just like any other, it's all legitimate; the contracts, the land purchase, the planning permission, the contractors, it's put together following every detail and letter of Majorcan law. You know how precise I am,' Chris says, trying to put Stephen at ease.

Stephen frowns. 'But your moral compass obviously doesn't subscribe to the letter of the law; it dances to the tune of a South American drug cartel.'

Stephen stands and paces around the office. He walks towards the window and looks down onto the street below. It is a normal scene, one that has become familiar to him; buses, taxis, cars, faceless pedestrians, just another normal day. Yet, the revelation that Cesar Ramos, the businessman behind the Spanish investment side of the project, is a major player in the trafficking of drugs from South America, exploded any remnants of normality this day had offered.

Cesar Ramos' company is based in Madrid and Palma, specialising in golf, spa clubs and luxury homes developments in mainland Spain and the Balearic Islands.

'Fuck, what's going on Chris?' Stephen cannot curtail his surprise and shock.

'Look we've all been working on this project for months. Cesar was offering to go 50/50 on the whole project. His companies are legitimate, you know that Stephen. He counts politicians and bankers amongst his friends. In

Cesar's world he's just expanding, all he is doing is gaining extra capital to finance his business deals for his legal companies.' Chris tries to sound convincing.

'Don't kid yourself, Chris. That kind of money is used for personal pleasure, houses, and cars, it feeds a certain lifestyle.' Stephen scratches his chin.

'So it comes with pleasurable benefits.' A conspiratorial smile crosses Chris' lips.

'What's there to smile about? I can't believe you waited until now to tell me. What were you thinking?'

'Look.' Chris moves to the edge of his seat. 'This is purely business, it's what we do. The Majorcan project is soundproof. This doesn't change a thing. We've invested time and money, signed the contract; legally it's watertight.'

This was not the first time Chris had revealed illegitimate business practice in the course of their partnership. Stephen had learned Chris was a shrewd vampire who sucked the blood from a deal, to gain a profit and by any means available to him. It was his currency and he was always looking for opportunities to expand the fortunes of Armstrong and Hastings. Chris took the risks, and to date, his business accolade had earned the company generous yearly profits. Over the years it had grown, as has their reputation, amongst the business community.

Chris Hastings was the son of a prominent banker and educated at Oxford. He graduated with honours in Corporate Law, and although his father harboured ambitions for him to carve out a career in politics, Chris instead embraced the yuppie culture of the early nineties to its extreme. His reputation soon grew amongst the boardrooms and wine bars of the city. It was whilst he was recruited by Union Capital Markets, whose services included corporate finance, commercial, real estate, and banking, that he first met Stephen Armstrong, who worked in a senior role as a partner in the Corporate Real Estate Team. The team's expertise centred on indirect real estate investment, such as onshore and offshore vehicles, tax-focused transactions, and disposals in real estate on a global basis. A friendship developed between them, based initially on their respect for each other's work and then, their shared ambition to progress to the highest levels in their profession. When Tony Blair came to power, the volcanic explosion of wealth that followed, made Union Capital Market a major player and both Stephen and Chris were involved in the growth that made it a dynamic and innovative company.

It was this success that fuelled their over-inflated salaries and yearly January bonus. Chris soon rose to equal Stephen as a senior partner. They thrived in the culture of expectation; the adrenaline rush of a highly charged office environment was the nutrient they craved to succeed in the marketplace. By their natures, they both became restless and developed the idea of starting their own business. The property market boom in London gave them the impetus to set up a property development company and their client base at Union Capital Market gave them access to potential affluent customers.

Armstrong and Hastings specialised in luxury homes such as Mayfair, Chelsea, Knightsbridge, Belgravia, St John's Wood, Hyde Park, Notting Hill, Kensington and Holland Park. It also had interests in commercial investments, potential sites, new developments and international property. Their client list comprised of Russian oligarchs, Middle Eastern oil billionaires, American and British businessmen, and European bankers.

From the beginning, they worked with their individual skills. Stephen managed international corporate finance, real estate, project management, creative vision, branding and the marketing, while Chris' expertise involved acquisitions, development, and financial control.

During this time, Stephen met Georgia, who was working for a leading firm of lawyers in Edinburgh. A quick courtship ensued and a year later they got married. Georgia continued to work in Edinburgh and they bought a townhouse in Stockbridge. She travelled to London on Fridays to spend the weekends at Stephen's Chelsea flat or he would fly up to Edinburgh. Such an arrangement suited both their interests until Dylan's birth a year later when

Stephen spent most weekends in Edinburgh. Motherhood won the tug of war over her career and after her maternity leave, Georgia took a career break that became a permanent arrangement. Stephen's earnings were such that they could sustain their two homes, therefore such a decision did not predict financial hardship.

'Come on Stephen, its business, we've bent the rules before, this is no different.'

'It's entirely different Chris. We could go to prison for a long time. Does that not scare you?'

'But we're not going to go to prison. There's something else bothering you. You've been short-tempered and a pain in the arse for weeks now.'

'What, so you think that will make it all right.' He scratched his chin. 'It's Georgia, this thing about getting Dylan a tutor and staying at the house in Corfu has been a pain in the arse. Opened a few old wounds actually, eventually, I gave into her. I could see how determined she was. I think it may be some kind of delayed grieving, a response to her mother's illness, that she kept it from us for as long as she did. She's had a hang-up about it for years, never got over it really. Georgia has always blamed herself, she feels guilty that she didn't do enough for her. This idea of going to the house may play a part in coming to terms with it all, a reconciliation if you like. And there's this bloody tutor business, and now drug trafficking and Columbians at that, Jesus Christ Chris, they don't fuck about, they kill people like flies.'

'You're making it sound like some Hollywood film.'

Their business interests in Majorca involved the purchase of land, developing the building program and design and obtaining public approval. Months of investment with architects, engineers, and contractors coordinating the environmental, economic, physical and political aspects of the project, saw them gain government approval.

'Come on Stephen, you met Cesar at the meetings with Phil in Madrid and Palma, he's a sound guy.'

Phil Douglas was Senior Negotiator in the company and the drive to extend their share in the lucrative international market is boosted by his fluent command of Italian and Spanish.

'It was during my last visit to Palma, we were out having dinner when Cesar approached the subject and expanded on the details'.

'What I don't understand is why did he tell you? If he was looking for someone to become involved, someone he could trust, then why did he approach you?' Stephen raises his eyebrows.

'I'll get to that,' Chris says, dismissively. 'After dinner, we went to his house, just outside Palma, I met his wife and kids all very domesticated; he even has a personal assistant, for Christ sake. Cesar proudly introduced me to the garage on the ground floor and his cars - an Aston Martin, Lamborghini, and Ferrari you wouldn't get much change from a million and they're just his toys, not the family cars. They're shipped over from his main house in Madrid, like pets. Anyway, the next day we went to the marina and had lunch on his boat, and when I say boat, I mean it was almost a bloody ship. He was drip-feeding me, priming me I suppose, with this opulent display of wealth and success. By most people's standards, we run a successful business and our lifestyles reflect that, but this was a different level altogether.'

'You've always had a taste for the extravagant. He must've known that was your week point.'

'The contracts were just about to be signed when he explained he'd other business interests that had proved very profitable for little investment, unlike this project. Initially, I thought he was backing out of the project, but then he went into the detail of it. At first, I was scared shitless, I thought *this isn't happening,*' but as he explained the actual mechanics of his operation, I found myself surrendering to his proposition.'

'And what was his proposition?' Stephen says dryly.

'Well, if the material trappings were the fishing rod, this was the bait at the end of his hook and I was about to be caught. It runs like clockwork. You see once the cocoa farmers grow the crop it's turned into crystallised cocaine and then from Columbia it's moved into Venezuela by couriers who take the real risks, but there's no short supply. Various members of the Venezuelan security forces are on the cartel's payroll as well; they make sure the drugs are trafficked across the border into Venezuela. From there, it's transported to the Atlantic coast and moved along the Venezuelan border to a place called San Cristobal, then to Puerto Cabello, where the cocaine is moved onto container ships. Once they arrive at Galicia, in North West Spain, the cocaine is unloaded onto speedboats and moved to the Spanish mainland. It's hidden in trucks, moved through Europe to Holland, where it's subdivided into loads of 10 and 50 kilos and from Zeebrugge, the drugs land in Britain. The cocaine is subdivided into smaller amounts and cut with cheap drugs making it only 30% pure by the time it hits the streets of London, Birmingham, Manchester, and Glasgow. So get this, this is the beauty of it, from a value of £50,000, one kilo, sold in gramme bags can fetch up to £150,000.'

Stephen sat in silence, an intent look crossing his face.

'Their markets are well established in Britain, except Edinburgh, Cesar's gateway to the rest of the country.'

'I think I know where this is going.'

'Cesar needs a foothold in Edinburgh. He needs someone he can trust to oversee that the supply meets the demand, the oil in the machine as it were. He has his foot soldiers in Edinburgh, the people who will sell the cocaine on the streets, but he now needs the generals to oversee and manage the process. We would earn 10% from each kilo sold. That's seven and a half grand each. We could make tens of thousands a week.'

'I can count,' Stephen says, in a steely tone.

'Look, if I didn't agree to become involved, the whole project was fucked, he threatened to pull out. The contracts were on the table for Christ sake. What was I to do?'

'So, he blackmailed you. You could've walked away, called his bluff even. Let's be honest, you couldn't resist that kind of money. Are you prepared to lose everything? You should've told me, Chris.'

'Listen, I took the initiative, we've worked our balls off on this project. We're expanding into a very profitable international market, and it's only the start. Cesar's keen to extend our partnership beyond this project, branching out to Portugal, Greece and the Balkans. Of all people, you know that fifty percent of bonuses paid out in the city are invested in overseas property. With our connections, we're sitting on a potential gold mine.'

'Hence the reason we're involved in overseas development. What are you getting at Chris? Are you willing to gamble everything? What if he gets caught by the Spanish authorities? Without his company's involvement, our project would sink and we've already taken sizeable deposits from very influential customers. As a company, we'd be fucked; we'd go down with him. No one would touch us.'

'But that's the beauty of it, he's invisible, other people take the risks, only his counterparts in Columbia have contact with him. He vets the individuals, who run the operations in each city, and then contact is broken, and other people run the day-to-day operation supplying the manpower when the drugs reach Spain and the rest of Europe. It is set up so that he is untouchable.'

'Ok, so tell me, what you have got us involved in?' says Stephen warily.

'There is a fertile supply of young professionals whose recreational pastime involves a night out fueled by drink and cocaine. It has become the '*in*' thing: if you want to be seen with the '*in*' crowd, it's the trendy thing to do.'

'So your target market can afford the goods.'

'Precisely, they can more than afford it. There's already a market, the glamorous middle classes. It's rife at house parties and dinner parties. They take cocaine as if it's a bottle of wine. I should know, I've been to a few. A lot of our clients are frequent users, especially here in London. We're talking about bankers, lawyers, business people, male and female, and they think nothing of paying large amounts of money to get their fix at the weekend. We'll just be the supplier of good times. Think about it, Stephen. Even if you're not in on it, I can do this on my own. I'm offering you an opportunity to make a lot of money and, if you're not interested,' He shrugs. 'Then that just means I take the full ten percent. It's good business for all of us, at the end of the day. We all get something out of it, the user, Cesar, me, you, even the little farmer that grows the crop.'

'Well, as a partnership, I reckon we should be sharing that ten percent.'

'I knew you'd see sense, Stephen.'

'I don't think sense comes into it, Chris. It's all about the money, it always has been.'

Chapter 6

Despondency Whispers

He glances at the clock on the wall. The lecture is scheduled to last an hour. His class consists of a nurse, a speech and language therapists, a social worker, special education teachers, an educational psychologist and a parent of a child with autism. The lesson comprises of the three main psychological theories that propose to explain the behaviours of individuals with autism.

'It's important to remind ourselves of what we covered in our last session before we move on. As you should know by now, autism is a lifelong, complex spectrum of disorders, with serious implications for the individual and often challenging to service providers.

'Society's awareness and knowledge of autism have increased considerably, along with research which has expanded our knowledge base on the influence of autism upon interpersonal, communicative, cognitive, imaginative, sensory, perceptual, physiological and behavioural processes.' As he speaks, Adam walks around the room, as is his custom, delivering his words, like an actor, to his captive audience.

He continues. 'This has infused a developing understanding of the perceived causes of autism, advancing diagnostic tools and cultivated a growth of interventions and approaches.'

He pauses as if gathering his thoughts and sits on the edge of his desk. 'As everyone here should know, autism is a pervasive developmental disorder that inhibits an individual's capacity to communicate, form relationships with others and react suitably in the environment. These individuals range from those with normal intelligence to those who lack any medium of communicating with others. Autism is regarded as a spectrum of disorders, enveloping a broad range of difficulties which led to the term Autistic spectrum disorders or ASD. Wing and Gould suggested a "triad of impairment" that comprises difficulties in social interaction, social communication and social imagination, such as restricted and repetitive behaviours and interests, inflexibility of thought and of play.

'These embody three wide and interacting features of ASD. Individuals diagnosed with Asperger syndrome share difficulties on the triad of impairments and these difficulties should not be undervalued in comparison with classic autism. These difficulties influence the daily activities of life, making it awkward for individuals to initiate and sustain friendships. They may experience loneliness and frustration, misread social situations, they may not appreciate that their interests are not shared by others, experience difficulties when they have to organise themselves and in understanding everyday social situations. Also, it's not uncommon to see individuals with an increased sensitivity to touch, sound, smells, taste and visual stimulation. All of these explain the world that people with autism experience on a daily basis.

'However, it's worth reminding ourselves there are those with autism who would advocate that these so-called impairments, are not perceived as difficulties by every person with autism, and they would argue that it's people who do not have autism, who they refer to as, neurotypicals, such as you and I, who display behaviours that are odd, peculiar and strange.' A ripple of laughter floats towards him.

'A mountain of research has been undertaken to explain what may be the source of these impairments, for want of a better word. And this brings us to the purpose of this afternoon.' He gestures to the powerpoint. 'There are three main cognitive theories that are proposed and these are deficits in a theory of mind, executive functioning and central coherence.

'Why should we concern ourselves with these proposed theories?' He pauses, waiting for a reply. There are none forthcoming. 'Knowledge of the theoretical underpinnings of ASD enables us to empathise with and understand individuals with autism. It opens a window into how they may experience the social and communicative world. It offers us the opportunity to develop imaginative and effective methods in working with individuals in daily practice.'

As he speaks, the room holds his words. 'Is anyone familiar with these theories?'

A handful of hands is shown.

Using the PowerPoint, Adam explains each individual theory. At times, he answers a question, forwarded by an eager and anticipatory searching face. Then he organises the class into three groups of four and distributes cards that contain specific social scenarios and each group's task is to show which scenario corresponds to each psychological theory.

Vociferous debates vibrate around the room, until eventually; Adam brings a sense of order, by raising his voice above the cacophony of infectious enthusiasm that draws a sense of gratification from him. What intrigues him, in this moment, is the wave of eagerness that punctuates each individual face. He too was once involved in their thirst to enquire, and as he stands in front of the smartboard, a harsh sensation of hypocrisy stabs him, as he attempts to muster an inconspicuous and dignified betrayal and coat himself in an assured portrayal of the committed lecturer, whilst all along, in his ear.

***

That morning, he left for the university with yet another drought from the letterbox. Several weeks have passed since the interview and each day cements his growing instinct he is, by now, not the favoured candidate. He will leave the university at the end of the week and he has two options open to him. One is certain; the other seems to ebb from him, like a receding tide.

Adam had intended to take a year out to concentrate on research, his area of interest pertained to families adjustment to their child's diagnosis of autism and their experience of services' involvement after the diagnosis. The research project had a year to conduct the research and write their report. Adam had all but agreed to become part of the team set to work on the project. However, since his interview with Georgia and with each passing day, he has thought of nothing else, relishing the logistics of a new challenge and the prospect of tutoring her son.

Chapter 7

Puddles and Snails

Dylan, small in stature, forms a miniature build for his fourteen years. His complexion is pale, in contrast to the healthy crop of brown hair that sits in no particular style upon his head. He inherits his mother's eyes.

It is raining steadily as he shelters in the doorway of a coffee shop, with the woman his mother has insisted he spends time with, for the next two weeks.

The month of May has arrived, shrouded in uncharacteristic and turbulent excesses. Snow has fallen on high ground; the sky seems to burst with rain each day, like a balloon overfilled with water. Hailstones mercilessly pound the ground, stinging exposed faces that the biting winds slap with indiscriminate hands, and temperatures refuse to creep past 10 degrees Celsius. The sun has hidden for days behind a ubiquitous greyness that covers and lacquers a heavy and sweeping sky.

'Is there anything troubling you Dylan? You seem to be preoccupied with your... eh, humming.'

Dylan shrugs. 'I'm fine now.'

'Well, you don't seem fine to me.'

'I'm fine because I am humming.'

'What do you mean?'

'If you had looked at the communication passport my mum gave you, you would have found under the section, 'sensory sensitivities,' that I don't particularly like noise. The sound of the rain on the tarmac, the cars and their tyres whooshing through the puddles hurt my ears. I hum to block it out.'

'But surely your ears must hurt from the noise when you have your headphones on listening to your music?'

Dylan does not look at her. 'It's not noise and it's not my music, it's Mozart's music and it's scintillating.'

'Of course, how silly of me. I didn't mean to infer that Mozart was noise.'

'But you did.'

'Did I? Oh, ok, well that's not what I intended. I'm just trying to understand how something like the rain or the traffic, for that matter, can cause you to feel distressed.'

'I thought you knew about these things. That's why you are with me. My mum trusts you to be with me.'

'Yes I do, but sometimes you need to understand the person and how they react to their surroundings. Like now for example.' She smiles nervously. 'I'd like it if you could explain it to me.'

'I can get disorientated in places that are busy with lots of things that are going on at the one time. I feel uncomfortable in crowded places, I don't like standing next to people, like now in this doorway. The space is too small. Your perfume is making me feel sick. I have never liked going to supermarkets or large shops. The humming of the fluorescent lights, the smell of fish and people bumping into me make my arms stiffen and my belly feel squidgy. I don't like the noises, it sounds loud in my ears, it hurts them so that's why I hum, it blocks out the noises.'

'I'll read the communication passport when we get back.' Then her expression brightens as the rain stops and offers a distraction. 'Look it's stopped raining. We should get you back home.'

'But there is only you. No one else is here,' he says, as a matter of fact.

'What do you mean?'

'You said 'we' but there is only you. Why do people never say what they mean?'

'I didn't mean it like that. I meant it's a good time to walk home now.' She feels suddenly aggrieved.

'Well, why didn't you say that,' he murmurs.

They step onto the pavement and as they walk, Dylan takes studious care to walk around and avoid the puddles, slowing their progress that etches a frustrated frown on the woman's face.

'Look how the sky is reflected in the water. I don't like that.' Dylan stops, intrigued, he studies the puddle.

'I hate when it rains like this, it brings out these huge snails. Look at them, they are everywhere. God, I've just stood on one.' She screws up her face.

'You've crushed its shell, it will be dead now.' Dylan pokes at the cracked shell.

'Good. Stupid creatures, they're slow and they take forever to get anywhere. They do nothing… except get stood on.'

'That's not true actually,' Dylan says. 'Snails move one metre an hour and can explore a garden in a night. We did a project about snails at school once. They have a strong homing instinct as well.'

'Well not that one,' she mews indignantly.

'Snails can only move by producing slime and other snails use the trail to get around. How neat is that? I read that their slime is good for your skin.'

'Aw, that's disgusting.'

'It's good for birds too, they eat it.'

'That's vile.'

'So snails do have a purpose. Also, they can carry a parasite that can eventually kill them.'

'Good.'

'That's not nice. I like snails and slugs… more than I like you.'

Georgia meets them in the hallway as they enter the house.

'Ah there you are, I was beginning to worry when it started to rain. I should've given you an umbrella, it's been threatening all day.'

'That's ok; we kept out of the rain thankfully and had a nice talk,' the woman says, smiling broadly.

'What did you talk about Dylan?' Georgia asks.

'We spoke about things she is supposed to know, but doesn't,' says Dylan, as he runs up the sweeping stairs towards his room.

'I'm sorry; he's not coping as well as I'd hoped.'

'It's fine, it must be hard for him,' she says politely.

'Yes,' Georgia says, as her eyes travel the stairs and she fights an urge to go to him.

Chapter 8

A Change of Mind

Adam sits at his desk in his study, a small box room that looks out onto the tree-lined street below. It is a bright morning, a welcome reprieve from the rain that even now, continues to leave its mark in damp patches on the walls of houses, dressing the soaked streets and pavements in a wet shroud. Adam cradles a cup of coffee, staring at the laptop screen and the e-mail he has opened fifteen minutes earlier.

The sender is Professor Samson, the clinician leading the research project. He needs to know if Adam has made a decision. He can only give Adam one more day of grace; it is imperative that the project begins with no delay. It is not an option. Professor Samson is not known for his diplomacy; he has built a prosperous academic career on doing things his way. His habitual unorthodox approaches are delivered with the air of a man who does not breathe the air of conformity if it conflicts with his sense of professional integrity. At times, it has brought him into conflict with colleagues and policymakers. It is a quality that Adam admires, but it now occurs to him he is the recipient of such confident and unswerving principles.

He looks out of the window and sees a man striding purposefully out of the park opposite his house. A gust of wind catches his coat and it flaps like a sail. Just then, Adam's mobile phone rings, vibrating on the surface of the desk.

'Hello.'

'Hello. It's Georgia Armstrong.' Already her voice is familiar to him. He feels a surge of elation.

'The reason I'm calling is… I wondered if you could come to Edinburgh, this weekend, and be introduced to Dylan. That's if you don't have other plans of course.'

He forces his mind to be active. 'That should be fine… I think,' he says, remembering the deadline Professor Samson has set. His elation seeps from him.

'You sound hesitant,' Georgia says. A hint of concern laces her voice.

'No, it's not that at all. Look it's not your problem, but I've until tomorrow to accept an offer of some research work. To be honest, I didn't think I was in the running as I hadn't heard from you.'

'I must apologise. Let's just say, things have not worked out as expected.'

'I see,' Adam says, deflated knowing he has not been one of the first two candidates. 'What happens now?'

'Well, that depends on you, Mr Newman. You can accept my offer and have a 50/50 chance of being selected or you can tell me you're not interested, in which case I'll trouble you no more. I don't have the luxury of time. We're leaving in two weeks. To be honest, I'd prefer to be beyond this stage. I should have finalised everything by now. I was thinking you could arrive around ten. Unfortunately, I need to move things along. It's not ideal I know. So I'll expect you for ten o'clock.'

'Yes, ten o'clock then.' He smiles, the decision is made.

'Good. I'll see you then,' Georgia says, a tangible relief clear in her voice.

Chapter 9

The Boy Who Hugs Trees (1)

Adam takes a train from Queen Street Station, arriving at
Edinburgh Waverly Station at 9.30 a.m. He buys a carryout
coffee from the rail station's concourse, heads for Princes
Street and hails a taxi Early morning shoppers and tourists
throng the pavements, cars and buses pass his window, like
stills in a moving film. He contemplates meeting Georgia
once again, and the thought is pleasing to him

The rubberised clapping of tyres on cobbles slows to a
stop as the taxi pulls up outside a townhouse on Dean
Terrace. Leafy trees spray silhouetted shadows as he pauses
and lingers on the doorstep. A lurking thought suddenly
accosts him. Is he embarking upon the right course of
action? An uneasy panic tugs at him. The research project
offers stability, the known, colleagues, and the academic
bubble, all of which are familiar to him. Once through this
door, he will set events in motion that will offer none of
these, but an unfamiliar journey, an invitation into the
unknown where events will undoubtedly accelerate. But
does that not add to the excitement? He is considering this
when the door opens. He clears his throat.

'Thank you for coming at such short notice,' Georgia
says, extending her hand, which Adam shakes, registering
its warmth and feathery grip.

'Not a problem.' He is aware of the irony that laces his
words. His recent lapse into self-doubt is replaced by an
undercurrent surge of excitement that surfaces and
reverberates in his throat.

She gestures for him to enter the house. 'I feel
embarrassed, actually. I wouldn't blame you for thinking
you're my last resort, but let me assure you Mr Newman
(He recalls she insisted on using his surname during the
interview) you were by far the most impressive candidate. I
was just not prepared to consider a man; it sounds absurd I
know. It was Dylan who persuaded me to interview you. He

said if someone applied, had the appropriate qualifications
and impressed me with their performance at the interview,
then that person should be given a chance. He was right of
course. I'm grateful that you've chosen to come, consider
this an apology.'

'There's no need to apologise, really.' He feels
uncomfortable and avoids her eyes.

They are still in the hallway. Georgia moves into the front
room and invites Adam to follow.

He thinks of asking whether her husband will join them
but reconsiders. She, too, already looks uncomfortable,
flicking a stray strand of hair from her face and he does not
want to add to the air of vulnerability that prowls around the
room.

He sits in the same chair as he did at the interview. The
room feels different to him, Georgia has a relaxed air about
her and it illuminates her face as she adjusts her sleeve.

'I've taken the liberty to apply for a disclosure. I hope
you don't mind, but as you can understand, I need to hurry
things along a bit. I'm not going to start his lessons straight
away. I thought I'd let Dylan have the first week, as a
holiday, before starting his tuition.'

Adam smiles. 'That seems the sensible thing to do.' He
calculates if offered the position, he will start in three
weeks.

'Please sit down.' She looks at him curiously. 'Did you
have time to look over the communication passport?'

'I did,' Adam says, sinking into the chair. 'I printed the
attachment you sent and read it on the train.' He smiles
reassuringly.

'Good.' A serious expression crosses her face. 'It's
important that this goes smoothly. If Dylan feels
comfortable with you, then, it goes without saying, the job
is yours, Mr Newman. I'll make the appropriate travel
arrangements and send you the details. As far as the
subjects to be taught are concerned, we can discuss that
later. I'd expect around four hours of study a day will be
enough. It's more important to concentrate on spending the
little time you have getting to know Dylan and for him to

feel comfortable around you.' Georgia looks at him studiously. 'This is not easy for me. I'm putting my trust in you. It's not every day Dylan spends time with a stranger.'

The door opens and Dylan enters the room.

'Dylan, this is Mr Newman.'

'Hello Dylan,' Adam says.

'Hi,' Dylan's hands flap subtly.

'I thought it would be a good idea to spend a little time in the garden. Would you like a coffee, Mr Newman?'

'That would be nice, but please, call me, Adam, I insist.'

She smiles at him. 'Very well, Adam it is.'

They walk to the back of the house and into a large spacious kitchen, the size of his flat, Adam thinks, as they go through glass sliding doors and onto a decking. At Georgia's invitation, they sit on a brown garden sofa and Georgia places a tray, she retrieved from the kitchen, on a glass table. Above them, Adam watches membranes of cloud dust the sky, like small ships on a bleached sea, as he breathes air, diffused in freshly mowed grass. A wall borders the garden, softened by geraniums and aquilegia, alongside a stone pathway that winds down to a row of conifers. Dylan strides through the garden, listening to his I-Pod, as the trees above him stir in the breeze, like the sound of water.

Adam senses Georgia has eased into an unguarded contentment and he asks, 'What would you like me to call you?'

Georgia takes a seat. 'Well Adam, since we're not being formal, please call me Georgia, everyone else does.' She smiles.

He nods and tastes the coffee from a white cup. 'You make a strong coffee Georgia'.

'Oh I'm sorry; I should have asked how you take it,'

'No, its ok, don't worry, I like it that way, strong and dark… Your garden's nice.'

'I'm afraid I can't take the credit for that. A gardener comes every two weeks, although I like to potter about now and again.' She thinks of the garden at the house in Corfu and feels exciting contentment.

'If I had to maintain a garden there would be more chips laid than grass grown. I like a well-kept garden, though. I can't believe the variety of garden furniture that people can buy now.'

'Unfortunately, we need the weather to appreciate it; there'll be no such problems in that department in Corfu. I spend most of my time living outdoors when we are over there.' She hears the elation in her voice.

'Yes, I can imagine that would be the way of life.'

'That brings me to an important subject.'

He detects a hint of excitement in her voice.

'I'm quite surprised you haven't asked where we are staying in Corfu.'

'To be honest, I haven't thought of the mechanics of it all. I suppose I didn't want to tempt fate.' Adam had an impression of a modern house, with a pool and sunbeds.

Georgia smiles. 'Don't worry; we'll get to all of that later.'

She thinks for a moment. 'I realised my mistake once Dylan became upset with the last lady. Interpersonal skills and knowledge go hand in hand. You can't have one without the other otherwise, it's a recipe for disaster, as I found out to my cost and Dylan's detriment.'

She runs long fingers through her hair, an involuntary ritual that Adam notes peppers her conversation. To his surprise, he finds it projects a seductive quality he reproachfully pushes from his mind.

Georgia walks over to Dylan, who has been walking with a bounce, up and down the garden. She touches him on the shoulder.

'Dylan, take your headphones off, it's time to sit with Mr Newman. Would you like a drink of orange?'

'Yes please,' Dylan says, removing the headphones from his ears.

Dylan sits opposite Adam, head bowed. Georgia pours a glass of orange and hands it to him.

'Thanks.' He takes the glass and holds it in both hands on his lap.

'I'll be inside if you need me.'

Adam is unsure if Georgia is addressing one or both of them. He raises the cup to his lips and savours the strong coffee. Adam clears his throat. He feels a pang of sympathy for Dylan. The boy must be unnerved by all this attention he thinks. Dylan sniffs. He does that a lot, Adam reminds himself, probably a tic.

'Dylan, my name is Adam and I'm here because I would like to teach you now you're not going to school. I know this must be odd for you, having to meet lots of people you've not met before.'

Dylan continues to stare into his lap. Adam tells Dylan about himself, where he lives, where he works, his likes and dislikes. There is a long pause. Dylan continues to stare into his lap.

'What is your favourite subject at school?'

Dylan shrugs.

'We can talk about something else if you want.'

'Computer lessons were practical, and I was content to be in the music class, but only sometimes.'

'And why would that be?' Good, Adam thinks, at least he will speak.

'If a subject doesn't interest me, then I don't see any reasonable explanation why I should learn about it. That would not be logical.' Dylan does not lift his gaze.

'Well then, you must have an interest in a certain musical style or topic, maybe.'

'Yes.'

'And what was that?'

'Wolfgang Amadeus Mozart.'

'Is that who you were listening to?'

'I only listen to Mozart.'

'I don't know a lot about classical music, but I've heard Beethoven's 5th Symphony. You know the one that everyone knows, the part that goes... Dan Dan Dan Dan.'

Dylan's head remains bowed.

'Do you know what? I'd like it if you could tell me something about classical music?'

'Well a symphony consists of four movements; it nearly always has a slow beginning, then an Allegro which is the most important movement as it develops all of the themes.' Dylan speaks with exuberance in his voice. 'The complete collection of Wolfgang Amadeus Mozart's music fills one hundred and seventy compact discs, which I actually have. Compare that with Bach, whose music fills one hundred and fifty-seven compact discs and then Haydn with one hundred and fifty. Now, what makes Wolfgang Amadeus Mozart the genius he undoubtedly was, is, Bach died at the age of sixty-five, Haydn at seventy-seven, but Wolfgang Amadeus Mozart was just thirty-six years old when he died on Monday, December 5th, 1791 of complications arising from a chronic kidney failure, rheumatic fever and a streptococcal infection.'

'That's a lot of music.'

'Mozart wrote forty-one symphonies, twenty-seven concertos for the piano, five for the violin, four for horn, two for flute, and one for the bassoon, oboe, clarinet, and the flute and harp. Twenty-four violin sonatas, twenty-five string duos, string trios, string quintets, string quartets, eighteen piano sonatas, nineteen operas, then there are keyboard works, sacred works, concert arias, canons, songs, serenades, dances, marches and divertimenti.'

'You seem to know a lot about Mozart.'

'As well as listening to his music, I have also read quite a lot of books on Mozart and his life. I wouldn't say I'm an expert, but I know a lot about him. When Mozart was my age, he had already travelled to and given concerts in Vienna, Paris, London and Italy with his father, Leopold. He spoke German, Italian, French and Latin. He was away from his home for three thousand seven hundred and twenty days. That is over ten years, one-third of his life.'

'Apart from listening to his music and reading about him, is there anything else you like doing or are interested in?'

'I like to walk beside the river opposite our house. The lady who mum sent away said it was dangerous, and she didn't let me hug the trees.'

'You like to hug trees?'

'Yes, I like the feel of the bark, actually.'

'We can go if you want if it's ok with your mum.'

Dylan glances at Adam then, 'Good.'

Dylan leads the way, his headphones clamped to his ears, as they cross Deanhaugh Street. At the foot of a clock tower, they descend metal framed steps and follow a path that takes them to Water of Leith, a river that cuts through Edinburgh. They stride along the embankment until they come to a small clearing. Adam has an unsettling momentary sense they are being watched. The charred remains of a small fire and discarded bottles of cheap vodka and super strength lager, litter the ground. Fragments of glass and decapitated bottlenecks lie scattered across the dry earth, like the dead on a battlefield. Adam's attention is snagged by a tree trunk arched over the water, its branches skimming the surface, like outstretched arms, as if poised to dive into the placid flowing current.

Dylan removes his headphones and lets them fall around his shoulders. He walks towards a dead tree, with folds of reptilian bark that creases and lines its trunk. He leans inwards, raises his arms, turns his head to the side and gently presses his cheek to the trunk. Dylan closes his eyes and greets his old friend with a smile, slowly sidestepping around the trunk.

'Look it's the tree hugger.' The voice comes from behind Dylan, projected provokingly.

Three teenagers run down the slight decline of a well-worn track and into the small clearing, the timbre of their voices buoyant at the prospect of taunting their unsuspected discovery. One boy bends down and grabs a small rock. With a flick of his wrist, he tosses it in the air and catches it in his palm, repeating the action several times, as he moves closer to Dylan, accompanied by a sardonic grin.

'We've got you this time tree hugger, there's nowhere to run.'

The other two boys stand behind their friend, laughing encouragingly. He moves closer. Dylan turns, facing the threat before him. Adam remains out of view. The boy moves to Dylan's side, juggling the rock between his hands.

Adam acts quickly, swiping the rock from the air in one swift motion. The boy seems genuinely astonished, as he stumbled backwards.

'Do you still feel big, now you don't have your little stone?' Adam smiles threateningly.

'Who the fuck are you?' the boy gasps.

Adam leans towards him, staring into the boy's blinking eyes. 'I'm your worst nightmare, you little shit, now piss off to wherever you came from,' Adam rasps in a steely tone.

They stare at each other and then, like a scared dog, the boy backs away, retreating to his friends and the wounded pack disappears, tails between legs.

'You swore Mr Newman; that conveys a lack of command of the English language.'

'It was a necessity that was effective, given the circumstances, I thought.' Adam tosses the rock into a clump of bushes.

Dylan bends his head to one side. 'I can see the logic in that, actually.'

'Do you know them?'

'No.'

'Does this happen a lot?'

'Sometimes.'

'Have they ever hurt you?'

'No. They call me names. They don't scare me. School is worse.'

'What do you mean?'

'I don't like school. Well, maybe not all schools in general. I don't know what other schools are like, I only know about the one I went to. I hated my school.'

'Would you like to tell me why?'

Dylan shrugs.

'You don't have to tell me. We can talk about something else if you like, while we walk home.'

'I was picked on... bullied... They obviously didn't understand me and I didn't understand them, but that's not a reason to do and say the things they did.'

Dylan paces backwards and forwards, staring at the ground.

'It happened every day, but they were careful not to let the adults see. I think about it a lot. I'm able to replay each incident, every detail. I store them in folders in my mind, like a computer. It brings back the feelings each time as if it were happening again. At first, I thought they were playing a game; this must be how people play I thought. I didn't really understand it. I felt confused. I said sorry a lot and that made them laugh, like a joke, but I didn't know why it was funny. I find it hard to know what people think about, actually.'

'Did you tell anyone?' Adam asks, sympathetically.

'No. They told me not to tell anyone. It was a secret and they said that if I told an adult, something bad would happen to me. I found lots of places to hide in. It's a big old building, but they always found me.' Dylan frowns. 'School is a confusing place. People break the rules or change the rules. School smells of disinfectant and the corridors vibrate with loud noises, they're often filled with lots of people talking and shouting. I couldn't make sense of the noise. I hate the corridors because people often bump into me and I find that to be painful, just like a shock wave running through me.

'I was made fun of by certain boys. I didn't know that at the time. They often followed me around the school at break times. They called me names like, '*freak*,' and '*geek*,' and emptied my school bag onto the ground. Sometimes, I'd try to push them away, but that made it worse and they would laugh. I was physically assaulted once, actually. They took money from me, to buy cigarettes to smoke within the school boundary. I told them that cigarettes can kill people. One boy, the biggest in size, said that if I told anyone, there would be only one person in danger of being killed. They all laughed again like they always did. I didn't understand what he meant. I said that I had to tell a teacher because rules were made to be followed not broken. That was when he hit me.'

'Did you tell a teacher or your mum?'

'The teachers were always saying things I didn't understand,' Dylan says despairingly. He hesitates. 'I was always getting into trouble because, in the classroom, I often looked at the wall or the floor, and the teacher would shout at me, saying I was ignoring him and not listening. When I said that I find it really uncomfortable to look at a person when they're speaking, he said that I was being insolent.

'A lot of the time, I focus on an object next to the person or behind them. If they are close, like you are now, I always look at their mouths, never into their eyes.'

Adam looks at him curiously. 'Does your mum know about the bullying?'

'Oh yes. Mum found out about the bullying because a teacher noticed my pack lunch box was always empty when we sat down to eat lunch. He asked me why this was and I said that it's part of a game I play with the other boys. I give them the food in my lunch box and that makes them laugh. I know now that we weren't playing a game.'

Dylan stops pacing and smiles awkwardly. 'Out of the entire people mum interviewed, she said that you were the best qualified. She should have picked you first, she was sorry she didn't, so you should know all about children like me, actually.'

'Not every person with autism is the same. For example, most of the children I taught liked school. They were happy to be there.'

'I would have liked school if the teachers understood what it meant to have someone like me in their class. The children in your class were happy. I would like you to be my teacher, Mr Newman, so I can feel happy like those other children.'

Adam looks at Dylan with a conspiratorial smile. 'I would like that very much, Dylan.'

Adam hadn't expected Dylan's frank disclosure. He feels a rising sense of pity for the boy, made all the more tangible by the ordeals he must have faced on a daily basis.

'Are you excited about going to Corfu?' he asks, trying to sound optimistic.

Dylan nods briefly. 'Mm, a little I suppose. It won't be like the holidays I've had there. I've never had to take school lessons there, that will be different. It won't be like school, which will be a good thing, actually.'

Chapter 10

Katherine

Adam was born in Manchester, the youngest of three children. His father was a lawyer in one of the larger and more prosperous firms in the city. Adam's mother worked part-time as a teacher, at the local primary school. His sister, Annabel, was four years older than Adam and ten minutes older than her twin sister Sarah. Adam attended the local primary school where his mother taught. His sisters looked out for him, protecting him like mother hens at every opportunity. He didn't mind their attention.

Adam's father spoke with a measured voice and was meticulous and a perfectionist in everything he did; attributes that advanced his career. When Adam was seven, his father secured a partnership at a prominent Glasgow law firm. The family moved to Kelvinside, a predominantly middle-class area of the city. Adam attended Kelvinside Academy, a private day school near the city's Botanic Gardens. The main school building was category A listed. He moved from the junior school to the senior school, playing in the rugby and cricket team. Adam became de-anglicised, adopting a soft west coast tone to his voice.

He discovered music and a few of his friends started a band. Adam played rhythm guitar. He wasn't proficient enough to master the lead brakes and intricate solos that are required from a lead guitarist; that was left to Jim. Jim owned a Marshall stack and at sixteen he had already cultivated the look of the rock star with his flowing hair and fluffy stubble, perfecting the poses of Slash from Guns n Roses, as he executed another screeching solo on the fretboard of his sunburst Gibson Les Paul. Adam was content to fill the spaces with his crunching chords and dream of stadium gigs and platinum discs.

It lasted a year, and they parted company citing musical differences, the usual footnote to a breakup. Adam had

become disillusioned with the local music scene, when he
realised it was only a small percentage of bands that
eventually secured a contract in the music business and,
even then, success is not guaranteed.

There was always an expectation on his father's part that
Adam would follow him into Law. His father was a serious
man, astute and disciplined. He seldom appreciated the
views of others, waving a hand of impatience if they
conflicted with his own. It was a trait that served him well
in his profession, but not as a father. Adam achieved good
grades that afforded him the choice of applying to several
universities. Instead of studying Law in Edinburgh, his
father's recommendation, he accepted an offer to attend
Jordon Hill College of Education, studying a BA Hons in
Primary Education.

Adam first saw Katherine in the student bar. It was
December and winter had settled over a shivering Glasgow.
Thursday night was usually the start of the weekend for
most of the regulars in the student bar. The band had just
finished playing, the last chords fading from the final
encore. Ordering a round of drinks, his attention was drawn
to a group of girls, who arrived discarding jackets and
scarves in animated gestures. It was so warm in the
diminutive surroundings that the walls often perspired when
the place was bouncing to the next big band to come out of
the city. Its nickname was, 'the oven' and on this night, it
felt like one.

She stood beside him and ordered three white wines, a
red, and half a pint of cider. Katherine was a few inches
shorter than Adam, an advantage that allowed him to scan
her up and down without being detected. He found her
attractive. She flicked her hair behind an ear, and he was
able to appreciate the structure of her face. Adam's drinks
arrived, he paid the barman and intentionally lingered as he
deposited the change into his wallet.

'Did you catch the band?'

'No, I've just arrived.'

'Oh, they were good.'

'I know. I've seen them before.'

'My name's Adam by the way.'
'Katherine.'
'You're American?'
'No, Canadian.'
'Oh sorry.'
'It's ok. It happens all the time'
'Where about in Canada are you from?'
'Toronto.'
'What are you studying?'
'Primary Education. I'm in my third year.'
'Ditto. I haven't seen you about. I'm in my second.'

She picked up her tray of drinks. 'Well then, maybe I will see you around, nice speaking to you Adam, bye.'

'Yeah, hopefully, see you around, Katherine.'

After that, he did not see her for a week, and then, one morning between lectures, he literally bumped into her in the library, sending a pile of papers hurtling towards the polished wooden floor. That second encounter was the start of their life together, although such a prospect was furthest from their minds, as Adam crouched beside Katherine, apologising profusely, as he helped her in scooping up the intermingled pages of her journal articles.

Chapter 11

Gracie

Coffee brown eyes, large and deep, stare at Adam. A melancholic look he finds captivating, but also doleful. There is a definite personality reflected through her gaze, he is sure of that. It radiates towards him, in warm currents, whenever they are together. The dog's head turns sheepishly towards the sound of a creaking door, her ears twitch, but she soon loses interest and again turns her attention towards Adam. Her nose twitches and nostrils flay. Adam pulls towards her eyes again. Eyelashes, short silk needles, blink involuntarily. Adam wonders if the dog is contemplating a decision to stay or move through the house in search of food, or a place to sleep.

She remains seated, content to feel his hand massage behind a floppy ear. She lifts her head and presses it luxuriantly against his kneading fingers. The dog yawns and smacks its lips.

'A dog's life, what a ridiculous saying,' Adam says, out loud.

The rain slides down the window; he watches its trajectory along the glass. Giant tears falling from the sky, he thinks to himself and grins at the poetic substance of his thought.

He will need to take the dog for a walk soon, and hopes for a break in the weather. Fifteen minutes is all it will take, but the sky looks stubborn in its leaded complexion.

'You had a long walk this morning, missing one this afternoon won't do you any harm,' he tells the dog, whose ears twitch at the word, 'walk.'

Adam remembers reading somewhere that dogs can recognise around twenty words. The dog's hopeful eyes scan Adam's body language for any sign he is about to undertake the daily routine of fetching the lead from the cupboard and pocketing snacks, a poo bag, and mobile phone. Sometimes, all it takes is for Adam to retrieve his headphones from a drawer, to send the dog into an excited stupor, running into the hallway, sliding the rug along the floor, and standing to attention at the front door, tail wagging in anticipation.

He gives the dog a small treat, a peace offering, and pats its head. 'Not to worry Gracie, this time, tomorrow, you'll be home again.'

For the past week, Adam and Gracie have been getting acquainted with one another, after Adam offered to look after Gracie, for his sister, who is due to return from a holiday in Gran Canaria the next morning.

Gracie's kennels were ravaged by a fire the day before Adam's sister was due to depart, and he felt obliged to look after the dog.

He has become acquainted with the local dog-walking community during his twice-daily walks. He ventures out at the same time each day, early morning and evening. Normally, he will come across the same dog walkers, offering a polite greeting: given their shared commonality, it feels the customary thing to do. Some often comment on Gracie, *what a lovely dog she is, so well behaved*, others ask after Gracie's age. The conversation graduates to Adam's, by now, well-recited monologue of how he came to be watching his sister's dog. These encounters skip around the periphery of conversation; after all, Adam is only a casual dog walker and will never be admitted into the Kelvinside fraternity of dog walkers.

He makes himself a coffee and checks his e-mails, one, in particular, catching his attention. A hot sensation jumps in his chest. He notices Georgia has sent it half an hour ago. It has his itinerary: flight number, flight time, Georgia will pick him up at the airport. She also reminds him to check in online a few days before departure and he grins at her thoroughness. It is now real. It will happen.

Chapter 12

The Professor's Letter

He is sitting outside at a pavement café, on Great Western Road; Gracie is slumped at his feet, slurping water from a bowl that a waitress has brought. Adam reaches for his coffee and leans back in his chair. Around him, murmured conversation blends with piped music that emits from the café's interior. His mobile rings. The rumble of the midday traffic and screeching brakes make the voice distant like in a tunnel; the woman at the table next to him laughs, a high-pitched falsetto that at once irritates him. He frowns.

'Hello, Sally, I can hardly hear you.'

'I'll be there in a second, I can see you.'

Adam looks. He can see Sally crossing the road, her mobile clamped to her ear. Adam waves. 'I've got you a coffee.'

'Lovely, did you get a slice of their lemon cake, I had it yesterday. It was to die for.'

'I followed your orders to the letter.' Adam grins.

'Oh, you're a darling.' Sally quickens her pace.

She sits down beside him, flicking strands of hair from her nose.

'I didn't know you had a dog.' She pats Gracie's head.

'She's my sister's; I'm looking after her while she's on holiday.'

'What's her name? She's adorable.'

'Gracie.'

Gracie pricks up her ears and turns to Adam, inquisitively hoping for food.

'I'm taking her home today; her holiday is at an end. No more treats for you.'

Gracie smacks her lips.

Sally takes a sip of coffee. 'Ah, that's better, my first caffeine injection of the day. So, how're things, Adam?'

'Fine.'

Sally brushes her hand through her hair then removes some stubborn strands from her face. 'I suppose I'd better put this out, don't want to be anti-social.' She nods towards the 'No Smoking' sign. Adam watches the smoke exhale from her mouth before she drops the cigarette into an empty can of coke.

'You would have thought the table would've been cleared before you ordered.' She shakes the can and her cigarette hisses. 'The standards have obviously dropped since it was bought over. I'm glad you phoned, I was meaning to do it myself, but work keeps getting in the way. We're so busy at this time of year, as you know, while you jump ship.' She smiles sarcastically.

'Thanks for coming. I wanted to explain why I'm doing this. It's not a reflection on the department. I wanted to make that clear.'

She lets a smile grow on her face. 'Adam, how long have you known me? I could tell for months you've not been happy. It happens to the best of us you know. I took a break once, call it a sabbatical or whatever, it doesn't matter, but what mattered was that I knew it was the right thing to do at the time and you need to be sure of that too.'

Adam seems astonished. 'What did you do?'

'I went off and met up with an old friend.'

'And who was this old friend?'

'Professor Tzakis Konstantinos, remember I told you about him at the restaurant? He teaches ancient Greek and Roman history in the History Department.' She raises an eyebrow. 'And guess where? At the Ionian University in Corfu. I was miserable, and he cheered me up...' Sally pauses for effect. 'We were both young and back then, well, I was impressionable. It was the happiest six months of my life.'

'Well, I never. Talk about skeletons in the cupboard.'

'We thought we loved each other, I suppose we did, in our way, but it wasn't real love, it was an escape, an escape from everything that was real. I thought I'd find all the answers to my questions. The answers were always there, inside me, I'd just not figured it out. You can't hide you see.'

'From what?'

'From the person you are.' Sally touches his hand. 'Are you sure about this Adam? You've turned down the opportunity to do valuable research that could change people's lives.'

'At least if it's a mistake then it's my mistake. I'll have no one to blame but myself.'

'Ah, self-responsibility, I like that.' She looks at him attentively.

'Dr Williams, Head of Autism Studies, eloping with her Greek lover. What a scandal.' Adam teases.

'It wasn't like that and I wasn't head of anything back then.'

'Well, what was it, intellectual flirting?'

'We're still good friends you know,' Sally says, drinking more coffee. 'After all these years, we've stayed in touch.'

'Do you still see him?'

'At the occasional conference… dinner and a nightcap. We're just two old friends now. There's been a lot of water under the bridge for God's sake. In between, we've both been married and divorced.' She takes a slice of cake. 'You must try the cake, Adam.' Sally pushes the plate towards him. She pulls a piece of paper from her bag. 'This is Tzakis' mobile number. I've already told him you're staying in Corfu. You can get in touch with him at any time. In fact, he'd love to show you the around the island.'

'That's kind of him, but he doesn't even know me.'

'He knows me, obviously.' Sally pauses and smiles. 'And I told him you were a dear friend I'd worry about, so he's more than happy to help.'

'It's unnecessary, but thanks, anyway.'

She studies him for a moment. 'Do you know much about the boy?'

'Enough.'

'And the mother?'

'I think this is hard for her. I get the feeling she's almost been pushed into this. She doesn't give much away.'

'Is she pretty?'

'Sally, it's a professional arrangement, I never noticed.'

Sally's nose creases as she laughs. 'Really, come on Adam, is she attractive?'

'Not in a classic way, but yes, she's agreeable to the eye.' Adam grins and then at once feels he has betrayed Georgia as if he has tainted their arrangement. He feels a sudden rush of guilt. 'It's not like that.' He corrects himself.

Sally grins apologetically. 'I'm sorry, I was only teasing. What about the husband, you've said little about him.'

'I know. I've not met him yet. I don't think he's around much. He seems to be always away on business.'

'Is he going to be in Corfu?'

'Not all the time. I feel a bit awkward about that. He has some project in Spain. He's into property development seemingly.'

'It's a long way from Spain to Greece. I couldn't imagine he'd do that every week.'

Adam shrugs. 'No, I suppose not.'

'So it's just you, the boy and his mother.'

'I suppose so, although, I think she gets some help around the house, there's someone who looks after it.'

The day Georgia offered Adam the job, she enquired if he had any dietary intolerance. Her mother's old housekeeper still kept an eye on the house in Corfu and would stock the kitchen ready for their arrival. He had wondered about the domestic arrangements, but Georgia reassured any misgivings he might have had by indicating that the house was large enough for everyone to have their own privacy; with five bedrooms and three bathrooms, they wouldn't be in each other's way. He welcomed this information with a mixture of relief and exhilaration; it allowed him to concentrate on the coming months. A new enthusiasm dominated his thoughts; he researched the North West of Corfu, the villages and resorts, he trolled the internet for any information he could find, pictures, posts, videos on YouTube, anything that would illustrate the landscape and its character, the satiety of colour that infused the sky and sea. All of these were important to him, such lucrative knowledge afforded him a glimpse, hinted at even, what it would be like to live on an island, in a strange house, amongst people, whom a month ago, were mere strangers to him, who he would have walked past in the street. Now, they influenced the trajectory of his life for the next three months, they dominated his thoughts with a tightening excitement in his stomach, ecstatically happy, but at other times, he found himself withdrawn into a cavern of doleful self-doubt. It was a reminder of the gravity of his undertaking.

'Have you any fears about this Adam? I mean, if it doesn't work out, for whatever reason, you'll find yourself in a bit of a mess professionally.'

Adam shrugs and then sighs. 'I might have just made the biggest mistake of my life, I know that, but if I don't do this, I'll never find out. I'm willing to take the chance; I don't want to live with the regret.'

Sally smiles sorrowfully. 'No, I suppose not, regret can eat at you. But you, you've always been so calculated Adam. I'm going to miss you. Come on, we're supposed to be sharing this cake. I've eaten most of it.'

Adam takes the plate and tilts its contents towards Gracie, 'Your last treat before you go home, Gracie.'

'I wonder if you could do me a favour Adam?'

'What would that be?'

'I wasn't being entirely honest with you about Tzakis. I gave you his mobile number because I'd hoped you'd give him this.' Sally hands him an envelope. 'It's a letter. If you don't want to I'll understand.

'Most people send text, e-mail or phone these days.'

'That wouldn't feel right. In fact, it wouldn't be right. It needs to be a letter. A letter is personal and intimate.'

'Why don't you post it then?'

'I need to know he's received it. I can't just speak to him. It's all in there.' She gestures to the envelope.

'Of course, I will. Not a problem.'

'Thank you, Adam, this means a lot to me,' she says with a relieved smile.

Chapter 13

Arriving

The air is warm as he walks out of the airport into a shroud of heat that seems to encase him. His shirt is already feeling uncomfortable and a burden. He flaps it to circulate the air. He knew it would be hot, but all the same, the intensity surprises him. As he walks, the brightness forces him to shade his eyes. Where did he put his sunglasses? I'm actually here, he says to himself, still not believing it.

He scans the immediate area, he can't see Georgia, perhaps she has forgotten the day of his arrival or even the time? That wouldn't be like her, she is too organised to make such an error. He has waited for her as planned, amongst the tour reps and smartly dressed men and women, displaying placards with surnames emblazoned in bold ink. He feels panic, which increases, as he pulls his suitcase towards a taxi rank. The address? He has no idea where he is going. Adam rummages in a small travel bag.

'Adam.'

He looks around; Georgia is walking towards him flustered, an apologetic look on her face. She pushes her sunglasses onto the crown of her head. She is wearing a lilac dress, sleeveless, that falls to just above her knees.

'There you are, I'm so sorry.'

'It's ok, you're here now.' Adam smiles, relieved.

'Theresa is watching Dylan for me; she was late arriving. I've parked over there,' Georgia points to a car park. 'It's a bit away. You should get a trolley for the suitcase.'

Adam swings the suitcase into the boot and, as they pull out of the airport, he can feel his shirt stick to his back. The air conditioning placates his discomfort, as Georgia describes how both she and Dylan have, by now, acclimatised to the somnolent pace of life, in contrast to the hyper-bowl of the city life they have left.

Dylan has now settled and is feeling at ease with his new surroundings. Now that her son is benefiting from his new environment, Georgia has relaxed with an effervescence that grows with each day.

As they travel, it is clear they both feel nervous. It is the first time they have been in such a confined space together. Georgia's arms are tanning; he also notices several freckles on her forearms as her hand taps the steering wheel to an inaudible beat. The change in climate has definitely agreed with her; he senses she is not as guarded as before.

'I was thinking, you should take a few days to settle in before you start teaching.'

'That's kind of you.'

'It's only right. How was your flight?'

'Oh, it was fine, not much legroom, though, it was good to stretch my legs once we landed.'

'Sorry, I didn't get you, first class.'

'I didn't mean it like that.' Adam says, apologetically.

Georgia smiles. 'I'm just kidding.'

This is the first time Adam has heard Georgia using humour. It suits her. He takes it as a good sign. She is relaxing in his company; he has to relax in hers now.

'Have you had anything to eat?'

'Just a sandwich on the plane.'

'Not a cucumber one then.'

They both laugh.

'I've asked Theresa to make some lunch for when we arrive at the house. I suppose if I was selling it, an estate agent would call it a villa, but it's always been "the house" ever since I went there with mum.'

'Great. I'm feeling hungry now.'

They drive along Riga Fereos, past retail buildings and farmhouses. Adam notices a street vendor has set up a stall by the side of the road, cooking meat on a spit. He catches the word, 'Apnaki' scrawled on a placard.

'Is it far?'

'It's on the other side of the island, close to Palaoikastritsa.'

'I've heard of that.'

'It's a nice resort, but it gets busy in the summer.'

Motorbikes, driven by helmetless males, weave dangerously through the traffic. They pass a basketball court and enter a residential area, where the vegetation thickens and courtyards sprinkled with pots and vases, palm trees and vines appear often. Adam notices a lemon tree or orange tree; from his viewpoint, it's difficult to decide which. He senses they are entering the suburbs of Corfu Town, as the mustard and white exterior of houses, a motorcycle shop, a kitchen store and several boutiques appear. They pass advertising boards and shop fronts with Greek lettering; as yet, he hasn't seen an English word. This is definitely not a tourist area he thinks to himself.

'Has the house changed much over the years?'

'Just cosmetic changes really. It's pretty much the same since mum and dad bought it, although we do have all the mod cons, flat-screen televisions, the internet, it's not all stuck in the '70s. The building itself has been renovated several times since it was first built. We have a pool now. We put that in several years ago for Dylan. I'm looking forward to doing the place up. It's overdue really. Theresa does her best when were not there. I've neglected the house. We haven't stayed as much as we used to, which is a shame. Life gets in the way I suppose.'

'It has a habit of doing that.'

On the left, a small church comes into view and scores of white crosses in a cemetery. They come to a crossroads where, for the first time, Adam sees a shop sign in English, 'DVD Planet.' They turn left, the length of the road packed on each side with parked cars. Here, the buildings are three floors high, the traffic heavier, nudging itself through the streets. A graffiti wall letters bold and large, border the road where it widens and Adam feels a sense of space again. Now the buildings do not crowd in on them, they look cosmopolitan, with their glass fronts and neat displays. The expanse of the sky is more visible here, as they pass Intersport and Mothercare, brands familiar to him, a reminder of home. The buildings thin out as the road to Palaoikastritsa evolves into two lanes, over a murky canal where traffic lights loom overhead. They skirt the coast and Adam catches sight of the sea.

'Do you visit every summer?' Adam asks.

'Sometimes, but we also come in the spring if we can. Corfu is beautiful in the spring. It's a shame people don't visit as much then. It virtually explodes with colour. Mum and Dad would often visit at Easter. It's a shame we've missed it.'

'I've heard Easter is more important than Christmas in Greece.'

'It's a special time. Bands and choirs play in the streets, epitaphs are paraded. I love the traditions, it's also a time for families. Corfiots are big on family.'

Further along, the road swings inland. Here the traffic is lighter and at times they have the road to themselves for miles.

For a time, they journey in silence. Adam, aware that the pause in their conversation has not elicited any strained or awkward side effect, is content to take in his new surroundings. His online research helped him form an impression of the island, but now, he truly appreciates the intensity of light that immerses him in pine and cypress, draping the landscape like a vast carpet. Now and again, a shaded olive grove sucks him into the loops and twists of their trunks. He senses that amongst the trees, the air is sweet, still and becalmed.

The mountainous landscape undulates, mile after mile, in a thick cloak of emerald trees, where they pass the occasional farmhouse and villa, ancient groves and modern rent-a-bike-car signs.

'We're coming into Palaoikastitsa.' Georgia smiles.

Tavernas became more populous. At the bottom of a steep path, Adam catches sight of his first swimming pool, shaped like the sole of a shoe. Suddenly, from behind a wooded hill, the sea appears. They drive past hotels, set off from the road.

The road now hugs the coast, as do the indigenous "Spiros" apartments and tavernas, where the turquoise sea melts into verdant headlands and sandy shores.

'We're almost there,' Georgia announces. 'The views are amazing, aren't they? There's a track that leads from the house to the beach. We often go there for a swim and a picnic.'

He is reluctant to move his gaze from the landscape. A thought enters him; Corfu looks as if a great quantity of green paint has spilt and gradually soaked into the fabric of the landscape.

The car twists and turns along roads and miniature streets, that weave upwards, through a village, until giving way to a single track, flanked by arching trees, where leaning branches make a canopy under which the sun's light spears the dust. To his delight, he can still see the sea and a sheltered bay below them.

A thicket of knots swells in his stomach, a growing combustion of excitement and hesitation. He wonders how the house will look. Georgia has not given him a photograph; his imagination has formed an image in its absence. He has tried to locate the house with 'Google Street View' but the image ends at the track they have just left. As the car swings to the left, it enters an opened iron gate between a stone wall, each fixed stone, pieced together in a masonry jigsaw, crowned in red and orange bougainvillaea.

'Here we are. From the terrace, you can see the sea.' Georgia brings the car to a stop.

An array of Ionian blue shutters illuminates the stone façade of the house. It looks better than he imagined.

Adam can see an elderly woman on the covered terrace. She is preparing a table and as she looks up, she waves.

'We won't be long Theresa; I'll show Adam to his room.'

They enter a large welcoming hall that leads off into a spacious high-ceilinged living room.

'I'll show you around first, so you know where everything is.'

Each room has beamed ceilings, solid tiled floors and French windows. Again, it's just as Adam imagined it would be, rustic on the outside, but modern and voluminous inside.

His room is pleasingly spacious and air-conditioned.

'We put the aircon in some years ago; it makes such a difference in the summer months. I'll let you get settled, lunch is just about ready. I'll see you when you come out.'

'Thanks, I'll just freshen up and change this.' He pulls at his shirt.

His is the only bedroom on the ground floor, the rest are upstairs. In his room, he finds a double bed and a large oak wardrobe. He crosses to a writing desk with many compartments; he opens one but finds it empty. The bathroom has a shower with glass screens, toilet and a handbasin, above which sits a large mirror, small blue tiles cover the walls and a supply of soap and shampoo fill a woven basket.

He slides open glass doors and walks out onto the terrace that seems to wrap around most of the house. It is then he notices his part of the house has been an addition at some point in time, complementing the older part of the house in design and materials. He can see mature pines, multicoloured oleanders and bougainvillaea. The air is still and he can feel the sun on his face. He goes back inside and unpacks. Once he has washed and changed he moves through the house, taking in the furniture and ornaments; most are modern, imposing Georgia's character and style into each part of the house. The house feels large and spacious; the rooms are wide, with an open feel to them, each one a continuation of the other, but each with a distinct feel of the individual character.

'So, he is finally here.' Theresa says, mixing a salad. 'Poor Dylan he will have to start his lessons now. No more playing in the pool for him.'

Theresa is a spritely woman, with a handsome face that defies her advancing years. Her posture is erect, statuesque even, she gestures with wide flowing arms to emphasise her words.

Georgia sits in a chair and takes a sip of lemonade. 'Actually, I've suggested Adam takes a few days to get settled in before he starts to teach Dylan.'

'Good. Is he joining us?'

'I hope so; he said he was hungry. It would be rude to start without him.'

'Sorry, I hope you weren't waiting on me I decided to unpack.'

'This is Theresa, Adam.'

'Pleased to meet you, Theresa.'

'I hope you can find something you like?' Theresa gestures towards the table.

'I won't starve. It looks lovely.'

'We won't stand on graces. Please sit, Adam.'

'Is Dylan joining us?' Adam asks.

'He's already eaten, about an hour ago.'

'I'll get going Georgia; I'm picking up Yanis and Effrosyni from school. A Grandparent's work is never done.'

'So it's just the two of us then.' Adam suppresses a smile.

'I had lunch with Dylan.' Theresa smiles. 'It was nice to meet you, Adam. See you tomorrow Georgia.' She kisses Georgia on the cheek and says goodbye in Greek. 'Andio sas.'

She scoops up her bag and, at an athletic pace, heads towards the gate.

Georgia tells Adam Theresa is like an aunt to her; as a child, she called her, *Thia Theresa.*

'The food looks amazing.'

Georgia smiles. 'Theresa is a wonderful cook. Here we have chopped tomato and cucumber salad with mint and feta, this here is gemista, stuffed peppers and tomatoes with rice, flatbread with hummus and green pea fava and last, but not least, grilled aubergine with halloumi.'

Adam smiles to himself; these were the moments he has dreamed of, dared to imagine even.

'I've got some lesson plans for you to look at.'

'That won't be necessary just yet. I'm sure they'll be fine. I thought we could introduce Dylan to the lessons gradually and then increase the time each day.'

'I'm sure that's the best way.'

'Good. Until then, you'll have some extra free time.'

Adam nods; he plays with his food.

'I thought you were hungry. Are you ok?'

'There's something I need to ask you.'

'What?'

'It concerns your husband.'

'Oh, I see.'

'The thing is, I feel uncomfortable that he's not here. I've not met him yet, but here I am, about to stay with his family and teach his son.'

'I can see your point,' Georgia says as she pulls her hand through her hair.

'I didn't mean to make you feel uncomfortable. Look, I'm not expecting you to explain the situation, it's none of my business, but it has bothered me. I just thought you should know, that's all.'

'No, you're right. I can see what you mean.' She lightly scratches her forearm. 'I'm afraid it's an occupational hazard these protracted separations. Over time we've both become used to it. Do you feel you might be pouring oil on troubled waters, Adam?' Georgia raises her glass and smiles at him. 'Well, you can find out for yourself. Stephen arrives tomorrow.'

Chapter 14

Elena's Vegetable Thieves

In the privacy of his room, Adam finishes unpacking. He turns on the laptop he has now placed on the desk, inserts a USB key and opens a folder. Adam has everything he needs, the materials, handouts and lesson plans. He will also rely on the internet and a printer... he needs to ask Georgia about that. She said there was a printer, but it is a few years old. Adam closes the laptop.

He opens the glass doors and steps outside, where he is struck by the continuous tempo of stridulating cicadas. Adam decides to take a walk in the garden and even there the sound is pervasive.

It is a large garden and well maintained. He doesn't know the names of the many flowers, but if he did, he would know that there were roses, marigolds, pansies and bougainvillaea. There is a herb and vegetable garden. Earlier, at lunch, Georgia told him that Theresa had planted a variety of herbs: basil, mint, thyme, chives, rosemary, and sage, all of which season the food they eat. The air is impregnated with their aroma. He notices artichokes, broad green beans and courgettes. A butterfly flutters past him. At the end of the garden, there is an olive grove; amongst its pathways Anemones, wild Tulips, Irises and Bluebells litter the ground, soon to wither in the summer heat. He is amazed to see tangerine trees; underfoot a Moorish Gecko scuttles under a rock. Beyond the garden, the hills are covered in Fig trees, Eucalyptus, Holme Oak and, sprinkled here and there, Cypress tower towards the sky.

From where he stands, through the intervening trees and shrub, about a dozen goats are foraging in the vegetable garden. Adam claps loudly. Several goats, mildly distracted, raise their heads and consider him for a moment. Others, unperturbed, ignore Adam and continue to eat. Adam moves towards them, flapping his hands overhead, he shouts at them and ponders his next move, as his efforts are treated with disdain, a minor irritation by the majority of the group. He looks past them, 'God there's more,' he sighs, as other goats encroach here and there and, annoyed at his lack of success, he reassesses the situation. Adam moves closer, sensing the need to escalate his approach. He considers lobbing a volley of rocks into their midst but then thinks it a step too far. As he draws nearer, he continues to flap his arms and shout like a deranged madman and, as each second passes, the goats continue to linger, almost sedated by their occupation of pillaging the vegetables. One goat in particular, larger than the rest, grunts aggressively and turns to face him. Fearing a physical confrontation, he bends and scoops up a rock, when suddenly a tirade of indistinguishable words is barked from the trees.

An old woman appears, hunched over a crooked walking stick. She hobbles down the small embankment and makes her way around the goats, prodding each one with her stick, encouraging them to move back up to the small track they have come. The aggressive goat ignores the old woman, who twists her wrist and with the accuracy of a sword fencer slices her stick through the air, in an arc, and strikes the goat's rump. It gives out a painful cry and hurtles towards the others. The old woman turns and, with yellow stalagmite teeth, she scowls at Adam and grunts what sounds like a curse. She hauls herself back up the embankment, where the goats are huddled along a dusty track.

Adam stands for some time watching them, relieved to see the goats disappear. The smell of flower and herb still fresh, he looks towards the house and sees Dylan jumping into the pool. He wonders if the boy will resent Adam being at the house, knowing his carefree existence is about to end.

'Hello Dylan, it's nice to see you again.'

Dylan pulls himself from the pool. Adam notices how skinny he appears.

'Hi.'

'Did you see the goats and that old woman?' Adam asks.

'Yes, you looked funny waving your arms about.'

'They were eating the vegetables. How often does that happen?'

'I don't know. Mum has spoken to the woman, but the goats still come back. The last time we were here, Dad shot at them and killed one. He says he was just trying to scare them.'

'That's a bit drastic.'

'The police came and took it away.'

'I see. Are you enjoying your stay so far?'

'It's good.'

'What have you been doing?'

'Nothing much.' Dylan shrugs.

'The pool looks lovely, is it warm?'

'It is now.'

'Oh, was it cold?'

'The sun heats it up like a thermostat.'

Adam smiles. 'That's a good way of putting it. Oh, by the way, your mum's told me we don't need to start the lessons straight away. We can start in a few days' time.'

Dylan wraps a towel around himself. 'Ok.'

'You've met our vegetable thieves then.' Georgia is walking towards them from the house.

'Ah, the goats.'

'I see you had the pleasure of meeting the delightful Elena,' Georgia says, in a sarcastic tone. 'I saw you from the upstairs balcony.'

'She was scary.'

'It's been a long dispute. Elena insists she has the right of way and can take her goats through our garden if she wishes. It all goes back to the time Mum and Dad bought the house. According to the deeds, that part of the land belongs to the house. Elena disputes this, saying that for generations it was used for grazing animals. Such traditions are built in stone apparently. For years it's never been an issue, Mum and Dad never used that land, so they never disputed it, the old tradition carried on and everyone was happy. Unfortunately, as you saw, some people don't recognise our right to use the land as we see fit. Elena insists she is perfectly within her right to let her goats eat my vegetables.'

'Disharmony in paradise.' Adam smiles.

'I told him about the dead goat,' Dylan says.

'Ah yes, we had several meetings with our lawyer after that. Things got a bit nasty for a while before settling down thankfully. The lawyer says we could prosecute if we wanted to but what would that achieve. Stephen is all for it of course. I don't want to make enemies. Mum lived happily here for all those years; it was a home to her. I want to continue that legacy and be accepted, not ostracised.

Adam scratches his chin, he needs to shave. 'Why don't you build a fence?'

'I thought about that but the local joiner is Elena's nephew, I'd have to get someone who doesn't live in the village, or do it myself.'

'I don't mind doing it.'

'It's fine, Stephen will sort something out.'

'Honestly, I don't mind. I just need the materials.'

'Are you sure? There's wood and things in the outhouse, they've been gathering dust for years. I'm sure there'll be nails and tools as well.'

'There you go then. It's not a big job. What if I just fence off the vegetables, make it high enough so that the goats can't get access to them and make a gate too, that's if we can find hinges and screws?'

'Handyman wasn't part of your job description.'

'No, but it'll make me feel useful and hopefully solve your problem.'

The door creaks open, throwing a patch of light into the dim interior of the outhouse. Inside, the air is sultry and a musk smell lays heavy around them. Through the wood-panelled walls, spears of light diffuse through dust, disclosing shelves filled with jars and crammed with all sorts of screws and nails. Pillars of paint, varnish and old oil tins lean against each other, rusting and peeling. Boxes gather dust, their contents undisturbed for years. Adam notices an archaic lawnmower and three bicycles leaning against each other. Instinctively, he presses a tyre which softens to his touch, deflated of air, with the lack of use. Towards the far wall, a pile of wood is neatly stacked.

'Here it is,' Georgia says. 'Do you think they'll be enough?'

'There's a lot of it.'

Adam crouches and opens an old toolbox, rummaging inside.

'Here we are,' he says triumphantly, holding aloft a hammer. 'It's a start.' He examines the shelves and the assortment of jars and containers. He coughs as disturbed particles of dust thicken the air.

'I remember riding that bike. We went for rides when I was young. Mum would pack sandwiches and drinks in a backpack and we'd spend the day exploring the countryside and shoreline. We use to pick herbs that grew wild, God I took all of that for granted; it seems magical now. It's funny how objects can generate certain emotions. Days full of happiness and adventure, that's what these bikes remind me of.'

'They still look salvageable, some oil on the chains and air in the tyres and they'll be good as new... almost.' Adam smiles.

'I should make a list of the jobs you could do.' Georgia laughs.

'Found them. How lucky is that.' Adam picks up an assortment of hinges and chooses two that match in size.

'These should do,' he says, examining them.

Georgia walks around, taking in the interior of the outhouse and its attachment to her past.

'This was never Dad's domain; he was never any good with his hands. Mum said he only used half of his brain, the artistic and creative side. It was Yannis, Theresa's husband, who accumulated all of this. He was our original handyman.' She smiles.

'Well, I think there's enough here for what we need. What was the wood going to be used for?'

'I don't know. It's been stored in here for years. I wonder if Mum intended to do something about the access to the land after all.'

Chapter 15

The Husband's Scorn

Moonlight snakes across the ceiling. Adam is lying still, but not asleep, his thoughts keep him from falling into its arms. Georgia's face, big eyes, hair falling around her shoulders, is smiling at him. This Georgia is not the self-protective, standoffish persona that sat in the airy room of an Edinburgh townhouse, driven by an intended purpose. Is this the real Georgia? Relaxed, open and confident, who has stepped from behind her veil? Has moving to Corfu, to this house, been the source of these adjustments, becalming her, as she moves through these rooms, with the light and shadows they throw, filled with endearing memories of childhood, adolescence, of being a daughter, wife and mother, surrounded by the familiarity of sounds, tastes and scents.

Lying in the room, he still feels that day's exhilaration of walking with the warmth of the sun around him and his wonderment at the landscape, igniting in colour before him. It's like being in an alternative universe.

For months now, there has been a weight pressing on him. Today, he has felt it ease slightly from his shoulders. There is a shift inside him, a physical presence, something is growing, it has pronounced itself, a pleasurable state that has removed his blindfold and embraced him. He came to teach, but this is far from his mind.

He inhales deeply, contemplating these threads of thought and their contradiction in wonderment.

Adam awakes early to an opaque sky. He sits outside his room and watches as a thin screen of skeletal cloud hangs, like a prehistoric vertebrate in a museum, luminous and tinged orange and salmon. It is a miraculous sight, his first morning. Gradually, the cloud disperses in the heat of the sun, until there is nothing left, but empty blue and the trailing contrail of a plane that stitches the sky.

Adam narrows his eyes and glances upon a gecko, motionless on a small wall. Each morning, it becomes a permanent fixture and Adam takes to calling it George. He decides he will walk to the village and maybe the beach.

That morning, before anyone is awake, he leaves the house. Lush vegetation fringes the single track that descends towards the village. In other places, patches of grass and dried earth encroach here and there. As far as he can see, an arresting shade of green, forested hills and sloping valleys scatter for miles. At one point, he notices a crude wooden sign, 'To the beach' carved into the grain, pointing to a narrow track that ventures amongst the tree trunks.

Stephen is arriving today and all morning Adam has thought of their meeting with trepidation; he can't shake it off. There is a feeling of falling, inside him. He knows Stephen played no part in recruiting him and Adam has the impression Stephen thought the whole venture expendable. A pervasive melancholy follows him until, through the foliage, he catches sight of the impassive sea, a curved bay and a white sandy beach. He is enthralled.

***

He can see the figure of a man facing Georgia, his back to Adam. Once Adam steps onto the terrace, his presence causes their raised voices to subside into an air of quiet belligerence. Adam can feel a fluttering in his stomach, like trapped birds.

'There you are. Stephen this is Adam.' There is a slight edge to Georgia's voice.

Stephen turns and gazes intently, looking Adam up and down, as if doing so would give an impression of Adam's personality.

'Hi Adam, Stephen, I'm Dylan's father.' He beams a smile that shows even teeth. He pauses before offering Adam his hand. 'Georgia tells me you're a dab hand with wood.' There is a menacing edge to his voice. 'I hope you're as good a teacher as well.' He smirks. 'Just a joke. What do you think of the place, Adam? Not bad is it?'

'What is there not to like? It's beautiful. I've just been down to the village, amazing views of the sea and that beach...'

'Remember, you're here to teach.' Stephen interrupts him. 'Not to appreciate the scenery,' he says, formally. Adam feels uncomfortable. Perhaps it is his smug countenance, but Adam takes Stephen's lack of social convention as emphasising an established hierarchy between them.

'We've just been talking about getting that printer you need,' Georgia says, embarrassed by Stephen's remark. 'I'm thinking of getting a laser one and colour of course. We're going into Corfu Town later today.'

'Thanks, that would help with the lessons.'

Stephen forces a smile. 'See, you're learning already. Georgia tells me you're from Glasgow.'

'Yes, that's right.'

'I've never liked the place. Not a patch on Edinburgh. Do you like rugby, Adam?'

'Not really, I played it at university but not with any real enthusiasm. The ball's the wrong shape.' Adam grins.

'Ah, you're a football man, never liked that either. Too working class, if you know what I mean.'

'You're building houses?'

'That's right, in Majorca. Could I tempt you with one?'

'Slightly out of my reach I think.'

Stephen smiled. 'Yeah, you're probably right, you won't get much change out of a million and that's the small ones.'

'Come on Stephen, we'd better get going.' Georgia takes his arm.

'I'll see if Dylan's ready, shall I? See you around Adam.'

Georgia looks like a parent apologising for her child. 'I'm sorry about that Adam. Stephen's has never been known for his tactful approach. He's still getting used to the idea of Dylan being tutored.'

Adam shrugs. 'It must be hard, especially the logistics. Flying to and from Majorca is not going to be easy.'

Georgia smiles at him and he feels drawn towards her simple gesture.

'He will come every second weekend if he can,' she says, combing her fingers through her hair.

Adam feels a sense of relief. The thought of Stephen not being around is pleasing to him. It is clear that Stephen resents him being at the house. Adam senses a rift between his employers. He has caused a ripple on the waters of their relationship, but he thinks what lies underneath is far more turbulent.

Chapter 16

The Priest and the Scholar's Mate

All along, from the beginning, the husband's absence has bothered Adam but that morning, Stephen's contemptuous manner had caught him by surprise. Afterwards, there had been a hint of reticence in Georgia. He scratches the nape of his neck and tries to rationalise his thoughts. Has he been naïve? It is an unsettling feeling, one that is in stark contrast to his morning walk. Then, he felt emboldened, awestruck by the glass luminance of the Ionian, where he saw a yacht appear to hover in mid-air, against the turquoise bay and sapphire horizon.

He has wandered through the village, where there is little movement in the narrow streets or behind open windows and their dark interiors. The paving stones are smooth, shining in the sun, straddled by furrowed gutters, that catch rain but on a day like this, he can't imagine it ever rains.

Even though the day is hot, he is eager to know how Greek coffee tastes. He climbs several steps of a Kafenion in the village square. Around him, several local men and a priest congregate at tables, sitting on blue wooden chairs in the shade, reading newspapers and discussing that day's news.

The heat has lodged itself inside the Kafenion, as he orders metriou (coffee), where the bar, shelves and rafters are painted a Mediterranean blue. It is the colour he associates with picturesque Greek villages in magazines and social media sites. He is served by a middle-aged woman who speaks little English but smiles cordially at him. Behind her, an array of spirits, liquors, pasta, bread and tins, crowd the shelves; underneath, religious icons are spread along the entire length of the wall. Copper pots and woven baskets hang above the bar, suspended from iron hooks that resemble miniature anchors. From outside, conversations wash into the Kafenion.

He takes his coffee and sits outside, unnoticed by the priest and men, as the day's news continues to circulate amongst them in a language that Adam finds hypnotising, even though he cannot decipher a single word.

He sips his coffee. It is strong and bitter, just as he likes. There is nothing worse than a weak tasting coffee. Adam smiles and feels this will become his local coffee haunt.

His mind shifts and a strange mixture of trepidation and excitement enter him as he contemplates the days ahead.

'You like the coffee?' the priest says, in English, his accent thick.

'It's perfect, hits the spot, which I like in my coffee.'

'I know of something a little stronger that does the same, but it's a little too early in the day for that. I've not seen you around, are you staying local?'

'I'm staying at Villa Katrina.'

'Ah, I didn't know it was being used for that. Theresa hasn't mentioned it.'

'No, the family are also there. I'm teaching Dylan, Georgia's son.'

'Teaching?'

'Yes, as in school lessons, over the summer.'

'I see. Is this your first time in Corfu or have you been before?'

'My first time. In fact, it's my first time in Greece.'

'I hope you enjoy your stay. I'm Nikolaos Chiotakis, the local priest as if you didn't know already.' He gestures towards his ankle hugging robe, grinning through his wiry beard, flecked with silver. Nikolaos has a long face and pronounced cheekbones that emit a youthfulness his years have failed to erase.

'You're not eating. Here, take one of these, it's called Loukoumi, it's a Turkish delight.' He passes Adam a plate.

'What's that sprinkled on top?'

'Powdered sugar, I hope you have a sweet tooth.'

Adam takes a generous bite. 'Mm… nice.'

Nikolaos seems casually content.

Adam licks his lips and wipes the sweet powder from the side of his mouth. 'I'm Adam by the way.'

'Do you play chess, Adam? There are only five of us today and I'm in need of an opponent.'

Adam looks towards the others, who are setting up three Greek mythology chess sets with metal pieces and bronze boards.

'Not very well, but I could give it a go,' he adds.

'Excellent, pull your chair over.'

'Like a lamb to the slaughter.' Giannis sighs in Greek, twirling Komboloi beads around his fingers. He is bald with a shadow of a beard over his double chin.

'Let us speak in English, so our guest is not left out,' Nikolaos says. 'Giannis thinks you are beaten already, Adam.'

'He has not lost for two years.' Giannis frowns, speaking English this time. 'He has God on his side.'

'How often do you play?' Adam asks.

'Most days, it depends on who can play. Mostly, we play in the afternoon, unlike today. Today there is only Stamatis who is not here.'

'I thought most Greeks played backgammon.'

'Just like every Scotsman wears a kilt. I love the Scots accent by the way.' Nikolaos grins.

'I get your point.'

Once the pieces are in place, Nikolaos claps his hands.

'Let's begin, you may go first Adam.'

Adam rests his hand on his chin and taps a finger; he moves a pawn forward two places.

Nikolaos studies the board, like a general considering his next strategy on the battlefield. He picks up a pawn and taps it gently on the board before sliding it forward onto the next square. Adam moves another pawn, mirroring his first move. A small smile creeps over Nikolaos' face; he moves his Queen diagonally along four opened up squares.

'You are trapped in the corner Adam, you cannot run, block or capture... checkmate. You are moving too quickly, you have no strategy.'

'That was only two moves.' Adam shakes his head in disbelief.

'Huh the hand of God is at it again,' Thanos says, without lifting his head from the board. 'He's one of a kind; when they made him that was it.'

'Yes, that makes me special then, a limited edition.' Nikolaos smiles. 'Take your time Adam. Study your opponent, predict my next move. You need to consider a different perspective Adam.'

Adam looks up from the board. 'That sounds as if it'll take time and effort.'

'We have all day.' Nikolaos shrugs. 'Now concentrate. We will start again and I will go first.'

Adam studies the board, his gaze flits from one possible move to the other. Eventually, Nikolaos moves a pawn forward two places. Adam moves a pawn two places mirroring Nikolaos' move so that both pawns are facing each other. Nikolaos slides his Queen diagonally four places and, folding his arms, he sits back in his chair.

'Someone is pleased with themselves,' murmurs Giannis.

'Ok,' Adam muses, his hand hovers over a knight and places it in front of a pawn.

Nikolaos activates his bishop and slides it diagonally four places. Adam moves another knight and Nikolaos' Queen takes a pawn.

'Checkmate, that move is called "*the scholar's mate.*"

'Not again. That was four moves.'

'You are improving Adam. Next time let's try to make it six moves.'

They play several more games. Adam loses each one in succession. He learns that Nikolaos grew up in Thessaloniki, the second-largest city in Greece, where he once taught History and English in a secondary school. To his surprise, Adam finds out that Nikolaos is married, which the Greek Orthodox Church allows if a man is married before he joins the priesthood, something Adam has never considered. There is a carelessness about Nikolaos; Adam decides its part of his charm as Nikolaos describes a recent wedding where the guests congregated in the square eating and dancing until late into the night.

Around him, he can see contentment in the faces of the men. The ritual of endless black coffees has been observed. The sky pours diffusing light from the sun's enervating glow, the fading grandeur of several buildings is offset by freshly painted blue shutters and whitewashed walls, the roofs are transect by sunlight, pots and vases cavort in colour, spilling pink and white, blood-red and orange, flowers indistinguishable to his eye.

A feeling presses against him.

A woman hunches over a stall, set up by the side of the road. She arranges fruit and vegetables with an ethereal delicacy.

The feeling presses harder.

He is afraid that if he blinks it will disappear. He tries to absorb it.

White steps climb towards sapphire doors. A bell tower and tiled Venetian roof of a church seem perched on the rooves of houses, like brooding doves. The air is honey-sweet. The feeling persists, as the hairs on the back of his neck stand up and gradually he is able to translate it, he is witness to a moment forged by a sense of place.

Chapter 17

The Boy Who Hugs Trees (2)

Dylan prefers being around adults, especially if he only needs to converse with one adult; when more are involved, he cannot make connections or links, these are Dylan's words for reciprocating conversation. He can concentrate on one link, but two or three at the same time is too much for him, he finds it difficult to process that information and then act upon it in an interesting way. He has told Adam this is why he prefers to be on his own. When he is listening to Mozart he does not need to be thinking of how to make these connections in the world of interaction, a world he finds confusing, where the codes of social conduct are observed by knowing what the thoughts, feelings and intentions of others are, just by looking at a person. To Dylan, these concepts are invisible, as opposed to the physical world around him, like trees. Their trunks are their body; the ridges of their bark remind Dylan of reptile skin, branches form arms and hands, clothed in leaves that sway and rustle in the wind as if speaking to one another. They have their own smell. Trees look different but are the same, they give him pleasure.

Dylan feels different. He does not feel like the other boys in his old school and there lies his dilemma, he would have liked friends at school. A good friend would have been someone who spoke about and listened to Mozart. He feels isolated and vulnerable and he understands this is why he was bullied at school.

It is awkward for Dylan to initiate and sustain friendships. This has made him feel lonely and frustrated.

Dylan is aware he often misreads social situations, and he struggles to understand that the things he is interested in are not necessarily shared by others. Everyone should like Mozart, Dylan thinks.

He has developed a system where all his Mozart CDs are divided into corresponding categories - piano concertos, violin sonatas, symphonies... all are ordered and catalogued into their chronological dates. This attention to detail makes sense to Dylan, yet in life, he struggles to plan, to choose, to prioritise or even organise and carry out simple tasks.

At times, Dylan struggles to understand his own behaviour, yet, he can also have a deep insight into how the environment affects his behaviour. He is acutely aware, as it has been pointed out to him on countless occasions by Georgia, that he lacks the ability to appreciate other people's mental states or the knowledge they may possess. This tendency to impose his unswerving perspective leads to conflict. Dylan has described this as his 'firewall' and if he believes something is right, or he has an opinion, it will be difficult for him to sway from that thought process and for others to penetrate his 'firewall.'

His inflexible thinking is also an attribute; it coats Dylan in a veneer of unshifting principles: he is always truthful, honest, punctual, what you see is what you get, there is no in-between.

Dylan's school has been an unwanted testament to his difficulties in reading deception, making sense of humour and being aware when others are teasing him. Dylan struggles to understand others' perspectives or even pick up on the emotions that others portray in conversation or through facial expressions. His teachers perceived him as insensitive or naïve, depending on the circumstance. Now he is older, he can recognise the 'big' emotions, such as happy, sad and angry, it's the subtle ones, the kind that needs intuition, an awareness of other people's body language in context or in the moment, that he seems blind to.

Dylan often cares about the feelings of others; it matters to him that his mother is happy or sad. What Dylan can't read is whether she is perplexed or dissatisfied, such emotions are too complex for him, in such instances, her face becomes a mask.

When Dylan was much younger, his literal interpretation of language was such that innocent everyday phrases like, *'He is the apple of my eye'* and *'Broken heart'* evoked such emotional reactions and confusion that they caused several public meltdowns, often to Georgia's embarrassment.

Sometimes Dylan finds it impossible to read the intentions and motives of people around him. Dylan cannot predict their behaviours or at times, even give reasons for his own. In Dylan's world, the instinctive flow that is social interaction is a maze of confusing words preceded by expressions, gestures and rules he now knows, through experience, influence how others think and feel.

The younger Dylan would often interrupt others and dominate conversations, with little regard to showing an interest in or questioning the person he was talking to. These conversations usually contained Dylan constantly talking about Mozart in sophisticated language. During these monologues, he rarely secured eye contact and was blind to the body language of the other person. He was never aware if the person was listening, and he was oblivious to their use of facial expressions and gestures that may have shown their displeasure or annoyance.

Dylan likes Adam, this new person in his life, who understands these things.

Chapter 18

On a Boat (The Gift)

The lessons are taught in a room on the ground floor of the house. Georgia insists that visiting this room each day will accommodate Dylan's need for routine, which has been absent since their arrival. For most of the morning, a large window bathes the room in light, from which they can see the garden and forested hills, silhouetted against the sky. Adam has set up his laptop and the printer Georgia bought in Corfu Town. Daily timetables are devised, each with an allocated time that allows Dylan several fifteen minutes periods to listen to Mozart. Each day, when the lessons finish, Dylan goes to the far reaches of the garden, past the vegetable patch and disappears into the thicket of trees.

Adam has found Dylan a pleasure to teach. At first, Dylan spent his time completing his work in silence, only speaking to answer a question, but gradually Dylan has eased into Adam's company.

The lessons are scheduled for the morning and Adam has the rest of the day to himself. It has taken him two days to construct the fence and gate around the vegetable patch. He has found working in the late afternoon more amenable as the heat of the day subsides and a draping shade from the trees protects him from the sun.

On one occasion Elena passed, herding her goats, one of which broke free, scuttling down the embankment towards Adam, and sniffing curiously at the ground. Adam shooed it away, unlike the discordant glare from Elena, as he felt another curse thrown at him; all the same, he is pleased with himself.

Adam has formed a communal bond with the chess players at the Kafenion. Most afternoons, he wanders into the village and takes his seat at the table where there is always the same empty seat awaiting him and a cup of steaming black coffee next to the chessboard. His chess playing has improved, although he is still no match for the studios Father Nikolaos, who wins every game he plays.

Adam has learnt that Thanos, who is often stretching and yawning, is a fisherman. He takes his small boat out each morning at dawn and unloads his catch by midday, which he sells to the local restaurants and tavernas. Giannis, owns the local grocery store, although as far as Adam can tell, it is always his wife, Eva, who is behind the counter and often berating him to her regular customers, who nod their heads sympathetically and make their purposeful excuses to guarantee a quick exit. Midas is a postman, tall and skinny with dark shadows under his eyes; he is often still wearing his postman's uniform when they meet. Midas has an aversive fear of dogs, ever since he got the tip of his finger bitten off.

As the week's pass, Adam has grown fond of their companionship; it is an emotional attachment he never expected to find. He has settled into the routine and looks forward to joining this mixed band of chess players most afternoons. He has become a familiar sight to the other villagers, who visit or pass the Kafenion. Many of them nod a greeting; others stop to talk to Father Nikolaos or Giannis, who always introduce him as Adam, the teacher.

'Do you like fishing Adam?' Nikolaos asks, holding a pawn over the board, contemplating his move.

'I've not been fishing since I was a boy.'

'We're going out tomorrow morning in Thanos' boat. You're welcome to come.'

'I don't have a rod.'

'No problem.' Thanos smiles, 'I'll bring an extra one.'

'It's my day off tomorrow. What time are you going?'

'It's an early start, at seven o'clock.'

The next morning, Adam wakes early and, after breakfast, he strolls down the lane to the village and thinks, with pleasant anticipation, about his day ahead. He inhales deeply, his senses stimulated. There is something extraordinary about the quality of light at this time of day. A soft, subdued pastel hue hovers amongst the trees and a huddle of houses, as the village draws near. The sun has not cleared the hills, its luminous light skirts the tops of trees that lurk in charcoal shadows. As he walks further, his eyes gleam, as a scattering of skeletal clouds proliferates the sky in orange, purple and lilac, infused like a furnace. It takes his breath away.

When he reaches the boat, Thanos invites him on board. Adam can see it is a working boat, the paint peels and there is rust here and there.

'What do you think Adam? Have you ever seen a more impressive boat?' Thanos grins, as he assembles the fishing rods.

Not wanting to offend his friend, Adam is economical with the truth. 'She certainly looks the part, a good boat for going fishing in... Where's Nikolaos?' he says.

'He's babysitting Midas,' Giannis moans, as he empties small silverfish into a bucket. 'Midas has overslept, he was out last night, I told Nikolaos we should go without him, but Nikolaos was having none of it and off he went.'

'There they are.' Thanos nods.

When Nikolaos and Midas reach the boat, Thanos has uncoupled the ropes and cranked up the engine.

'You look like shit.' Giannis frowns.

'I feel like it,' Midas mumbles and crumples into a seat, cradling his head.

Nikolaos slaps Adam on the back. 'Kalimera Adam. How are you this morning?'

'Better than Midas I think.'

'He'll be fine once he has one of these. Fishing's thirsty work.' Nikolaos opens a hatch on the deck. Inside it's full of bottles of Mythos (Greek beer) that drip water, like condensation. Adam realises it's a cool box.

The water laps against the boat as it moves away from the small harbour and gathers speed. Adam can already feel the sun's heat on his neck as the horizon wobbles like liquid.

'How far are we going?' Adam asks.

'That depends on where the fish are. I track them with my sonar,' Thanos says proudly.

After fifteen minutes Thanos silences the engine. 'We'll try here.'

Colour has returned to Midas' face. He has spent the time in silence, abandoned, barely lifting his head. Now he stands, looking surprisingly refreshed.

'You must have had a bucket load last night,' Giannis scorns.

'I was sober; I only had a few beers and some wine before I went out.'

'Not your classic definition of sober then,' Giannis says.

'I remember everything about last night,' Midas says defensively.

'So, how did you get home?' Thanos asks.

'Ah, everything except that part.'

'You were slumped against your front door, the key in the lock, unopened. It took two of us to get you into bed. It was fortunate I was passing,' Nikolaos says.

'What are friends for? Thank you all the same,' Midas says impishly.

'It's part of the job description.' Nikolaos smiles.

'Come on, the fish won't hang around forever.' Thanos passes the rods out, impatient to start. 'Now Adam, you remember how to fish? You don't need to cast too far; it's not a competition to see who can cast the furthest. Nice and gentle.'

They catch a lot of fish, so much so, that their initial elation fades and even the enjoyment of it deserts them after a while. They spend the rest of the morning drinking beer, except Nikolaos who drinks water from a bottle. After two cans, Adam feels the alcohol numb his head and decides to drink water.

'You don't want to dehydrate Adam. Good choice,' Nikolaos offers.

Adam closes his eyes. His head feels fuzzy against the gentle sway of the boat, 'There's nothing worse than a hangover, especially in the afternoon. Water will do me fine.'

'Unfortunately, that lot are not as wise.' Nikolaos stands and stretches his legs. 'Once again, I'll be taking us back.'

'I wondered about that. Thanos has drunk quite a bit,' Adam says.

A burst of laughter erupts from Thanos and Giannis who, smiling broadly ruffles Midas' hair.

'They've made up,' Adam says.

'They're worse than a married couple,' Nikolas says, and he starts the engine.

Adam is aware, as Nikolaos steers the boat towards the shore, this is the first time he has seen his friend without his black tunic. He is wearing jeans and a t-shirt and in this moment he looks ordinary, he could be anybody.

'You look different today Nikolaos. I was trying to figure out why and it's just struck me.'

Nikolaos bends forward, picks up the water bottle and takes a drink. 'What is it then?'

'You don't look like a priest.'

'Ah, my cassock. I'm off duty.' Nikolaos smiles.

'Why do you have to wear it, anyway?'

'It's all about the symbolism. Black is the colour of death, so I'm dying in order to rise and serve the Lord. It reminds me I die to the world every day and immerse myself in the teachings of the church. It's the flag of the church... it also hides stains.' Nikolaos points to a small stain on his t-shirt and laughs.

'That's the difference. Without the outward symbolism, that identifies someone being a priest. You could be anybody. You could still be the teacher in Thessaloniki.'

'Some days I wish I was, but not often. I've found my place in the world. I'm still a priest but in ordinary clothes. What about you Adam? That was a big decision you made, leaving a good job and heading into the unknown.'

'Mine only lasts for three months; yours is a lifetime.'

'Maybe so, but yours could be life-changing. Imagine wakening up to this. Every morning is a gift.' He gestures with his hand. 'Have you found your place in the world?'

'Before a few months ago, I thought I had.'

Adam looks around, they're heading towards the shore and he can see the houses of the village grow in detail with each passing minute. He finds the contrast between the green vegetation and the azure sky striking. The water reflects a glass image of the village and land, delicately balanced to perfection. Adam looks like he has found a valuable treasure soaked in sunshine. A gift.

Chapter 19

Mozart's Mind Map

'I've got a sore head. I need a drink of water.' Dylan disappears into the kitchen. When he returns, he is holding a glass of water. He sits down and takes a long drink.

'Ten more minutes until your break,' Adam says looking up from the laptop screen.

Dylan shakes his head. 'I think you get a sore head when you're dehydrated. When there's no fluid between your brain and skull, your brain bounces off your skull and gives you a sore head. When you drink water, it fills the space and stops your head from feeling sore.' He takes another drink and his expression seems to ease.

Adam raises his eyebrows. 'You need to drink lots of water in this weather. It's a bit warm in here today.'

Adam opens the doors into the garden and immediately it feels as if he has opened them into another world. The light slides into the room and Dylan watches him for a moment. It occurs to Adam that he has not thought of home for some time.

'Do you miss Edinburgh, Dylan?'

Dylan purses his lips. 'I miss my room.'

'What do you miss about your room?' Adam returns to his seat.

'I talk to people online.'

'Who?'

'There is a group of us, we all like Mozart. We found each other on various blogs and soon we were having group chats.'

'How many people are in the group?'

'There are five of us.'

'Do they stay in Edinburgh?'

'Oh no, actually they live all over the world.'

'Really, whereabouts?'

'Josh and Amanda live in America, Boston and New York, Zak lives in Brisbane, Australia, Liam is in Oxford and Rasheed lives in Bradford.'

'Wow, that's a diverse bunch. How often do you meet up, I mean, speak online?'

'Every night. We can see each other on the screen.'

'And do you think of these people as your friends?'

'Of course, they are.' Dylan does not look at Adam's eyes when Adam speaks to him. Instead, he concentrates on Adam's mouth, watching his lips part and glimpses of his teeth. He finds it uncomfortable to look into another's eye, he can't explain why.

'But you have not met them?'

'No, but we know lots about each other.'

'Do you have friends at home?'

'There are so many things to do to make friends, so much work, it's stressful remembering to contact people I've not spoken to in a while and it's difficult, not natural. There is a pressure of figuring out what you have to say. What if I'm not interesting? It feels natural to go online and speak. I don't have to work out what to say, you don't have to speak if you don't want to. On Vent or Skype, anyone can jump in; it's not like two people just sitting there trying to figure out what to say.'

'So you speak to your friends online here?'

'Yes, but it doesn't feel the same. At home I'm surrounded by my things, my room, I feel secure.'

Adam stands and walks towards the opened doors, pondering a thought. 'I think we will start a project. How would you feel if I said it could be about anything you wanted?'

'That would be amazing. It would be about Mozart of course.'

'I never thought it would be anything else.'

Dylan smiles broadly, his headache no longer an intrusion on his thoughts. It's the first time Adam has seen him so animated as if some wonderful thing has leapt inside him.

'We'll start off by doing a mind map. Do you know what that is?'

'No, but I've already got lots of ideas about what I'm going to do.'

'Good, you'll need them.'

Adam takes a sheet of paper and sits beside Dylan. He draws a large circle and writes Mozart in the middle of it.

'Now, what we need to do is start to think about the different parts of Mozart's life, from when he was young until he died. So, we can start with his family, who they were, where they lived, what did they do?'

'That's easy. I know all of that.'

From the circle, Adam draws a small line and writes *"Family'"* He then draws another and writes *"Mozart's early years"*

Within half an hour, the paper is covered with headings, subheadings and scribbled notes.

'There, that's your mind map done.'

'It looks a lot when it's written down.'

'That's ok. I'll put it in your timetable for each day. There's plenty of time. You don't have to have it finished for a certain time.'

'Oh that's good then,' Dylan says, relieved. 'I can't wait to tell Mum.'

'Tell me what?' Georgia says. She is standing at the doors to the garden, not quite in the room; she has on a large floppy hat, a set of pruners in her hand and a small woven basket hanging from her forearm.

'Guess what? I'm going to do a project about Mozart,' Dylan says, cheerfully.

Georgia looks at Adam and smiles.

'That sounds wonderful dear.'

Dylan picks up the sheet of paper and crosses the room towards Georgia. 'Look, Mum, we've done a mind map. How cool is that?'

He shows it to Georgia as if Adam has just given him an unsuspecting present.

'That will keep you busy. There's a lot there.' Georgia places her hand on Dylan's head.

'I don't mind, it's going to be great.'

'I'm sure it will be.'

'We're finished for the day Dylan,' Adam says, as he leans towards his laptop and turns it off, closing the screen.

'Can I start tomorrow?' Dylan asks.

'Like I said before, I'll put it on your timetable. It'll be the last thing you do each day.'

'I can't wait. Can I go in the pool after lunch Mum?'

'Only if you put sun cream on. Ask Theresa for some, she's in the kitchen.'

'Ok.'

'That's the happiest I've seen him since we arrived.' Georgia says as Dylan leaves the room. 'Do you have plans for the rest of the day?'

'I thought I'd go into the village and play chess.'

'Ah yes, you're almost a local now, I've been hearing.' Georgia grins.

'What about you, a bit of gardening?' Adam nods towards her basket.

'I'm finished now. After lunch I'm going to tackle the attic, clear it out, there are things up there as old as the house.'

'Do you want a hand?'

'No, I'll be fine. I'm looking forward to it. I've no idea what I'm going to find up there.'

Chapter 20

A Proposition

It is at Palma, at the harbour, that Stephen and Chris meet with Cesar on his luxury boat for their arranged meeting. They are reclining on cream leather sofas, under a white canopy that shades them from the sun. The spires of La Seu, Palma Cathedral, dominate the cityscape, while around them, a fleet of boats and yachts shimmer and clink in the midday sun. On their arrival, they are escorted by a young man, dressed in a white shirt and black waistcoat, to the upper deck, who informs them Cesar, will join them shortly.

Chris smiles. 'Nice piece of kit, don't you think?'

'Certainly put him back a few million.'

'It's one of the biggest boats in the harbour, a bloody ship really.'

Stephen feels the quality of the leather on the sofa. 'Well, we're not here to appreciate the view or the trappings of Cesar's wealth.' Stephen scoops the air with his hand. 'It's business as usual.'

'Stephen, Chris.' Cesar appears from glass sliding doors. He moves towards them with a confident swagger, offering his hand to each of them before sitting. He takes his sunglasses off and places them on the table. Stephen notices the Armani logo and approves of Cesar's taste.

'I'm glad the both of you could make it. Sorry about the short notice, I know how busy you are… but aren't we all?'

A waiter approaches.

'What will it be? Wine, beer, or a whisky perhaps?' Cesar offers.

'I'll just have a glass of water,' Stephen says.

'I wouldn't say no to a beer.' Chris smiles.

'My usual,' Cesar orders, and the waiter nods his head before leaving.

'How are the houses coming on, still on schedule?' Cesar spears an olive with a small fork.

'We're a week behind, an issue with suppliers, it's not a problem we can't fix and we can make up for lost time in other ways,' Chris says consolingly.

'Good and the sales?'

'There are only two houses unsold but there's interest from two overseas clients. Should be tied up within the week.'

'Excellent,' Cesar says, encouraged.

The waiter returns with their drinks and an ornate cigar box. Chris hands out a document from his case and directs Cesar's attention to various figures and coloured charts.

'Well, this deserves a celebration.' Cesar leans forward and opens the lid of the cigar box; he gestures for Stephen to take one.

'The best of Cuban.' Cesar wags a large cigar at them.

'Not for me.' Stephen waves his hand.

Cesar strikes a match and puffs until the embers are fired into life with an orange glow. He sits back, satisfied, and exhales a plume of smoke.

'You've got to admire our South American cousins. They make nothing less than quality.' Cesar looks at the cigar in admiration. 'I've only two addictions in life, these magnificent cigars and making money, lots of it.' He gestures around him with the hand holding the cigar. 'As you can see, I'm good at it.' Cesar looks at Stephen, observing him seriously. 'On the other hand.' He upturns his free hand. 'One man's addiction can be his strength, but another's weakness. I don't trust those who can't recognise their weakness, such a man doesn't have the vision to turn it to his advantage.' He puffs enthusiastically on his cigar.

'What is your weakness, Stephen?' Cesar asks.

'What is my weakness?' Surprised, Stephen waivers, he cannot think.

Chris has already lit a cigar and crumbles into a fit of coughing as he inhales. 'Christ, it's like a train hitting your throat.' He gasps. Cesar laughs.

It feels like a reprieve, as Cesar hands Chris a drink of water.

'Our venture in your fine city of Edinburgh has been very successful and profitable for us all; it hasn't gone unnoticed. I have a proposition for you that will strengthen our partnership, our alliance. All propositions need an investment of some sort and this one proposes an investment of your time but crucially, my money.' Cesar's eyes widened.

'Sounds interesting. I'm not one to shy away from a profit,' Stephen says.

'I know, but, this is slightly different. Let me explain. New markets are opening, Albania, the Balkans, the Middle East. Trafficking drugs from Albania to Greece is an arduous business, moving it through forests, mountain paths and inaccessible areas of the borders. Illegal border crossings have made it easier to move the merchandise and get it to the customer. I'm talking about cannabis, marijuana, hashish, these all end up in Greece and Italy. Heroin from Afghanistan and Pakistan is smuggled into Greece through the Balkan route. Geographically, Greece is the country of transit for drugs from the Balkans and Asia, usually passing through ports in Greece on their way to Western Europe. There are gangs in Greece. The Greek police have been successful to an extent in breaking up these operations; however, many of the police officials are involved in the trafficking.' Cesar explains that the cost in the effort of manpower and time to establish a hold in these markets is an option that is not on the table. He already has Cocaine from his South American operations that can be smuggled into Greece by sea, directly from Spain. The consignment will be camouflaged as a trade deal, coffee from South America. He has contacts in the Greek Coast Guard who will see the safe passage into Piraeus port and into warehouses. Another route is being established that will see a foothold into the Middle East market.

Stephen looks at Cesar and asks why he is telling them this, but even as the words come out of his mouth he knows his connection to Corfu is fundamental to Cesar's ambitions.

'I'll set up the meeting in Athens, all you need to do is be there, make sure the arrangements are met and those on the Greek side know the protocols, who's in charge and everything is agreed and signed, all above board. Chris will make sure all parties subscribe to the terms of the contract. They will be paid in cash, a substantial sum of money to begin with and thereafter, instalments through several bank accounts as each load is successfully brought into the country and then distributed to the next link in the chain.'

Stephen looks over the railing towards the bow of the boat where two men have stood since their arrival. He views their personas differently now. There is an air of menace about them, they are there to protect the man sitting opposite him. How many others are on this boat employed to do the same?

Cesar motions with his hand to the waiter. 'Bring more drinks.' Turning his gaze to Stephen he says, 'We need to cement our new venture with a toast.'

Chapter 21

The Discovery

Georgia is standing on ladders, and with a little effort, she pushes the hatch open. She climbs into the attic space and, remembering where the light switch is, she flicks it on. She can stand upright; as she does so she coughs, as particles of dust catch her throat. It is warm; the air is stale and sultry, the smells of faded grandeur pressing heavy against her skin. It's been several years since anyone has been up here, she thinks, probably her mother being the last.

Georgia scans the area; an excited knot pulls at her abdomen. It's either going to be an Aladdin's cave or just piles of junk. There are stacks of old yellowing magazines, cardboard boxes and distressed chairs. Several pictures lean against a beam and, incredibly, toys from her childhood are scattered along the floor: a pram with a doll still sitting upright, staring into space, a doll's house with its miniature furniture and a figurine family with their pet dog. It's like stumbling across a child's museum. They bring back instant memories. Her mother bought the pram and doll's house in Corfu Town; she remembers it as if it were yesterday. Georgia moves around the attic, opening the lids of boxes: one is full of old vinyl records, LP's and seven-inch singles, pristinely kept, as the day they were placed in the box. She comes across an old typewriter, her father's; she types her name, the sound of the keys instantly bring forth an image of him, not recalled, but rather, from the stories her mother has told her. Georgia can see him sitting on the terrace, studiously typing with a cigarette between his lips and a glass of vodka or whisky; he wasn't choosy, sitting next to him, keeping him company. She brushes her hand along the typewriter's keys, several letters have faded: L, E and C. The angled white line of the letter N is still visible, as if in defiance. Georgia traces it with the tip of her finger. She has never looked into her father's eyes and the typewriter is a reminder of this.

In a corner stand jars full of seashells and more jars filled with pebbles and sea glass. An old trunk snags her attention, reminding her of old movies, foggy train stations, steam trains hissing and porters wheeling cages stacked with trunks, similar to the one she now kneels next to. She opens the lid and is surprised at how heavy it feels. Inside, placed with care and attention, females clothes are folded into three piles. Mustiness permeates her nose, the smell of abandonment and confinement, in contrast to the vibrant colours that have refused to fade with age. She feels the material between her fingers, soft and smooth. She admires the stitching and patterns. Georgia lifts a dress from the trunk and standing, she places it against her body, a perfect fit. She loves the colour, ice blue; it reminds her of the sky.

A pocket on the underside of the lid catches her eye; she thinks she detects the shape of a book. She reaches in and pulls it out. It is brown and leather-bound, with a gold lock, a diary or a journal, she tells herself. She tries to prise the lock open, but it is stuck fast. A key, there should be a key. She places her hand once again into the pocket, deeper this time and explores each corner. Nothing, it is empty. Disappointment slips inside her, like a snake.

It takes Georgia an hour to move the items from the attic that require minimum exertion, the items that are heavy and bulky will wait until Stephen arrives later, at the end of the week.

In the kitchen, Georgia pours herself some lemonade and sits at the table. She is gazing down at the curiosity that is the book she has plucked from obscurity; she runs her fingers over the leather cover; it feels luscious to touch. Georgia picks up the book and turns it in her hands several times and while doing so, she debates a decision. She is aware of the silence in the house. Georgia takes a drink of lemonade; it numbs her forehead and momentarily her head feels weightless. Half of her wants to return the book to the attic, dissipating the guilt of the thief, but there is another side to her, urging her to take the initiative, tugging at her fascination for what may lie within its pages and with some finality, her decision is made.

She takes a knife from a drawer, the biggest one she can find, and wedges it under the lock; she makes several attempts to free it, only for the lock to squeak in protestation as the blade slips each time. She is becoming more frustrated with each failed attempt and is about to abandon the idea when suddenly the leather creaks and the latch gives way. Georgia gasps in wonderment, finding no regret in her action, as an instantaneous bubble tickles her stomach.

She sits for some time staring at the book; her euphoria has wavered, replaced by embers of doubt. Maybe there is nothing in it, not a diary or journal, just an empty notebook that someone has stored away, but then, she at once amends her thought. What if it was not spur-of-the-moment or impetuous? But a calculated and deliberate attempt to conceal, to hide and forget? In such case, was it of value to someone? Was it that precious that it could not be destroyed, burned or ripped into tiny shreds, but also at the same time not be read? There is only one way to find out. Eventually, with her thumb, she flips the book open, the spine creaks as if new. To her surprise the first page is blank; she adjusts her position on the chair.

The sun beams an angular light across the floor and, in the surrounding silence, she can hear herself breathing. This time, she picks up the book and turns the next page. She can see a date and a year; *Friday, 2nd June 1972*. The page is full of writing, her mother's handwriting, the indistinguishable flicks and exaggerated curves are undeniably hers. She always had beautiful handwriting, Georgia remembers. It feels like her mother has entered the room.

At that moment she can hear someone come into the house. She closes the book and covers it with her hands as if surrounding it with a protective screen. Bare feet slap the tiled floor Dylan runs and then stops at the entrance to the kitchen; he performs what the onlooker would describe as a subtle jig before he crosses the threshold into the room. It is a ritual he has conducted since a toddler, moving him from one room, from one space to another.

'Dad's here, look what he bought me.' He is staring at the cover of a book. 'It's called, Mozart's Letters, Mozart's Life. Selected letters edited and newly translated by Robert Spaethling.' Dylan starts to jump up and down on the spot, flapping his hands. 'This is going to be great for my project. Imagine Mozart's letters in here, in this book, that's amazing. I can't wait to tell Adam.'

'That's wonderful honey.'

'It's me,' Stephen bellows from the hallway. 'I managed to get an earlier flight.'

'You're two days early.'

'I thought I'd surprise you.'

Stephen is in the kitchen now. He throws his bag on the floor and kisses Georgia on the cheek.

'Chris sends his love. I told him he should visit.'

'That would be nice; it's been some time since I've seen him.'

'You know Chris, always up to something. I'm dying for a drink.'

Georgia reaches for the lemonade jug.

'I mean a real drink. Is there any beer in the fridge?'

'I think so. Dylan likes the book you bought him.'

'I saw it in the airport. I wasn't sure if he had it... but obviously, he hasn't.'

'Talking about books, look what I found in the attic.' Georgia lifts the book. Stephen glances at it as he opens the fridge.

'What were you doing up there? Ah perfect.' He pulls the ring of a can and the beer hisses, a gush of foam erupts over his hand. 'God, someone's been shaking this. What is it anyway?' He nods in Georgia's direction and sucks the foam into his mouth.

'It's a diary I think. Mum wrote it, I've not read it yet, but it says 1973.'

'That was before you were born. I wonder what it was doing up there?'

'Mum must've forgotten about it. I found it in a big trunk full of her old clothes, some really nice dresses in fact. I might take a closer look later on.'

'What else is up there, anything interesting?'

'One of Dad's old typewriters.'

'I bet that'll be worth something.'

'Actually, I was quite surprised; there was some furniture and some of my toys, a pram and dolls house. I couldn't believe it when I saw them, they look brand new.'

'Your mum wasn't one for throwing things out. It took us weeks to clear her house, remember? It'll be interesting to know what's in that little book.'

'Yes, I suppose it will be.' She touches the cover as if it is a thing already precious to her.

'Dylan looks happy. How are the lessons going?' Stephen sits down and takes another drink.

'He's doing a project about Mozart, it's really motivated him. It was Adam's idea.'

'Maybe he knows what he's doing after all.'

'Dylan likes him and that's the main thing.'

'Mm… I suppose so.'

'Look, Stephen, we're here now, it's happening, Dylan is being taught by Adam, just get used to it. For God's sake, Dylan has.' She points out.

'Ok, I'm sorry; it's just that I'm not here all the time, that's all. You know, it's difficult having a man I don't know living in the house, alone with my wife and child.'

'He's not a convicted rapist or paedophile, he's a lecturer, he teaches, and he's a nice person.'

'I can see Dylan's ok with him, I just need to accept it.'

'If you actually spoke to Adam civilly and took the time to get to know him while you're here, you'd feel a lot better about it. He's not a threat to you.' She realises she is defending Adam and wonders what this means?

'I will, I promise. I'm going for a shower.' Stephen crushes the empty beer can and lobs it into the bin. 'We should eat in the village tonight.'

Later that night, after they return from their meal, Georgia invites Adam for a drink on the terrace. Stephen has been drinking all night. He pours a generous amount of wine into a glass and offers it to Adam before topping up his own to the brim.

'There you go, get that down you.'

'Thanks.' Adam sits opposite Georgia. 'How was your meal?'

'It was nice.' Georgia smiles solicitously.

'Never had a bad one there so far, have we Georgia.'

'No, we haven't,' she says warily. Georgia is slightly concerned, Stephen can become argumentative if he drinks too much, but it's late now to ask him to slow down.

'Shouldn't have had that fudge cake, it's coming back up on me.' Stephen burps.

Georgia is regretting asking Adam to join them and wishes they had gone straight to bed. She offers Adam a slice of melon cake Theresa has made that afternoon.

'Not for me.' Stephen gesticulates with a hand. 'I hear you've been fishing Adam.'

Adam smiles. 'Yeah, I went this morning. I brought some fish back, Theresa gutted them for me. I wouldn't have a clue what to do, she's going to cook them for lunch tomorrow.'

'Excellent, I'm quite partial to fish.'

Adam eats some of the cake. 'Mm, very tasty.' He is feeling emboldened.

'So you're settling in then, making new friends, playing chess, going fishing, God, you've even built a fence but most importantly, Dylan seems to like you.'

'He's a nice lad; we're getting on just fine.'

'Good, I'm glad to hear it; puts my mind at ease.' He drains his glass.

'That's the bottle finished, we'll call it a night I think,' Georgia says.

'Nonsense, Adam hasn't finished his drink. It would be rude not to have another.'

'You're fine, I don't mind, here have some of mine.'

'I'll get my own, it's a bottle I need.' Stephen stands and stumbles against Georgia as he heads inside the house.

'I'm sorry Adam, Stephen's always like this; he doesn't know when he's had enough. I don't know what I was thinking; we should have just turned in.'

'It's alright, you don't have to apologise. It's fine, honest.'

Stephen returns brandishing a bottle of wine, 'What happened in Glasgow Adam?'

'What do you mean?'

'Something must have happened, what are you running away from?'

'Stephen,' Georgia intercepts, prickly with alarm.

'You don't just give up your job on a whim and decide to run off to teach someone you don't know and in another country. Doesn't make sense to me Adam. What are you hiding? Should I be worried?' There is a steely tone to his voice.

'You've got it all wrong Stephen. It wasn't like that,'

'Oh really, then how was it?'

'That's enough Stephen. I think it's time we all went to bed.'

'Oh I don't think so Georgia, I'm just getting started. I want to know what's in his filthy little mind. Do you fancy her is that it? When you're all alone with my wife, who wouldn't look at her. She's any man's dream. Are you just waiting for the perfect opportunity, or is it, Dylan?'

'For God's sake, that's it; I've had enough of this. I'm so sorry Adam.' Georgia stands and moves towards Stephen who turns to face Adam.

'You bastard,' Stephen growls and swings the wine bottle.

Adam moves to the side as the bottle just misses his head and, as he tries to stand, Stephen is already moving towards him. Adam attempts to avoid him but, in his confusion, his shoulder strikes Stephen's chest, who stumbles backwards, winded. The bottle drops from his hand, smashing into sharp fragments, covering the floor in a blood-red stain.

Georgia grabs Stephen's arm. 'Enough.' There is steel in her voice.

'Mum, what's going on. Why are Dad and Adam fighting?' They all turn. Dylan is standing in his pyjamas.

'It's ok Dylan,' Georgia says soothingly.

It is enough to bring Stephen back to his senses.

'We're just mucking around, playing a silly game, aren't we Adam?' Stephen says needy.

'Your Dad's right Dylan.'

'There's blood on the floor, why is there blood on the floor?' Dylan turns and runs into the house, the darkness swallowing him.

Georgia and Stephen have not returned, leaving Adam who remains outside, trying to make sense of what has happened. After a while, Adam decides to tidy up. When in the kitchen he can hear muffled voices from upstairs that gradually become heated. He feels a concern for Georgia and is undecided what to do when there is a silence which lasts, a truce has undoubtedly been established and the house remains silent.

Once he has cleaned up, Adam sits outside on the terrace. Four small crumbs have fallen from the cake Georgia ate and lie scattered where she sat. It is the only physical evidence to show that she sat in his company.

When he looks at her, he is overwhelmed by a want to touch her, trace her skin, feel her in his hands. It is a desire he has fought, taking the breath from him. She speaks with her eyes and he is mesmerised by them; the whites of her eyes, the inscrutable green irises converse with him. Only now does he appreciate what is meant by the *window to the soul*, for he is plunged into mesmerised reverence. He observes every detail, the wavy shine of her hair as it sways and falls brushing her shoulders, the shine of her lips, the crease in her nose when she laughs and smiles; all of these things he studies, his senses unfurl like electricity, he is alive.

After tonight, there is a sense of having been caught. There is a pulling in his chest, summoning an undercurrent of emotion that quickens inside him. He feels a pronounced protectiveness towards her but he knows it is impossible for him to stay in the house, not now. He feels his world has deflated around him. Tomorrow he will go to the village and find somewhere to stay until he can make arrangements to leave the island.

Chapter 22

The Search

It is morning. Voices, faint at first, travel through the house. The closed door obscures their timbre. Adam encounters Theresa in the hallway.

'It is Dylan.'

'What about him?'

'He has not slept in his bed. He has gone. Georgia is phoning the police.'

In the kitchen, Georgia is speaking on her mobile. She glances at Adam and then looks out of the window as if something has snagged her attention. She looks vulnerable, like a child.

'Where is Stephen?' Adam asks.

'He has left, to look for Dylan. We should do the same.' There is an urgency to Theresa's voice.

'No, the police are coming, they need a photograph of Dylan, some details also,' Georgia says, fiddling with the mobile. 'I need to find a photograph, something recent.' She waves her hand in despair and averts her eyes. A feeling of panic has tightened around her heart. She needs to keep busy. Georgia looks pale, her eyes red, blotchy and brimful of tears.

'Look, I don't need to be here. I'll go into the village and see if anyone has seen him.' Adam doesn't wait for Georgia's approval.

He walks down the lane, scanning the trees and immediate landscape. He has the feeling that his altercation with Stephen is responsible for Dylan's disappearance. His guilt forces him into a jog.

Upon seeing the beach, he decides to check there first. His feet sink into the sand. He thinks about removing his shoes but in his indecisiveness, the sea has lapped over them. The beach is empty and, because of this, it feels bigger than it looks from the lane.

Adam calls Dylan's name. The rippling surf is all that
answers. Georgia's pain looked insufferable; as he watched
her exterior crumble, it felt palpable. His instinct was to
console her, cradle her grief and dissolve it in his arms. As
he walks, he feels shameful that he could do nothing; it
covers him like a shawl. He can't imagine how Georgia is
feeling; the thought stings him. He wants to be with her, not
on this beach, that on any other day would be an idyllic
retreat.

A pervasive melancholy sits on him as he reaches the end
of the beach. He scans the rock formations that sit at odd
angles, like giant boulders resting in the sea; secluded inlets
and a menacing cave offer shelter and a place to hide.
Frothy foam cascades over deep indigo rocks, wet and
slippery. He looks up towards the tree-covered hills and
speculates that if Dylan left the house during the night, he
could be miles away by now.

In the periphery of his vision, something moves in the
thicket.

'Dylan is that you? It's all right, no one is angry with
you, your Mum just wants you home. She is worried, we all
are.'

He quickens his pace and almost stumbles. The sand is
deeper, holding on to each step, it has become an effort, the
more he tries, the slower he progresses, like the unsettling
dreams he had as a child. There is no sign of Dylan, just
bushes, dust and trees. It is then Adam remembers Dylan's
routine after his lessons. Dylan goes to the bottom of the
garden and into the trees. Amongst the pine and cypress,
there is a small clearing where a tree stands alone. The tree
Dylan hugs.

When he reaches the clearing, he is exhausted. Sweat
stains his t-shirt, tracing his spine. He slumps against the
tree; a pulse in his head threatens to explode as he tries to
catch his breath.

'Dylan, where are you?'

'That's the question we'd all liked answered,' Stephen
says, walking towards Adam. 'The police are at the house,
I've just seen their car.'

'Let's hope he hasn't gone far. I went down to the beach and thought I saw something but it was probably just an animal, I'm going to go into the village, someone might have seen him. Do you want to come?'

'I'd better go back to the house and see what the police intend to do.' He looks at Adam a moment longer. 'Georgia will need me.' He starts to walk away and then turns, 'Oh and by the way, I'll tell Georgia we've made up but, between you and me, I've seen the way you look at her. You keep the fuck away, do you hear me?'

'Look, Stephen, I don't know what you think you saw but you've got it all wrong.' Adam argues in his defence.

'Well then, treat this as a warning. The best thing for you to do is stay as far away as possible from Georgia. Now since you're living in the same house, that's going to be difficult.'

'You don't have to worry about that. I'd intended to look for a place to stay this morning.'

'If it was up to me, you'd be on a plane back home by now but Georgia values your teaching. It's the only thing that's keeping you here.' Stephen walks off towards the house.

Is it that tangible or just coincidence? Is Stephen just paranoid? Under normal circumstance, Adam would feel his position weakened but considering Stephen's behaviour of late, Adam attributes Stephen's threats to Stephen not wanting him around. His anger towards Adam has been like water hissing in a pot, eventually boiling over.

Adam believes Stephen is denying his own misgivings and camouflaging his failings by using the made-up scenario that Adam is attracted to Georgia as a threat, even though Adam thinks Stephen doesn't believe it himself.

But there is the irony of it all. Stephen is right, of course. Adam has imagined kissing her clavicle, tracing the construct of the bone, copiously brushing the skin of her shoulders with his lips and then the spot where her throat subtly protrudes, the curve of her neck and finally her lips luscious to his eye.

Not much is moving when Adam walks along the main street of the village. He passes the empty Kafenion. He closes his eyes. When he opens them, he rubs them, they are beginning to ache. The sun is hot on his skin. He catches sight of the sea between the buildings, shimmering in elastic transparency, reflecting the sky and saturated in deep lucent blue. How can it look so perfect, at a time like this, as his life crumbles around him? As do the lives of others: Georgia, Theresa, even Stephen. Dylan's disappearance has a rippling impact, like a stone thrown into water. His mind curdles with possible eventualities.

Adam tells himself he has a purpose here, in this landscape, in the lives he has touched. He looks around, reflecting, thinking. There is a period of stillness. The sun has warmed the air and is breaching the rooftops of terracotta tiles and solar panels. A line of trees follow the street; beyond them, the street curves, shimmering like liquid. Tables set for customers' sit, shaded by draping vines. Here and there, purple bougainvillaea colonises archways, above cobbled lanes where sturdy doors and window frames pepper white-washed walls in leprous blue, prominent and intense as if splashed from the sky. Adam catches sight of Giannis' hunched shoulders as he tends to a display of fruit and vegetables outside his shop. Adam walks over to him with purposeful strides.

'Kalimera Adam, You are not often in the village at this time of the morning.'

'The boy I teach, Dylan, he's gone missing.'

'That's terrible. Have you been in touch with the police?'

'Yes, his mother has. I've been out looking for him.'

'What was his name again?'

'Dylan, he's thirteen and small for his age.' Adam wishes he had a photograph.

'Is that you talking to someone again instead of working? Hurry up; I need you to move those boxes in the back room,' Eva instructs from inside the shop.

'Eva, the young boy at Villa Katrina has gone missing. Have you heard anything?'

'No, but I will phone Vasso, she might have heard something.'

With a lazy shuffle, Giannis makes his way to another stall where an array of melons is displayed.

'Do you want me to help you? I can do with the walk and the change of company.' He nods towards the shop and Eva's relentless chatter. 'A plague of blisters wouldn't stop that stubborn tongue.'

Adam fears Giannis would slow him down. 'No you're fine, just keep an eye out and if you do see Dylan, let the police know.'

'I will Adam. I hope the boy is found soon.'

He is making his way along a coastal path that fringes thick shrubs and an army of pine. A clutch of anxiety sits in his stomach.

He remembers last night when Dylan saw the scuffle. Dylan's face is freeze-framed in Adam's thoughts, a fragment of clarity, as vivid as the surrounding scenery. He recalls Dylan's static confusion, his dancing eyes intoxicated with fear. Adam is driven by guilt, from which there is no negotiation; it prevails in profound waves.

Occasionally, he catches himself wondering if he should have stayed in the house this morning. Georgia's grief was like a vice around him. He felt an imposter; most of all he wanted to preserve her dignity and that could only be rescued by allowing her the privacy to be alone. He had ached to comfort her; all he wanted to do was embrace her and melt the tension from her, clasp her face in his hands and kiss the tears from her skin. That is the world he cannot enter; he's not even sure if Georgia has sensed his gaze upon her and read the intent in his eyes.

The sun is blinding as he squints upon a dark figure. He draws nearer and to his surprise, it is Elena; she is crouched over, looking down a steep slope that falls into an olive grove. She points an assertive finger, 'Ayopi.' (Boy)

Adam is immediately overwhelmed with an urgent need to run. When he reaches Elena, he peers in the direction of her outstretched hand. Her goats are grazing amongst the olive trees; for a moment he is disorientated. His eyes are wide, anticipatory, darting from one tree to the next.

'Ayopi,' Elena spits.

It is then Adam catches sight of a small bundle lying beside the twisted trunk of an olive tree. He scrambles down the slope and thicket, stumbling over a rock, but managing to stay on his feet.

'Dylan, are you alright?' Adam shouts, gasping for air between his words.

Dylan is motionless, and a fear seizes Adam. When he reaches Dylan, he can hear the boy moan; he hunches beside him and shakes him by the shoulder. He puts his ear to Dylan's mouth and can see his chest rising and falling. Adam watches Dylan's face. Dylan's eyes flicker and half-open, heavy with effort.

'Thank God, are you hurt?'

Dylan moves and tries to sit up. 'Aw, my ankle it's sore.'

Adam helps him to sit against the tree and then inspects Dylan's ankle.

'I think it's just a sprain. There doesn't seem to be any bruising.'

Dylan looks gaunt and tired; Adam can see a few tiny scratches on his forehead and his hair is matted with dust.

'What were you thinking? Your mum's in a terrible state. Why did you run away?'

Dylan stares at the ground, he fiddles with the zip on his jacket.

'I'm hot, I need a drink.' Dylan screws up his face in pain.

'I need to get you back to the house,' Adam says, concerned.

'I know you were fighting with my dad so don't lie. I saw the blood.'

Adam thinks for a few seconds. 'No. That was wine.'

Dylan is quiet. 'I thought... I thought it was blood. I don't understand why you were both fighting. People fight when they don't like each other.'

Adam tries to be diplomatic. 'I think your dad would prefer a woman teaching you and not me... a man.'

'I've been taught by men before… at school.'

'He views this situation differently, it's not like school. You went home after the school day. The teachers didn't stay at your home.'

'So Dad doesn't like you because you're staying with us in the house. Well then, you can find somewhere else to stay.'

'I'd planned to look for a place in the village before you took off.'

'But I've not been on a plane.'

'Sorry, I didn't mean it like that. I meant when you decided to leave the house last night.'

Dylan nods.

'Your mum is really worried about you Dylan.'

'That's not a good thing. I want Mum to be happy.'

'Then you need to come home.'

Adam feels a presence behind him. He turns. A smile that stresses the lines on her face crosses Elena's mouth as she looks down on them. She hands a bottle of water to Adam.

'For the boy,' Elena says, her English surprising Adam. Her voice is soft and motherly. Adam gives the water to Dylan and Elena smiles at Dylan while he drinks.

Adam does not recognise this manifestation of concern and human charity offered inquietude. He has only known Elena as a retributive figure who scorns at them with every opportunity, like an ogre. Adam wonders if the war is over or if this is just a truce. He prefers this Elena and acknowledges this with a grateful smile.

Adam returns with Dylan in a taxi. Released from her torture, Georgia throws her arms around the boy and weeps. Dylan stands still, arms by his side. He feels a panic rising, an urge to wriggle free but knows to stay in his mother's arms is the right thing to do until he is released from her embrace.

Georgia does not entertain any suggestion that Adam leaves the house. Dylan has been through enough psychological trauma and she is determined that he will remain unscathed from any deviation to his normal routines. Arrangements are to remain intact, especially now.

Adam has no desire to contribute towards any further tensions between Stephen and himself and with Stephen's restraint agreement, it is the best thing to do, under the circumstances; it is Dylan that matters. Stephen's thaw makes Adam's decision to stay, easy to make. Yet, he has felt the weight of Stephen's falseness towards him, knowing that one drink too many will crack Stephen's veneer.

A few days later, Stephen leaves on a business trip to Athens.

Chapter 23

Moving Closer

Adam's days have a reposeful continuity about them. Stephen's absence has brought a settled and soothing quality to the rhythm of each day; these purifiers float in the air permeating through the house. He has a newfound enthusiasm since censoring the thoughts that remind him of Stephen; he dismantles them and waves them away.

Georgia is rummaging in the fridge, a gleam has returned to her eyes.

'There's orange or lemonade, which do you prefer?'

'I'm not fussy.' Adam shrugs.

'Both then.' Georgia takes the two glass tumblers and gives them to Theresa who is setting the table on the terrace.

'I thought I'd take Dylan into Corfu Town after lunch. Would you like to come?' Georgia asks enthusiastically.

'That would be good. I haven't been yet,' Adam says, placing a bread knife on the granite bunker. 'Do you think that's enough bread?' He has cut the bread into thick slices.

'More than enough, you're not feeding an army.'

Dylan and Theresa are already at the table when Georgia and Adam sit down.

'Can I eat now, I'm starving?' Dylan asks.

'Yes and take your time. Are you remembering we're going to Corfu Town after lunch?'

'Yes, Can I take my Mozart book to read in the car? I'm almost finished it.'

'Of course dear, oh and Adam's coming with us too. He hasn't been before.'

Dylan nods his head and spoons bean soup into his mouth.

'The soup's lovely,' Adam says.

'It's called Fasolatha, it's Theresa's favourite. It's a winter soup, but she makes it all year round. Don't you?' Georgia smiles at Theresa.

'And I'm glad you do, it's too good just to keep for the winter,' Adam says.

Theresa nods her head in agreement. 'I learnt the recipe from my mother; it has to be nice and thick, very filling, yes?' Theresa asks.

'It's perfect,' he says with immense satisfaction.

After lunch, Theresa clears the table and Dylan goes to fetch his book.

'I'm glad you decided to stay, I would have understood if you hadn't though. Stephen can be like a spoiled child at times.'

'It wasn't what I wanted, but I felt I had no choice. Dylan is what is important not how I feel,' Adam says.

Georgia looks away, towards the garden, as if to avoid an unheard thought. Even in the shade, Adam squints against the light, but he can detect a change in her posture, her shoulders hunch, she flicks her hair behind an ear, an explosion of firecracker corkscrews.

Adam smiles. He inhales the scents of the garden for it is all he can do to stop himself from reaching out and touching her.

'Are you happy Georgia?'

'Sometimes.' She hesitates. 'When he is away.'

Her remark nips the bud of anger in Adam. 'Does he often get aggressive... I mean like the other night when he drinks?'

'Not always, but his drinking has got worse. He can get verbal, sometimes nasty.'

'Has he ever hit you?' He catches her eye, and she turns away, tracking the garden.

Adam looks at Georgia carefully, her silence unease's him.

She nods her head. She is flushed.

'The bastard.' His eyes flick over her. The temptation to reach out and touch her is so strong. He has to clasp his hands together.

'It was only the once, in Edinburgh, he cried like a child afterwards and promised it would never happen again. He says he hated himself. You can never tell anyone of this

Adam.' She looks at him now as if to strengthen and give meaning to her words.

He takes a long drink of lemonade. Georgia smiles at him nervously. 'We better get a move on.'

In the car, there is a prevailing silence, as Adam contemplates Georgia's disclosure. In a perverse way, he feels a quiet satisfaction that Georgia can convey such an intimate revelation to him. They are moving closer, she trusts him, it is a bond he does not want to suppress, although he wishes the circumstances were different.

They are travelling from west to east, from the coast that looks towards the Heel of Italy towards the coast that fringes the fledgeling democracy of Albania. Vast ornamentations of mountains, wooded havens and wildflowers remind Adam of Tuscany. The cypress, head and shoulders above every other tree, nudges towards a light that Adam would find difficult to describe to his friends back home. It hovers, halo-like, fringing magnificent forested hills where it melts into an oasis of blue sky.

A nervous somnolence sits between them, a presence in the car that can't be concealed; an unwanted passenger, an intimidating stranger.

Dylan is buried in his book amongst the letters he devours studiously. He looks up for the first time since they set off, oblivious to the static tension of the adults. He launches into an indulgent monologue about Mozart.

'Mozart is in Paris with his mother and every time he writes to his father at the end of each letter he puts, *"I kiss your hand 1000 times and embrace my sister with all my heart and remain your most obedient son."* This must have been how they wrote in eighteenth-century Germany.'

Georgia finds a new confidence well inside her and feels oddly excited. It occurs to Georgia that a transition has taken place, an adjustment. She has moved from a dark corner into a bathing light and it has a profound effect upon her.

Adam is intense, an intellectual, the opposite of Stephen.

She turns to look at him. He has a look of uncertainty about him, a perplexed expression. Georgia is certain it was right to tell Adam, but so unlike her. It came from nowhere but she wanted the truth to be told; it felt right to tell Adam, she has not even told her closest friend. Georgia ponders this for a moment. It has changed the way they are together; even in this short time, she can feel it. Adam is the only person who knows, and he doesn't know how to react. He has been so quiet; he looks like a child pondering what to say. Georgia feels sorry for him and in doing so she struggles to fathom this emotional investment. She will break their silence.

'Did you know that Corfu is only forty miles long and at its greatest breadth it's twenty miles, not big at all really.' she smiles at him.

'No, I didn't. It looks bigger than that, maybe it's because the landscape is so green, it gives the impression of space. I wasn't expecting that.'

Georgia pauses. They both smile at each other then.

Whatever was between them now recedes.

'Corfu has a population of a hundred thousand or there-about, not a lot of people really. It has the population of a small city,' Dylan says, as a matter of fact, without lifting his gaze from his book. 'And just over thirty-nine thousand people live in Corfu Town. It's on the UNESCO World Heritage list, actually.' He turns on his I-pad.

Adam feels an irrepressible desire to sigh with relief.

There is a settled air around them now and for the first time, he relaxes in his seat. He looks out of the window. The traffic is heavier, and he glimpses the sea.

'I'm glad I told you.' Georgia glances across at him with a smile.

'You are. You don't regret it then?'

'No, I've needed to tell someone for a long time but it had to be someone that cares.' She hesitates a moment 'Someone I can trust.' There is a certainty of affection to her voice and no repercussion of regret. 'You'll love Corfu Town, especially the old town.'

There is now a build-up of houses and shops, mini supermarkets, hotels and tavernas. This semblance of civilisation encourages Georgia to tell Adam of her favourite places to visit and to eat in Corfu Town; it helps to dispel for good the gulf that has sat between them since lunchtime.

The road widens and soon they are parallel to the sea where two small islands, like anchored ships, seem to float on the placid water. Reefs sprout by the side of the pavement tapered like Spartan spears. Georgia points out to Adam the port, where a ferry is about to dock.

Soon they are on foot, ambling through the cobbled stone lanes of the old town. Green and blue shutters, some sunburnt turquoise, like the Ionian itself, sprinkle the walls with fading grandeur. Many of the buildings have wrought ironed balconies and at three and four stories high, the walls shade the luminous stone pavements from the sun. There are tourist shops selling cheap trinkets, ceramics, t-shirts, blouses, fridge magnets, handbags and sun hats. They stumble upon churches, quaint cafes and restaurants where tables with newly pressed table cloths sit next to peeling banana-yellow walls. They turn one corner to find ceramic vases populate a stone staircase with flowers that explode in an array of purple and orange, white and red and above Adam's head, from one building to the next, washing lines dangle clothes in the eddied air.

They pass St Spyridon's church, with its domed tower, Kremasti square and then the Jewish quarter. Dylan complains that there are too many people and he is hot. They buy ice cream and sit on steps. Dylan escapes the sounds around him by listening to Mozart on his I-pad.

'He seems to be coping well.' Adam nods towards Dylan.

'He is. We visit the town often when we're here, he has got used it. Actually, the places I've shown you are where we normally go when we visit.' Georgia smiled.

'Ah, I see, keeping to routine then.'

'Very much so. It makes life easier. He's not too bad at the house; he has his own rituals throughout the day as you've probably seen.'

'Yes, I've noticed he likes to visit a certain tree and hug it. When I first met Dylan, and we went for a walk along the waters of Leith, he showed me the tree he hugged there. I'd never come across that behaviour before, not in children with autism. The more I thought about it, I began to understand why. It de-stressed him from having to be continually sociable in his efforts to communicate with others throughout the day.'

'He's come a long way. I'm really proud of him, given what he's had to cope with. When he was younger, it was different then. He wouldn't interact with people he didn't know and sometimes he didn't even speak with those he did know, like Stephen's parents. That was really frustrating and embarrassing, especially for them; they struggled to understand him anyway.

'Social settings were nearly always excruciating affairs. I'd answer for him, so there was no need for him to interact with others, which of course just reinforced his difficulties. Why would he communicate with others when I was doing all the talking for him?' She looks at Dylan and gives a little smile.

'As a parent, it was hard, especially before his diagnosis; we didn't have a reason why he behaved the way he did. We struggled to understand him but that changed when he was eventually diagnosed. We started to look at the world around us from Dylan's perspective; it's amazing how different it looks and feels. I walked around in his shoes for a day and tried to experience the world from an autistic perspective. After that, I read as much as I could, I went on the internet hungry for information, but there's so much of it.'

'Were you given any information when he was first diagnosed?'

'We received an information pack, and I went to a parents' group. Stephen didn't. No surprise there. I was surprised at how many people there were. I was able to speak to others who didn't view me as a neurotic mother. They empathised and shared their experiences. I'd discovered other parents who were going through similar experiences and emotions. That was powerful, a "wow" moment. Before then, I hadn't let anyone help me or break into my inner circle, as it were. I thought if I asked for help, I'd be failing him as a parent.'

Adam shook his head. 'You're not the first to think like that, it's common.'

'The group occasionally invited guest speakers to discuss various topics. I remember one quite vividly. She was talking about communicating with your child, being responsive, she called it. As parents, we constantly want to help our children, it's our natural instinct. We do particular tasks or even when we're showing them what to do we end up doing it, anyway. But this was what was wonderful about her talk. She spoke about tuning into your child, finding the correct frequency, using what motivates them, being aware of what they're doing and do it together. Share in their focus of attention. She urged us to take advantage of family routines and rituals as a means to encourage interaction and communication.' Georgia wipes her hand with a napkin.

'And so, that's what I did. When Dylan was five he developed an interest in listening to classical music, well, initially it was a compilation CD of classical music that we got free with the Sunday paper. I use to play it in the car and he'd always ask for number 5, which was Mozart's symphony, Jupiter. Eventually, I was so sick of hearing it, I bought him a compilation of Mozart and it just grew from there. He wouldn't listen to anyone else; it had to be Mozart. I used his obsession as a motivation for good behaviour. We had a reward chart on the fridge and if Dylan achieved five stars at the end of the week, we'd go to a shop and buy him another Mozart CD and so Mozart became the impetus for our interactions. We'd listen to the music together and he started to interact. There was a common link. Now, of course, we've graduated to full conversations'.

'What about Stephen?' Adam asks the question gently.

'Stephen was carrying around this overwhelming guilt that his son was not normal, that Dylan was not the perfect child. God, no child's perfect. I, on the other hand, coated myself, I found an inner strength and all those people who were judgemental and critical of the way we dealt with Dylan ceased to have a negative effect on me. I stopped questioning myself.' Georgia stands up and stretches her legs. 'I'm sorry for going on so much. I don't know why I'm telling you all this.'

Adam looks up at Georgia, her face framed in the Venetian splendour of the buildings all around them. 'It's really interesting. A lot of what you're saying reflects a lot of parents' journeys. Some don't adapt as easily as others. You've done a good job. You should be proud of yourself.'

'Oh, I don't know about that.'

'Dylan's a credit to the way you've brought him up.'

She waves her hand in the air dismissively. 'Shall we get something to eat?'

They eat outside, seated at a small table with a red checked cloth fastened at each end with plastic clasps. They order meatballs seasoned with thyme and sage, spaghetti served in white bowls, salad with shredded lettuce, carrots, onions, cucumber, feta and olives. Bread arrives in a basket, fresh and with a crispy crust. They drink bottled water and when they have finished eating, they sip dark coffees, whilst Dylan savours two scoops of strawberry ice cream.

Georgia cradles her cup in both hands and smiles at Adam. He notices for the first time that her nose creases slightly when she smiles.

'The perfect end to the perfect day,'

'It was delicious, good choice,' Adam says.

'Another one of Dylan's routines. He won't eat anywhere else.'

'Ah, I should have guessed.' Adam's eyebrows rise. His eyes meet hers and for a moment they linger.

'Can we go now?' Dylan asks.

'Yes dear, I'll pay the bill first.'

Adam reaches into his pocket. 'It's my treat, Adam.' Georgia insists.

On the journey home, they zigzag along serpentine roads and, to Adam's delight the sky is fused in lingering orange and red. Gradually the light drains, leaving a crimson ribbon of cloud that scorches the horizon. The sinking sun fades to pearl and before long, darkness falls like a black curtain, blotting the landscape that is now familiar to Adam.

'I can't believe how quickly it gets dark. One minute its light and then suddenly pitch black.'

A broad smile suffuses Georgia. 'It took me a while to get used to it. I don't even notice the change now.'

When they arrive at the house, Georgia has to wake Dylan, who has fallen asleep with his earphones plugged firmly in place. Drowsily, Dylan shuffles towards the house as Georgia instructs him to, 'wash, teeth cleaned and bed.'

Georgia touches Adam's arm. 'I'm glad you decided to stay Adam.'

He is conscious of the gesture and smiles, 'So am I. Thanks for today. It was wonderful.'

'It was my pleasure and thanks for listening to me. I thought I might have scared you away earlier on.' She removes her hand.

'Not at all, it took a great deal of courage. I might even tell you one of my secrets one day,' he says as if it was an everyday occurrence.

'Sometimes, the moment just feels right, that's how it felt, anyway. I didn't wake up thinking I was going to tell you.'

'No, of course not.'

'And as I said, it was a one-off, it hasn't happened since. So, how do you feel towards Stephen now?'

'I felt shocked at first, outraged and then anger, but now, I suppose I pity him in a strange kind of way.'

'You do?'

'He must feel insecure right now. I feel guilty about that... Georgia, if you ever feel threatened by him, tell me. Now I know, I couldn't stand by and do nothing.'

Georgia seems a little taken aback, her lips tighten and she nods slightly, her eyes brim with tears. She flicks her hair behind an ear and it is a gesture that even now, tormented by the knowledge of what Stephen has done, stirs an imperceptible desire in Adam. He wishes passionately that he could kiss her.

They move up the steps and onto the terrace to the metallic sound of crickets.

'School day tomorrow, Dylan's eager to get on with his project.'

'I suppose I'm in it for the long haul then,' Adam says and grins sheepishly.

'I like the sound of that,' Georgia says and smiles back at him.

Chapter 24

The Diary

The diary has always been on Georgia's mind, nudging her
at certain moments of the day. With the incident on the
terrace and Dylan's disappearance, reading a diary that
concerns the past felt an indulgence. There was a reluctance
to open its pages when the present demanded so much of
her attention. Also, the thought of Dylan running away and
spending that night afraid and confused could have been
avoided if she had only gone to his bedroom and checked
on him; she could have comforted him in her arms. Guilt
had bruised her and it felt raw but now a rhythm has
returned to their days. Dylan is settled and the worst is over.

She sits on the edge of the bed, the diary in her lap. She
draws her breath in sharply and thinks of her mother,
writing the words on each of the pages, in this very house.
A warm feeling encases her, Georgia smiles to herself and
opens the book…

1972

Emily Rossa tentatively turns the key of the lock and the
book opens with a creek, a sound that announces its
newness as a pleasing current passes through her and
Emily's lips curl into a broadening smile. She flicks a wisp
of hair from her face and then, picking up her pen, she
begins to write on the crisp white paper.

Corfu, Friday 2nd June 1972.

*We arrived at two in the morning, after a bumpy landing at
Corfu airport, and then travelled across the island in a
Mercedes that we bought in advance of our arrival. I told
Paul it was a bad idea and we should just hire a car at the
airport, but he was having none of that. It doesn't look like*

the same car, in the photograph, that was sent to us. I think the car had been in its prime when I was at Primary school. It constantly grumbled and groaned as the crunching of its gears echoed through the countryside that was constantly hidden from us in the darkness.

I was unable to see if the outside of the house was indeed in need of the coat of paint Theresa mentioned in her last letter, as Paul brought the Mercedes to a halt, turned off the engine and extinguished the lights, as the rhythmic sound of a cricket pulsed in the pitch blackness. I did not even have the energy to unpack and fell into bed exhausted, where sleep consumed my senses, until late this morning.

I had intended to have breakfast with Paul, outside on the terrace where there is an old solid oak dining table but, as usual, he was up early and left a scribbled note in his spidery handwriting that announced he was out buying food and supplies in the village.

After a breakfast of eggs, toast and coffee, which Theresa had supplied for our arrival, I wandered around the grounds and ultimately felt dismayed and saddened at what I saw. The garden is in need of immediate attention and the paint on the window frames and shutters is indeed flaking in parts. Thank goodness Theresa has been coming every week to clean and air the house. Domestically, the house has an air of being lived in, during our absence, which is a blessing.

Due to Theresa's frequent correspondence and much to Paul's amusement, I have already made a list of the jobs that need to be done. He says that I should allow myself to settle into the slow pace of life that is the genetic predisposition of all the island's inhabitants.

We bought the house three years ago and have been coming back ever since, in the summer months, enjoying the climate, tranquillity and landscape that surrounds this beautiful area.

As I write, the air from the opened window is suffused with the hint of fragrant scents from flowers and herbs we abandoned to their own devices when we left last October. The olive and fruit trees in the orchard have harvested an

abundance of oranges, lemons and olives and I wait, in
fervent anticipation, for them to caress my palate with their
riches. The lawn garden is in need of the lawnmower's
blades, which reminds me; I need to check on the garden
tools in the garage.

I should mention that Theresa is our housekeeper;
actually, that is unkind, she has become a dear friend and I
know that it is reciprocated on her part too. I put an advert
in the post office in the village and she replied to it. I was
expecting an old woman dressed head to foot in black to
come hobbling up the hill from the village with deep creases
lining her face like a road map. Instead, to my surprise, this
young woman, slim in build, with long ebony hair appeared
at our door. That was three years ago and Theresa has been
looking after the house ever since. Her husband, Kyriakos,
tends to the lawn and is a general handyman who visits in
between his other jobs. She has two lovely children, a boy
and a girl and while she works, her mother looks after them.

This is the only place that Paul feels he can truly write.
He has written his best books here. Back home, he suffers
from constant writer's block. He calls it his affliction; it
infuriates him, but the moment we arrive, he begins to
construct plots, themes and characters, at such a rate, that
he will have written a new novel, pored over several drafts
and have it ready for editing once we return to the cold
climate and rain of Edinburgh. I suspect that when he
returns from his shopping trip this morning, he will have
constructed the entire novel in his head and spend the rest
of the day surrounded by the constant clicking of his
typewriter.

As well as writing, he also reads while we are here, at
least ten books, obsessively. He says it loosens the creative
spur in him and generates his inspiration.

For my part, I am enthralled by the beauty of the
landscape and agreeable climate. Most of all, the house
keeps me coming back. The original house dates back over
300 years, but it has had many transformations since then.

The local people would call it a farmhouse. It was once,
but it has grown in size and now its purpose is more

recreational. Like most similar houses on the island, they
are called holiday houses, which I surmise, is to attract the
tourists who are now beginning to arrive each year in
alarming numbers.

We are surrounded by spectacular views of pine-covered
mountains and undulating verdant countryside. The house
is perfectly peaceful and hidden, tucked away from a
country lane and only reached by negotiating a single
winding track that snakes up the hill from the village to the
haven that is this house. Her mellow coloured two stories
clad exterior radiates a subtle rustic charm that sits in
eloquent and compelling surroundings. In the gardens,
mature pine trees impregnate the air with scented pine.
Colourful shrubs, herbs and citrus fruit trees populate the
ground around the house, as well as the fruit orchard, with
its abundance of orange and lemon trees.

The house has four bedrooms, a small reception room,
large kitchen, that we modernised with new appliances, two
bathrooms, dining room, lounge, garage and covered
terrace, with cooking facilities and stone built BBQ. Each
room is dominated by oak beamed ceilings and tiled
terracotta floors.

We were attracted to the location as Paul wanted
somewhere he could write that would offer seclusion,
privacy and be off the beaten track. The house perfectly fits
these requirements and more. It is tranquil and ideally
quiet which is often complemented by birds singing during
the day and the flutter of butterfly wings.

I'm planning to give the place a makeover, nothing too
drastic of course, a bit of paint here and there, freshen the
place up a little. I have decided on painting the interior
walls terracotta and over the next week or two, I will source
out some locally crafted fabric from the village. Paul has no
eye for such things however, he has one stipulation. He is
insisting on retaining the interior stone wall features and I
must admit they do complement the oak beamed ceilings
rather well.

I am expecting Theresa today...

'Yassou.' The voice carries its way to the bedroom where Emily has just finished casting a satisfied critique over the page.

'Theresa,' Emily cries out. The sound of the voice draws Emily down the stairs, her flip flops smacking the tiled steps as she hurries to embrace her friend.

'You look beautiful, as always,' Emily says, as she steps back and regards Theresa in admiration. She has large and wide eyes full of happiness.

'And you too. The house has been too quiet without you,' says Theresa in her perfect English.

'How is Kyriakos, and the children, I bet they're all grown up?' Emily asks excitedly.

'They're all well, but driving me crazy,' Theresa says with a smile.

'You can tell me all about it over a glass of lemonade.'

They sit outside on the covered terrace and drink ice-cold lemonade that has been made from freshly squeezed lemons from the orchard. The morning air is already warm and scented with the sweet aromas of the garden.

'There are many opportunities now. Kyriakos has started to work for a company who are building lots of hotels.'

'That's wonderful.'

'It's long hours and hard work but the money is good. He won't be able to come as often to help around the house and garden.'

'Oh, don't worry about that, Theresa, we'll get by. If it comes to it, Paul can do his fair share in between his writing.'

'I saw him on my way here. The car is very noisy.'

'The thing's a death trap. He's taking it to the garage he bought it from. I told him it was a bad idea to buy a car he'd never seen,' Emily rebukes, rolling her eyes. 'But you know Paul, once he gets an idea in his head there's no moving him. It's a Mercedes, he said, what can go wrong.'

They both laugh.

Emily pours more lemonade; she loves the way light makes the ice cubes glisten, like diamonds, she thinks.

'I've had some thoughts on redecorating the house, a lick of paint, cosmetic touches really, nothing too drastic: cushions, a splash of fabric, the place needs to be brightened up a bit.'

'I have just the place for you. A new shop has opened in the village, it would be perfect, just what you need: local handcraft, fabrics, ornaments, pictures, cushions, even clothes.'

'It does sound perfect.'

'It's owned by a friend of mine, Gabriella. She creates and designs all the clothes she sells. In fact, I bought this dress from her. Tell her I sent you, you might even get a discount.'

Emily admires the soft sheen and cut of the fabric and how the pale yellow dress delicately hugs Theresa's figure.

'She certainly has a talent. Your dress is perfect. I was going to visit the market this Sunday morning, I should pop in then.'

Chapter 25

The Boy Who Hugs Trees (3)

'I read a book written by a boy who has autism. It is quite good. There were sections in it where I thought, that's just like me, I do that or I think like that. I saw online that some people with Asperger's call themselves, Aspies, and they call people who don't have autism, neurotypical.'

'Have you ever met another person with autism?' Adam asks. It is another hot day, and the lesson is almost over.

'When I was eleven, I went to a social skills group with a bunch of other kids with autism. After eight weeks, that's how long it lasted, we called each other friends, but we never kept in touch. Mum phoned the other mums, and we all met up at each other's houses, but it didn't last.'

'That's a shame. Would you have liked to stay in touch with them?'

'We were all different.' Dylan shrugs. 'They hadn't even heard of Mozart.'

Adam smiles. 'I suppose they liked more modern music.'

'I don't know, but just because we had autism doesn't mean we're all going to get on.'

'No, that's true.'

'I know lots of people without autism, but they can be odd at times. They say things they don't mean, mum calls it a white lie, that's not logical. How can a lie have a colour?'

'It can be confusing; it's just an expression people use. Sometimes people don't always say what they mean so as not to hurt the other person's feelings.'

'People should tell the truth, it's not nice to lie. I don't lie, I always tell the truth.'

'That's a good way to be.'

'I can't tell white lies. Mum says I don't recognise other people's feelings, but it's hard for me to work out how they feel by looking at their faces. I don't know what they're thinking when they do something or say something, I don't know what they actually mean a lot of the time. It's hard enough just trying to understand the words they use. Most people don't actually say what they really mean, anyway. I spend all my time trying to work out why someone's doing what they're doing, not how that makes them feel. I don't know because I don't know what they're going to do, I don't know what they might say and if they say something, what am I supposed to say back? It makes more sense just to talk about Mozart. I know lots of things about Mozart.'

'Do you have a favourite piece of music by Mozart?' Adam asks Dylan.

'Several actually. At the moment: Piano Concerto No.20 in D minor by the Philharmonia Orchestra. The Concerto lasts for 39 minutes and 14 seconds.

'What do you like about it?'

'It gives me a warm fuzzy feeling.'

'Music is good at that. It can make you feel different emotions, it can also trigger memories.'

'When I'm happy, I think of the colour blue.'

'So when you feel an emotion, do you always see a colour?'

'Yes,' Dylan says, warming to the theme. 'I see the colour in my mind. Sometimes yellow is happy because it reminds me of the sun and I like when it is warm.'

'What about feeling sad?'

'Black,' he says, without hesitation. 'Always black.'

'When I was a teacher, I knew another boy who thought like that.'

'Did he have autism too?'

'He did, but he was older than you.'

'People with autism look the same as other people, we just think differently. You can't tell someone has autism just by looking at them. I find it difficult to look at a person's face when I have to speak to them. I'm getting better at it now, but only because mum told me it was polite to look at the person who is speaking.'

'Did you ever get into trouble at school because of it?'

'I did. I would often look at the wall when the teachers were speaking, and the teachers thought I was being rude, but I wasn't. I've never felt autistic, I'm just me. I can't help the way I think. It's like, it takes me a long time to work things out, especially when people say lots of things at the one time and use lots of words that are confusing, they just get jumbled up in my brain. Mozart's music is the complete opposite of that, it makes me feel that everything is ordered. It relaxes me, like a drug, well I've never taken drugs so I don't really know about that actually. I've just heard people say that.'

'It's called "*a figure of speech,*" you used it in the right context.'

Dylan nods his head, but there is a quizzical look about him.

'Now, about your project. We need to decide how you will present all the information you've collected.'

'I want to do it like a timeline. That would be cool.' Dylan flaps his hands excitedly.

'You need to plan it, get the dates, the information in the correct order.'

'That's easy, I know it already. Within each section, I could put in the detail and some pictures,' Dylan says, eagerly.

Adam stands up and walks over to a table. He picks up the mind map they made earlier and places it on the wall.

'We need blue tack to stick this to the wall. It's best if it's visible, you can use it as a blueprint.'

'I've already written a lot about Mozart's Italian tours. He was thirteen when his father, Leopold, took him on his first one. They started out on the 12th December 1769, but before then, he had played in Vienna, Munich, Paris and London and he was given lots of accolades and distinctions. He met lots of famous people too: composers, violinists, singers; it's all in my notes.'

'Excellent. Well, the next stage is to get all of that information into a visual format, so that's what you can do now.' Adam replaces the mind map on the table.

'Adam, I'm going to my special tree after we have finished today. Would you like to come?'

Adam looks at Dylan, who has started to write in his workbook. 'I'd really like that, but are you sure?'

'I wouldn't have asked you otherwise.'
Adam smiles. Of course, you wouldn't have.

Walking through the grove they are watched by ancient
olive trees. The hypnotic rush of gentle waves is dulled, as
they venture further, encased by a canopy of branches and
underfoot a fine film of fallen leaves and pine needles
lightly crunch with each step they take.

'Why do you hug trees, Dylan?'

'Sometimes I like trees more than I like people. I get a
nice feeling inside me. I can smell the bark, feel the ridges
on my face, and it feels like the tree is holding me. It's a
nice warm feeling.'

For a moment Adam is silent, he looks at Dylan, whose
eyes are closed; his arms embrace the tree as he rests his
cheek against the bark and it occurs to him that Dylan is
happy in his world amongst the trees, cocooned from the
social world of conversation, of reading others' body
language, predicting others emotions, deciphering the
meaning of words within sentences that jump around in his
head, a confusing mass of misinterpretation. In his world of
hugging trees, Dylan is safe in his sanctuary.

Adam steps forward and places his hand on the tree. He
hasn't really given much thought to trees; they are just
there, part of his scenery, but as he feels the texture of the
brown ridges of the trunk and looks up to the sprawling
crown of branches that reach towards the sky, he feels
dwarfed by its presence and by its magnitude.

'I like your tree, Dylan.'

Chapter 26

Athens

Stephen smiles confidently, even though his stomach churns, as he shakes the outstretched hand of Spiro Rossis, an Athens lawyer and his contact. Spiro is tall and thin, with receding grey hair; he wears spectacles and is dressed in a dark suit, white shirt and blue tie. Stephen puts him at about fifty, but the hair could deceive, the late forties maybe.

They stand in a spacious room, minimalistic and clinical; the floor to wall glass offers a panoramic view of a sprawling Athens, shimmering in the summer heat.

The villa is perched on a hillside, an affluent northeastern suburb of Athens; it is just one of many upmarket properties camouflaged by trees and vegetation, fortified by imposing walls and gates.

Stephen had taken a taxi from his hotel and gained entrance to the villa by relaying a password into the speaker on the wall. The villa sequestered amid lush green trees and capacious lawns. The whine of the security camera, as it turned and followed his progress along a winding driveway to the entrance of the villa, unnerved him, his heart thumping wildly.

He asks himself, what is he doing here? Even in the asking of such a question, he knows the answer. It is just another venture, a transaction, it is business; the merchandise and marketplace are different, the rules remain the same.

Spiros smiles back at Stephen, with what seems like genuine warmth. 'Please take a seat, Stephen,' Spiros gestures with his hand. Stephen notices the Rolex watch.

'How was your journey from Palma?'

'A bit bumpy, but fine.'

'Ah, first class can be a bitch at times.' A sarcastic smile crosses Spiros' face. 'Where are staying?'

'At the Royal Olympic Hotel. It's nice.'

'It should be at those prices.'

'I thought it was hot in Majorca, but I wasn't prepared for this.' Stephen loosens his tie.

'Even for us Athenians, it is warm. Would you like a drink?'

'Water would be good.'

Spiros speaks in Greek to one of two men sitting on sofas at the far end of the room.

'All the arrangements are in place. As I told Mr Ramos, there'll be no problems at this end.' Spiros smiles reassuringly.

'I'm sure he already knows that that's why you are involved.'

'Precisely,' Spiros says with an air of self-worth.

'Shall we get down to business? All we need to do today is make sure you're happy with the contracts and sign them. I'll inspect the warehouses tomorrow and we're good to go.'

Stephen's water arrives. He places his briefcase on the glass table in front of him, flicks open the latches and hands Spiros a fold of papers. Spiros scans the documents and Stephen notices small beads of perspiration on Spiros' forehead.

'Everything seems to be in order.'

'That's your copy; we need this one signed too.' Stephen places another contract on the tabletop. 'Take your time; there's nothing there that hasn't been agreed.' Stephen takes a long drink of water.

Spiros nods his head confidently. 'Mr. Ramos is a very thorough man; I'm sure everything is how it should be.'

Spiros continues to study the documents for a few minutes more. Stephen sits back in his chair. It is his first time in Athens and, as he looks out, he is surprised at the expanse of the city. Eventually, Spiros takes a silver pen from his breast pocket, 'All in order.' He smiles exposing perfectly aligned teeth.

Stephen wonders if the smile cost Spiros several thousand Euros.

'Let's make it official shall we?' Spiros signs the documents with assertive flicks of his pen.

Stephen takes out his mobile, scrolls his contact list and activates the letter 'C.'

'It's done. We're live.'

Chapter 27

Evaluation

The days pass and stretch out in a languorous haze. Now and then a light breeze ruffles the trees, nudging oranges and lemons, daring them to fall. The sun dazzles in the sky, leprous in blue, and the sea flits from displays of dazzling azure to pellucid turquoise.

Georgia often tends to the flower beds, adorned in irises, white freesias, jasmine and white roses, mauve and blue flowers, an illustrious play of colour, spraying the garden in an iridescent quality that seems to have appeared in a short space of time. Butterflies skirt from flower to herb adorned in yellow and blue, black and white. The Jacaranda tree with its blue flowers gives way to the grove of lemon and orange trees. The pervasive heat stops everyone from becoming too energetic and a sedated pace settles into the life of the house.

Georgia has begun to redecorate. She has bought bed linen, throws, natural shades of paint, a new sofa and fridge, several pictures and a large mirror, all delivered from Corfu Town.

It has taken the painters a week to finish sanding, varnishing and painting the house. The walls of the house have a fresh look about them, complemented by the Corfu light that seems to have a special quality all of its own. Outside, the wooden shutters have been sanded and painted, brightening the exterior of the house where they look new again.

This fresh look to the house and Georgia's interior design skills have given her a sense of achievement and, now that Dylan has recovered from "*the incident*," as it is referred to, Georgia feels a period of normality has been enjoyed by all. Stephen's work in Majorca and now the additional trips to Athens has meant his visits have been less frequent. Normally, such absences were cause for discontent; however, Georgia knows it has influenced the air of contentment that has descended around them. With each passing day, the house has become a haven for her; quietude prevails, the likes of which she has not known in years.

There is a constant equilibrium. Yet, there is something else, and it prods at her now and again. She is sitting on the terrace looking at the garden, at the hills and terraced olive groves. Something inside her has changed, and she pinpoints it to the moment she closed her mother's diary after her first reading.

Georgia is thrilled to discover her mother was also in the middle of decorating the house, but the more she reads the diary, she is unprepared for the detailed accounts of her mother's thoughts and feelings that pepper the tone and pace of her prose.

Georgia has found the diary to be, not just a record of events and happenings, it is an intimate transcript of experience and discovery, and intense personal revelations, but, also light-hearted and frivolous. It celebrates the bonds of friendship; it ponders decisions to be made; the cracks appearing in her mother's marriage are portrayed with all their warts.

Georgia has wondered why her mother never spoke of the diary, or of its existence. As it languished in an attic, did she just misplace it and as time passed, forget about it? No, when Georgia discovered the diary in the trunk, it had been deliberately put there amongst other possessions that were folded and ordered, not carelessly or randomly; there had been a systematic approach towards the packing.

Georgia feels privileged to learn about this period of her parents' lives. The diary is giving up the stories it has held and kept secret. Georgia wonders if it was written for others to read or for personal gratification. Why did her mother keep it hidden in this house? Was it precious to her?

She has thought a lot about her mother and concluded that reading the diary has begun a process of evaluating her mother's identity. There is the mother of Georgia's childhood, her adolescence and into womanhood. She does not know this other woman that the diary reveals. Georgia has entered another world, her mother's private space.

These thoughts and others like it, accompany her day, like close companions.

In the past, her mother often glossed over the time she spent at the house, before Georgia was born, preferring to reminisce about the times Georgia was there as a child. Now looking back, it is as if she erased from her memory what the diary now discloses. When she considers such things, Georgia is aware that, even now, Theresa is also often evasive about her mother's past.

Georgia rarely thinks of her mother's connections to this house, but the last few days have changed that and resurrected feelings and memories that have been submerged deep inside her for years, raw and undisturbed until now.

Chapter 28

Gabriella

1972

Sunday 4th June 1972

Paul has been reading, under the covered terrace all morning, Eudora Welty's new novel, 'The Optimist's Daughter' He tells me with great interest that the book's main themes involve death, class, grief, love and loss within a family context. I'm not sure whether I would enjoy the story, it sounds rather a heavy read; anyway, I have far too many pressing distractions to occupy my mind.

It seems to have stirred his creative juices though. After lunch, he spent a successful afternoon writing, which seemed conducive to his celebratory mood this evening, and the two bottles of wine he consumed before falling into bed in an unsavoury fashion.

This morning, I took a walk into the village below us. It is only a brief five minutes on foot and constitutes a leisurely downward gradient. However, the return journey is less agreeable. Walking in flat shoes was not as easy on one's calves and, with the added addition of the afternoon sun and two overflowing bags, I soon regretted the irresistible urge I gave into, the purchase of a consortium of fruit and vegetables and the many fine items from Gabriella's treasure trove of a shop. Their combined weight dug into and pulled at my fingers, so much so, I had to stop frequently to stretch my fingers and dull the burning ache in my shoulders.

As I eventually and thankfully entered the welcome coolness of the house, I stood there, wordless in my discomfort, as droplets of sweat trickled down my spine and dampened my dress. Paul chuckled and said I looked like I had just walked out of the shower.

My morning in the village was worth the arduous walk
back home...

Emily walks the declining gradient of the dirt track that
leads to the village. She can feel the morning sun growing
increasingly warm on her shoulders, its presence a welcome
companion, as the scent of pine floats around her, like
feathers. Emily wears a strapless white dress that sways at
knee length with each step. She fingers a small lucent cross,
a birthday present from Paul, wrapping the chain around her
forefinger. Contentedly, she contemplates the morning
ahead.

Ochre-coloured stone buildings meet her, as she leaves
behind the crackle of pine leaves underfoot. Their facades
stand decorated in iron-railed balconies where blue and
white wooden shutters sit imprinted and bold, like the
features of a well-known face. Emily wanders through a
labyrinth of narrow cobblestoned lanes that twist and turn,
revealing tavernas and bars around each new corner.

She fights off the irrepressible urge to enter a baker's
shop, whose decorative displays of cakes and pastries have
already lured an unsuspecting small crowd with its
indistinguishable sweet aromas. She almost trips over two
skinny kittens, as they chase each other, blindly darting
between ceramic pots that border her path, watched by the
dozing eyes of their mother who spreads herself across a
shiny stone step.

Emily's eye is drawn towards a window and a dark blue
dress that hangs like a picture. She admires its cut, the
delicate detail of the embroidery and the quality of the
fabric.

Emily looks at the sign above the doorway and an
inevitable realisation comes over her, 'Gabriella.'

'It couldn't have been anyone else,' she smiles and
delicately steps over the somnolent cat.

She is met by an unannounced coolness of air that blows
over the inside of the shop by a fan on top of the counter.
The walls are stripped back to their original stone and
whitewashed. Perched in each corner of the ceiling, two

small white speakers immerse the shop in the deep bass resonance of Bach's Cello Suite No. 1.

Compartmentalised shelves house assorted fabrics and cushions, their rich colours intensified by the backdrop of the white walls. Emily is particularly attracted to the tasteful ornaments and sculptures that project a distinguished style, some might think overly pretentious, but it is very much to Emily's liking. A glass case houses rings and necklaces, which she studies. Then several railings of clothing consume her interest. She shifts the fabric between her fingers, holds a blouse to her chest and admires the reflection in a walnut framed mirror.

From an archway, Emily is aware of a figure. A young woman moves towards her.

'Yassas.'

'Oh hello… Yassas.'

'You are English?'

'Yes, I was just admiring your clothes. Well, everything really.'

'Thank you. Can I help you with anything? There's a small room in the back you can use to try on the blouse, or anything that catches your eye.'

The young woman inclines her head and flashes hazel eyes over the garment. Emily notes she ties her hair back with a red ribbon. She has an attractive face and a small frame that her tight jeans accentuate. A fine gossamer plume rises from her cigarette which she extinguishes in an ashtray on a nearby low counter.

'If you don't like the colour, I can make you one in the colour of your choice.'

Through the archway, Emily notices a sewing machine and shelves, stacked with uniformed rolls of cloth, a rainbow of fabric: orange, lemon, purple, white and green.

'I like the dress in the window. Could I try it on?'

'I have one I've just finished. I'm sure it will fit you.' She disappears through the archway.

'Where are you staying?' She calls from the other room.

'Just outside the village. I'm freshening the décor of the house so I thought I'd have a look around. Actually, you were recommended.'

The young woman leans out of the arch. 'You are the woman Theresa works for?'

'Yes, I am.' Emily smiles, the affirmation she is Theresa's employer leaves her embarrassed. She swings her gaze to the cushions, avoiding the subject. She has always considered Theresa a friend, as opposed to an employee.

'I love the detail in the embroidery on the cushions. I think I'll take these two and this fabric as well.'

'My name is Gabriella.' Gabriella emerges holding the dress. 'Do you like the colour?' She gives it to Emily.

'I call it ice blue.'

'It's perfect.'

'Try it on,' Gabriella urges, casting an eye over Emily. 'It will fit you perfectly.'

Emily follows her to a small changing room.

'Theresa speaks fondly of you. Your husband is a writer?'

'He is. This is our third year in Corfu. We visit each as much as we can. I adore the place.'

'Yes, we're lucky to live in such a beautiful village, but unfortunately, we don't attract the number of tourists that Corfu Town does. I'm moving there to open a boutique.'

'I'd better buy some of your dresses before you do. This one is beautiful,' Emily says, emerging from the changing room.

'It's made for you. I'll give you a ten percent discount today.'

'I wouldn't dream of it,' Emily says.

She looks in the mirror. The dress fits perfectly. I'll wear it tonight, she thinks. She is having dinner with Paul in the town square to celebrate Paul's recent news. His agent has just secured a new publishing deal in the States after the recent success of his book there.

Gabriella folds the dress and places it in fine wrapping paper. She puts the cushions and throws into a separate bag emblazoned with the logo 'Gabriella'.

'What about that ten percent discount?'

'No. How are you going to open a shop in Corfu Town if you give away discounts to everyone that knows your friends? If Theresa asks, I'll say you gave me a discount.'

'Then take this.' She hands Emily a ticket.

'What's this?'

'I'm having an exhibition of my work in two weeks. I'd be grateful if you would come. Theresa is going. It's always better to have people at these things that have actually bought from me. It's good for business.'

Emily looks at the ticket and smiles. 'I'd be delighted.'

Emily sits in the square, under a white umbrella that shades her table from the sun, the bags from Gabriella resting at her feet. She orders a coffee and a slice of walnut cake. There are only several tables occupied, the lull before lunch. She congratulates herself on her purchases and promises herself she will return soon. She takes the ticket from her purse and looks at the venue; it isn't a name she recognises. She thinks of asking a waiter but then reconsiders; Theresa is going as well. They could go together, as friends, and she looks forward to the prospect, full of ardent anticipation.

Chapter 29

Inhabitations Melting

Above their heads, strident bougainvillaea and vines populate trellises that shade them from the heat. It is midday and Adam and Georgia are sitting enjoying a coffee. The owner of the taverna, Pandelios, an old friend of Georgia's mother, has taken their order. He is in his seventies, his hair is silver and thinning on top and he walks with a stoop and limp. He is unshaven with a forest of grey whiskers on his chin. Georgia feels his gaze, a kind look that enjoys her presence.

'I'd heard from Theresa you were staying at the house. It's nice to see you Georgia. The news of your mother's passing was a shock to us all. She was a good friend.' Pandelios bows his head and crosses himself solemnly.

'She loved coming here, the house, the village; they were all special to her. She always regretted that she didn't come more often.'

Georgia remembers this was her mother's favourite place to eat. It reminds her of the summers they spent at the house. She feels an effervescence run through her body.

Pandelios shrugs. 'That is life, getting in the way of the things we enjoy.'

'This is Adam; he is giving school lessons to Dylan.'

Pandelios shakes Adam by the hand. 'Ah, the teacher, I've seen you at the Kafenion. Father Nikolaos speaks highly of you but not of your chess.' Pandelios grins and Adam shakes his head, enjoying the old man's humour.

'What will you have?' Pandelios asks, licking the lead of his pencil before it is poised to take their order.

'Two coffees, two bottles of water and… I think I'll have a Baklava.'

'Your favourite.' Pandelios smiles.

'You remembered.'

'How could I forget? It's all you ever asked for, but you had to promise your mother you would eat all your main course first.'

By his expression, Georgia realises Adam hasn't a clue what they are speaking about.

'A Baklava is a dessert. I love it. It's crisp pastry layered with a filling of walnuts and drenched in aromatic honey syrup.'

'One or two? '

'We'll share. Could you bring two forks?'

'Share! Georgia! Your mother had to always steal a piece.' Pandelios shakes his head in amusement.

'My daughter, Christina is getting married next Saturday.'

'That's wonderful. How old is she now?'

'Twenty-one.'

'Gosh, it's incredible how time flies, she's a woman already. I still remember her as a young girl. I've not seen her for years.'

'It would please me if you came to the reception; we are having it in the square after the church service.'

'But that's just for family and friends.'

'You are the daughter of Emily, which makes you family. Bring your husband and Dylan. Adam, you come too. Theresa will be there also.'

'Well, if you're sure, I'd be delighted.'

'Good, that's settled then.' Pandelios turns to head towards the counter where a young woman is cleaning glasses.

That morning, Dylan awoke with a pasty face and a film of perspiration over his body. He complained that his arms and legs were sore and returned to bed. Georgia made him drink a glass of water and tucked him into bed. It was a Saturday, so there were no lessons. Georgia had planned to pack a lunch and take Dylan to the beach. She had been looking forward to it, but now turned her attention to domestic matters.

When Theresa arrived at the house, she insisted she would watch Dylan and encouraged Georgia to take time to herself, there was nothing she could do that would change how Dylan was feeling and he had slept most of the morning, anyway. Georgia accepted Theresa's offer.

She met Adam as he finished his game of chess with Nikolaos. Adam saw Georgia walking towards the Kafenion and joined her, accepting her invitation of a coffee.

As they walked, a smile twitched at Georgia's lips. 'Don't worry; we've been the topic of conversation since the day you arrived. Let's give the chattering classes something else to talk about.'

Pandelios arrives with their coffee and pastry. 'Kali Orexi.' He smiles and shuffles towards another table.

Adam wonders why the old man continues to work at his age. Pandelios' face lights up; enervated by an explanation or a set of directions he has just given, as he chats to a family. Adam overhears they are staying at a hotel in Paleokastritsa.

Pandelios is active, his mind is alert, he converses with his customers, his life has meaning. In fact, that's it, Adam decides; he probably feels liberated from old age by the life he leads. Adam smiles as he feels Georgia watching him.

'Have you any plans for the rest of the day?' Georgia asks.

'No, not really. I thought I might go for a walk later on.'

'I was on my way to the beach for a swim, I love the sea compared to our pool; it's too restrictive. The beach is never busy, tucked away and hidden, that's why I like it. Would you like to join me?'

'I'd like that, sure.'

He smiles to himself; a euphoria of joy tickles his stomach, he feels a desperate elation. Her presence strains his capacity for self-control. He wants to subside to the urge of tracing every part of her delicate skin; it seems a natural response that delights him with its possibilities. The intelligent side of him errs on the side of caution but he can't drag his eyes from her.

Georgia reaches into her leather lattice bag and retrieves her purse. 'I'll pay for these. My treat.'

The thought of being rational could easily evaporate from him. He knows she has not reciprocated in words or gestures the way he feels about her, but that is not to say she does not harbour a purity of feeling for him, beyond mere friendship. Something is developing, he is sure of it. There is a palpable acceptance on her part that Adam is now more than just the employee hired for the purpose of teaching her son. Would he jeopardise that? What if he kissed her, would she yield to him, be embarrassed, or worse still, recoil in shock and find him weak and vulgar? The loss of dignity would be inflicted upon them both. The thought is insufferable. He could not put her through that. Yet, he is constantly in a state of riotous passion, absorbing her every detail. He draws his breath in tightly, to deny his desire is to deny who he is. For now, he exists in a moral no man's land.

The heat is intense and subsiding occasionally by a tepid breeze that seems to evaporate too soon on the sizzling sand. The only means of cooling off is to swim or lie where the sea meets the sand. The beach is sparsely populated and sits in a bay sheltered by wooded hills and terraced groves.

Adam is sitting on a towel, watching Georgia. They have bought a bottle of wine and drink it from polystyrene cups. Her inhibitions are melting, he tells himself, as she steps out of her shorts and unbuttons her blouse, revealing a bathing costume. She has climbed onto a large rock where she stands poised. She bends her knees and then with a spring, she dives, like an arrow and enters the sea. Adam is impressed by how majestic and seamless the dive looks, but then the sensation fades as Georgia doesn't surface as he expects. His eyes widen, he leans forward and cranes his neck, casting worried glances over the calm surface. Just as he is about to get to his feet, Georgia emerges a considerable distance from where she entered the water. Her hair is flat against her head, shining in the sun and she is smiling broadly.

'Come on in Adam, it's lovely and warm.'

Adam gestures towards his shorts and shrugs.

'They'll dry in no time,' Georgia says reassuringly.

He is warm and the thought of cooling off is tempting.

'Ok then, but I'm just coming in as far as my knees.'

He draws his t-shirt over his head and walks to meet the sea, the sand hot underfoot. Consciously, he pulls his stomach in.

The surf ripples softly and reminds Adam of the contours of a tortoiseshell; flecks of sunlight, snow-white in the pellucid surf, dance around his feet. The water is just below his knees and swells against him dampening his shorts. He cups water and lets it fall between his fingers. Georgia has slipped under the surface and emerges a few feet from him. A sense of wanting to be near her flushes him in anticipatory pleasure, pushing him into a dive, and he is submerged into the warm water.

'See, I told you it was warm,' she says, with a grin.

'It's like a bath,' Adam says.

Georgia moves a piece of hair from her face. It is the first time Adam has seen her like this as if she has just stepped from the shower. As he draws near her, his hand brushes her arm. It is not deliberate, but it sends an accomplished feeling through him. He wonders if Georgia feels the same.

'That was an amazing dive.'

'I used to do competitions when I was younger; I stopped when I was fifteen, but it's like riding a bike, the skill never leaves you.'

'How do you stay underwater for so long?'

'I hold my breath,' she says, grinning sarcastically.

They are the only bodies in the water. The beach, too, is almost deserted, apart from a couple and a family of four, the mother reading a novel while the father helps his two children, a boy and a girl, build sandcastles and a network of roads in the sand with plastic spades and buckets.

From the water, the bay looks different; the tree-covered hills seem magnified and stretch into the distance, touching the sky, a blue so intense, sharp and crystal that Adam feels he is looking at it for the first time.

Once they dry themselves with towels, Georgia slips into her shorts and applies sun cream to herself.

'You haven't always been a mother. What did you do before you were married?' Adam asks.

'I was a lawyer.'

'Really?'

'Does that surprise you?' She takes a drink of wine.

'No, not at all.'

'I worked for a law firm in Edinburgh, specialising in property deals, real estate, that kind of thing.'

'When you interviewed me, you had a professional air about you. I can see now that was your professional side. You didn't come over as being a mother if I'm to be honest. Don't take that the wrong way. What I mean is, it was like a real job interview.'

'My background helped. I slotted into the role quite easily.'

'You did.'

'I wasn't too harsh I hope. Did I come over as being clinical, uncaring?'

'No, you didn't.'

'Good, it was quite nerve-racking. It's different when it's your job; you have an identity, a professional role, there's not that personal bond involved.'

'Is that how you met Stephen, through work?' Stephen would be furious if he knew about this: the coffee, the beach and the swim, Adam thinks.

She nods. 'It was. He was a client. I worked for him in London, several contracts,' she pauses. Adam notices she doesn't say his name.

'He offered me a job. I was based in Edinburgh and he had a place in London. When we married, I went part-time and when Dylan was born, I just did enough to keep myself up to date and registered. Then, when I realised Dylan had his difficulties, I gave him all my time. I couldn't work, anyway. I wanted to give him the best I could. By the way, being a full-time mum is the hardest job in the world.'

She thinks of her own mother, and the diary, and imagines, what it must have been like bringing up a child on her own. Sometimes Georgia feels like a single mother,

Stephen is always away on business. She wonders if it affects Dylan.

'I found a diary in the attic the other day,' Georgia informs Adam.

'That sounds exciting, whose was it?'

'My mum's. She wrote it in the early seventies when she stayed here in Corfu with my dad. I've not read it all, but it's really detailed and personal.'

'That must feel weird, but good at the same time.'

'It's strange. I'm intrigued to find out what she's written, but I'm conscious I'm prying into something that's personal, that wasn't meant to be read.'

She sighs. 'It's not just that. It's stirred a lot of things from the past... when she died. I kept a memory box, jewellery, a bracelet, a brooch, that kind of thing. I've got her reading glasses as well. If they were not on her head, she was always walking about with them in her hand. They were forever being waved in the air when she spoke, like a conductor's baton.'

There is a hint of reticence visible and then Georgia gives a small resigned smile. 'I miss her terribly. It's been thirteen years; it feels like thirteen weeks. I wish I'd given her more of my time. I regret that now. It eats away at me. I remember the important things. It's the small mundane details I've forgotten or didn't even notice. It catches me, like a cramp. There's still times when I wonder what mum would have thought about this or that, just silly things. I wish I could ask her, just listen to her voice once again. I don't know why I'm telling you all of this.'

'It's ok, I don't mind. It sounds as if you need to talk about it.'

Georgia nods. 'Yes, It still helps... to talk about her. I feel quite comfortable talking like this with you. I don't know why. You've grown on me, Adam.'

His eyes linger on her longer than they should.

'I've thought about this and on the surface, it probably seems obvious, but there's a deeper current to it and it bothers me. What I've learnt, and to my own cost, is that the time we share with those we love is a gift, it's precious, yet it slips from us unnoticed and we can't stop it; it has a life of its own. If I'd known that my mother's death was imminent, that we were hurtling towards our last days together, then every second, every tiny detail would be logged in my head, encased in my memory.' She taps her head with a finger.

'Instead, those little details have melted from me. Nothing is permanent, time doesn't stop. Don't you think time distances you from people? When Mum died, I thought about her every day, but now it's different; she feels distant from me and I feel this incredible guilt.' Georgia looks away. 'My memories of her are not just the images I have in my mind... they evoke profound emotions, and the trouble is, I'm left with the guilt. I feel I didn't do enough for her. She suffered so much and kept it to herself until that suffering became physically visible and the choice was taken from her. There are things I should have said.' Her words make her feel ashamed. A silence follows.

'She said she didn't want to worry me, burden me, or as she put it, "*infest my every thought with her cancer.*" She once said it was like a computer virus, once planted in your conscience, it spreads, and there's not a second of every day that its presence isn't felt, it hijacks every thought and decision. She didn't want me to go through that; she wanted to delay it for as long as she could.'

'She was just protecting you. It was her instinct. She was your mother, Georgia.'

Tears well up and glisten in Georgia's eyes. She rubs them away. 'God, I didn't realise I felt so emotional, I'm sorry, I'm being stupid.'

'No, you're not; you'll only start to feel better if you talk about it. Call it D.I.Y. therapy; it's good counselling, part of the healing process. Think of it as going on a journey, but one you don't have to experience on your own, it can be shared. You have to travel along that road before you can reach the end, a conclusion.'

'And what would my conclusion be?'

'Acceptance.'

She recoils a little. 'Will you travel with me… on my journey?'

'For as long as you want me to.'

Georgia reaches out touching Adam's hand. 'Thank you.'

He wasn't expecting the physical contact, her hand is warm. He takes a deep breath.

'I use to dream about my dad, not a lot now. They were recurring dreams. Some were different, but he's always alive and, in my dream, I know he should be dead, and it's like he came back to visit me. In each one, I hug him as tight as I can, and he cups my face in his hands and kisses my forehead and whispers, *"Love you to your bones."*

'It was something he never did when he was alive. He wasn't that kind of man, he didn't do emotion. And then there were other dreams where the roles reversed and it was me who held his face and whispered: *"Love you to your bones."*

'That kind of affection never passed between us. I often thought he was emotionally barren as a parent when I looked back to when I was younger. He was cold. There's a phrase, 'refrigerator parenting' that describes him to a tee. I didn't really know him; I feared him in a strange way. Maybe those dreams helped me come to terms with the guilt that always seemed to be teetering on the edge. I was carrying it about, like a jacket, I wore every day. I think in some way, subconsciously, I was trying to atone for all the things I'd never said to him when he was alive; I was breaking down the emotional barriers that were always there between us. Life's too short to have regrets Georgia.'

'Since we're both being honest with each other, apart from your father, what regrets do you have Adam?'

'I've had some.' No words pass between them for what seems like an eternity. Georgia worries that she may have upset him.

'I was married,' Adam says, eventually. Georgia looks at Adam as if he has just revealed some great secret.

'I wondered about that when we first met. It crossed my mind during the interview when you said you weren't married and I thought, does he mean, not now or has never been, but obviously, it would've been wholly inappropriate to ask.'

Adam thinks back to the interview. That Georgia is someone from a different time, not this woman in front of him that he has grown more than fond of.

'If you don't mind me asking, what's her name?

'Katherine.'

'Were you married long?'

Should he tell her? He suddenly feels cold, an unnatural feeling in the heat.

'We were; five years in fact.'

'Where did you meet? How did you meet?' Georgia says, enthusiastically. She smiles vivaciously. She's starting to feel tipsy, that initial numbness that frees inhabitation.

'We were both at the same university. I literally bumped into her.' He remembers with a smile.

Georgia registers affection in his tone. 'Do you still love her?'

'She died in a car crash,' he pauses. 'She was six months pregnant. It was six years ago now.'

Georgia's jaw drops, aghast. 'Oh my God, I'm so sorry Adam, how awful.'

'I stopped the car and got out to help a woman who was on the hard shoulder, struggling to change a wheel. And then, I saw this car on the other carriageway swerving erratically. There was a long screeching noise that seemed to go on forever and suddenly it was heading towards us. It swerved again and hit my car head-on. She died instantly. He had been drinking.' He rubs his forehead and his fortitude begins to waver. Georgia feels an urge to reach out to him.

'She was the most perfect, beautiful person I'd ever met. She was my life, my love, and my best friend. I know she would have wanted me to live my life to the full and have no regrets. We've all lost loved ones; we deal with that in our own ways at the time.'

'I can't imagine how that must have felt.'

A smile forces its way across his face. 'Time helps, not that it gets any easier; medication can numb the pain, but that's not the answer. Life continues, it doesn't stop.'

'And is that how you coped, by getting on with life?'

'Eventually... It took a long time. At times, the grief is unbearable, but on a day like today, talking about it is my weapon.' He looks at her steadily. 'Why don't you write a letter?'

She looks at him quizzically. 'A letter?'

'Yes, to your mother. Write everything down, as if you were talking to her again. Tell her how you felt then and how you feel now.'

'Do you think it will make a difference, I mean, will it help?'

'It may help to put things into perspective. You need to be truthful. Make peace with her, with yourself.'

She considers what Adam has just said and embraces the idea. 'Yes, you may be right,' she says with joy and relief.

She raises an eyebrow. 'And you... have you written a letter, to your wife... to Katherine?'

'I did, and yes it helped.'

'Good. I'm glad.'

Adam is surprised by her concern. 'I've still got it. If you do write a letter, make sure you keep it safe. At the beginning, I read it a lot. Not so much now, though.'

'I will, definitely. I think it's something I need to do.'

It takes Georgia three days to organise her thoughts and summon the courage to write the letter.

Dear Mum,

By writing this letter, I hope to start a healing process that will allow me the grace to understand and come to terms with the insurmountable loss your departing has left.

Where to begin?

If only you had confided in me, I would have been prepared; I would have been there for you, in the beginning. I could have helped more. I may not have eased your pain or its advancement, but at least I could have comforted you. You would have had the opportunity to share your thoughts, your pain, and your anger. Why did you only disclose your cancer when you knew your time with us was ebbing away and your body had been defeated by this disease? Why mum? Were you trying to spare me? Shelter me from the inevitable until the time came when it was impossible to do so? Were you sheltering from our pity?

I am being selfish. I am only thinking of myself, my feelings.

I could never imagine what you must have gone through. To daily live your life with the dignity you portrayed. Each living minute, hour after hour, day after day, conveys the person I could never be, but only look towards in admiration. In my heart, I know you wanted to spare us the immense turmoil this disease brings but, in doing so, you made the end so much harder to accept.

I was not ready to lose you… to let you go. If only I knew that those days were to be our last together, I would have absorbed every detail of every second, every minute and hour. I could have recorded our times together so that, in some way, you would be with us, amongst us, and then I would be able to revisit those precious times together.

I say this because, as time passes, sometimes the clarity of your image softens and gets harder to define, and it does not matter how hard I try, I cannot focus on your face, your eyes, your mouth, the subtle colours of your hair, the tone of your voice fade, like a balloon rising into the sky, as it slips from a child's hand. I feel like that child.

Regret haunts me with its bitter taste. I am endlessly revisiting the times when I should have told you I loved you but didn't. Not just with words, but with actions as well, the giving of affection, the smallest gesture can say so much. Did you look for this from me?

I still have cherished memories. I loved the way we spoke about the little things in life- what are the best flowers to plant in spring, where to shop for that dress, discovering an authentic Italian restaurant, the shows and plays that *inspired you to go out nearly every evening during the Edinburgh festival.*

When I was a teenager and had broken up with a boyfriend, you were always there to place a bandage on my broken heart, or to help me with a decision I had to make that seemed, for me at the time, to be the most important thing in my world. At that moment, you made it yours too, just by being there and listening, understanding and never judging, but always offering sensible advice that was comforting and always right. Each and every day, you were always there for me, and I will spend each day living by your example, by always being there for Dylan, to support, encourage and love. This will be your legacy.

I will never get over your death, but I will try to live by your example, and if I can emulate just some of your courage, your grace and your wisdom, I will be a better person for that.

Until we meet again,
Always, you're loving daughter,
Georgia.

She lays down the pen and exhales deeply. She has hoped for a feeling that will lift the weight from her, but none is forthcoming. It's a beginning, she tells herself, small steps first.

Chapter 30

Nothing to Declare but my Genius

1972

Tuesday 6th June 1972

Earlier tonight, we ate in a local restaurant hidden amongst a small network of lanes in the village. Everything looks different at night; there is a glow of light that radiates from the streets, shops, restaurants and tavernas, as the locals call them. In my ignorance, I don't know what the difference between the two is. On this visit to Corfu, I'm determined to immerse myself in local history and customs. I'd picked up several phrases of the Greek language on my earlier visits and it's my goal to eventually be able to converse with the villagers and hold a conversation. Since I hear the language every day, I'm hoping that it won't take too long. Theresa has been teaching me almost daily, which has been a tremendous help.

At dinner tonight, we ate in a local restaurant hidden amongst a small network of lanes. Paul's mood was elated...

'I received a phone call from my publishers this morning when you were out shopping. It looks like I might have to go away, for a week or two at the most. They want me to go to New York, capitalise on the book's success and make the most of the moment, that kind of thing.'

'That sounds marvellous, Paul.' Emily smiles.

'The New York Times want an interview. No doubt they'll want a picture as well. I'd better take a good suit. You don't mind Emily, do you? I'll be back before you know it.'

'When do you have to go?'

'I'm waiting on confirmation, but it looks like they want me over next week. I need to go to London first, and then travel on to New York. I know it won't be good for you dear, the timing stinks; after all, we just arrived.'

She waves away his concern with the flick of a hand.

'Oh, don't worry. I've enough to keep me occupied here, freshening up the house for one thing. You won't recognise the place when you get back and, besides, I've got Gabriella's exhibition to go to as well.'

'It'll be good for you to socialise. I'm sure Theresa will look after you. If anything it'll get you away from the house without me tagging along.'

He drains the wine from his glass. 'I'm glad you're ok about it. Shall we order another bottle?'

'Not for me. I'll just have a coffee.'

He lights a cigarette. 'Well, you won't mind if I do then.'

Paul calls the waiter and orders another bottle of wine and a coffee.

Light drains from the sky and leaves a crimson ribbon of cloud that scorches the horizon.

'An article in The Telegraph claimed, rather opaquely, that Scott Walter was lured from Scope Publishing to Randolph House by an outrageous advance. I always knew he was motivated by money; it resonates with mercenary overtures.'

'You never liked the man,' Emily suggests.

'That's not true,' Paul replies without hesitation.

'You once said, he could only sell books because of his good looks and media-friendly personality. There was a hint of resentment there. Am I not right?'

'He's acting like a rock star, not an author, and the media treat him like one. I could almost accept his celebrity if he'd written anything of quality. He's not exceptional, not even average. He's abandoned the novel and married money instead.'

'Oh come on Paul, you can't complain about that. You've done quite well when it comes to making a good living out of words. But is that important? Should it not be enough that people enjoy his books and there's a lot who do, let's be fare. Are you questioning their literary judgement?'

'Well yes.' Paul fills his glass.

'That's pompous Paul. You've become a literary snob. I don't read a book because it meets with the approval of the author's peers, or because of its intellectual stamina, or its beautifully crafted prose and cinematic scenery. I read it because it entertains me.'

Paul sighs. 'If it doesn't meet, as you so eloquently put it, with the skill of our craft, then it shouldn't be printed on paper. The novel should have a potent effect on the reader, emotionally, psychologically and spiritually. It ought to be layered with all the elements that tease out what it means to be human, absorbing the reader into the pages with beautifully crafted scenes, iridescent language and characterization. It's an art form, not a piece of disposable junk.'

'When you hear a song you like, do you enjoy listening to it?'

'Obviously.' Paul shrugs.

'So, when you're listening to that very song, are you analysing the chord sequences, the chord changes from major to minor, are you critiquing the quality of the musicianship or debating if the lyrics are thought-provoking? No- and that doesn't make the song any worse. The song connects with you on a simple level, it has a hook, a catchy chorus, you may even identify with the lyrics but essentially you listen to it because it entertains you.

'It seems to me that fame has replaced religion in the public consciousness. It's because of the Scott Walters of this world that people are addicted to celebrity. Wouldn't you like a slice of the fame cake?' Emily asks, raising her eyebrows.

'Certainly not,' Paul says, suddenly aggrieved. 'I'm respected for my work not for worshipping at the altar of celebrity.'

Emily looks at him seriously. 'But going to America could change all that. I'm not suggesting for one minute that's your reason for going, but success will expose you to the inevitable roller coaster that is the media machine.'

'In that case, I'll have nothing to declare but my genius.'
He throws his head back and laughs.

***

The water flow cascades over Emily and dispels the soap
lather, leaving her skin glistening in the pallid glare. The
shower sings like a waterfall. Persistent images slide across
the surface of her thoughts: Paul sleeping silently, contented
rasps of breath escaping his nose like a soft breeze,
anticipating the imminent rise and fall of his chest, the
involuntary flicker of his eyelashes. Is he dreaming in his
wine-induced slumber?

Soon she will fall exhausted into bed. She has become
irritated with his complacent disregard for his "*hobby*" as he
refers to it. Some men like gambling, some even take a
mistress, some drink, and some do all three. Paul just
drinks.

She banishes the image from her, replacing it with
brilliant sunlight and market stalls emanating a banquet of
colour. She browses each display, deliberating over each
item, like pictures in a gallery. Red, yellow, and green
peppers, purple aubergines, blood-red tomatoes freshly
plucked from the vine, onions the size of cricket balls,
melons with green mottled and yellow skin, red
watermelons, oranges, lemons and apples. Redolent bread
shaped and baked that morning evokes a snapshot of her
mother's kitchen. Bulging bags pull at her joints. She
negotiates her way through the stream of locals and tourists,
a lingering contentment soothes and dances within her.

Once dry, she wraps the towel around herself. The
darkness presses against her. In the bedroom, she studies
Pauls' face; his bottom lip is loose. She sighs into an angled
pool of gilded light offered by the distant moon.

There exists an absence between them, a disconnection; it
has become a customary feeling they both accept. She is
captured within the rituals of their suffering. There is no
pause or rescue from the distance between them.

Chapter 31

Reconciled

Swallows are constructing nests in the wooden eaves of the veranda, darting in theatrical arches, swift twists and aerobatic turns. In the trees, birds flutter and sing. If Adam knew their names he'd recognise Jays and Golden Orioles.

Theresa has placed on the table a dish of Sofrito (beef casserole) and courgette cut into strips, glistening with oil and lemon juice.

Adam made a coffee in the kitchen and now stands to look over the garden. He looks down at the table still to be set, and it dawns on him how he has become used to the domestic routines of the day. He does not feel alarmed at how effortlessly he has eased into this new life like a hand fits a glove. Some euphoric pleasure rushes through him. The sensation reminds him of the satisfaction he felt when a lecture was delivered well. It is a sentimental memory, but it does not bring a longing to return to that life, quite the opposite. An understanding has grown in him; he belongs here, there is a familiarity about the house, the village and the people that stir a feeling inside him and grows with each passing day. Such thoughts are often superseded by a small anguish and the anticipation of a visit by Stephen, but recently his visits have become less frequent and brief.

Stephen has kept himself to himself, often reading alone, playing with Dylan in the pool or taking messages on his phone. It is obvious to Adam that Georgia and Stephen are just going through the motions. When Stephen is home, Adam does not dine with them. It is a decision he has made and one that Stephen has not confronted. He can detect a strain on Georgia's face that gradually ebbs once Stephen has left.

Theresa is still setting the table, fetching a jug of water and instructing Dylan on where each individual piece of cutlery is placed.

Adam decides to take a walk through the garden and, as he does, it occurs to him that his recent conversations with Georgia have become emotive, to the extent that at times, tears prick at Georgia's eyes. He often feels an impulse to reach out to her and glide his hands through her hair. He has dreamt about her only the once since he arrived.

In his dream, they are on the beach, watching the surf, as Dylan swims with Stephen. It is a warm day. Sally, Dr Williams from Adam's university, is walking with Elena, whose goats weave in and out of the trees, foraging for food. Georgia smiles at Adam and delicately draws her fingertips across his lips and kisses him. Stephen says something, but it is inaudible. He is smiling broadly and then throws Dylan into the air who laughs, arms and legs flying, like a doll, before splashing into the water. He does not understand what the dream signifies, and he has never been a believer that in deconstructing one's dreams; hidden meaning can be got. None the less, he often lingers on the kiss, playing it over in his mind and holding on to the illusion.

He has accumulated happiness beyond anything he has felt for years, not since his marriage to Katherine. There is a sense of continuity to their days, a permanence that merges each hour with formality. Each morning, he is eager to indulge himself in her glorious face, hear her mellifluous voice. His feelings are instinctive, primaeval.

In Georgia's company, he is whole and balanced, so much so, that he wants to announce his feelings, but he is fearful of her response. Would such a situation confirm a mutual attraction? This is his daily dilemma, and he is not a gambler. Curiosity is a powerful thing, but he will not jeopardise their emotional intimacy. There can be no compromise, for the moment at least, he has to be logical in his reasoning, just like Dylan, Adam smiles to himself. He is reconciled to being passive to the complications that reside within him.

Adam continues to wander through the garden and stops at the vegetable patch, where he tests the fence with his hand and is glad to feel it is still sturdy. He turns and looks back at the house. Georgia is now helping with setting the table. Dylan is wearing his earphones and Adam knows that Georgia will soon tell him, 'No Mozart at the table.'

Georgia looks towards him. 'Dinner will be ready in five minutes, I hope you're hungry.'

Adam smiles back at her. He is glad he has told Georgia about Katherine. He never thought he could ever love unconditionally again as he did with Katherine. The thought of meeting another woman that could fill the void she left scared him. What was between them was immeasurable; their connection was so that they could often tell what the other was thinking. Such pairing was a once in a lifetime happening, a phenomenon that could never be recaptured. Adam thought he would never again touch the rapturous sensation that confirms that kind of love until now, on this day, in this garden.

He watches the way Georgia tilts her head, as she listens to Theresa. He gazes upon the involuntary motion of her hand as it weaves through her hair and lets it fall, like sheets, back into place. Adam is attuned to the curve of her neck and the sway of her hand when she walks. All of these intricacies are visible to him, they are pronounced in every detail.

Adam is not the only teacher at the house, for Dylan has taught him about the letters of Mozart from the book Stephen gave him. Dylan has read it assiduously each day and, as timetabled, he lurches into a lengthy monologue.

'On the 14th January 1775, Mozart wrote that on the previous day, the 13th January 1775, his opera La Finta Giardiniera, was received with tumultuous applause and shouts of 'Viva Maestro.' Mozart was not just a musician who performed and composed, he also taught others how to play the piano and violin.' Mozart would often describe musical techniques by giving it a human quality so when he was improvising a certain piece he said that he was 'taking it for a walk,' It took me a while to work that out, but I got there in the end. Actually, I asked Mum, but I know what it means now.'

When he reaches the terrace Dylan has removed his earphones. Beside him on his chair is the well-thumbed book '*Mozart's letters Mozart's life.*' There is an inch rip on the front cover along the spine.

'Stephen is not going to be back for the wedding.' Georgia is telling Theresa. 'He phoned this morning. He's stopping off at Athens to finalise the contract for the new houses.'

'He seems to be spending more time in Athens and Spain than he is with you and Dylan,' Theresa says disapprovingly.

'It's only for the short term. Once it's up and running he won't have to visit as often.'

Theresa spoons some Sofrito onto her plate and tuts.

'That looks delicious Theresa,' Adam remarks, as he sits beside her.

'Thank you. Your mother loved it Georgia, it was her favourite meal,' Theresa says wistfully.

'I'm reading more of her diary now.'

Adam notices Theresa's face changes, a look that is quickly rubbed out.

'You're in it quite a lot, Theresa, did mum ever speak to you about it.'

'Not really. I knew she was writing something but she never spoke about it.'

'Whatever happened to the woman called Gabriella? She owned a shop; I think mum was quite fond of her.'

Theresa took a deep breath and played with her fork. 'Ah Gabriella, yes, she set up a clothes shop in Corfu Town and eventually moved to Athens.' She speared a piece of meat.

Adam looks at her, Theresa definitely seems uncomfortable; her expression is muted.

'I find it fascinating, I wasn't sure if it was the right thing to do when I started to read it, but now, I find myself looking forward to reading it. It's a part of Mum I knew nothing about. She never really spoke about that time; she always glossed over it.'

'It was such a long time ago; a lot has changed since then. Look at me, I'm old now.'

'You're still a beautiful woman Theresa. I hope I look half as good as you when I'm your age, and you still have your health.'

'I do and I hope the good Lord keeps it that way.'

'Mm this is delicious; it's fast becoming my favourite too.' Georgia smiles. 'Have you any plans for tomorrow Adam? Playing chess again?'

Adam grins. 'No, I'm actually going to Corfu Town. I've got a letter I need to deliver for a friend.'

'Oh, to who?' Georgia says intrigued.

'To a professor in the Department of History at Ionian University. I know it's odd, considering there are easier and quicker ways to get in touch with people, but it was given to me by a colleague who trained with him; she insisted I delivered the letter personally. I was wondering if there's a car hire in the village. I've not seen one yet.'

'You don't need to, I'll take you and I can do some shopping.'

'I don't want to put you out. Are you sure? I could hire a car, drive around and see some of the island.'

'That's a good idea, I'll take you, honest, Dylan can come along and we can make a day of it. Would you like to go to Corfu Town Dylan?'

'Sure.'

'I'm buying lunch this time,' Adam insists.

Chapter 32

A Letter, Augustus and the Beginning of Possibilities

The Department of History is a modern three-storey
building in Ioannou Theostoki str, a residential area of
Corfu Town.

Above the entrance, the national flag hangs still and limp
in the dry air. Adam takes a seat, while the receptionist
phones Tzakis Konstantinos' office. He is grateful for the
air conditioning, as it is getting hotter by the day, and to his
annoyance, he has left his bottled water in Georgia's car.
They have arranged to meet again in an hour's time. While
waiting, he holds the letter and is relieved that he is about to
fulfil his promise to Sally.

The foyer is a hub for students between classes, a meeting
place before heading for lunch in the canteen. Adam
observes a constant flow of bodies, coming and going, and
wonders if it is ever quiet. He is aware of a man exchanging
words with the woman at the reception, and then the man
turns and strides towards Adam. As he draws near, the man
extends his hand.

'It's Adam, isn't it? Pleased to meet you. Thanks for
getting in touch. I'm Tzakis Konstantinos.'

Adam stands and shakes his hand. 'Nice to meet you. It's
a hive of activity.'

'They keep us busy; they have a thirst for knowledge.'

Tzakis is a tall man, with short grey silver-flecked hair.
He has a long straight nose and deep-set eyes. He is wearing
a well-fitted suit and white shirt, opened at the neck.

'We'll go to my office, it's quieter there.'

Adam follows Tzakis, who takes long purposeful strides.
When they reach a set of stairs, he takes two at a time, as if
it's part of an exercise regime.

Tzakis' office is considerably spacious, not like Adam's
office at the university back home. There is a large window
that allows a generous amount of light into the room. One
wall is covered in books encased behind sliding mirrored

doors. The desk is uncluttered and sparse, a framed picture of two teenagers, his children Adam assumes, on one side, on the other, a bust of the Roman emperor Augustus sits at an angle. Other than a computer screen and a writing pad on the desk, it is otherwise bare and uncluttered. Adam gets the feeling that Tzakis likes order with a minimalistic approach. There is an absence of the academic; it feels more like an executive's office.

'Can I get you a coffee?' Tzakis walks over to a coffee maker that Adam has not noticed. 'I despise instant coffee, especially out of vending machines. How it gets called coffee I'll never know. How do you like yours?'

'Just black and no sugar, thanks.'

Tzakis hands Adam a small cup and invites him to sit. He slips his jacket around his chair, sits down and sips his coffee.

'Now Adam, I believe you've got a letter for me.'

Adam hands him the envelope. Tzakis places it on his desk in front of him and taps it with a finger.

'I'm afraid the letter is just a prop. In fact, it's not a letter at all.'

'What do you mean?' Adam shifts in his chair.

'It has served its purpose.'

'I don't understand.'

Tzalis smiles. 'Its purpose was to get you here, in front of me, so I could meet you.'

'This is not making any sense.'

'Let me explain. Our dear friend Sally, Dr Williams, asked if I wouldn't mind keeping an eye on you. She is worried, you see. She didn't like the thought of you being in Corfu, on your own, just in case something happened to you, or you weren't settling in as well as you thought you might. It's one of her virtues; she acts like a mother to those she cares about.'

Adam smiles.

'The only way to get us to meet was to construct the story about the letter. She says you wouldn't have got in touch with me otherwise. Was she right?' Tzakis asks casually.

Adam nods, still coming to terms with Sally's ingenuity.

'She was worried when you hadn't contacted me, but relieved when I phoned to say you eventually got in touch.' As he is speaking, Tzakis opens the envelope and takes out a piece of folded A4 paper. He smiles and shows it to Adam, who immediately recognises Sally's handwriting, '*Thank you. xx*'

'I should have known. What a woman. She's right of course; I wouldn't have got in touch with you.'

'Then it was her insurance policy.'

Adam nods towards the bust. 'Augustus?'

'It is. Are you interested in history?'

'I am. I've always had a fascination for the Roman period.'

'We're a match made in heaven; I'm a professor of Greek and Roman history. Sally knew what she was doing. How's the coffee?'

'It's perfect.'

'We're the only university in Greece that is solely dedicated to history, now that makes us special. Personally, I've got a soft spot for Augustus. He was Rome's first emperor and under him, Rome really prospered, he's a fascinating character. I'm writing a book about his life and Rome, during that period; it's going to be published early next year. We're expected to publish our work, but I don't find it to be a task. I wish I could dedicate more of my time to it.'

'It must be satisfying.'

'It is. I'd be interested to know about your interest in ancient Rome.'

'It's not the great personalities of that time that interest me. What does, though, is the ordinary man and woman, and what would life have been like for them in the Roman world, living in towns and cities.'

'You should come to a lecture. I'm sure it would interest you.'

'Would that be possible?'

'Sure, why not? After all, I'm the Dean of the department.'

'I'd love that.'

'Whenever you're free, let me know and I'll arrange it.'

***

'How did it go?' Georgia asks brightly, as Adam gets into the car.

'Actually, it was not too bad, but not what I expected.'

'What do you mean?'

Adam explains about Sally's motivation behind the letter, Tzakis, and their shared passion for everything Roman.

Georgia smiles. 'I like Sally. She's obviously a woman who knows how to get things done.'

'It's made me realise just how much she cares about me, but I had to go to the other side of Europe to find out.'

'Sometimes we don't see what is in front of us.'

'And sometimes we do.'

She turns her gaze from the road and looks at him quizzically, studying him with liquid green eyes.
He takes a deep breath and feels he is crossing a kind of boundary, but then he retreats.

'I mean,' he says, trying to retrieve the situation. 'I feel we've become good friends. I see it that way and I know that's not what you initially intended. Obviously, you were just looking for someone to teach Dylan, but, as time has passed, I think we've become quite compatible.'

'Yes, I suppose we have and I'm glad.'

They travel in silence. Adam feels they have connected on some level and when he looks at Georgia, she seems preoccupied. He wants to know what she is thinking.

'I'm hungry and my stomach's getting sore,' Dylan complains.

'Lucky for you then, we're just about there.' Georgia glances at Dylan in the rear-view mirror.

'Where is just about there?' Adam realises he hasn't asked where they are going.

'To my favourite restaurant and remember it's your treat.'

Georgia smiles brightly, and an uplifting feeling passes through him to see her look so happy.

At breakfast the following morning, it occurs to Georgia
that Theresa has not enquired about the diary, nor shown
any interest in it. She is puzzled by this and, as she clears
her plate and cup, and deposits them in the sink, she frowns.
She decides to tackle Theresa, later in the day. The
thought she might be avoiding the subject stings Georgia, as
they have always been close. Georgia has known her
practically all her life and Theresa has always been part of
the family, even though they are not related;
Theresa has always been regarded as a special aunt.

Georgia takes an orange from the fruit bowl on the
granite counter and peels it. She picks up the diary and
leaves the kitchen, enjoying the explosion of citrus juice in
her mouth. As she walks through the house, she delicately
wipes her mouth and steps out onto the terrace, sinking into
a cushioned seat.

The diary opens with a creek. Images of her mother
sitting in this very place and writing the words Georgia is
reading, entangle themselves with thoughts of Theresa's
lack of interest, or even curiosity in the diary, or its content.
Georgia cannot imagine why this is so, but she is
determined to find out and dissolve her personal bafflement.

Chapter 33

1972

An Encounter that Involves 356 Steps

Saturday 10TH June 1972

*It has now been a week since Paul left. He has called
several times from New York, but each time, the connection
was so bad we had to abandon the call. I'm going to
Gabriella's exhibition this evening...*

The clothes exhibition is set in an upper floor room above
the main square. During the daytime, it is bright and
spacious. A soft evening light defuses through the large
windows, insulating the room in a warm glow. Emily is
standing beside Theresa, sipping a glass of wine, its taste
encouraging her with a light enthusiasm for the night ahead.
This is the first night she has been out without Paul since
arriving on the island. She is wearing the dress she bought
from Gabriella. Theresa smiles at her encouragingly.

'You look lovely Emily.'

'I don't feel it. I'm surrounded by young and glamorous
woman.'

'Nonsense. Half of them would die to have a figure like
yours.'

Small groups cluster around the room, sipping drinks and
talking. Emily's eyes are drawn to a man in a dark blue suit
and opened neck white shirt. He moves from person to
person, indulging in polite conversation as if holding court,
she thinks. A woman laughs, throwing her head backwards,
in an exaggerated gesture. The man in the blue suit smiles
politely, turns towards the woman's male companion, and
bends his head to the man's ear. For a few seconds, a
pensive mask crosses the man's face, and he nods in
agreement.

Emily wonders what words passed between them. She feels drawn to this man, with his shiny black hair combed back from his forehead, curling at the edges. He walks with a dignified and confident posture. Gentleness occupies his authoritative gestures, almost a contradiction she ponders, and, to her surprise, she finds this attractive.

'That's Stelios Karagounis,' Theresa offers, noting Emily's interest. 'Gabriella's benefactor. He's going to open a shop for Gabriella in Corfu Town.'

The evening's highlight is a fashion show. Gabriella's clothes are modelled by young women that have been hired from Corfu Town. The show is a resounding success and Gabriella smiles constantly as everyone vies for her attention.

Waitresses light candles and move amongst the guests with trays of drink and food. As Theresa mingles with friends, Emily hugs the environs of the room in an unsettling flash of vulnerability.

'I feel like some air. I think the wine has gone to my head.'

'You're an amateur, Emily.' Theresa smiles. 'I'll come with you. I need to go to the toilet first.'

'It's fine. You stay and enjoy yourself. I've had a great time. I'll see you tomorrow.'

'Are you sure.'

'Of course.' Emily leans towards Theresa and kisses her on the cheek. 'I'll be in bed and sleeping before it finishes.'

She inhales the still quality of the air, as she steps outside. She loves this time of night. The evening light is stolen by a sudden darkness that engulfs the village. Soft lights from bars and restaurants blot out the night sky and Emily thinks of her house, where visible stars, like hundreds of pinpricks of light, will be at this very moment, suffusing the opaque sky. Emily looks around, and for the first time since Paul left she feels lonely, exposed even and the vulnerability she felt at the party returns, like an unwelcomed visitor, her concern surprises her.

Emily notices intimate couples, families and groups milling around the square. She tries to settle her mind. She turns and heads towards a staircase of steps that rise into the night. Emily stands for a few seconds. Small lanterns protrude from stone buildings spreading shafts of light. In places, she is able to make out tall trees that stand like sentries.

'There are three hundred and sixty-five steps, a step for each day of the year.'

The voice startles her.

'I saw you at Gabriella's exhibition and noticed you had left. I was speaking to Gabriella and enquired about you. She told me your name was Emily. I, too, slid out, for five minutes.'

Emily bows her head, avoiding his eyes.

'Where are my manners? My name is Stelios Karagounis.'

He offers his hand. Unexpectedly, his skin feels soft and smooth. His hand lingers in hers, for a moment. Nervously, she touches her earlobe. She observes that the taut angularities of his face convey a menacing look that becomes smoothed by his extravagant and friendly smile.

'I was about to take a walk.' He points with a finger to the top of steep stairs. 'The view of the village is breathtaking. Would you like to join me?'

'I was heading that way anyway.' Emily says, trying not to sound too eager.

They amble at a leisurely pace.

'I hope you enjoyed our little show.'

She notes the way he says 'our.'

'Gabriella tells me you have a house here,' Stelios says.

'Yes, that's right.'

'Are you staying long?'

'I'm not sure. For the summer anyway, that's the plan.'

'Are you on your own?'

'No, I'm here with my husband.'

'Ah, I see, your husband, he was not at the exhibition. Not his thing then?'

'Oh no, Paul is away on business, for a few weeks at least.' A quiver of uncertainty goes through Emily. She has revealed too much.

Stelios registers her reluctance. He bows his head courteously and the light from a nearby lamp catches his profile. His eyes are smiling at her, Emily thinks, almost beseeching her. Emily's head races, how unsuspecting it is appreciating another's attractive composition. Emily chastises herself for allowing such thoughts to float over the boundaries of acceptability. '*You can look but not touch*,' a voice from the past whispers. She laughs at this childish thought, her rebuke dissolves, and she becomes more relaxed. There is an enchanting sophisticated quality about his presence, a graciousness that emanates from him in the gentle way he speaks.

'As I said, there are three hundred and sixty-five steps all the way to the top. We can count them if you don't believe me.' Stelios smiles broadly.

'I think just walking up them will be enough.' She looks at him then, olive skin, three deep lines on his brow, deep-set eyes, high cheekbones and pencilled lips.

Pools of light from decorative lamps follow their progress.

'Did you like the exhibition?' His face turns towards her, he is smiling.

'I did, Gabriella is a talented designer. I've already bought one of her dresses.'

'Then you should visit her shop in Corfu Town, once it opens.'

'I hear you are her benefactor.'

'She has a wonderful talent. It pleases me to help her. I am giving her the medium to reach a wider audience, that is all. I admire creative people and it also helps she is my niece.' Stelios smiles. He places his hand on the base of her back, guiding her past a woman, who has stumbled from a shop into their path.

'Forgive me, my intention was honourable,' he says with a dignified courtesy that leaves Emily momentarily embarrassed. She allows his hand to linger a moment longer.

'There's nothing to forgive. It was kind of you,' she says, trying to put him at ease.

'You are English?'

'No, I'm Scottish.'

'Oh, I'm sorry I just thought…'

'It's ok; I wouldn't be able to tell the difference between someone from Spain and South America, even though they share the language.'

'Where do you live in Scotland? Glasgow?'

'No, Edinburgh.' She smiles courteously.

'I've always wanted to go to Scotland, see your mountains and eat haggy.'

'Haggis.' She corrects with a grin.

'Yes, haggis, what does it taste like? Is it true it comes from sheep's stomach and blood?'

'That's what they say. It's spicy and has a soft texture. I don't like it much.'

'I have a restaurant in Corfu Town maybe I should put it on the menu.'

'Put it in the Moussaka.'

'Yes, what a good idea.' Stelios smiles broadly.

They walked for a minute without speaking and then Stelios asks, 'How long have you been coming to Corfu?'

'For several years now. It's like a second home.'

'I like that idea, a second home. One can have several houses but that doesn't mean they all feel like home.'

'It sounds as if you're talking from experience.'

He shrugs. 'If I had my way, I would never leave this island. Unfortunately, life dictates otherwise.'

'Yes, it has a habit of doing that.' She thinks of the house she will return to tonight and, even though she will be alone, a secure feeling stirs within her; the thought of leaving it, at some point, and returning to Edinburgh troubles her.

'Has your husband returned to Edinburgh?'

'No, he's gone to New York.'

'New York. It must be important business, to travel so far and leave you on your own.'

'He's an author.'

'I see, what's his name? I may have read his books.'

'He has a pen name, Paul Hudson.'

'I'm afraid I haven't heard of him. Is he famous?'

'Amongst the people who read his books, I suppose he is.'

'Has he sold a lot?'

'He's a best seller.'

'Then he has sold a lot of books… but not in Greece,' Stelios grins. 'And you, what do you do when your husband writes?'

'I use to own a chain of fashion shops, women's clothes and accessories, that kind of thing, but I recently sold them.'

'Really, now that's interesting. Why did you sell?'

'I received an offer I couldn't refuse. It was a good business deal, and came at the right time.'

'So what do you do now?' Stelios asks, intrigued.

'At the moment, I'm in no rush to begin anything new. I'm enjoying the rest I suppose.'

'Once you have had enough of resting, you should let me know. I might need some advice with my venture with Gabriella. I know nothing about the fashion industry. How fortuitous it is that we have met.'

They reach the top of the steps. She turns around, pleasingly disoriented for a moment. The view enthrals her.

'We made it just in time; the darkness will soon steal our reward for climbing all these steps.'

She is sucked into the landscape; she feels like a grain of sand on a beach.

Later, Emily accepts Stelios' offer of a nightcap at a bar with only a few customers. The sparse clientele eases Emily's sense of guilt that has sat in her stomach since they met.

'Why don't we meet up tomorrow? I'll take you for lunch, not to one of my places, of course, I know a lovely restaurant in Corfu Town. I have tried to steal their chef but they have just given him a pay rise. He says I will have to better it if he is going to come and work for me. I like that. Good business sense. Come tomorrow and try the food. Tell me if he is worth the extra drachmas. I'd value your opinion.'

Emily feels her face go hot. 'I'm no food critic.'

'Two heads are better than one.' He tilts his head.
'Ok, lunch it is.'

That night Emily sits outside on the terrace feeling the wine race through her. Her thoughts are splintered from clamorous pangs of guilt to bubbles of excitement. For a fleeting moment, she rebukes the idea, but then tells herself there is no harm in it; a bit of fun, that is all it will be. She takes a long deep breath and lets it out.

Chapter 34

The Keeper of a Secret

A heavy feeling seized Theresa, the day she learned about Georgia's discovery in the attic. Her face had turned pale; she exhaled shakily and tried to maintain an air of nonchalance about her.

As the days pass it continues to burn in her, like indigestion and it lingers on. The past should remain in the past. Nothing good will come from digging it up and analysing the details decades later. She wrestles with such thoughts; they intrude upon every single day.

She is the keeper of a secret. The only one left alive, now that all the others have died and left her with the knowledge of a past that now permeates the present.

Each passing day brings Georgia closer to the discovery of the truth within those pages. Theresa feels fatigued. It wears her down and in a way, she will be relieved to share her burden and expel it from her. That day is coming; it gets ever closer. With each turn of a page and with every word read, the veils of the past diminish with time.

She is exhausted with the pangs of guilt. It frustrates her, she will have to confront the truth after all these years it lay submerged. It happened so long ago now, the secret that was the casualty of a loveless marriage. Theresa had always been reluctant to think badly of her friend. At that time, Emily said her life could truly begin, she had a purpose once again, her life meant something. It had worth and it filled her with the most incredible joy and it did, even if the ramifications were of volcanic proportions.

For years, Theresa thought she was safe, the burden of disclosure did not fall on her shoulders; it was not her responsibility, nor was it her place and she would never go against Emily's wishes. As the years slid past, Emily seemed to refrain from the truth. When they reminisced, Emily often excused herself by referring to 'When the time is right' and she was serious, but the opportunity never seemed to arrive and in some strange way, Theresa felt, as time passed, Emily was content to let it lie. There was always sombreness around these discussions, and it became evident to Theresa that Emily's perceptions of that time changed, as Georgia eventually matured into a young woman. Within their conversations, it became less prominent, almost terminated from thought.

How things changed when Emily learnt her illness was terminal. Telling Georgia then would have been the cruellest blow, she did not have the desire by then. Emily would take her secret to the grave and Theresa was happy to comply with her friend's wishes. Until now, that is, because the discovery of the diary changes everything.

Chapter 35

A Wedding in the Square

On their way to the village, Georgia, Adam and Dylan pass the small white church where earlier the bride and groom were married. Through the opened doors of the church, an old woman kisses an icon, and then makes the sign of the cross in front of incense candles, that flutter and burn a yellow light across a gallery of frescos. It is moments like this, that Adam feels privileged to witness such personal affirmations at faith, even though he has none himself; it will leave a lasting and genuine impression on him.

As they reach the square, Georgia comments that it looks like the whole village is invited. The square is refurbished and decorated for the occasion. A row of tables, strewn with food and drink, is decorated with a white tablecloth, running along each side of the square. Adam notices familiar faces, Midas and Thanos, already fuelled by substantial amounts of beer, raise their glasses in greeting. Giannis has a forlorn smile on his face, as he watches the young men and woman dance energetically, while Eva, his wife, stands amongst a huddle of old women, gossiping and brooding.

The large tree that stands in the centre of the square is lit with small white bulbs, twisting around its trunk and across its sprawling branches. A band, dressed in white shirts, black waistcoats and black caps, play violins and bouzoukis with an enthusiasm that is contagious. The music reverberates around the square, people are clapping and dancing; the music, quick in tempo, is building to a crescendo, a finality that the dancers anticipate with sweeping gestures and exuberance.

There's Father Nikolaos,' Georgia points out.

Nikolaos is sitting at the table reserved for the groom, the bride and their parents. He is dressed in his long black robe and deep in conversation with the groom who is a handsome looking young man, broad-shouldered, with a fine complexion and neatly trimmed stubble.

Pandelios waves them over and hugs Georgia affectionately. 'Georgia thank you for coming, please sit at this table. Let me get you a drink, what will it be?'

'No, no, I'll buy you one; after all, it's not every day your daughter gets married.'

'I insist. I'm so happy you could come, I've paid for all the drinks anyway.'

'A red wine then.'

'I'll bring you a bottle and you, Adam?'

'I'll have a beer.'

Pandelios ruffles Dylan's hair. 'You're getting taller by the day Dylan. What would you like to drink?'

'Just a glass of water please.'

'Good choice.'

Dylan shrugs; he always drinks water.

'Stephen is not coming?'Pandelios asks.

'No, he's still in Athens; he'll be back in a few days, though.' Georgia says, aware that Pandelios has only seen Georgia with Adam.

'He is working too hard, he needs to relax more and enjoy the company of his family.'

Adam is relaxed and contented, but the reference to Stephen stabs him; he shifts in his chair.

Georgia hands Pandelios an envelope. 'For the happy couple, Christina won't remember me. Could you give it to her?'

'No problem. I'll introduce you later; I'll get those drinks.'

'What was in the envelope?' Adam asks.

'Money. It's a tradition; the guests at a wedding give the married couple a "fakelaki," an envelope with money in it.'

'Maybe I should've given them money.'

'It's fine, one envelope is enough, but if you want to give them money, we've still to pin money to the bride and groom's clothes.'

'What! Pin money to their clothes?'

'Yes, the last dance of the night is reserved for the bride and groom, and guest's pin money to their clothes!'

'I find customs and traditions fascinating, it builds identity, makes us who we are. It's really important, don't you think?'

'I don't suppose you've ever been to a Greek wedding?'

'No.'

'There's lots of traditions and symbolism in the ceremony. That's what I love about Greece; the people, their customs, the Orthodox Church, they're so intertwined; it's the fabric of life, especially on the islands.'

Adam has not heard such passion and enthusiasm in Georgia's voice. She explains that there are certain times of the year that Greeks can't get married in a church. This includes the first two weeks of August which is devoted to celebrating the Virgin Mary, the forty days preceding Christmas, the forty days leading up to Easter and several holy days.

She explains that before a wedding, money (for prosperity) and rice (for putting down roots) are thrown on the bride and groom's bed and then a baby is rolled across the bed to guarantee fertility! And whether that is a boy or a girl, the sex of the baby used, will be the sex of the couple's first child.

'And does it work?'

She smiles. 'I've no idea, but the odds are short.'

Georgia continues to explain that on the day of the wedding, the best man, who is called the "*koumbaro*" will shave the groom and then the groom's friends will help to dress him.

Likewise, the bride is similarly prepared by her *koumbara*, the maid of honour – and dressed by her friends. Then the bride writes on the bottom of her shoes the names of all her unmarried friends. The names that get worn away by the end of the night are supposed to be the women who will marry soon themselves. The bride will smash a glass, signifying the finality of leaving her parents to begin her new life and finally, when she leaves the house, she has to look back at the house to ensure her children take after her side of the family.

'During the wedding ceremony, the couple hold candles and, I find this bit really touching; two gold crowns, called "*Stefana*" are connected by a strand of ribbon and swapped three times, back and forwards on the heads of the bride and groom, symbolising their union into a married couple and equal partners. The priest gives them a single wine glass – and the bride and groom each take three sips from it. The wine symbolises life, and, by sharing the glass, the couple will share in life together. Isn't that beautiful? Then, still wearing the crowns, they walk around a table that has the cup, the Bible, and the candles on it. They're led by the priest in their first walk together as husband and wife; it's also a symbol of their commitment to stay with each other, no matter what life throws at them.'

'Now I know so much, I feel I've been to the wedding.' Adam jokes.

'Have you heard of the evil eye?'

'That wouldn't be Elena and her goats would it?'

Georgia laughs and explains this is the term used for bad wishes, jealousy, and unsavoury or evil thoughts.

She tells Adam that if he were to compliment the bride's dress, he would then have to spit to ward off the evil eye, or the bride could be in danger of ruining her dress by spilling food or drink on it.

'Have you seen the little blue eye symbols in the shops, on magnets and necklaces?' she asks.

'Yes, they're everywhere.'

'That's to ward off the evil eye; I've got one in the house. Theresa brought it years ago.'

Pandelios has brought their drinks. 'I hope you haven't eaten, there's a buffet over there.'

'I'm fine Pandelios. Are you hungry Dylan?' Georgia asks.

'I could eat a little bit.'

'Well, it's my first time at a Greek wedding, so it would be rude not to try something,' Adam says. 'Come on Dylan let's see what there is.'

Adam is amazed at the amount of food on display, split up into three courses on hot plates.

'Look at this Dylan, there's so much food I don't know what to eat.'

'I'm going to have one of those pies,' Dylan says and puts a feta pie on his plate.

There is a line of guests eagerly filling their plates. Next to Adam, a young man smiles at him and spoons some Keftedes (meatballs) onto his plate.

'I see you're having trouble choosing.'

'It would help if I knew what everything was.'

'Let me help you; these are stuffed vine leaves, falafels, those are butter beans and my favourite, chilli peppers stuffed with feta. You should know these: that's pitta bread, mixed olives, of course, the dips, tzatziki, hummus, Strofilia and olive pate. Over there are the main dishes: moussaka, chicken skewers, beef stifado, bekri meze, spetsofy and finally the sweets: baclava, kataife and karidopita.'

'Thank you,'

'No problem. Try the beef stifado, you won't be disappointed.'

'That's a plate full,' Georgia says, as they return their seats.

'There was so much choice; I thought I'd have a bit of everything. Either the plates too small or I'm greedy,' Adam says whilst setting down the plate.

'Your eyes are bigger than your belly, you'll never eat it all,' Georgia added.

'We'll see.' Adam grins.

'I'm thinking I might stay longer. There's no great need to return to Edinburgh. How would you feel if I asked you to stay? I could extend your contract.' Georgia says eagerly.

'For how long?

'The end of the summer, September maybe, it's just a thought at the moment. Dylan needs the stability and structure you have given him. It's good for him and I'd like that to continue.'

'I don't need to rush back to the university,' Adam says reflectively.

'I'm not expecting you to commit yourself just now, but it would give me some peace of mind to know you could be flexible. Actually, Adam, we don't need to be formal anymore. Your word's as good as any contract, let's forget the whole contract thing. It doesn't feel right anymore. Unless you still want one, of course?'

'Are you sure you'd like me to stay?'

'I've never been surer of anything in my life. Do you need time to think about it?'

'No, I'd love to, that would be great,' he says, feeling a spasm of happiness.

'Then let's seal it with a drink.'

They clink their glasses. 'It's a deal.' He can't stop smiling.

'That's a relief. You've made me very happy Adam. Thank you,' Georgia says cheerfully.

'That makes the two of us then.'

A satisfying exhilaration courses through him. Adam indulges in the feeling, as around him the tempo of music quickens its pace in a flurry of notes and, as the melody fills the square, it urges many to dance.

'Let's dance.' Georgia pulls his arm.

'I've got two left feet.'

Dylan looks confused and stares at Adam's feet. 'That's a weird expression.'

'It's an idiom,' Adam says. 'It means, I can't dance.'

'Oh, then why didn't you just say that?' Dylan shakes his head, perplexed.

'It doesn't matter if you can't dance, just copy the others.' Georgia is already standing and pulling Adam to his feet. She is smiling broadly.

Adam feels clumsy and disjointed. He notices the young man he met at the buffet and tries to mimic the movement of his arms and legs but feels his body has a mind of its own. He thinks he probably looks ridiculous, but Georgia is still smiling at him encouragingly. He must be doing something right, after all, and he concentrates on his feet.

'You're doing fine,' She raises her voice above the music.

'I don't feel it.' He looks down towards his feet and grins.
'Is anyone laughing?'

He smiles and looks around the square. 'Not yet.'

'Well then, enjoy the music. You're in Greece.'

Adam is relieved to return to his seat.

'You were right, you can't dance,' Dylan says as he
fiddles with his I-Pad.

Adam takes a drink of beer. 'See, Dylan noticed, and he
was listening to Mozart. That's how obvious it was.'

Georgia leans forward and touches his forearm. 'Thank
you anyway, that took courage, looking like a fool in front
of the whole village.'

'I thought you were on my side.'

'I am. It was courageous of you.'

'I'm learning about myself every day.' Adam grins. For a
moment, he wonders what it would be like to touch her lips
with his; he hesitates and settles for her smile.

'Are you glad you came to Corfu Adam? It was a gamble
not knowing if it was going to work out. I know Stephen
has been intolerable at times, but apart from that, is it how
you thought it would be?'

'To be honest, I thought coming here would challenge
me.'

'And has it?'

'Yes, but not in the way I expected.' He averts his eyes
and takes a deep breath.

Georgia raises her eyebrows. 'And what does that mean?'
Her face is rueful, sympathetic almost.

Earlier in the day, Adam had been listening to David
Gray on his I-phone, and a line in a song resonated in his
head, repeating itself and walking with him most of the day.
Now it returned, *"Feels like lightning running through my
veins, every time I look at you."*

He wants to respond by telling her how he truly feels. He
aches to see her face each morning; just to be near her and
share the rituals of the life they share in this house which
holds him in a dreamlike state. It is enough just to be able to
smell her perfume, ravage each detail of her face, each
expression, gesture, the subtle movements of her lips, the

shine of her eyes. He is witness to all of these things, his heart swells and it could burst.

Adam feels a hand on his shoulder, it is Giannis. 'You dance like a demented goat, it's almost as a bad as your chess. Come and have a drink with us.'

'You go.' Georgia smiles rather sadly. 'I need to speak to Theresa, I've not seen her all night, and it's almost time for Dylan's bed.'

Chapter 36

Enough for Now

When Adam returns to the house, Dylan is already in bed. In the kitchen, he meets Georgia.

'I'm just having a coffee, would you like some?'

He sits at the table and observes Georgia pour the hot coffee.

'Did you see Theresa?' he asks, accepting a cup of her.

'Yes, I did.' Georgia sits next to him.

'Did she enjoy the wedding?'

'I think she did until I spoke with her.'

'What do you mean?'

'It's been troubling me for some time now. Theresa hasn't asked about mum's diary. I thought she would be interested in it; even just to ask if she's in it.'

'I suppose, so what did you say?'

'Well, I just came right out with it. She seemed to be quite elusive about it and said it was a private thing between Mum and me. She looked uneasy as if something was troubling her, I think, I don't know, it was hard to tell. But I wasn't convinced.'

'It must feel strange, reading your mum's thoughts after all of this time.'

'It is. I wasn't prepared for how I'd feel. The moment I opened the first page, she was alive again, but it's bittersweet. Reading her words, I feel her presence around me, and I'm learning things about her I never knew or was never meant to know. It's like she had another life. She's still the mother I know; only now, I'm beginning to think of her differently, and I don't know where that's taking me.'

Georgia tells Adam that it has brought back feelings of guilt and loss. She explains that her mother was diagnosed with Myeloma, a blood cancer. At the time, neither of them had heard of it. Emily eventually became worn out by the heavy doses of chemotherapy and Steroids, complaining of having to take a pharmacist's shelf load of tablets every day.

Once the cancer spread to her brain, it really took its toll on her. She started to slur her words like she had a stroke. Until that point, they had lived with the threat hanging over them and by all accounts, she lived a normal life. Now, this was the start of the end. She was articulate, her mind was alert; she did the crossword every day, spent hours in the garden, digging and planting, and if she could, she would walk everywhere, rather than take the car or get the bus. She transformed from a spritely, active woman, fit for her age, into a withered, shrunken flower, who couldn't take more than a few steps, before crumpling into a wheelchair.

'We never really got the chance to share the gift of motherhood. She died soon after Dylan was born. Apart from her death, that was the absolute heartache.'

Adam leans towards Georgia, he wants to reach out and take her by the hand.

'Stephen is staying on in Athens, just a little longer, he phoned just as I got back.'

'Oh.'

'I've noticed that when he is here, we don't see much of you.'

'It's better that way, for everyone.'

'It's difficult for me Adam.' Georgia looks away, she seems almost frightened.

'Stephen's going to be pretty pissed off when he finds out I will be staying longer. I feel guilty about that, it's the last thing I want. Maybe it would be best if I finished as we planned.'

'No, I won't have that. I need you to stay and to teach Dylan. You're a good teacher Adam. You're gently insistent and Dylan has benefited so much from you. He's almost a different boy... and... I need you.'

They sit in a silence that permeates their pores. He feels an exhilaration rush through him, as he gazes into eyes that are inscrutable green and in return, she holds his stare. Instinctively, Adam lifts his hand to her face and gently slides his fingers across her skin.

'Nothing makes sense without you,' he whispers unashamed.

She touches his fingers, a light fleeting graze.

'When did you know?'

'The night Dylan ran away,' she answers. 'I thought about it all night. Stephen was reckless, but there was something about you, your reaction. Stephen was just clutching at straws, he was drunk. You were a threat to him; you reminded him, he is hardly ever with us. You saw Dylan more than he did; you spent more time with me than he had in months. Stephen was using you to deflect from the truth, his failure as a father and husband. But there was something in your eyes, I saw it.'

'It's a relief.' Adam sighs. They have moved on to the next step. 'I had no idea how you would react. I've wanted to tell you for so long and I nearly did several times, but the thought of driving you away, or of having to leave, was a gamble I wasn't prepared to take.'

'Oh, Adam.' Georgia squeezes his hand. 'I need time. I need to think this through.'

'It's enough for now. You know how I feel, I'll settle for that.'

Chapter 37

An Offer is made

1972

Wednesday, 21ˢᵗ June 1972.

I have woken to the sun spreading its light into every nook and cranny, every corner of the house. How can I feel lonely when I have as companions, imposing hills all around me, clothed in the fabric of luscious trees, like a sea of emerald embroidery, undulating against a halo of transparent light that kindles the birth of each new sky.

I embrace the harmonious evolution that reinterprets each morning. I find the process intriguing; it is profound as much as it is unpredictable. It is extraordinary, altering brightness and contrast, colour and light.

The bougainvillaea has claimed the garden as its own; colonising great sways of it in rich purple, orange and reds; words can't describe the intense richness of it all. The family of swallows, above me, in the eaves, dash in and out of their nest all day long. I wonder if their young have hatched already.

I often catch myself wondering how I will feel once Paul returns. I have thought about this intensely for the last few days. I have peeled the shell of who I am and exposed the membrane of possibility. I like this new me, I am in a state of contentment.

This morning, I sat drinking my usual cup of coffee on the terrace. Even by its standards, the sun was already hot, pressing its heat into the garden. As always, I was immersed in the scents of herbs and flowers. I felt enormously invigorated, but at the same time, such joy brings with it a reminder it is not a permanent state. It elicits an uncomfortable self-evaluation of my marriage. I will not leave Paul, that would be inexcusable, but the door has been closed on salvaging anything of value, it is too late

*for that. We are both responsible for eroding what little is
left between us.*

*I never gave it a thought really, the prospect that I could
be attracted to another man, after all these faithful years
with Paul. There was no conscious deliberation. I didn't
wake up one morning and decide today is going to be the
day. It just happened. The gradual disintegration of any
real attempt to salvage what was left of our marriage, the
lack of reciprocal communication between us, made it
easier, I suppose...*

The wooded hill gently unfolds beyond the garden. Her
senses tingle, as she watches the oranges hang heavy in the
branches, circular little moons in a canopy of green leaves.
When she thinks of meeting Stelios again, Emily feels a
pleasant shifting in her stomach, a pleasing contracting of
her sphincter. What surprises her is she does not feel a
sense of guilt and, even if that was so, her enthusiasm for
the day ahead is so profound, she would probably suppress
it. Her curiosity is palpable.

The distance between Paul and Emily has grown as each
week and month has passed. Coming back to Corfu and
staying at the house is, in a way, a test; could they be
reconciled as a couple? Could they save their marriage?
Was it salvageable?

There are days when the house feels cut off from the rest
of the world. Tucked away from the village, days can pass
without seeing another living being, apart from the birds
and butterflies of the garden.

Over many visits, the house has become her home. It is a
place to relax, to take stock, become refreshed and absorb
the natural properties of the Corfu climate. It is an
enchantment she craves.

It is not that they bicker or niggle at each other; they have
passed that stage. They have grown into a bubble of
acceptance that, at some point, became the norm. It can still
be painful, this detachment from Paul, and that can be
bruising, for their marriage had been fulfilling; they had
been in love, once. She accepted long ago that their

relationship is disfigured by a natural decline that has been exacerbated and accelerated by motivating forces. They are almost separated in every regard. Emily makes a resigned face and checks her watch.

He had lustrousness eyes that lit up when he smiled, that was the first pull of attraction, and it encouraged her to stay in his company longer than she would normally have and accept his invitation to lunch. He exuded an old fashioned courteousness that amused her but, most of all, she enjoyed his company and, being honest, she liked the attention he afforded her.

It brought home how barren her relationship with Paul had been for all these months. Expressions of intimacy, both cognitive and physical are no longer shared with warmth and affection; they have become mechanical processes, which fulfil some primaeval instinct that is now expressed less frequently and is harder to capture as time moves on. When they are together, more often than not, they retreat into their own islands of solitude.

Emily contemplates these thoughts, as she ambles along the streets of the capital. She takes in the many influences that define the architecture of the facades, grand buildings and walkways that flourish in the town. She could be in Venice, Naples, even France.

Emily once got lost in the maze of narrow streets, and her instinctive panic subsided with each new discovery; an old chapel, a square riotous with flowers, Roman and Greek-influenced archways and old mansion houses, peeling paint.

Above her, the sun is a blazing yellow orb. Summer has truly arrived and the town's cobbled streets are thronging with tourists and visitors from the island's many resorts and visiting cruise ships.

She stands outside the restaurant, '*Ionian Skies*' and it is familiar to her. She thinks she has eaten here before, with Paul and some friends from Edinburgh, who were staying with them for part of the summer, several years ago.

Stelios is sitting at a table in the open air; he is smoking and extinguishes his cigarette in an ashtray when he sees Emily. He waves to her and smiles.

'I'm glad you came.' Stelios is still smiling as he pulls out a chair gesturing for her to sit. 'When you insisted on making your own way here, I must admit, I thought you wouldn't come.'

'To be perfectly honest, I did deliberate whether I should come or not. I'm not in the habit of accepting invitations from strangers.'

'I hope we can change that… me being a stranger that is. I would really like to get to know you better Emily.'

She bows her head. Were her cheeks reddening?

'This place looks familiar. I think I've eaten here before.'

'Was it good?'

'I can't remember.'

'I told the chef I was bringing a food critic from the UK to help me make a judgement on his cooking.'

'You never did.'

'I did, I think he is feeling ill. I might have put him off the whole idea of working for me.' He laughs rapturously.

'That wasn't kind, poor man.'

'I want to see what his cooking is like when under pressure.'

'Surely just cooking for you must be an ordeal in itself?'

'Maybe, but I want to know he can attain certain standards. I have a reputation to think of. After all, my success as a businessman will, in part, depend on his skills in the kitchen.'

'I see your point, but me, a food critic?'

'You work for The Times, by the way. I thought it would give the afternoon an air of authority.'

She looks at him, aghast.

'I'm kidding.' He smiles, raising his palms in front of him.

Emily laughs, feeling more comfortable now.

Lunch is a success. Stelios declares his intention to offer the chef a position as head chef and, during coffee, he asks Emily if she would like to see the shop that is being refurbished for Gabriella.

'There is still work to be done, but it's almost finished. I would value your opinion on a few matters… around the retail side of things.'

'It's been a long time since I worked in that business. I'm not sure if my opinions would be valid anymore.'

'They would be valid to me and that's all that matters.'

The shop is in an upmarket quarter of the town, sandwiched between a jeweller and a trendy bar. When they arrive, the electricians are completing the wiring and the interior is almost complete, apart from some cosmetic fixtures. Several floor to ceiling mirrors gives the illusion of a vast space, complemented with leather sofas and marble counters.

'What is your first impression, Emily?'

'I like it, it's very chic, some shops over glamorise their image with their brand but this is very subtle and at the same time, it gives the impression of a certain confidence, so the customer immediately will get the impression of who we are and what we sell.'

'I couldn't have put it better myself. That's exactly the ambience Gabriella was looking for and what she wanted to create. She'll be thrilled to know that's what you thought.'

'Yes it certainly works,' Emily says, taking in her surroundings.

'Gabriella has done well, her designs are popular, but she now needs to take her business to the next level. I can give her all of this,' he gestures to the shop. 'But what I can't give her is the knowledge to be a player in this market. I don't have that experience.' He trails his hand over the marble counter and looks at Emily. 'My point is, Emily, you do, and I wondered if you would consider mentoring Gabriella, just for a little while. What do you say?'

'What does Gabriella think about this? Does she know you were going to ask me this and is she in agreement?'

'I didn't even know myself until two seconds ago. This is not her little shop in the village, it's a different league. Now that the shop is almost finished, she is going to need good, impartial guidance. She is employing staff and she'll be concentrating more on the designing aspect of her business.

I think she would welcome your involvement with open arms, but you are right, don't give me an answer just now, I will speak with Gabriella first.

Chapter 38

Being Honest with Ourselves

The days that proceed have an air of avoidance around them. Adam understands why Georgia needs time; they have not spoken about that night and, although he finds it difficult, a weight has lifted from him.

They didn't ask for this to happen; it is what it is. Both, in their own ways, have resisted their feelings for each other, but there is no consolation in abating what is an undeniable attraction. He has tried to push it to the back of his mind, but his senses tingle every time he finds himself in her presence. Adam often glances at Georgia, as she tends to some flowers or picks oranges in the orchard, and he feels a closeness towards her, even though a respected distance has emerged between them. He knows there will come a time this will become unbearable, and he fears what may become of them.

One morning, Dylan saunters into the room where Adam is waiting to begin their lessons. He waits until Dylan sits down.

'Good morning. I didn't see you at breakfast.'

'I'm tired.'

'Oh, you didn't sleep well?'

'My brain was working too much and I couldn't get to sleep.'

'What do you mean, working too much?'

'I couldn't stop thinking about things, I do that that sometimes and it stops me from sleeping.'

'And what were you thinking?'

Dylan answers with a question. 'Are all people with autism direct, and too forthright with their opinions on things?'

Adam scratches his chin. 'Why do you ask?'

'Because I know I am and I was trying to work out why. At school, I was told I didn't consider other people's feelings. All I was doing was being honest. I think it's good, to be honest. I can't understand why people can't be honest.'

'There's times when it's better to be aware of how honesty may affect other people. You can think it, but you don't necessarily have to say it.' Adam thinks about Georgia.

'I don't see what the difference is and anyway I can't lie. If someone is fat, then they are fat. Just thinking about that doesn't change the fact that, physically, they are fat and they will remain so whether I say it or not. If someone smells, then they smell. Lying about it makes no difference, actually, they will still be smelly.'

'Yes, that's true.'

Dylan sits down after a while he says. 'I don't think I'll ever get used to the way people think.'

'It's going to be another hot day, I'll open the doors.' As Adam does so, he asks Dylan, 'How are you getting on with your project?'

'I've been online and found a great video. It's about Mozart's opera, Don Giovanni, and how the opera looked and sounded in 1787, during its first public performance in Prague. That's where the premier took place. Since then, it has been restaged and invented throughout the world's opera houses since the 18th century. Mozart's operas express what it is like to be human; it's about the human soul. I can understand that and relate to people in operas more than I can in real life.'

'I've never heard a real opera. Have you?'

'Yes, I went with Mum once when we were in London, it was my birthday present. It was Don Giovanni actually.'

'What was it about?'

'Well Don Giovanni, he is the main character, and he likes lots of women. He's not a nice man, really. His sins catch up with him when he commits murder and because of this he finally unleashes, what could be described as, vengeance from beyond the grave.'

'It sounds like a lot of modern-day films.'

'The first performance was on a Monday, the 29ᵗʰ
October 1787, at the Nostiz Theatre in Prague. It was a
sellout and Mozart conducted the orchestra; it received three
standing ovations. At the time, he was just thirty-one and in
today's money, he was paid thirty-five thousand pounds.
Mozart not only made audiences listen to the singing and
words. The music is just as important. The music expressed
the characters of the opera. He was a genius really. The first
performance was postponed because the set was not ready.
The stage was lit by candles, they even had special effects,
and they would put brandy in oil burners and blow a powder
solution over it which would cause a large flame. A local
newspaper reported that *Prague had never seen the like.*
Do you know that when Mozart died in 1791, four thousand
people attended a requiem mass in Prague?'

'You have been doing a lot of studying.'

'I enjoy learning new things about Mozart. I've read that
some academics think he might have had autism. I don't
think so. He was very sociable actually. He was always
looking for some sort of company, he hated being on his
own. He never liked to eat on his own. I do, I quite like it,
being on my own. I don't feel alone when I'm hugging
trees, I like the feeling it gives me. But you know all about
that.'

After the lessons, they have lunch on the terrace; Dylan
leaves to swim in the pool and Georgia sits back in her
chair, looking at Adam. It is the first time they have been
alone since the wedding.

'What?'

'Nothing.' She smiles.

'Come on, what are you thinking?'

'Did you enjoy the wedding?'

'I did, it was vibrant and energetic. I think that's a good
way to describe the experience. What about you, did you
have a good time?'

'Yes, I love Greek weddings; they always remind me
why we keep coming here. Life is celebrated with tradition
and family. I like that; it fosters a feeling of belonging and

identity. Living here is such a privilege, it's difficult to describe.'

'I know what you mean. Sometimes a place just feels right, you know, everything fits together perfectly. The people I've met are so open and welcoming; nothing seems too much of an effort, everything is done with genuine human spirit. I'd love to put in a bottle, what it means to be Greek, and take it with me wherever I went and release it; spread it all over the world. It would be a nicer place.'

'You've certainly settled then.'

'It's wonderful. I feel attached to the place; the village, the landscape, the people I've met, they are now my friends but, most of all, as time passes, this house feels more like home, every time I leave and return, and then, of course, there is Dylan. But most of all, there is you,' he says, truthfully

'We need to be careful Adam. I don't want to jeopardise what you have with Dylan. What we have, what we have become, it's special to me, but I can't let it get in the way of Dylan's happiness. I'm frightened of the consequences if we give into this... if I surrender to it. I can't rip my family apart.'

'What about Stephen? Can you continue to live like this, Stephen's unpredictable behaviour hanging over you every time he returns?'

'I don't have a choice.'

'You do. There's always a choice Georgia. Making the right one was always going to be the hard part.'

She looks away from him and towards Dylan who is still in the pool.

'Can we continue as before, for now at least? Is it possible?'

'Stephen's back on Friday?'

'He is.'

'I don't know Georgia. It might be better if I stay with Tzakis for a while. If you want, you can tell Stephen I'm visiting a friend, but I think you need time together, as a family, without me around. You can tell me to leave and I'll go back to Glasgow if that's what you want.'

'No, I don't. What will I tell Dylan?' she asks quietly.

'Tell him, we are being honest with ourselves, he'll understand that.'

Adam looks at her mouth, the curve of her lip, he longs to kiss her. He feels an anger swell that is replaced by a heavy sense of grief. He is impatient; he wants her now, not these complications. Adam wishes for the hundredth time that things could be different. His anger is directed towards Stephen, his grief is unimaginable. His lust is specific; he takes in the angle of her chin, the soft skin at the nape of her neck, the slant of her shoulders, and the curve of her breast beneath the fabric of her dress. He wishes he could change things. Adam looks at her, she suddenly looks exhausted, pained even.

A breeze picks up from the sea, dry and hot but, despite this, Adam feels chilled. Georgia opens her mouth as if to speak, but no words' spill from her.

Chapter 39

Slipping from her in Corfu Town

The flat is on the third floor of a building in the centre of town. It has a bachelor feel, the opposite to Tzakis' office at the university. Adam finds this odd and Tzakis has told him that a woman comes twice a week to do the cleaning and washing. There are many books littering the bookshelves, most of them interest Adam, the ancient Greek and Roman period. Tzakis has told him to read what he wants but not to take any books with him when he leaves the flat. His room is small, a single bed and a wardrobe make it feel even smaller, but Adam is glad Tzakis is pleased to help him.

Adam has found a small bakery, Panetteria Starenio, which sells pastries and pies. He has tried a different pie each day: spinach, chicken, pesto, next will be the feta or parmesan. The coffee is delicious; it is the best he has tasted, and he visits most days. Adam spends an hour or two watching people coming and going, as it offers a good vantage point, just outside the old part of town. He has bought a pocket tour guide and, in the afternoons, he wanders the old streets and sites. Adam has taken a historical and heritage tour, visited the archaeological museum, Spianada Square and the old fortress.

Each night, he has eaten in a different restaurant and spends the rest drinking in bars. He has developed a taste for Mythos beer that has contributed to his late risings and morning hangovers.

He is confident he will return to the house soon but, under what circumstances, he is less sure about.

Now he has told Georgia how he feels, he is accosted daily with the real prospect she will not leave Stephen. But can he stay under such circumstances? Each day would be agony for him and intolerable for Georgia. The realisation is like a curse.

He thinks of such a reality; he could not live in the house and teach Dylan. But also, he is not prepared to lose her. It is a thought he tries to put to the back of his mind.

The exhilaration he felt when they revealed their feelings to each other was short-lived. Adam has awoken each morning with dread and guilt, each night's excesses has not dulled the intensity of his fears; it has only stained his dignity. He trembles at the thought of returning to an empty house, Georgia gone with Stephen to Majorca or back to Edinburgh. It makes him feel light-headed, or is it the hangover, it's hard to tell. He is sure of one thing, he has wallowed long enough in his self-pity and last night was his turning point.

Adam found himself in a small bar, hot and noisy, a TV hung from the wall, and it was on but impossible to hear, as music blared from the bar's speakers. Not that that made any difference to the clientele, few paid it much attention; most were locked in conversations, preferring the company of friends.

Adam was on his third Mythos when he picked a euro from the floor that had fallen from a young woman's hand.

'Efcharesto.' She smiled as Adam handed her the coin.

It was then he noticed how attractive she was. Her hair fell to her shoulders, in black curls, her eyes were dark and piercing and he was drawn to her full red lips. She wore a red dress that hugged her slim body, cut low, where her cleavage drew his eyes.

'I don't speak Greek, well not much.'

'It's ok. I speak English, but not very well.'

'Let me buy you a drink,'

'No, I buy my own.'

'I insist, what are you having?'

She looked at him speculatively. 'A vodka and orange then?'

'Of course, it's my pleasure.'

They sat at a table outside.

'What's your name?'

'Chrystala. And you?'

'Adam.'

'Are you living here, working or just visiting?'

'I'm working but not in Corfu Town.'

'What do you do?'

'I'm teaching a young boy, he doesn't go to school, I teach him at his home.'

'How unusual. Do you mind if I smoke?'

'No, not at all.' She offered him a cigarette.

'Not for me, thanks. I gave up years ago.'

As she lit the cigarette, he noticed her nails were painted red. She tilted her head back and exhaled the smoke.

'I try to not blow it in your direction.' She smiled again.

'Do you work?'

'Only at night.'

'Oh, so this is a day off then.'

'Not exactly.' She tilted her head, a smile flickering over her mouth.

'Ah, I see.'

'You did not know?'

'Afraid not,' he said, embarrassed.

'I'll take that as a compliment.'

He took a long swallow of beer. He is seized by an incredible feeling of wanting this woman. The thought of making love, no, having sex, because that's all it would be, seized him. His heart is racing.

He followed her to a door and they go up a set of steps. Inside the room, she placed her handbag on a chair. Adam's breathing was fast, she smiled at him. The shutters were closed; there is a dull light in the room. Adam looked around the room; there is a bed, a bedside table, the chair with her handbag and a bathroom.

'It is extra if we kiss.'

He pulled her towards him, his hands resting on her waist. He found her mouth, her lips were soft, he could feel her warmth, smell her perfume, taste her. His hand slide over her dress, he felt her breast through the material. She unfastened the button of his trousers and pulled on the zip. He could feel her hand on his skin, her fingers trailing inside his trousers.

He pulled away from her.

'I can't do this.'

She looked at him, frowning slightly. 'That's a shame; I was just beginning to enjoy myself.'

He was appalled with himself.

She trailed her hand through her hair. 'It is ok; I have been with enough men and done this long enough to know the difference.'

'What do you mean?'

She smiled. 'Some do this for the thrill, others because they are not getting it at home and then there are the few who do it as a reaction to their confusion, their deceptions, betrayal, anger, grief, whatever.'

She reached into her bag and lit a cigarette. She sat on the bed and looked at him. 'Do you love her?'

'More than the world, but she's married.' His chest is a vice.

'Is she happy in her marriage?'

'No.' Adam said faintly, looking down at his feet.

'Then there is your answer.'

He took 50 euros from his wallet.

'I can't take that.'

'Why not?'

'I've not earned it.'

He placed the notes beside her bag. 'But you have. Thank you.'

Walking back to Tzakis' flat, Adam can't believe what he has just done. He will lose Georgia before it has begun. What was he thinking? He wasn't thinking, that was the problem. It had been illogical thinking. And what about tonight? He has never been inclined to be with such a woman. What has gotten into him?

Adam nurses his hangover, with his second coffee of the morning drank outside Panetteria Starenio. His phone rings. It is Tzakis, inviting him to attend a lecture he is about to deliver that afternoon.

When Adam arrives, the lecture room is large and almost full. He finds a vacant seat and settles himself as Tzakis is about to begin. Adam finds the lecture illuminating; its subject, *'the lives of ordinary Grecian and Roman woman,'* concentrate on their lack of legal standing, why they could not vote, and their exclusion from advanced education. Tzakis touched on marriage, the dowry and sex.

'Romantic love was not necessarily an essential component of marriage. However, parenthood was taken very seriously and women were expected to tolerate their husband's excesses such as alcohol abuse, gambling and womanising.' The lecture lasts an hour.

Over coffee, Adam congratulates Tzakis on his lecture.

'I really enjoyed that.'

'Did you learn anything?'

'Yes, I didn't realise you taught in English.'

'Ah, we don't, this was a special lecture for a group of foreign students who are visiting the university, so we lecture in English. That's why I invited you. Normally we speak Greek'

'I didn't know that women could own land.'

'Yes and, although they needed a guardian to oversee the business and make the legal contracts, this didn't hinder them in the slightest.'

Adam feels embarrassed. 'Look Tzakis, I need to thank you for putting up with me. I would've been at a loss if you hadn't let me stay and I don't always spend my nights going out to get drunk.'

'It's not a problem Adam, I'm glad I could help. Any developments?'

'I've not heard. Stephen never stays more than four days. Georgia said she'd phone me.' He gives out a long sigh.

'You've got yourself into an awkward situation. I hope it turns out agreeable to all concerned. Do you think she'll tell her husband?'

'I don't know. Shit, we haven't even kissed; you can't break up a marriage on as little as that.'

'No, probably not.'

'Hopefully, she'll phone soon.'

'You're welcome to stay as long as you want or need.'

'I've overstayed my welcome, you're too kind. Look as a thank you, let me buy you dinner tonight.'

'You don't have to do that. I've hardly seen you as it is.'

'You've put yourself out and you didn't have to. It's my way of saying thank you. I promise I'll only drink water. I don't know what I was up to. I think I was trying to anaesthetize myself with drink. I'm not going back to that place again.'

Chapter 40

A Peculiar Mix of Relief and Uncertainty

She has never been intimidated by Stephen but there is something different about him now; he is like an elastic band that has been pulled so tight he may snap at any moment. It is a threat that accompanies their conversations and the long silences.

She has explained Adam's absence as visiting an old friend in the capital. Stephen does not question this; he seems uninterested, disengaged almost. Georgia has asked him if he is taking on too much work, with the commuting from Majorca to Athens and Corfu. He dismisses her concern with a casual nonchalance that has only increased her worry. He moves through the house as if distracted. At other times he stares into space, a distant expression suffusing his face, like someone who is carrying a great secret. She has asked about this and each time he either dismisses her concern with an off-the-cuff remark, 'I'm fine,' or, more seriously, he clams up, folds within himself to a place she cannot reach. Georgia feels he is contained in his own world.

They have spent time together as a family, driving through the countryside, stopping for impromptu lunches at tavernas and swimming in the sea, when they discover a little cove or stretch of beach. On these outings, Stephen is more himself, the husband and father roles instinctively played. His phone rings constantly and, jokingly, Georgia has threatened to throw it into the sea. There is an edge to him; she senses a change in him, an unbalanced spark that could easily ignite a fire. When she looks at his face, it expresses a permanent strain and irritated frown.

She dreads the evenings. A glass of wine before dinner, the bottled drained, and another uncorked during their meal. He becomes less tolerant of Dylan. It loosens his tongue and he does not hold back, his eyes unfocused, glazed over, his voice less coherent.

She wonders if Stephen still loves her. He does, she thinks, in his own way, but it is a love of convenience and of habit. They are not in love, not anymore, there has been no intimacy for a long time.

Georgia has gone to bed early, avoiding Stephen's gradual decline into a stupor. He comes to bed late. She is awoken by a clatter in the bathroom and Stephen cursing. A shiver runs through her, as she turns onto her side, away from his side of the bed. He fumbles his way to the bed; Georgia can smell the alcohol still lingering under the toothpaste on his breath. She feels his hand upon her, moving from her thigh, over her stomach and eventually holding her breast. He kisses her shoulder and moves onto his elbow, taking his weight.

'You're drunk Stephen, go to sleep.'

'I'm not drunk, I'm horny. I want to feel myself inside you, it has been too long Georgia.' He leans towards her and kisses her cheek.

'No, not tonight, please Stephen, just go to sleep,' she says, more insistently this time.

'For fuck's sake Georgia, you must be getting enough of it from teacher boy. Now I'm not good enough anymore,' he snaps incredulously.

'What!' she turns to face him, 'How can you say that? What a stupid thing to say.'

At that moment, Stephen's face clouds, she doesn't recognise it as the man she married, the father of her son. This is a stranger.

He grabs her face and pushes it away from him.

Georgia gives out a cry, more in surprise than pain.

Stephen crawls over her, and stands up, grabbing her by the arm and pulling her from the bed.

'Stephen stop, you're hurting me.'

He swings his arm and slaps her across the face. She falls backwards onto the bed. Shocked, in disbelief, her face stinging, she leans forward. He slams his knee into her chest and straddles her, pinning her to the bed. His weight crushes her, she struggled to breathe. Her eyes peer in horror, through the dim light, at the demented figure towering over her. She struggles, thrashing from side to side but he has a hold of both arms now, his hands vice-like on her wrists. She screams then and the pain that follows is excruciating, his knuckles smashing into her eye socket.

'Shut the fuck up, you whore, you fucking bitch,' he hisses in a controlled low voice, which stuns her more than his fist.

For a second, she can feel he is off-balance, as he tries to position himself over her. With all the energy she can muster, Georgia flings herself onto her side, sending Stephen tumbling over the bed and colliding with the bedside cabinet, sending a lamp tumbling to the floor. She gets to her feet, escape her only thought. To her horror, she feels the cold clasp of his fingers around her ankle; he forcefully yanks on it, sending Georgia crashing to the bedroom floor. The tiles are not kind to her hip bone and her fall is painful, her nightgown riding above her thigh. She screams again, he is standing over her now, and she doubles up in pain, as his foot thuds into her abdomen. She muffles her pain this time, fearing Dylan will hear. He strikes her again, and she thinks she will die and then it stops.

Stephen sits down on the bed, he falls onto his back and within seconds his breathing is deep; he does not move. Georgia spends the night in the guest bedroom. She does not sleep.

During the night, it occurs to her if Stephen were to be sick; he could choke on his own vomit. At that moment, she does not care whether he lives or dies.

The sun is blinding as she steps outside. She slides her sunglasses from her head covering her eyes. Her sunglasses shade her from the glare of the sun, but they serve a dual purpose. She has told Theresa she walked into an opened cupboard door, but the look of concern on Theresa's face questions this.

The sky is a deep blue, her favourite colour; she can spend hours just watching it. She walks over to the pool and slowly bends; she winces and then trails her hand through the water. When she was a child, there was only the sea to play in; the pool has been a later addition.

Georgia loved visiting the beach with her mother, building sandcastles and swimming in the warm Ionian. She would often read and occasionally join Georgia in the water. These memories cloak her with a warm sensation but also sadness. Georgia turns and looks at the house, it is well proportioned, not much has changed and her mother would still know the place. It was here that Emily was at her happiest. When she died, Georgia brought her mother's ashes back to Corfu, back to her home and buried the casket in the garden as was her mother's wish. They planted a tree in memory of her, in Emily's favourite part of the garden. As the tree has grown and matured each year, it has been a constant reminder of the years that have passed.

Georgia misses her mother dreadfully; her ache is sharp, especially when she reads the diary it only compounds her loss. She would give anything to be wrapped in her mother's arms once more, inhale her familiar scent and hear her voice bring clarity to Georgia's questions. She feels a tightness, a coiling inside her.

Georgia lowers herself tentatively into the wicker chair, her abdomen is tender, the bruising fresh. She tries to settle into the seat and winces as she reaches over to get a glass of lemonade. Stephen has gone, back to Majorca or Athens, she doesn't know, she doesn't care. The following morning after the attack, Stephen was like a child overcome with grief. He didn't know what got into him, it wasn't him, he didn't recognise that person, he would change, he told her he would stop drinking. He pleaded with her and when she told him it was over, he blamed her, accused her of teasing Adam, of having an affair, it was her fault this had happened, she was responsible for his rage.

There was no more violence, to her insurmountable relief, he packed, said his normal goodbye to Dylan as if nothing had happened, and left for the airport.

She is glad for the shade of the umbrella which hovers above her. She rarely sits by the pool, preferring the terrace or the patio at the far end of the garden with its unrestricted views of the Ionian, but she promised Dylan she would watch him swim the ten lengths of the pool he has gradually built up to. The pool is only fifteen metres, but for a child that spends most days in the solitude of his room when he is at home in Edinburgh, it is an achievement she wants to celebrate with him.

To her great relief, Dylan heard nothing of the night before. He has seen the purple and orange colouring that stains her eye, commented on it, as a matter of fact, and accepted Georgia's explanation of the rogue cupboard door. Her makeup can hide the physical remains of Stephen's hate but not the scarring inside her.

Dylan has asked when his lessons will begin again; he hasn't shown concern that Adam has been absent. He is eager to continue with his Mozart project.

She thinks of phoning Adam. Is she ready to tell him? She feels ashamed, she doesn't know why; after all, she is the victim in all of this.

Once Dylan swims his ten lengths and receives Georgia's praise, he takes himself off to his room to listen to Mozart.

She shifts slightly in the chair, attempting to calm the pain in her stomach. She wonders if she has ruptured an organ, and thinks of internal bleeding but then tells herself she is being overdramatic, she is bruised, nothing more.

Once again Adam enters her thoughts and, even after all she has been through, there is a flutter in her stomach.

She remembers the day of the interview, opening the front door to Adam; he looked apprehensive and unsure, with Stockbridge behind him. She felt something move inside her as she welcomed him into her house and, unknowing, into her life.

Even then, her marriage to Stephen had developed the habit of just going through the motions, just existing. They had both withdrawn from one another and filled the void with other interests.

She reaches for her mobile, scrolls down to Adam's name and presses 'call.' She takes a deep breath and composes herself.

After the call, she feels a peculiar mix of relief and uncertainty. Georgia watches swallows gracefully arc and glide over the garden, the rainbow infused butterflies fluttering from flower to flower and, in the grove, one of Elena's goats is stretching its neck nibbling on an olive. Georgia is overcome with a sudden need to be near to her mother.

Chapter 41

An Outing on a Boat

1972

Sunday 2ⁿᵈ July 1972

Stelios has invited me to go out on his boat and see Corfu from the sea. We will travel around its coast and find an ideal spot for lunch. He said he has a few places in mind, but will leave the decision to me. He is looking forward to showing me how beautiful the island is from the sea. I must admit, I'm quite looking forward to it.

Paul has been asked to do an extended book tour around a few American states. He said he wouldn't do it if I was against the idea and wanted him back in Corfu. I told him not to worry about me; he needs to ride the crest of the wave with this new book for as long as he can, so to speak. I think he was relieved. In all honesty, I'm enjoying my time alone at the house. I see Theresa most days and Kyriakos has been working in the garden for the last few days. It has been nice to see Theresa and Kyriakos together; I normally just see one or the other.

Theresa has been curious about my friendship with Stelios. She wants to know all the details and she is quite taken aback that Paul doesn't mind. She said that no Greek man would put up with such a thing. I haven't told Paul. I let Theresa think I had; it is better that way I think. It made me feel better, but now I feel a mixture of guilt and dread.

When I'm with Stelios, I feel reassured; I feel a confidence in me I have not felt in years. He makes me, dare I say it, feel like a woman again. When we are together he is not distracted with mundane things, he is focused on me and me alone. It is as if he is owned exclusively by me. I find myself craving his attention. How strange it is. It is not infatuation. It sounds like an adolescence crush, but it is graceful and pure, "bewildering" comes to mind. I have tried to extrapolate what it means, what does it accomplish? I have come to the conclusion it bathes me in a sexual excitement that I have not felt in years.

He is not patronising in his compliments; he is considerate and genuine and I like that about him. I have also registered that I am more inclined to accept his invitations without hesitating which, in itself, says something about me. I think I might be falling in love.....

Stelios' boat is a 1969 Islander 37/SL; it sits in the cove looking every inch the perfect specimen of its kind. Stelios has rowed to the shore in what can only be described as a dinghy that gets towed at the rear of his boat. He jumps into the shallow water and pulls the dinghy towards Emily who is standing with an amused expression.

'Your taxi awaits.'

'When you said you'd pick me up, I wasn't expecting this.'

'It's only the baby. What do you think of the mother?'

'Impressive, but it's the baby I'm worried about.' She gives an edgy smile and looks uncertain.

'You'll be fine. Here, take my hand.' He presents her with his hand and then swiftly withdraws it. 'You can always swim?'

'The baby it is then.'

Emily is surprised at the buoyancy of the 'baby' as she sits with her knees together. Emily is wearing a red sleeveless dress, which falls to her knees, white flip flop sandals, with a jewelled slip and a wide-brimmed sun hat. She places her plaited bag on her lap. The bay is calm and translucent in turquoise and blue. Emily can see little crops of seaweed and rock, elsewhere on the seabed is sand.

As they move closer to the boat, Emily is surprised at its size. She can make out the writing on the side, '*Ionian Queen*'

'You didn't tell me she was royalty.'

'You'll have to be on your best behaviour then.'

'I'll try but I can't promise,' Emily says, smiling.

Emily feels the warmth of the sun on her face as she scans the landscape. It is the first time she has viewed Corfu's coastline from a boat, and she lets her eyes wander along dark and green foliage that covers the land, like skin. Along cliffs and rocks, the sea is a magnificent blue that melts into turquoise, crystal clear, transparent and glasslike. Emily has perched herself on a cream leather seat and feels happy. From this position, she can see the sun's light dancing on the surface of the Ionian, like sparkling stars.

'I've never seen the island from the sea like this before. It seems to magnify how lush and green it is. Look at the colour of the sea, it's like the Caribbean.'

'You mean the Caribbean is like Corfu.' Stelios smiles.

'Yes, precisely.'

Stelios is sitting in front of Emily, steering the boat.

'Would you like to try and hold the wheel?'

'Oh no, I don't think so.'

'It's easy, come on, it won't bite.'

Tentatively Emily holds the wheel.

'Not too tight, nice and gentle, just like you're driving a car.'

Stelios stands behind Emily and places his hands upon hers. 'There, I told you it was easy.'

Emily can feel her heart race. She can feel his breath on her neck and his stomach against her back. She forces herself to concentrate on the front of the boat.

'Look, Emily, over there; dolphins.'

To their left, three dolphins glide alongside them, slicing through the sea effortlessly.

'Let me take the wheel.'

Emily moves to the side of the boat and watches in disbelief as the dolphins arch in and out of the water beside the boat.

'Wow, they're really quick, but look how graceful they are.'

'Sometimes there are twenty, even more, all racing alongside the boat, It's a pity there is only three.'

'They are spectacular.'

She reaches into her bag and retrieves a camera.

'I need to take photographs of this.'

Emily takes photographs and, as soon as the dolphins appeared they are gone.

'Did you enjoy that?'

'It was marvellous. I hope the photographs do it justice.'

Stelios turns and smiles. 'I'm sure they'll turn out fine.'

'Can I take your picture?'

'Sure.'

Emily raises the camera to her eye and runs off a series of photographs.

'I thought this would be a good spot to have lunch.' Stelios says.

He glides the boat into a small inlet; it is narrow and has a small sandy beach.

'This place is beautiful.'

'It's perfect, I love this spot.'

The engine dies and the pulse of the crickets is constant as Stelios throws the anchor overboard.

'I've got sandwiches in the galley. We can eat lunch here or on the beach.'

'We've got it to ourselves; it would seem a shame not use the beach.'

Stelios takes two towels, and what is essentially a picnic basket onto the dinghy and once Emily has sat down rows the small dinghy towards the beach.

The basket has several compartments, holding plates, forks, knives, sandwiches, biscuits, cheese, and olives. He opens another compartment and produces a bottle of wine with two glasses.

'You've been busy.' Emily grins.

'Not exactly, my housekeeper made it up for me.'

'Oh, I see.'

Stelios pours two glasses of wine and hands one to Emily.

'Thank you.'

'Cheers,' Stelios says and clinks Emily's glass.

'What do you think of the wine?'

'It's lovely.'

'I'm glad. Are you having a good time?'

'It's wonderful Stelios. What is there not to like? Look where we are. It's beautiful, good food, good wine and you make an excellent host.'

He smiles widely. 'Good. Let's eat. Try some cheese, it's my favourite.'

During lunch, they speak about their respective pasts. Stelios is frank and open. He tells Emily that, although his upbringing was a poor one, his parents had a work ethic and valued the sanctimony of the family. His father was a baker in the village, but they moved to Corfu Town and his mother worked as a maid for one of the wealthier families. They lived in a poor area of the capital. Stelios shared a bedroom with his two older brothers. He had two younger sisters who shared another room. There was a small kitchen, just big enough to cook in and a living room where they ate, read, discussed their days and played when they were younger.

An uncle who had emigrated to Britain died and gave each of his nieces and nephews £200, a lot of money for a twenty-year-old from Corfu Town. Stelios invested the money, used it as a deposit to buy a flat in the town. Within two years, he had a portfolio of six properties. He opened his first restaurant in the capital a year later. By the time he was twenty-eight, he owned properties all over Corfu and had expanded into building houses, hotels and restoring townhouses. Today, he is one of the richest men in Corfu.

'What do your brothers and sisters do?' Emily asks.

'They work for me. I look after my family. They each have their own talents they bring to my businesses.'

'That's a noble thing to do, looking after your family in that way.'

'If they were in my shoes, each one of them would have done the same. How are you getting on with Gabriella and the shop?'

'I'm really enjoying it. I have a purpose again and she is like a sponge. I didn't realise how much I missed it: the buzz, the decision making. Well, I just advise her really, I don't have the final say.'

'Has she ever questioned your advice?'

'No. She has always taken it on board and used it.'

He smiles. 'Well then, that says it all. Gabriella has told me, she would like you to become a partner in her business.'

'She has.'

'Well, why not. It makes perfect sense.'

'I'm not sure if I want to get fully involved in running a business again. I like the freedom of just dipping in and out.'

'I think that is all she is looking for. She values your contribution and your knowledge. When do you see her next?'

'Tomorrow.'

'Speak to her then about it. I think she will be happy just to have you around for as long as she can.'

'And I'm happy to do what I've been doing.' She sips her wine.

'What do you think of the wine?'

'It's nice. I like a dark fruity wine.'

'I thought about dipping my toe into winemaking, but the problem is you can't just dip your toe into it, it's the whole leg approach, and so much investment, it takes an eternity to see any return. So, for now, I'm happy just to drink it.' He grins.

'Has there been someone special in your life?'

Stelios lets the sand fall through his fingers. 'Once.'

'Were you married?'

'No. I have a six-year-old daughter. She is the only good thing that came out of it. Her name is Pavlina. She lives in Athens.'

'With her mother?'

'No, although I love Corfu, but it's better she stays in Athens. I have a house in the city.'

'And her mother?'

'We do not see each other anymore.'

'Has she abandoned her daughter?'

'It's complicated. What about you Emily, do you want children?'

'I do, one day. Paul needs to concentrate on his work for now. We have decided to wait.'

'It's a decision not to be taken lightly.'

Emily looks away from him.

'I get the feeling that this is more Paul's idea than yours.'

'It's difficult. We are going through a tough time at the moment. If I'm to be completely honest, and I feel I can with you Stelios, but my marriage has been over for a long time now.'

'Then why are you still together?'

'I'll always be with him, he needs me.'

'Like a mother.'

'Something like that.'

'Do you love him?'

Emily pauses. 'I care about him.'

'There's a difference.'

'I know.'

'Let's finish up here.' Stelios clears away the plates and cutlery. 'We can stay here or move on, it's up to you.'

'I don't mind,' Emily says.

She feels a tremendous drag of guilt. What would Paul think if he knew about her day with Stelios? What must it look like? She massages the back of her neck and sighs. But it is precisely because of Paul and what they have become that she finds herself here, she reasons with herself, and she has not felt this kind of exhilaration with Paul for as long as she can remember. Emily wonders how long can their pretence continue. There is a momentary pang of sadness. She loves Paul, she knows that, but not as she should.

She looks off to the side, to where the beach sweeps into the sea. Her guilt suddenly dissipates as she observes the striking quality of light against the sand and sea and she wishes she could capture this moment, like a photograph. She looks at Stelios, who is smiling to himself, a congratulatory gesture that accompanies the closing of the basket. 'There, all done.'

'I'd like to go for a swim. Not here, from the boat.'

'You don't have a bikini,' Stelios says, out of curiosity.

Back on the boat and in the bedroom, Emily undresses down to her underwear and bra and wraps a white towel around her. Hesitantly, she makes her way to the deck where Stelios is standing in nothing but his shorts. His chest is covered in fine wiry hair that glistens in the sunlight. He politely turns his back as Emily, self-consciously, slides the towel from her and lowers herself into the sea.

'Oh, it's only cold for a second and then it gets warm,' she calls out to Stelios.

Stelios is still standing looking at her. He is smiling. A beautiful warm smile.

'What is it?' She asks quizzically.

'You look so happy. It suits you, Emily. I never want to take the smile from your face,' he dives into the sea then and resurfaces. 'How long can you hold your breath for?'

'I don't know. I've never tried. Why?'

'There's another world below us. It's beautiful. Hold your breath and follow me.'

With each new dive, Emily is able to hold her breath a little longer, and she is amazed at the different variety of fish, the rainbow of colour, the pellucid light and clarity of the water.

'It's amazing Stelios,' she laughs as they resurface, again and again, her vanity dissolving with each dive.

She sits with her back to him, the towel once again in place. She runs her fingers through her wet hair.

'It won't take long to dry in this heat,' Stelios assures her.

'It can take all day. It's a shame it has to end.'

'What?'

'Our day. This, being here, it's perfect Stelios. Thank you.'

She can feel the sun penetrate her shoulders and realises she needs to apply sunscreen. She rummages in her bag.

'Let me,' Stelios says, taking the sun cream from her.

He spreads the cream in slow deliberate wave-like motions, across her shoulders, down to her shoulder blades and then sweeps up along her neck. His touch is a charge that races through her. She arches her head backwards, and he slides the cream across her clavicle. He bends forwards and puts his lips to the nape of her neck. She makes a small sound, anticipating his touch. His lips are light and feathery upon her skin. She draws in her breath.

'You taste delicious,' he whispers.

The towel slips but she makes no attempt to straighten it. Instead, she turns her head towards him; he runs his finger along her arm and then lifts her chin so that their mouths hover an inch apart. She opens her mouth and feels his breath, warm and moist upon her lips. She savours the moment her mouth touches his, their tongues pass over each other, as every fibre of her body melts into him.

Chapter 42

Returning

Anger is a strange thing. It manifests in different forms and guises. It searches out our flaws and imperfections. Adam has felt its touch upon him and now it is ruthless.

When Georgia phoned, her voice was measured, but also strained, as she tried to convince him that although she was sore, she was fine; there were no cuts, just bruising and a little swelling.

He cannot bear to think of the scene she described. To his dismay, he tries to imagine what he would have done if he had been in the house. He blames himself; he compromised, it was what he wanted, insisted upon even. Now he struggles to understand why he left her alone to face him. To his distress and incomprehension, the pain of it makes his mind ache; it disturbs him and fills him with remorse. There is only one thought on his mind and that is to return to her. In his eagerness, he left without telling Tzakis.

He can't recall the car journey back to the village. He drove with a desperate urgency. His mind consumed with images of Georgia panicking, his thoughts relentless with, *if only I had stayed this would never have happened. She must have been terrified, and I wasn't there, she was alone.*

His regret is palpable; his anger is a rage that grows in strength with each new thought. There will be no forgiveness, no pity for a drunk that beats his wife; only retribution. Adam passes through the village square almost trembling; he is near to her now. He doesn't see Nikolaos wave a greeting from the Kafenion or the old lady, dressed in her black mourning clothes, buying aubergines and tomatoes at the little market stall. Adam drops a gear and puts his foot on the floor as the car screeches along the lane. Eventually, he is through the gates and the car skids to a halt. Even before the engine has died, Adam is running up the stairs, onto the terrace and through the door.

'Georgia, Georgia.' His voice resonates through the house seeking a reply.

Adam searches every room downstairs; he thinks of trying the garden but then takes the stairs two at a time. He finds her in her bedroom. Georgia is sitting in a large comfortable chair. This is where it happened, is the first thought that enters him. They hold each other's gaze. She can see the tension in his body and wishes she can take it from him.

Georgia looks at him silently; there are tears in her eyes. She has her mother's diary in her lap.

'She had an affair,' she says calmly.

'Who?' Adam's face is flushed but perplexed. He is relieved he has found her.

Georgia places both her palms over the diary. 'My Mum.'

Chapter 43

A Welcomed Ending

Stephen flies straight to Athens and caught a taxi to the Royal Olympia Hotel. He drops off his case in his room, washes and changes into a clean shirt and walks across the corridor to Suite 125. He knocks on the door and waits. Chris opens the door. 'Stephen come in. I've just ordered room service; look at the amount of sandwiches they gave me. Do you want one?'

'No, but I'll have a drink. Where's the minibar?'

Stephen opened a small bottle of vodka and a can of coke. He sinks most of the glass and refills it.

'Go easy Stephen. You need to keep a clear head for today. This is it, your last time in Athens, it's easy money now. After today, you won't be coming back.'

The operation in Athens was now well established. One final meeting set up to finalise the arrangements and Stephen's involvement was over.

'What we have done is a bad thing Chris, it's evil, it's tainted us. Drugs are not a crime in themselves, but what is a crime is that they ruin people's lives.'

'Don't get all sentimental on me now Stephen, it's a bit late for that. There has been some resistance from the Albanians. They want more than Cesar is offering. Cesar will not move on the figures, he'll go ahead without them if he has to. Other arrangements have been made that will allow us to open up The Balkans. Spiros has assured me that it's not a problem.'

'That doesn't concern us. We've done what we agreed to do, let them fight it out amongst themselves. I've had enough of this shit; the deal didn't involve a fucking drug war.' Stephen drains his glass and pours another.

'Go easy on the drink Stephen; we both need to keep a clear head. Are you ok?'

Stephen walks out onto the balcony and takes in the vast expanse of Athens.

'My marriage is over.'

'What?'

'I've done some terrible things and said things I can't take back, not now, it's too late.'

'What are you talking about Stephen? I've never known you or Georgia say a bad word about each other.'

Stephen massages his forehead. 'It's such a mess, Chris. I've had this thing in my head that Georgia is having an affair with Adam, the tutor. I couldn't help it and it just grew bigger, they are virtually living under the same roof, seeing each other every day. To be fair, it's not just that, we've been living almost separate lives for a long time now.'

'Georgia wouldn't do that Stephen.'

'It's the drink. I can't control myself. I don't know where the anger comes from.'

'I never knew. Why didn't you say something?'

'I need help. I was good at hiding it. I'd developed my own strategies. I thought I was in control of it, but the drink controls me.'

It feels as if a weight has finally lifted from him.

'There's a clinic in The Borders. They've got a good reputation, bloody expensive, though. I don't know how long it takes, but when I get back home, I need to refer myself. That's the plan, anyway. It means that you'll need to run things in Majorca on your own for a while.'

'You do what you have to Stephen. God, we all like a drink, I didn't think it had got that bad.'

'Neither did I, but I don't recognise the person I've become.' He looks at the glass in his hand. His hand is shaking. 'After today, it's finished with. I need it for now, especially today. '

They are picked up at the hotel and driven to the villa, in Filothei. Instead of going inside, they are shown to the rear of the villa, to a lavish terrace area, where Spiros is sitting on a large cream leather sofa.

Spiros gets to his feet when he sees Stephen, 'Good to see you, Stephen. This must be Chris.' He extends his hand.

'Come take a seat. Would you like anything to drink, a coffee perhaps?'

'A coffee for me,' Stephen says.

'I'm fine.' Chris takes a file from his briefcase and leafs through it.

Around the house, Stephen is aware that there are more guards than usual, strategically placed. Stephen feels an upsurge of concern. Normally, when he has arrived at the gates, he is met by one guard; today, there are two. He notes the holstered guns under their suit jackets. Stephen thinks it wise not to mention this to Chris. He wonders if Spiros is armed.

Stephen sips the coffee Spiros has poured into a small china cup. Stephen wonders if Spiros has a family. They have never spoken of such things, they are just acquaintances brought together by a common interest. He observes the façade of the villa; it is two stories and large, a modern design, with a plethora of glass, like a gigantic greenhouse, Stephen thinks. The walls are white, brilliant in the sun and this reminds him of the panoramic view from the Acropolis, a sprawling Athens, flat and white but softly muted. The interior of the house is spacious and open planned, marbled and pillared.

He is an intelligent man. How did he end up like this? A drunk who beats his wife, who orchestrates the flow of drugs through cities and countries. He despises what he has become. There was once a sense of pride in his work, it made him what he was, it was his identity. A melancholy knot sinks deep in his chest.

When he thinks of Dylan, the sense of failure is enshrined in the guilt of the absent father, the absent husband.

Spiros has taken off his glasses and is pointing to a paragraph in the document, that sits on the table in front of him. Stephen hasn't heard a word they have said.

'I need to move fast on this one and demonstrate that we don't negotiate.'

'What do you suggest?' Chris asks.

'A little persuasion can go a long way. Leave it with me. The Albanians are out of their depth on this one.'

A crack punctures the air. The body hits the pool, and the water changes colour as if red ink has just been poured into it.

In that moment, Stephen doesn't care if he lives or dies, and the choice is about to be taken from him. Another crack, then another, 3, 4, 5, like firecrackers,

'Jesus,' Chris screams, as he and Spiros scramble towards the villa.

The guards run for cover, P90 submachine guns spraying the garden indiscriminately.

Stephen sits motionless. He has focused on a Judas tree at the other side of the garden. He has betrayed those he loves. How apt that he now stares at that particular tree. Like Judas, he thinks he, too, deserves to die. He is hollow, unconnected to the world around him.

'Stephen, for fuck's sake,' Chris screams.

Envy, guilt, suspicion, bitter self-pity, rage, he has experienced them all, but now he feels nothing.

'For Christ's sake,' Chris' voice shrills as he and Spiros scuttle into the villa.

Loyalty to the company, loyalty to ambition, loyalty to the pound and dollar was all that mattered to him, until now.

A burning sensation rips through his shin, like a hot poker. He feels the air leave his lungs. A second bullet enters his shoulder, catapulting him backwards. He feels he has been hit by a truck. He welcomes death and the last sight of beauty bestowed upon him. He can see the sky, a timeless canvas.

Chapter 44

In the Garden

Adam has never seen colours like it; shelves of turquoise and aqua blue that define the Ionian, as it slides leisurely along rippling sands and the occasional underwater island of vegetation, so clear to the eye it defies all logic. He finds it almost indescribable. Walking further, he looks across the sea towards the horizon that blends effortlessly into a stunning blue. He exults in the glare and dazzle, a lingering luminescence where the sun shimmers in the silver light.

Adam is relaxed, for the first time in days. He wonders how different his life would have been if he had taken the offer of the research post at the university? He strides through the village, past the church, with its vast wooden doors and domed tiled roof. An image of the Madonna and child is painted into a recess beside the front door to a house where two elderly women sit on wooden stools, gesticulating wildly; one laughs, throwing her head back. Adam wonders what might have been said to cause such a jovial display of emotion, some village gossip or rumour that is gathering pace.

He has slept little in the past few days; it has been a time of readjustment, of aligning himself to the possibility that given time, Georgia and him, will leave behind the complications of the past. He feels he no longer needs to repress his feelings. In his mind, he lingers on an image of Georgia; he contemplates upon it, and it is enough to know they are both moving forward towards a new beginning.

Recently her words have encouraged him, everything has changed.

From the moment he saw her, he became interested in her. It was not just about tutoring her so; she held the centre-ground. In the beginning, he tried not to allow himself to think of her sexually, but sometimes when he did, he banished such thoughts from him. But now, as time has passed, he has become impatient with such self-discipline. It has also been reciprocated by Georgia, and although discreet, it is measurable.

She is married, and this sacred institution, the bond between husband and wife, is no barrier to his thoughts, to his feelings. How extraordinary, he tells himself. Her marriage, its aftermath, its debris, has made it easier for them both to acknowledge their feelings for each other.

In the midst of all this, there is Dylan. Adam smiles sadly to himself. He envisions the boy trying to make sense of the recriminations his father's actions will undoubtedly entail. Will Dylan find his father's aggression inexcusable? Will he be able to understand the motives? Will Dylan be apprehensive of his mother's fear? Will he grasp the gravity of the situation?

Dylan will not think emotionally; his conclusions will be driven by a one-dimensional thought process. In Dylan's world, there is no grey: only black and white; no compromise; only right and wrong.

What will he make of it all? Dylan occupies a different pole when experiencing the world around him. Will he be subdued by it all, frustrated? Dylan will find his shelter in other ways, ways that are deeply satisfying, only to him, this boy who hugs trees.

Adam dodges an open-top jeep and heads towards the Kafenion. Sitting in their usual seats are Giannis, Thanos, Stamatis, Mida and Nikolaos, sipping dark coffee and putting the world to right.

Thanos frowns. 'Never trust a politician, they are all liars. They even lie to cover up their lies. We need people in Parliament who are genuinely interested in working to better the lives of ordinary Greek families: better education, better schools, wages that reflect the value of a job to society, like teachers and nurses.'

'Thanos, you should run for the local council elections,' Stamatis says, winking towards the others.

'What's this?' Adam asks, pulling out a chair and sitting down. When he is amongst them they speak English.

'Thanos has found his vocation in life. No more catching fish for him, he is going to catch people's votes.' Stamatis laughs.

'I was just saying, there are very few people in public life who have any morals these days. Politicians say one thing and then do another.'

Adam smiles. 'They've been doing that since democracy began. Since democracy was invented by the Greeks, politicians lying must be a Greek invention.'

'Be careful, you're a guest on this island.' Giannis smiles a slow gap-tooth smile.

'We've not seen you for a few days, Adam. I was beginning to think you had gone back to Scotland,' Nikolaos says.

Adam is not sure whether his friends have heard about Georgia, given that gossip and news are celebrated in some quarters of the village as a valuable commodity to be shared at every opportunity, Adam is cautious in his answer.

'I visited a friend in Corfu Town, stayed a few days and took in the sites.'

'Everything ok at the house then?' Stamatis asks what they are all thinking.

Nikolaos gives Stamatis a scornful glance.

'Yes. Why shouldn't it be?' Adam says, finally.

Nikolaos sighs. 'You know what it's like in the village Adam. Someone begins a little rumour and before you know it, it's the property of the whole village. Some people have made it their occupation to know everyone's business. Nothing good comes of it.'

Adam wonders if he is being warned.

'Giannis wife, Eva, saw Georgia's husband leave the house early the other morning in a taxi, and he wasn't looking very happy.'

'He comes and goes all the time, almost every weekend.'

'The woman, Georgia, she had a big black eye. I saw it when I delivered her mail. She tried to hide it,' Manos says.

Adam's face flushes with irritation. 'Ah yes. I think she said, she had an argument with a cupboard door and she came off the worst.'

'Exactly what Theresa said, remember Manos? So let's drop this whole disagreeable interrogation and get on with our game.' Nikolaos leans back in his chair. 'Shall we?'

The morning stretches out, hot and airless. Adam is glad of the reprieve the chess brings, from the current fascination and interest in the goings-on at the house.

'Have you got anything planned for the rest of the day?' Nikolaos asks.

Adam shrugs. 'No. I'll probably have lunch at Pandelios.'

He has given Georgia some space, time to come to terms with what has happened. She has sought solace in Dylan; he is one of the good things her marriage has produced. They need each other right now. Georgia wants to soften the blow of Stephen's sudden departure. It is a task Adam does not envy but has given Georgia the courtesy of being alone with Dylan to accomplish it.

'Good choice. I'm having shrimp pasta at home. You're welcome to come along. It's Sofia's speciality; you haven't met my wife yet, have you? She loves cooking for others. She'll be thrilled. Linguini pasta, a tomato sauce, herbs, garlic, basil, feta cheese and of course lots of large shrimps.'

'How can I refuse? It sounds delicious.'

'Good.' Nikolaos looks at him steadily. 'We can have a talk; we've not caught up for some time.'

Adam knows Nikolaos' motives, and he welcomes the chance to speak candidly, in the knowledge it is far from prying ears. After all, Nikolaos is a priest; Adam smiles to himself. It will be like a confession.

Nikolaos' house, a whitewashed building with a terracotta tiled roof, is next to the church. Once inside, the aroma of aromatic tomato sauce, basil, and shrimp infuses a trail they follow to the kitchen.

'Sofia, we have a guest. Adam, this is Sofia.'

'Pleased to meet you, Sofia.'

'Ah, Nikolaos' chess prodigy. Yasou. I hope you like shrimps, Adam?'

'I do. It smells amazing.'

'Would you like some lemonade, it's cold? I've just taken it out of the fridge'

'I'd love some, thanks. Your house is lovely.'

'It belongs to the church, but we have tried to put our individual touch to it,' Sofia says, whilst pouring the lemonade into three glasses.

Sofia is curvaceous. She has an attractive oval face and wavy brown hair that falls down her back. She doesn't look like a wife of a priest. Her looks don't conform to his preconception of how a priest wife, in general, should look, but then again, this is Greece and he has never met the wife of a Greek priest, until today.

'It's too nice to eat inside; we'll eat out in the garden,' Sofia says.

They eat their lunch, shaded by an old olive tree. The garden is small, enclosed by a wall and decorated with several clay pots that sprout coloured flowers.

'It's rumoured that this tree is over five hundred years old,' Nikolaos says, between mouthfuls. 'It was part of an ancient olive grove before the village was built. This was the only remaining tree, so the church was built next to it so that the faith would always remain a constant presence in the life of the villagers, just like the tree. Eventually, the wall was built to protect it and then latterly, the house, for the priest.'

'How long have you lived here?'

'Oh, coming up for five years now.'

'It must have been quite a change, coming from a city to a small isolated village.'

'It was to start with. I couldn't get used to the pace of life. It was too quiet, everyone knew everyone else's business, and even if you didn't want to know, it was hard to escape it. Gradually, I started to appreciate the sense of community and I saw that there was a tremendous amount of charity amongst the villagers. People help each other out; it's not seen as a chore or a burden, but given freely and there is an enormous amount of worth in that. Don't get me wrong, it's not perfect; we live in the real world after all. Sofia is a teacher also, so she made the greatest sacrifice.' Nikolaos touches Sofia's hand.

'What did you teach?' Adam asks.

'I was a primary school teacher. When we first arrived, I taught here at the school. It helped to supplement the two good wages we had both lost.'

'Are you still teaching?'

'Not anymore, I taught for two years and then because of falling pupil numbers they had to make savings; I was one of the first casualties.'

'Do you miss it?'

'I used to, but it's been three years now and I've filled my time doing so many other things I don't even think about it now. How do you find going from teaching a class to delivering lessons to just one boy?'

'It can be a challenge, but rewarding all the same,' he says genuinely, thinking of Dylan.

'My friend, Eirini, has a son who, although not diagnosed, probably has autism. His name is Fanis, he is only five; she's going through a really difficult time with him. I wondered if I could pick your brains, take advantage of you while you're here?'

'I'd be happy to help if I can?'

'Eirini calls them "*meltdowns*." Fanis will just drop to the ground and start to scream, sometimes he goes into a rage and it doesn't matter what Eirini does, he can't seem to stop himself. She says that when it is a bad one, it's as if he has to get to the other side of it until it is finished and then he acts as if nothing happened; he forgets all about it.'

'And what causes this behaviour, does she know?'

'It could just be the simplest thing. He doesn't like change very much, especially if it happens unexpectedly. Things have to be done in a certain way, he likes routines, and he also has little rituals that he has to go through before he can move on to something else. They can't just go to the shops. Fanis will only go a certain way; it has to be the same route every time, or he gets distressed about it. What would seem trivial to you or me can be upsetting and stressful for Fanis. Eirini does her best, but sometimes you can see she is struggling. I don't know how she manages.'

Adam has a vivid picture in his mind of the countless parents who over the years have told him similar stories. This description was not unique, but rather a retelling of an individual story that resonated with familiar aspects pertinent to that family, but also very similar in its detail and the expressed concerns. Each had an emotional, physical and intellectual need. It was a case of improvisation regarding each individual family's need, guided by knowledge and pre-set strategies.

Adam explains that Fanis needs to be warned in advance about any changes to his normal routines or activities, although this would be more problematic when change is unpredictable, as can be the norm in daily life. Adam describes people with autism as in the main, visual learners, who need any advanced change to their routines represented with photographs, Velcro symbols or written lists if they can read. Also, Adam suggests using apps that are free or reasonably priced, and easy to use on mobile phones.

They spend a considerable amount of time going over particular aspects of Fanis' behaviour and Adam contributes several strategies Eirini can use which Sofia writes in a note -pad.

'This is wonderful Adam, thank you. The way you've described why Fanis behaves as he does in given situations, and what Sofia can do to help him, makes so much sense.'

'Fanis is only reacting to his environment. If Eirini can make his environment autism-friendly, by considering how he might experience the world around him and why he is reacting to that environment, she can reduce the unwanted behaviours. Fanis is only communicating a need. His behaviour has a function and, once Eirini works out why he uses that behaviour and what function it serves for him, then she can teach him new behaviours and skills that will help to get his needs met, but in a manner that is acceptable and appropriate.'

'I can't wait to tell Eirini. I hope I can make sense of my scribbles. I think I've got it all written down.'

'Let me have a look.' Adam offers.

'It's in Greek.'

'Ah, never mind. If there's a problem you can just let me know.'

'If you don't mind, Nikolaos, I'd like to go round to Eirini's. She'll really appreciate this Adam.' Sofia kisses Nikolaos and promptly leaves.

'That was a good thing you did Adam.'

'It was nothing. I'm glad I could help.'

'You've probably just changed Eirini's life. Hopefully, it will make things easier for her.'

Adam smiles, a self-reflective smile, and amongst the metallic rhythm of the cicadas, and the rose, white and yellow flowers of the small garden, he feels a small eruption of self-worth, a strange enchantment that has been missing from him this last week.

He is pondering this new feeling when Nikolaos says, 'Stamatos and Manos asked those questions because they're concerned about you, as I am. Is everything ok Adam?'

Adam pauses and then relates the events of the past week. Nikolaos does not interrupt him. When Adam is finished, he wipes his brow. Nikolaos sits quite still as he takes the information in.

'So now you know. I'm in love with a married woman.'

'So it would seem.' Nikolaos sits back in his chair and takes a cigarette from a packet. 'Do you mind if I smoke?'

Adam shakes his head.

'Are you sure she feels the same? Have you thought of the possibility you could make a fool of yourself?'

'She does, but she hasn't said it in so many words. The last few weeks have been difficult for her. I don't want to put her under more pressure. She doesn't need that, not now anyway.' Adam feels weary.

'Yes, I can see how that can be. Be cautious Adam. Don't let your heart rule your head, let Georgia take the initiative when she is ready. She will be feeling very vulnerable at the moment.'

'So you don't disapprove then?' He waves away a persistent fly.

'Have you been intimate together?'

Adam smiles at him. 'No. And I wouldn't, not yet anyway, not after what has happened.'

'Look, Adam, you haven't done anything wrong, you are only admitting to what you feel. You are not responsible for what has happened; by all accounts, their marriage was over before you arrived, irrespective of what you feel for Georgia. It's a delicate matter, respect her dignity. The last thing we ever learn about ourselves is the effect we have on others, and sometimes that knowledge comes too late.'

Chapter 45

A Momentary Lapse of Common Sense

1972

Friday 7ᵗʰ July 1972

A few days ago I took a trip to Corfu Town. I had lunch and walked around the old town for a while before plucking up the courage to enter a shop and hand over the film of negatives of my boat trip with Stelios to get developed. I felt a mixture of excitement and then incredible guilt. Even now, I find it incomprehensible, unbelievable that I have allowed myself to become involved in such a way with another man. It wasn't until I arranged for the developed photographs to be delivered to the house that the realisation dawned on me, I may have compromised my standing as a married woman and exposed Stelios as the other person. I hoped that the shop owner would be discreet, but all the same, as my heart raced, I decided to tell Stelios of my momentary lapse of common sense.

He laughed, and I felt affronted, almost devalued in a way, and then with the thread of a threat, and contempt that laced his language, Stelios said it would be more than the man's job was worth, to spread such malice gossip. At that moment, I was beginning to appreciate the standing Stelios carried amongst the island's business community. His dismissive attitude unsettled me, with a nervous perturbation, and I wondered how far his influence reached and in what manner?

I saw something in his eyes; a reassurance, protectiveness, and I knew then, I was falling in love...

Stelios walks over to a chair and sits down next to Emily; he crosses one leg over the other and lights a cigarette. With the tip of the cigarette, he lights another and hands it to her. His eyes seem to glisten like emeralds and he has a smile that is satisfying. The housekeeper has brought two glasses of red wine that sit in front of them on a glass table. Stelios reaches for one and takes a sip. He is looking at her now, his smile still in place.

'Emily, thank you for coming. I was afraid you might not.'

She hesitates, trying to find the right words. 'I must admit it crossed my mind,' she pauses; she cannot deny how she feels. 'I thought it would be rude not to. Besides, I did say I'd give you the photograph.'

She reaches into her handbag and takes out a cream envelope. She opens it and hands him a photograph.

He looks at it for a while and still looking says, 'you look beautiful Emily and happy.'

She smiles with her lips together. 'I still am.'

He looks at her then. 'I want you to know I'm not in the habit of inviting a woman to my house.'

She rubs the side of her neck as if there is an itch. 'I'm glad to hear that. And I want you to know I've never been unfaithful.'

'I know.'

'How could you know?'

'I can't explain it at this moment, I just know.' He feels an overwhelming protectiveness towards her. 'Are you sure this is what you want?' He stubs out his cigarette.

She stares into his eyes. 'I've never been more certain in my entire life.'

Stelios slides from the chair and kneels in front of her. He hesitates and then brushes his hand through her hair. Stelios traces his finger along her eyebrow and down her cheek. Emily's breathing grows faster, she inhales deeply. He brushes his fingertip over her top lip, her mouth opens slightly and she kisses it, and then another, the fullness of her lips sending light tickles through his abdomen. Stelios moves his other hand to her stomach and then feels her breast through her dress. He hasn't taken his eyes from her; he bends his head and their lips touch, delicately at first, and then deeper. Emily pulls away from him.

'Not here, take me upstairs,' she whispers. He takes her by the hand and she follows him.

In the bedroom, one of the double glass doors that lead to a large balcony is open; a slight breeze floats towards them. She can feel its touch upon her arm. The room is large and spacious and white sheets cover the bed. There is a smell of lavender. Stelios stands in front of her and touches her face with his hand. He leans towards her and unbuttons her dress; he slides it from her shoulders and lets it fall, abandoning its concealment. He kisses her neck and then her shoulder, Emily raises her head, her lips slightly part and a small sound escapes her.

She holds his head in her hands. 'My turn,' she murmurs into his hair.

Emily unbuttons his shirt with light flicks of her fingers and slides it from his shoulders. Her heart is pulsing inside her. She bends her head and kisses his chest, the hairs tickling her lips. The smell of his skin fills her nostrils. They move towards the bed and, in that moment, there is no confusion to her thoughts, only intentness, and an eagerness to feel him inside her, her inner space, and melt into him.

Chapter 46

Finding Something Precious

It will be another hot day; the forecast warned of an impending heatwave and Georgia thinks it has already arrived, for as she leaves the coolness of the air conditioning and strolls into the sweltering garden, it feels as if a hairdryer is blowing hot air around her.

The lemon grove is her favourite part of the garden. She likes the way the sun's light filters through the trees. She stands still and then reaching upwards, her fingers slide along a perfectly shaped lemon, a bulbous golden sun. Some have fallen and litter the dry earth.

She cherishes these moments, especially today; she closes her eyes and inhales. Georgia recognises the fragrance of rosemary and thyme, these smells are a comfort to her. They trigger fond memories that stretch to her childhood, of playing in this garden, and later, to the present day, picking herbs that will season a dish for a meal bringing together family and friends. How extraordinary, she thinks speculatively, how certain aromas can conjure such profound feelings and imagery. This house has seen her grow from a child into a woman; it has been a haven of attachment, a secure bond, and it has defined her life.

She wraps her arms around her waist, her eyes fill with tears; it is a moment of weakness she allows herself to have. And then she straightens her posture, there is no room for sentimentality, not now.

On the morning Stephen left, he read the anger on her face, heard the disgust in her voice. She feared his usual self-justification that always followed the morning after his verbal onslaughts of abuse but this time, unlike the others, his abuse had been physical. He had pleaded with her in consternation, a panic that laced each word; he said he was tormented by guilt, by jealousy. Georgia surprised herself but, clearly afraid, she told him it was over and he was to leave that morning; she never wanted to see him again.

Until that is, the phone call she received that morning from a policeman in Athens who explained that Stephen was in the hospital with gunshot wounds and was under arrest for money laundering, drug trafficking and several other charges she failed to process as he launched into a detailed monologue.

'I've had a call from the police in Athens. Stephen has been arrested, he's been shot and he's in the hospital.'

'My God, what happened?'

'They wouldn't tell me. Chris has also been arrested. I phoned the office in Majorca. They said that both Stephen and Chris were in Athens on business.' Georgia looks pale.

'Are you alright?' Adam asks.

She sighs. 'I feel exhausted. I can't take any more of this. Shot! What has he been up to that someone wants to kill him? The police mentioned drugs.' She rubs her forehead. 'I'm going to Athens; Theresa will look after Dylan for me.'

'I'll come with you.'

'No, I'll go on my own. I don't even know if they'll let me see him.' Her voice is trembling.

'You're in no fit state to travel on your own. I'm going with you, I insist, end of.'

Georgia looks at Adam; she has no desire to argue with him, she is tired and confused. 'You're right. I'd like that.' She smiles and touches his arm.

'Good, I'll arrange the flights. When do you want to go?'

'Today, tomorrow… as soon as possible really.' She pauses. 'I've been filled with self-doubt, loathing myself and blaming myself. I need to see him, even lying in that hospital bed, I need to see him, I have to face him and tell him what I should have said years ago, that he is a sad and pathetic excuse for a father and a husband. I've protected him far too long, I've been delusional all these years, thinking that somehow it would get better, that he would eventually change and become the husband and father both Dylan and I never had. He's such a wanker.' She glances sharply at him. 'Does that surprise you?'

Adam smiles. 'Only the part where you called him a wanker. I've never heard you speak like that.'

'Does it suit me?' Georgia smiles back.

'It suits you when you're speaking about him; otherwise, no.'

A short silence follows and then she says, seriously, 'Was it obvious? I mean, I tried to make us look like a normal couple, but at times it was hard. We've been living together, just, but in reality, we co-existed like two different people. In public we were a couple, it was a deceptive veneer, but I've become tired of pretending, tired of apologising for his behaviour. He has never hit me before. That was the first. It will be his last.'

As she speaks, Georgia looks sad and forlorn, but when she speaks the words, "*it will be his last*," her voice projects a rush of venom.

'When I think back to that night, sometimes it doesn't feel real like it was a dream, but then I remember the pain, the humiliation. There's a thing I must do, a final deliverance. It's not with compassion I will stand by his bedside. I'm going to enlighten him about the pain he has caused this family and then I'm going to tell him, to his face, I want a divorce. I want the house in Edinburgh; he can have the flat in London. This house is mine, thank God, he can't get his hands on it. I want half of what he's worth; I think I've earned it.'

As Georgia speaks, Adam feels he has let her down, he did not do enough. The feeling encases him, and he promises himself it would never happen again.

'Have you spoke with Dylan, about Stephen?'

'Yes, I have.'

'How did he take it?'

'He has been very subdued; I know he ruminates about it when he is on his own. I've heard him talk to himself going over and over it. I don't think he can articulate it.'

'It'll take time.'

'I know.' Her voice cracks slightly as she looks towards the garden.

'My mum loved this garden; she spent a lot of time in it. I remember helping her when I was little, planting flowers, picking the oranges and lemons. Then as I got older, it felt more of a chore and I hated the dirt in my fingernails. Now, I always wonder if mum felt sad that I stopped helping her, I became interested in other things that, in a way I suppose, stopped us talking as much as we use to.'

'But that's just part of growing up, we all did it.'

'I know. But now, I regret it. As a mother, I know how that must have felt for her. The sad thing is, I can't get those times back.'

She takes her sunglasses off, and in doing so she is allowing Adam to scrutinise the extent of the bruising around her eye.

'I don't want to live my life in fear anymore; I don't want Dylan's memories of this beautiful place to bedevilled by Stephen's actions; there will be no more bruised faces.'

He reaches out, and with the tip of his finger, he traces the orange and purple bruise as if it is a delicate flower. 'No one will ever hurt you again, I promise.'

There are tears in her eyes, and for the first time he sees a tangible relief suffuse her face, and each muscle physically relax. Adam is aware of becoming aroused; it's a mysterious thing, he thinks, how he can feel his love for this woman grow. Instinctively he embraces her and he feels willingness on her part as she does not pull away. Adam threads his fingers through her hair; he feels intoxicated by the smell of it, she tilts her head and looks at him, her eyes are wide, drawing him into her with their shine. He thinks her eyes are beautiful, stunning. Adam wants to weep for her, for her vulnerability, her grief, and for her anger. He bends his head and their mouths open, almost touching but not yet, he has not taken his eyes from hers. Adam has never been surer in his life, not since his wife was alive, that he has found something precious, which has meaning beyond mere words; it has touched his soul, there is no other way to describe it.

Chapter 47

Butterfly

It was Adam's first visit to Athens. They stayed at the
Emporikon Hotel, a neo-classical 19th-century building. The
police allowed Georgia only five minutes with Stephen and
then asked her questions, most of which she didn't know the
answers to. She expected the questioning, but not the short
time she was had with Stephen. They were not alone, a
poker-faced policeman sat in the corner of the room the
entire duration of her visit and Georgia noted he spoke
perfect English. Adam waited for her at a café bar across
from the hospital. On her return, Georgia refused his offer
of a coffee, preferring instead to take a taxi back to their
hotel. He smiled and was about to ask her how she got on
but thought better of it; he would wait until she was ready to
talk. When they arrived at the hotel, Georgia said she
needed to walk, so they spent time in the Plaka, amongst the
tourist shops, jewellery shops, street musicians and flower
sellers. Adam thought it felt like a village in the middle of
Athens. Gradually, Georgia talked, and they looked for
somewhere to eat. They sat at a table outside the Vyzantino
restaurant and ordered red lentil and aubergine moussaka.

'I saw him for five minutes; a policeman was in the room
the entire time.'

'How did he take it?'

'He was expecting it; it came as no surprise. He asked
about Dylan. Stephen knows he will go to jail for a long
time.'

'Did he speak of what's been going on, why he was
shot?'

'No, only that he was up to his neck in it and that he was
ashamed of his behaviour. He only said that he had got
caught up in this other world, he said it was evil, a
revolving door, one he could not get out of. Adam, he
wanted to die. When the shooting started he didn't move, in
that moment he willed a bullet to kill him. I wasn't

expecting to hear that. He is ill Adam. Whatever he was up
to it was obviously illegal. I was misled by a lie. He has let
us all down, especially Dylan.'

'He misled himself, what's that saying… as long as it's
sunny you don't have to mend the roof… something like
that. You've been through a tough few weeks.'

'I've got through it because of you. I couldn't have on my
own.' She bends her head and feels tears in her eyes. She
has felt hollow for weeks, but it is only with Adam that she
feels a warm radiance growing inside her.

'I know it's a cliché but a great weight has lifted from
me. I can look towards the future now with a smile inside
me and I haven't been able to do that in a long time.'

He leans forward and takes her hand. 'I'll never take the
smile from your face.'

She gives a little smile and her face becomes warm.
'Good, because now I've got it back, I intend to keep it. Do
you want to do the touristy thing? You can't come to
Athens and not see the Acropolis and the museum. My
favourite is the National Archaeological Museum, I must
show you The Temple of Zeus.'

Adam laughs. 'It sounds like we'll need to stay for a
week.'

Later that night, in the hotel bar, Adam asks Georgia
if she has travelled much in Greece?

'A little; the usual postcard islands, Santorini, Mykonos,
but to be honest, for me, nothing compares to the Ionian
Islands, they're lush and green, the sky and sea melt into
one another. I'm biased of course, Corfu being the best. It's
not until I'm back in Edinburgh that I realise just how much
I love it.'

'I'd love to see more of Greece.'

'Then you should start with the Ionian Islands. I've
visited the main ones. There are seven of them, they are
called Heptanese-seven islands, but there are many smaller
ones. Each has its own distinct personality, especially the
landscapes, and then there are the dialects, the different

customs and traditions. You'll have heard of Cephalonia and Zakynthos?'

'Yes, I know them.'

'Well, apart from them, and Corfu of course, there's also Ithaca, Lefkada, Paxi, also known as Paxos, and Kythira. You should visit Zakynthos and Cephalonia to start with. We should do that sometime.'

'I'd like that very much.'

'And so would I. It could be like a holiday, just you and me and nothing but the day in front of us to do whatever we want.' She finishes her glass of wine and pours them both another glass. 'That's it finished, shall we order another?'

Adam smiles. 'Why not? We can pretend we're on holiday.'

'I think the majority of the people in the hotel are. It's getting noisy in here; do you want to sit outside?'

'We could do, I'll order another bottle.'

They both stand up and Georgia sways a little. Adam reaches out and steadies her. Her skin feels warm, and he fights an impulse to kiss her.

'Oh, the wine's gone straight to my head.'

'You didn't eat much at dinner, that's why. Are you sure you want another bottle?'

'Probably not, I'll just have this glass.'

They settle into their chairs in a small rectangular seating area, with little bulbs positioned in raised flower beds that just give off enough light to allow Adam to scan a menu.

'Do you want olives or nuts?'

'No, I'm fine.' She looks around. 'It's nice out here.'

There are only a few couples around them; most are engaged in hushed private conversations. Adam wonders if, like them, they too are viewed as a couple.

'I think I'll get olives when the waiter comes over again.'

Adam takes a drink and looks at her face shadowed in the in the muted light. Her head is bent. As she checks her mobile for messages, a curtain of hair has fallen and covers an eye. He wonders, briefly, if her heart leaps every time she is near to him, but then, almost instantly, he feels ashamed that he has doubted her feelings.

She takes a swallow of wine as she reads a text. 'It's Theresa. She says Dylan's in bed now and sleeping.' She visibly relaxes in front of him.

'Good, you don't have to worry now.'

'But I do. When he has asked about what happened to Stephen, he wants to know what type of guns were used, did anyone get killed and if so how many? He seems fixated on it, he doesn't really ask about Stephen.'

'He struggles with understanding his own emotions at the best of times. His interest in the guns is probably his way of trying to communicate his confusion and sadness. He's just trying to understand his own feelings; it's his way of crying out for help.'

There is a silence between them, it is not uncomfortable or awkward, there is no intense need to fill every gap with conversation, it is a milestone in how far they have come.

'Look, I've no doubt he knows you are upset, but he probably doesn't know how to comfort you because really, he doesn't know if his dad will live or die and because of this he would feel he is telling a lie, so he can't say anything; he doesn't know what to say.'

'You understand Dylan better than I do?' she says, honestly.

'I don't, I'm just aware of what his thought processes are likely to be because of his autism… but I could be wrong,' he says, unable to resist a smile.

She gave out a small laugh, enjoying his sense of humour.

'I bet you were a good lawyer.'

'What? Where did that come from?'

'I can imagine you in your power suit; it's a pleasing image by the way.' He raises an eyebrow. Recently he has become more daring with her.

She meets his gaze. 'Well, you'll just have to keep imagining it.'

'Do you miss it?'

She shakes her head. 'Oh God no, I've never felt envious about that at all or that I'm missing out. There's far more self-satisfaction in bringing up a child. We learn from our children and such lessons are the most important gift we'll ever get. I felt nothing like that when I practised law.'

'That's actually quite beautiful.'

She looks at him steadily. 'What about you? What is more satisfying, teaching a class full of students or teaching Dylan, one to one?'

'They're both different.' He feels they have crossed a line, in a good sense. He is encouraged to be more intimate with her in his thoughts, which is a relief to him. 'I prefer teaching Dylan. At first, it took a while to get used to, but it has become very rewarding and most importantly I think Dylan enjoys it too.'

She nods approvingly. 'And that is the highest compliment.'

He smiles broadly. 'And so is seeing how relaxed you are about it now, I know how difficult it was for you in the beginning.'

'It was. Each day I expected the worse, and I had no idea what I would have done if it didn't work out, but thankfully you just seemed to connect with him, or he connected with you, it doesn't matter. I felt this incredible relief and I knew by coming to Corfu I had done the right thing, but what I didn't expect was the effect you were having on me and as each day passed I couldn't help the way I was feeling. I knew I was falling in love with you.'

'Is this right? So soon after what has happened? I don't doubt my feelings for you, it's just the timing that's troubling me.'

Georgia raises her shoulders so that her posture is erect and sets down her wine glass. 'It's not wrong and we shouldn't chastise ourselves.'

She looks at him with purposefulness and asks a question that is laced with intent. 'Shall we go to my room?'

The joy of anticipation courses through him, like a rapid river. It is an unexpected invitation but one that excites him with the possibilities he has only ever dreamed of in the intimacy of his thoughts. He is astonished at how bold they are becoming. They can never return to the people they were, it is different now. They have entered a new universe, one whose doors are unlocked.

He reaches over the table and takes her hand, feeling its warmth, and in doing so, he is consumed by a profound need that aches inside him. She raises his hand and bending her head, ever so lightly her mouth opens and she presses her lips to his skin. In that moment he thinks it the most erotic image he can imagine.

Georgia is lying in bed and studies Adam as he pulls his t-shirt over his head. He notices she is awake and looking at him. He asks if she wants to go for breakfast or he could phone room service if she likes.

She lies with her hands behind her head, her left breast exposed above the sheet; to her vague surprise, she is not embarrassed.

'There's no rush, we don't have to be at the airport until three. Breakfast in bed would be romantic. You choose.'

He sits beside her and lifts the phone on the bedside table.

'Room service… oh good morning, I wondered if it was possible to order two Eggs Benedict and fresh orange to drink… Yes, perfect, thank you.' He replaces the phone and looks at her. 'You are so beautiful.' It is something he has wanted to tell her for a long time, but couldn't until now. Her face grows hot. 'No, I'm not.' She bends her face into the pillow; it has grown flush.

'I love you.'

'I know you do. I have done for some time.'

'When did you first know?' he asks intrigued.

She raises her arm and strokes his face. 'At Pandelios' wedding. The way you looked at me was different; there was something in your eyes and in your smile. I saw it all over your face and in your demeanour.'

'It was that obvious?'

'I knew you liked me, put it that way.'

'And what about you?' His voice is quiet. He feels the softness of the bedsheet as he luxuriates in the scent that is unmistakably her, every time she enters a room or is close to him.

She speaks slowly. 'Love is an enigma; it can be fragile and beautiful, it can be tentative or brutal. I have only ever truly loved two people in my life, unconditionally, my mother and Dylan. I know now I never loved Stephen in that way. I believe he loved me in the only way he knew how. What I feel for you is instinctive and overwhelming, it is frightening but infectious, there is a transformation inside me Adam Newman. You make me feel like there is a trapped butterfly in my stomach. I felt that butterfly the day you returned with Dylan when he ran away.'

He bends forward, she opens her mouth, and he kisses her, her breath brushes his lips as they part. 'I can feel the butterfly's wings.'

Chapter 48

I Have Discovered Something Today

1972

Thursday 31ˢᵗ August 1972

Paul has returned from his tour of the States, which then included stop off trips to Munich, Paris and then a further week in London, negotiating a new contract with his London and New York publishers. He is happy with the outcome. He is now selling more books in America than his sales in the U. K. and Europe combined, so he could virtually name his price. I have never seen him so upbeat and positively brimming with confidence in such a long time. He returned two weeks ago and slept for a solid twelve hours. He has been physically exhausted but, at the same time, he is full of purpose. His notebook is full of ideas, scenes and dialogue for his next book which is due to be published next May. So far, it is untitled.

There seems to be a palpable euphoria about him, compounded by his consumption of wine during the day and whisky in the evening. There is a certain time of the evening I retire to bed and leave him to his own devices. I fear it is only a matter of time before his thoughts will be accompanied by a state of melancholy and once again, as they always have done, his demons will return and cloud his mind. Until then, his writing is giving him real pleasure.

My involvement with Gabriella has brought a mixture of intense purpose and remorseful impulses. Let me explain.

I am now working for three enchanting days of the week in Corfu Town. I have a small office above the shop, where I work on the promotion and marketing side of Gabriella's business while she concentrates on the designs and the day to day running of the shop. It fills me with such effervescence it frightens me at times.

I was travelling each day to and fro from the house which, at first, was manageable; however, I soon realised it could not be a permanent occurrence. I've never been a confident driver in the dark, and Gabriella and I often stayed late working on a specific project. The haphazard road home filled me with such a desperate panic that something had to be done.

The solution came when Stelios insisted that I stay at one of his apartments in town on the days I worked. To my surprise, Paul was amenable to this arrangement.

Stelios and I are always cautious and discreet; we go out for dinner on occasions, Gabriella accompanying us before heading off to some bar or night club with friends leaving Stelios and me alone.

In the mornings, I make him breakfast, which we eat in bed and I am always mesmerised by the shafts of sunlight that spear the shutters. Other times, we have coffee on the balcony which faces a quiet and small square that is always deserted at that time of morning. After breakfast, we often make love and his touch and grace enfold me like a shawl. Afterwards, it is a struggle to get washed and dressed and resume our normal lives, until we met again for lunch or dinner.

We talk continually; Stelios is always interested in my life before I met him; Edinburgh, my job, my business. He is fascinated and listens with intent but, at the same time, he seems duly perturbed if I mentioned Paul and he never asks about him. That troubles me; he is blanking Paul from his mind and the association is always with us, lurking in the background. I feel the weight of guilt and I assume Stelios does too, but we have stepped over the threshold, two willing adults. I often wonder what is going to become of us. But mostly, I feel humble with gratitude for this pleasant existence, this new life has given me. I know I am being outrageously unfair to Paul, who seems indifferent. I suspect he knows, but is content to allow me my indulgences as I allow his.

I have discovered something today that will change the course of my life. It was one of those dramatic moments that live with you forever. I had suspected it but I needed confirmation and there it was, facing me, I am pregnant.

Chapter 49

Learning to be Humble

Georgia walks as fast as she can, breaking into a small run, as she hurries down the lane. She is not aware of the beach being busy that day; a coach full of tourists has arrived, descending on the village and its trinket shops, eating lunch at Pandelios' and now most of them are populating the beach and swimming in the small, tranquil bay.

Georgia's mind is preoccupied with thoughts of her mother and the revelations of the diary that have been kept from her all of her life.

It pains her to think of Paul, her father, did he know the truth? There is only one person alive who can answer that question.

Georgia glares around the square. She knocks into the shoulder of a young woman, taking a photograph of an older woman and man, who pose awkwardly and stiff, the woman is smiling the man is not.

Georgia makes her apology without stopping, determined to carry on. She turns left into a small warren of lanes, and runs. Her face is flushed; she stumbles, avoiding a skinny black cat that has jumped into her path from a step. Georgia's heart is pounding; she can feel rivulets of sweat run down her spine.

Suddenly, she is standing before the door of a modest two-storey house. It has been years since she has been here. She raises her hand to knock and realises she is terribly afraid. For a brief second, she considers turning around and walking back towards the square, but something in her demands she knocks on the door.

'Kalispera Georgia.'

'I need to speak with you, Theresa.'

'I know, I've been dreading this day ever since you found your mother's diary. Please come in.'

Georgia looks around the kitchen. It is smaller than she remembers, but then again she was all but a child when she used to visit Theresa to play with her two children, Elpida and Aris. Theresa has poured two glasses of lemonade but they remain untouched. Georgia looks at her. Theresa's hair is long, thick and wavy; she has a touch of red lipstick and eyeliner. She looks extraordinary for her age, Georgia thinks.

'Why?' Georgia asks.

Theresa reaches over and takes Georgia's hand.

'Oh, Georgia. She wanted to tell you, ever since you were old enough to understand, but somehow life seemed to always get in the way.'

'I don't understand.'

'The last time we spoke.' Theresa hesitates. 'It was just a few weeks before she died. It haunted her for years. She agonised over it but, in the end, she felt content within herself. She came to realise that telling you the truth would be the same as betraying the memory of Paul, your father.'

'But that's the point, he was not my father.'

Georgia was only four years old when Paul committed suicide with an overdose of pills and a bottle of vodka at a book fair in London. It was his third attempt by then; he had refused all medical intervention for his alcoholism and depression. It was 1976. Emily did not return to Corfu until six years later. During that period she rented out the house as a holiday home, Theresa continued to clean and supervise its upkeep.

Posthumously, Paul's books sold well. The steady income from their royalties and the house allowed Emily the privilege of bringing up Georgia secure and comfortable.

Gradually, Emily returned to Corfu and the house, spending the school holidays there, summer, Easter and Christmas and it was the first time Georgia could remember the house feeling cold and Emily bought portable heaters to heat the rooms. Georgia grew to know the house as her second home and it became a treasure trove of fond and happy memories.

'Emily didn't want to cause you any pain. The thought of hurting you with such a revelation would have been something she would never have come to terms with. The last time she tried to tell you about your real father was on the day you told her you were pregnant with Dylan. How could she rip that joy from you? By then, she knew she was dying and the truth would die with her.'

Georgia's eyes are wide, her hands tremble. She struggles with conflicting emotions that surge within her. As a daughter, she can only think of this man, who is her father, but as a mother herself, a part of her is also sympathetic towards her mother's plight.

'Georgia, what would it have achieved?' Theresa squeezes Georgia's hand. 'Another father you didn't know, a stranger to you? Emily wanted to spare you that torment.'

'Did Dad know?'

Theresa sighs. 'He did. You need to understand Georgia. By then, that part of their married life was non-existent, and it had stopped long before Emily became pregnant. They loved each other in their own ways, but as a marriage, it was over by then.'

'And he accepted it, Mum being pregnant?'

'It was hard for him at first but, yes he did, and in his mind, you were his daughter. He loved you as if you were his own flesh and blood.'

'Even when he knew who the father was? Did Mum stop seeing Stelios? Did Stelios have any contact with me as a baby?'

Theresa looks at her as if she has just seen a ghost. 'You don't know?'

'Know what?'

'What else was in the diary?'

'Nothing. It stopped there, although mum must have written more as the last pages were missing. It looked like they were removed.'

'Oh my child, Stelios was killed in a car accident the very day your mother found out she was pregnant.'

Georgia bends her head and begins to sob; sharp tears behind her eyes. Theresa kneels and embraces her and Georgia buries her face into Theresa's hair.

'Oh Theresa, that's awful, so unfair. My God, how did she cope?' She says in a small humble voice.

'She was a remarkable woman Georgia. How can we even contemplate what she must have gone through? That's why you shouldn't judge her, you were not there... I was.'

'Why did she keep the diary at the house? Why didn't she destroy it? She must have known it would be found.'

'Those were her memories. I suppose it kept Stelios alive. As time passed, she felt that was where the diary belonged, in Corfu, not in Edinburgh. She knew it was a risk.'

'Maybe she wanted me to find it... Oh, I don't know.'

Georgia sighs and wipes the tears from her cheeks.

'It has come as a shock; you need time Georgia to accept what you have learnt.'

Georgia looks at Theresa, her green eyes wide and filled with tears.

'Emily made a brave decision. She knew Paul would know the baby was not his, yet she told him she was pregnant. An abortion was out of the question. She was willing to lose everything she had, everything she loved, the life she knew, for her unborn child, for you Georgia. She was prepared to face the consequences, however terrible they were, and she did, with grace.'

'What happened when Stelios died, how did she cope?'

'It was terrible. She hadn't told Paul by then; she had only just found out she was pregnant. Paul had just returned from America, obviously, he had no idea what was going on or what had caused this immense grief in Georgia. The funeral was a big affair; he was an important man in Corfu. Of course, Emily could not go. How could she? She didn't know his family, they didn't know her and certainly, no one knew of their affair. It was devastating. I stayed with her that day and did my best to console her.'

Georgia tries to imagine how her mother must have felt, but she can't contemplate the enormity of her grief and loss.

'So you see Georgia, Emily lost the man she really loved, but she was also prepared to lose Paul. You were all that mattered to her.'

Georgia is seeing a different Emily, one who projected unconditional love in the face of adversity. She now thought of her with admiration.

'This is all too much Theresa. I didn't really know her.'

'Of course, you did. This is the woman who brought you up on her own with love and security; you are who you are today because of that. I see a lot of your mother in you, Georgia.'

Georgia smiles. 'She knew me better than I sometimes know myself.' She pauses for a moment. 'I had two fathers, and I didn't even know them. I've very few memories of dad, but I remember sitting on his lap as he wrote on his typewriter. He got me to type my name. He showed me where the letters were, I could have only been three years old. Other than that, there is nothing, apart from photographs at Christmas, my birthday and some taken at the house. In my mind, I can't remember what he looked like. I only know because of the photographs.'

Theresa brushes Georgia's hair with her hand; she rises stiffly and sits back on her chair.

'Apart from Mum you were my family,' Georgia says. 'I loved coming to Corfu and playing every day with Elpida and Aris, collecting cockroaches and insects. They all ended up in the same jar, we even tried to catch lizards but they were always too quick for us. Remember the sleepovers at the house, one night would become two and then before we'd know it, a week had passed? Mum loved having them over.' She smiles at the thought.

'It's good to see you smile. Elpida often speaks about that time when she is home.'

'She lives in America now?' Georgia asks.

'Yes, Boston, she loves it. She's married now, she met Bill at work, and he's a doctor as well. They visit when they can. I've told them that when they have children, they will have to visit more often and I want my grandchildren to speak Greek as well as English of course.' Theresa laughs. She takes a sip of lemonade and sets it down, thinking. 'Our happiness doesn't depend on the things that have happened to us Georgia, but on the way we view those things, your mother knew that. Knowing what you do now, please don't judge her badly.'

Georgia rubs her eyes. 'I don't, in fact, I feel humbled.'
And then she remembers. 'Mum took photographs of
Stelios; she mentioned it in the diary.'

'I've never seen them.'

'I wonder if she kept them. I didn't see photographs in
the trunk. I'd like to have a reminder of him, something
tangible. In the diary, mum described what he looked like,
and his nature comes over in her writing, but it's not the
same as having something physical. There's one more
thing.'

'What's that?'

'Stelios had a daughter. Theresa, I have a sister.'

Chapter 50

The Need to Feel Connected

At the first glimmerings of dawn, Adam wakes. Recently, sleep has not come easy and when it has, it has been a troublesome affair. In the kitchen, he makes himself a coffee and drinks it on the terrace, watching the pearlescent light of the morning arch over the sky. For some reason, one that is not entirely clear to him, he remembers a holiday in Menorca, his wife, still sleeping in their apartment, Adam on the balcony, watching the sunrise, when from the apartment next door, a small man appeared, receding hair and overweight. During the succeeding conversation, Adam discovered he was of Ecuadorian nationality, his wife, Finnish, and they lived in France, had two children, three grandchildren, all born in France; they spoke French as their first language. He was a microbiologist and spoke Spanish, French and, as it transpired, very good English. It occurs to Adam, all these years later, he never found out his name.

Adam leaves the house and walks towards the small dirt track that Elena often uses with her goats. He moves through the lemon grove, past the vegetable patch, that is now rich in carrots, aubergine, cucumber, sage and oregano bushes. It has become his custom to inspect the fence he built, and he smiles with a deep satisfaction as it remains sturdy and robust. Approaching the dirt track, he jogs up a small incline. The track is shaded by pine trees. However; the sun's light has penetrated the canopy of branches and is already warming the air. Adam looks skywards and his heart quickens with pleasure at the inexhaustible blue.

He notices the clearing where Dylan goes and thinks of the boy hugging his tree. Adam has known Dylan has spent more time here. Adam knows why; the last few weeks have been trying for them all, especially Dylan. Georgia has been cautious with the truth, only telling Dylan what he needs to know, without revealing the detail.

'Is my dad a bad man?'

Adam is startled; he hasn't noticed Dylan standing in the small clearing.

'Ah, Dylan… he has done things most people wouldn't do.' Adam pauses and says reflecting, 'If he had the choice, I'm sure he'd want to be here with you.'

'Is he going to jail?'

'Yes, I'm afraid so.'

'A Scottish jail?'

'No, it will be in Greece. Most probably Athens.'

'I'm not going to see him for a long time, am I?'

'You could visit him sometimes. He would like that.'

'Mum is sad. I know because she cried. Sometimes, when people cry, it means they are sad, other times, it can mean they are happy. For someone like me, that's confusing. But I know mum is sad because she told me.'

'How are you, Dylan? How do you feel inside?' Adam points to Dylan's heart.

'I haven't cried, so I don't know if I'm sad. I think I am. It's easier just to say I'm sad. Words make it easier I suppose, it's more relatable, it's a common language, whereas, it's hard to describe how I'm feeling. If you're sad, you're just sad.'

'I'm going for a walk, do you want to come?'

'I'd rather hug the tree.'

Adam smiles to himself. 'After you've done that, you can walk with me.'

'Ok.'

Adam watches Dylan, and he is amazed how the boy physically relaxes. It looks like it is the most natural thing in the world to wrap your arms around a tree.

When he is done, Dylan asks, 'Where are we going?'

'I don't know. We'll just walk and see where it takes us.'

'How long will it take?'

'Thirty minutes.'

Dylan looks at his watch. 'So that will be eight thirty-two exactly.'

'Eight thirty-two exactly it is then. I'll text your mum, just so she doesn't worry.'

Sometimes the trees thin and the sky comes into view as they meander along the dirt track. The air is heavy with the scent of flowers and wild herbs and, with each step, they crunch pine needles underfoot. They come across an old house; the exterior is in such a bad state of repair that Adam is not sure if anyone would live there. Several small wooden shutters, the colour of red wine, hang loosely from their hinges against a wall, peeling with blue and mustard paint, at intervals; thin branches creep along the cracked exterior. Dylan is fascinated by the walls. 'It looks like a map; the blue is like the sea and the yellow colour could be land.' Dylan smiles to himself.

'Do you like living in Corfu?' Adam asks as they walk further.

'Yes.'

'What do you like about it?'

'Mm, I don't know.' He thinks and then says. 'I like the house, and swimming pool, and going to the beach. As long as I can listen to Mozart I'm fine, although it can get too hot at times, but that's ok, it's better than rain and snow. It doesn't rain much in the summer, but you know that you've been here a long time now, so I like it. I don't like puddles and, in Edinburgh, it rained a lot and when I went out, I walked around a lot of puddles. I can't walk through them, not big ones. I don't like the way they reflect the sky, buildings and people. I'm ok with the pool and the sea, though, they're really big compared to puddles.'

Adam is surprised that Dylan has expanded his answer.

'This is my first time in Corfu.' Adam says, with a curious intention. There is a silence, a long pause, one in which Adam expects, an answer. Dylan has to acknowledge an interest in finding out more information. Social chit chat is difficult for Dylan, but sometimes he will reciprocate and maintain a conversation out with his interest in Mozart. This is not one of those. Today Dylan just wants to talk, not with Adam, but at him.

'Things happen for a reason not by chance. It wasn't by chance that Mozart was a composer of exceptional expressive talent, his music creates a dialogue that is nonverbal. Some people think the universe was created by chance, the right set of galactic conditions, just at that precise time. How can something as big and as mysterious as the universe not have a reason to exist? That's not logical.

'I was born with autism, but if you meet one person with autism, it doesn't mean that the next one you meet will be the same as that other person, we're all different. I'm not like those boys and girls at the social skills group I went to, just like they are not like me, but that's a good thing and I believe there is a reason for that. It's like when Mum sent me to that school if I hadn't gone to that school Mum wouldn't have thought it was a good idea to come to Corfu and you wouldn't have gone for the interview to teach me, but because all of those things happened, when the bad things happened to mum you were there to take care of her, so you see, everything happens for a reason.'

Adam smiles. 'That's quite a compelling argument Dylan.'

'Yes, it is.'

'If you could think differently. If someone said I've got the cure for autism, would you want it?' Adam is curious.

'Why would I want to cure me? The way I think, the way I speak is normal to me. I don't know what your normal is, but I'm happy with my normal.' Dylan thinks for a moment.

'There is one thing I'd like to be better at.'

'What would that be?'

'I'd like to have friends. I'd like to know how to make friends. Friends are people who care about you, for who you are. I don't know how that feels. I can feel sad about that. Mum and dad are the only people who care about me.'

'Are you happy, Dylan?'

'I am only truly happy when I listen to Mozart or hug my tree.'

They return to the house and Dylan looks at his watch. 'It is nearly eight thirty-two.' He pauses. 'There on time and now it's time for breakfast.' He runs up the steps just as Georgia steps onto the terrace carrying a tray.'

'Oh, careful Dylan, stop running. Your breakfast nearly ended up on the floor.'

Dylan finds this funny and laughs. 'We saw a wall that looked like a map.' And with this, he runs into the house.

'That's nice. Wash your hands now,' Georgia says after him.

She places the tray on the table and distributes plates of toast, cheese, and poached eggs.

'Could you get the coffee and juice, Adam, it's all made up in the kitchen?'

'Sure, I'll be two ticks.'

When Adam returns, he asks Georgia if she wants a coffee or a soft drink. He pours the orange into a glass and hands it to her.

'Freshly picked from the orchard?' Adam asks. 'You wouldn't get orange this fresh for breakfast in Edinburgh.'

'No, that's true,' Georgia says dolefully.

'Is everything ok?'

She sits back in her chair. 'I'm not sure I want to return to another bleak winter in Edinburgh. I love it here; it's my home as much as Edinburgh is. Look around you Adam, why would I want to leave? I can wake up each morning to the sight of tree-covered hills, the beautiful sea that's only a minute away. I have friends here that I have known all my life, they are my family when I'm here and then there is this house, it is my home. I can feel my mother in every room, not like a ghost, or anything like that. What I mean is, every inch of this house holds a memory of her, it was a place she loved, it was precious to her and I didn't realise the real reason until a few days ago.'

'What do you mean?'

'You know I'm reading Mum's diary. Well, everything has changed. I haven't quite come to terms with it myself. Back in the early '70s, Mum had an affair with a businessman. His name was Stelios… she got pregnant by him, it was an accident. Anyway, I was that baby and Stelios was my father… my real father, but he died in a car accident before knowing that Mum was pregnant. I've spoken with Theresa; she's the only person I could talk to about it.

'Theresa told me Stelios was buried in the village he grew up in... it was our village. When my dad, Paul died, it took mum six years to return to the house. When she did, she visited Stelios' grave almost daily, making sure that there were always fresh flowers on his gravestone. Theresa said it took her that long to return, it was too painful for her, too raw, even after all those years. She wanted to tell me, Theresa was insistent about that, but she thought it died with her. I suppose if you think about something long enough, eventually you start to believe it's the right thing to do, and I believe she thought that.

'Stelios had a daughter, she is four years older than me. Mum knew about her. Her name is Pavlina, I don't know if mum ever met her.'

'So what are you going to do?'

'I can't let it go,' she says, quietly. 'I need to feel connected to her in some way and, whether that's possible or not, I won't know until I find her.' There is a decisiveness about her.

'And how are you going to do that? Do you have any information about her?'

She smiles wanly. 'It'll be difficult I know, but the last few pages in mum's diary were torn out. By whom? Probably Mum, but why, I don't know. I'm hoping if I find them they'll lead me to Pavlina. Mum took photographs of Stelios. They might be in the house, somewhere, possibly the attic.'

Adam takes a mouthful of toast, it crunches in his mouth.

'Life is never dull at the villa Katrina.'

'There's one thing I have to do.'

'What?'

'Find my father's grave.'

Chapter 51

Missing Photographs

'Here we are,' Nikolaos says as he places a large book, that looks like a ledger, on the table. On the cover is inscribed, 'Deaths, births and marriages.'

'I've already found the page,' he says, opening the heavy book where a bookmarker with the portrait of the Virgin Mary identifies the page.

With a finger, he traces the names until he comes to the one they are interested in.

'Here we are; Stelios Karagounis, born 1942, died at 3 p.m. on Tuesday the 1st September 1972, aged thirty years old. Death occurred in Paleokastritsa; the cause of death, road traffic accident; residence- Corfu Town; occupation- businessman; religion- Greek Orthodox; citizenship- Greek; father's name- Eleftherios Karagounis and mother's name- Ekaterini Karagounis.'

There is a sharp take of breath and then a moan; she is not prepared for this reaction. Tears sting her eyes, she grabs hold of Adam's arm to steady herself.

'Are you ok?' Adam calls, startled.

'I feel faint.' Her face has gone white.

'Here, sit down.' Nikolaos guides her to a chair. 'Do you want some water?'

'I'll be fine in a minute.'

She looks at Adam and tries to smile encouragingly. 'It was the shock I think, hearing their names, the details. Suddenly it was real, and they were real, the family I never knew I had.'

'Are you sure you want to see the grave?' Adam asks.

She nods. 'Yes, I'll be fine now.'

Behind the church, they find the small graveyard; a mass of white crosses and headstones littering the ground.

Nikolaos walks in front. 'It's just over here.'

They walk a few yards. 'Here we are. I'll be in the church if you need me,' Nikolaos says.

They stand for a moment and take in the cross that stands on a rectangular marble block. A cracked ceramic vase holds flowers that have withered and decayed.

'Someone has been here,' Georgia says in disbelief. She reaches out and takes the dried flowers out of the vase, replacing them with the roses she has brought from her garden.

They stand in silence. After a while Georgia says, 'I feel a comfort of some sort.' But there is a note of sadness to her voice. 'What might have been if he hadn't died? How different would my life have been?' Georgia finds the thought painful; she is discovering she is not as strong as she thinks. She feels a trembling begin, a sudden ache. Her resolve begins to waver. Georgia inhales the air. Adam tries to reassure her, telling her there is no point in thinking like that. She tries to compose herself and agrees with him; she tells herself he is right. Georgia wipes the tears from her eyes. She finds it incomprehensible that, for the most part of her life, when she stayed at the house she was less than a mile from this place. The world is shimmering in the sun, and nothing has changed.

From the kitchen, the French doors are open to the garden where the air is hot and still. A motionless cat is sprawled out on the terrace, sleeping in the shade. Adam can see the green roll of the hills. They are more vivid in this light, he thinks.

He scans Georgia's face. He anticipates a sign, an indication of how she feels, but it is unreadable. He does not know what to say, he senses her agitation. She is holding the diary. It has changed everything, unlocked a secret, questioned the familiar and left a wide hollow space inside her.

Again he examines her face where a quick flash of disappointment is visible. Outside in the garden, he can hear the call of a bird.

She takes a sip of water and sighs. 'I can't find them; I've looked everywhere, they're not here.'

'They could have been at your mum's house in Edinburgh.'

'No, I'm sure they weren't. When mum died, it took a week to empty the house. I found boxes full of photographs, all in chronological order; she was like that, I'm sure she had OCD. I spent an entire night looking at them, so I know they weren't there. They must be here in this house, somewhere, she would have kept them, I'm sure of it.'

'When was the last time she stayed here?'

Georgia sits thinking. 'She was here the year she died. In fact, I remember now, I was pregnant with Dylan; we came out to stay with her for a week. We knew about the cancer then, it was during Easter, I remember the celebrations. I thought she was saying her last goodbyes to the house, the village and her friends, which she was, but now I think she felt she needed to be here, to be near him, in a spiritual way. Does that make sense?'

'Absolutely.' Adam looks genuinely relieved. 'I think you're right Georgia, she was saying her goodbyes and, if that is so, wouldn't she bring the photographs and the diary to the place where it started. This is where they belong. They have got to be in this house.'

'I've been wondering who put the flowers on the grave; it was quite recent. They were only a few weeks old.'

'Does Stelios' family still live in Corfu?'

'I don't know. I'm sure Theresa would have mentioned it.' It seems inconceivable to think Theresa would not have brought it to Georgia's attention.

Georgia looks down at her lap where the diary rests. Adam can see her desperation.

'Why are pages missing? What was mum trying to hide? I'm not sure of anything anymore. I can't go on like this.'

'We'll find the photographs and then, when you're ready, we'll look for your sister.'

She raises her eyes to his. He kisses her but it is more than a kiss, it is a pouring of himself into her.

Later that day, Adam finds Nikolaos alone at the Kafenion,

'Adam, how is Georgia? She seemed quite upset.'

'She's better thanks; it's a lot to take in but she's a resilient woman.'

Nikolaos raises his hand. 'Rina, another metriou, for Adam.' He turns to Adam. 'Or would you like something stronger?'

'No, a coffee is fine. I need to ask you something. Before Georgia was born, Stelios had another daughter, and I wondered if the birth is registered in the church records.'

'If the mother and father lived here then, it should be. We can find out if you want?'

Adam nods his head. 'Good, have you got time?'

'Always for a friend.'

Rena puts a cup on the table. 'Careful, it is hot.'

'Thank you.' Adam sips it cautiously.

'And how are you?'

'Oh, I'm fine; it's Georgia I'm worried about.'

'And you and Georgia? The last time we spoke, things were, shall I say, developing. I heard about her husband, the poor woman, she's had a lot to contend with.'

'It's brought us closer.'

'Ah, I see.'

'We feel the same about each other. She loves me.'

Nikolaos smiles. 'Good, you both deserve some happiness. I couldn't help notice, when you're together, there's a certain connection, it's quite evident.' Nikolaos rests his hand on Adam's shoulder. 'And endearing, I might add.'

'I can't imagine how she feels right now.'

Nikolaos squeezes his arm. 'Come on, drink up, let's see if we can find this name in the register and put a smile on her face.'

Chapter 52

Truth

He studies her hand on the pillow, her fingers are long and elegant, her nails neatly manicured, painted red. He considers the slight wrinkle of the skin at the knuckles and the raised veins; he can see the bone flex as a finger jerks slightly, like an involuntary pulse and he wonders if she is conscious of the slight movement.

The room is bathed in a subtle light; the shutters sedating the sun's reach. Georgia is on her side, facing him, her ruffled hair covering a closed eye. Her lips are cherry red and, if he looks closely, he can see small lines that emphasise their fullness. Georgia's breathing is deep and steady, with a faint rising of her shoulder; the skin there is taut, and he can clearly distinguish the shape of her clavicle. Her face has a sedating quality to it, an expression in stark contrast to her despondent disposition of late.

Adam drifts in and out of sleep, and then suddenly, a small jolt of alarm passes through him as he recalls the fruitless search of the church register. Despite his best intention, the news of this forced a look of desperation on Georgia's face that spiked his heart. Every small smile is like a treasure to him and he hopes today's meeting with Theresa will bring them closer to one.

Last night, Theresa seemed flustered on the phone and Georgia had asked if she was feeling unwell, as Theresa apologised excessively, about what, she did not reveal, but it left Georgia sympathising for Theresa's apparent unsettled state of mind. Theresa is determined to see Georgia, and they agreed to meet the following morning.

Georgia is stirring; she stretches her arms and lets out a low muffled sound. Her eyes blink several times before focusing on Adam.

'How long have you been watching me?' She smiles embarrassedly.

'Not long.' He moves the hair from her face. 'You looked so peaceful. I was scared to move in case I woke you. Now you're awake, what would you like for breakfast?'

Her mouth forms a grin. 'Preferably you, I feel ravenous.'

Emboldened by Georgia's enthusiasm, he leans towards her and trails his finger along the curvature of her breast.

'We need to be careful; Dylan could be up and about.' Georgia says.

They have slept in Adam's room.

She opens her mouth, and he kisses her, he raises an eyebrow. 'You'll just have to be content with breakfast then.'

At the end of the garden, there is a paved patio, where a small stonewall and two olive trees separate the order and neatness of the garden from a precipice of wild shrubs and bushes that descend towards the sea. From here, the views are uninterrupted and spectacular.

Georgia is sitting on a wicker sofa, looking out towards the sea and she can feel the beginnings of a headache. When she was younger, she suffered from migraines and spent hours in a darkened room, hoping for the pain to recede. She shut her eyes. It's probably just a build-up of stress, she convinces herself. Has she the courage to carry on with this? And what does Theresa want to tell her? Theresa phoned again that morning. She was distraught, Georgia could sense the desperation in her voice, and it has unsettled her.

Georgia takes a deep breath and tries to calm herself as the possibilities push against her.

A diffuse sunlight filters the light so that the sky is emblazoned in a pastel tinge, against a glass aquamarine sea. From where she sits, Georgia can see a slice of the beach that then curves away from her view. A family has set towels and what she thinks looks like a picnic basket upon the sand. Two children are paddling in the shallow water observed by the protective gaze of their mother. Georgia is moved by such instinctive love. She wonders about the generations who have enjoyed this place, this geography. Georgia understands what it is to embrace precious moments. She has played on those sands with her mother and, as a mother herself, with Dylan. She is seized with an ache for the loss of such moments as time moves untouched.

'She is just over there on the patio,' Adam says, directing Theresa.

'Georgia, I need to talk with you.' Theresa hesitates and Georgia understands her reluctance refers to Adam.

'It's ok. Adam will be staying with us.'

Adam pulls out a chair and Theresa sits with a resigned sigh. She seems to sink into the chair as if it is swallowing her.

Her eyes are heavy and shadowed and, uncharacteristically, Theresa has no makeup on and it looks like age has suddenly caught up with her. It is the look of remorse Georgia decides.

Theresa is flustered and apprehensive, but finally, she speaks. 'I've sat here with your mother and on many of those occasions, we spoke of what I am about to tell you. Emily loved this view. She said it was a joy to awake each morning so close to the sea.'

Theresa said she had imagined this day ever since Georgia discovered the diary, and when Georgia came to her yesterday, she had gambled with her silence. She was shaken by their encounter and disturbed by the sudden notion she was hiding something that could be of immense value to Georgia. She has decided to put that right.

Theresa pauses, gathers her thoughts, and continues telling Georgia that Emily was not the only one who loved Stelios. Theresa had known him most of her life. They had grown up in the village, Stelios was eight years older than Theresa was. He would never stay and settle in the village and, when he was twenty, he moved to Corfu Town, and became successful in business, buying and selling property at first, and then his interests branched out, not all of it legal, but that gave him a certain aura. Stories were circulated around the island that increased his reputation and influence; some of them wildly exaggerated and off the mark, but most were true. The night of Theresa's brother's wedding was when it started. She was eighteen, Stelios was twenty-six. The whole village was invited. Stelios had grown up with her brother, and it was important for him to be seen at such local festivities it connected him to his roots and the community he grew up in. As the night progressed, before she knew it, they were dancing together, drinking, and talking. At first, she was infatuated by his reputation, but it became much more and as the drink increased, her initial infatuation gave way to a mutual attraction which culminated in both of them spending the night together.

After that, they met often. Theresa was immensely happy and Stelios told her he was too, but theirs was never a public relationship; it was built on a secrecy that his public persona demanded. Theresa was in love and even if she couldn't express her love publicly, it was a price she was more than willing to take.

Stelios' business interests took him to Athens and he would be absent for days on end, weeks even, but this did not matter to Theresa. When he returned, he showered her with gifts, and having him back was all that mattered.

As the months passed, Theresa began to realise she was never going to have a proper life with him, they never planned for the future, so gradually she constructed a course of action she was certain would force him to marry her. She was young, with no real experience of what lay beyond her village and in her restricted world. If she became pregnant, Stelios would have no choice but to marry her.

Stelios was furious; it wasn't the reaction she was expecting. He did not see her for two days, but then he summoned her to his house in Corfu Town, sending one of his men to escort her in his treasured Mercedes.

He spoke to her, and she listened in shocked disbelief. She would stay at his house in Athens until the baby was born. She would tell her parents she was working for him in a domestic role. Once the baby was born, she would leave and return to Corfu. Stelios would arrange that she would be given a generous amount of money in monthly instalments. Her family would want for nothing. She would travel to

Athens to see the baby on the last weekend of every month. He would arrange and pay for the travel expenses. The child would be raised and schooled in Athens. Beyond that, he was unsure how to proceed; whatever he decided would depend on Theresa's co-operation. Such an arrangement appalled and devastated her. She found it exceedingly difficult, and she was shocked into a mind-numbing paralysis that lasted for weeks whereupon, she contemplated the gravity of her position and reluctantly accepted Stelios' conditions.

As the years progressed, so too did Theresa's life. She married Kyriakos, the baker's son. She was twenty-one but felt she had already encountered a lifetime of tribulations. He was patient, kind and he accepted her for the woman she was and the complications of her past.

'When Emily started to see Stelios, well, it was a nightmare. He knew I was working for her; it put me in an impossible position. I could not tell her the truth; it would have broken her heart. She was so happy, the happiest I had ever seen her. I couldn't do it. Then she told me she was pregnant, it was happening all over again. I couldn't believe it, and then there was the accident and it changed everything, for both of us.

'Months later I told her the truth, it was awful. Life imploded. Once Stelios died, obviously, the money he gave me stopped, Emily left and did not return for years; she rented out the house as a holiday home. I did not hear from her for all those years. And then, one day, she returned, I met her in the village square and she embraced me like a sister. She forgave me and from that day until she died, it never came between us; in fact, it brought us closer. I worked at the house again. By then, I had a family, so I welcomed the extra money, but it was our friendship that was most important to me.' Her voice wavers. 'You have to understand. When I met Stelios it was a different world, those were very different times. I was young, and I was poor, he was powerful and rich, he was interested in me and back then, that made all the difference. I know this is hard for you Georgia.'

Georgia breathes in deeply. 'I'm just trying to absorb what you're saying.' It's an incredible story and one that Georgia has difficulty comprehending. She does not relate to the social intricacies of that time, it is an unknowable thing to her and inconceivable that Theresa would allow someone to dictate such drastic events. A part of her knows that Theresa's choices were limited by the prevailing ignorance of that time.

She catches her breath. She is consumed by questions. *Pavlina, your daughter is my sister. Your children, do they know? Does Pavlina remember Stelios? Does she know about me? About Mum's photographs and the pages missing in the diary?*

Theresa tries her best to answer all of Georgia's questions. Pavlina and Theresa have met regularly over the years. She is the one who placed the flowers at the grave, Pavlina does so each time she visits. Theresa explained everything to both her children, Elpida and Aris, once they were old enough to understand. And, as adults, they have all met. This information causes Georgia to exhale deeply and bite her lip. Theresa knows the pain this truth has caused, and she can see the anguish on Georgia's face.

'Very few people knew who your real father was and, as I explained yesterday, your mother didn't get the chance to tell Stelios she was pregnant.'

'Pavlina doesn't know about me.'

'No, I'm afraid not.'

A bubble of anguish surfaces and breaks her composure; Georgia turns her head and gazes out to sea.

'I have something to show you Georgia. In amongst all of this devastation, it might help to ease your pain.' Theresa takes an envelope from her bag and hands it to Georgia.

'What is this?'

'Open it.'

The first photograph shows Emily reclining on a white leather seat that curves along the angle of a boat. She is wearing a shirt, a man's white shirt, it is baggy on her. It covers her thighs, which are bare, and she has crossed her legs. Her elbows rest on the top edge of the seat; it could almost be described as a sofa. Emily has on a floppy sun hat, and she is looking at the camera in sheer delight.

Georgia is struck by how happy and content her younger mother looks. Georgia arranges the photographs on the table. In another one, Stelios is standing at the wheel of the boat. His posture is erect, his gaze steady as he looks out to sea. He has on the same shirt that is in the first photograph; his cuffs are rolled up along his arms, exposing dark hair and tanned forearms. His shorts are tight-fitting, the fashion of the day, Georgia thinks to herself. She looks at his face and feels a slight anguish at first. His hair is swept back from his face, revealing a forehead with several prominent lines. She can see his eyes are dark and piercing, with shallow wrinkles at the edge. His chin is angled and strong and there is a masculine attractiveness that obviously drew her mother to him. He is smiling broadly.

A torrent of emotions burst to the surface. Her hands shake, she can feel tears hover on her eyelids and then tickle her cheek as the image of her father blurs. She wipes her eyes and focuses on the image once more. Theresa muffles a sob with her hand.

There are other photographs: evidence of another life - a picnic on a beach, Emily reclining on a towel, Stelios diving into the sea from an outcrop of rocks, and one of them together in Corfu Town. He has his arm around her waist, Emily's head rests on his shoulder and they look like any normal couple, as they smile into the camera. Georgia can tell they are in love.

Georgia's voice wavers. 'How long have you had the photographs?'

Theresa looks away towards the sea and then back again where she gazes upon Georgia. 'Emily gave them to me, well, to be truthful, she threw them at me. When I told her about my past with Stelios she flew into a rage; she screamed at me, we were right here, on this spot. Emily ran into the house and I was so distraught, I went home. The next day I came back, I wanted to put things right. I didn't know if Emily was in the house, but she didn't answer and the house was locked. I went to the patio, and the photographs were still scattered on the ground. I took them, I had nothing of him. I thought it would ease the pain I had carried within me for all of those years.

'Years later, when Emily returned and we made our peace, she told me to keep the photographs if I wanted; she still had the negatives. I don't know if she ever developed them, she never spoke of it. But what I know is this, they belong here with you.'

Georgia moves her eyes from the photographs and looks at Theresa. She breathes in and lets it out slowly. She extends her hands across the table and cradles Theresa's hands.

'The missing pages are still a puzzle. I may never know what they contained.'

'I'm sorry, I can't help you Georgia, I wish I could.'

Georgia thinks about what she now knows about the past, events that profoundly resonate in the present.

'It's harder for me; I know about Pavlina but she doesn't know about me.'

Chapter 53

Her Need to Search and Find

'Why do fish smell so bad when they spend all their time in water?' Dylan asks as he walks passed a stall selling a variety of fish, octopus, and crab at the village market.

Adam smiles. 'I don't know, I've never really thought about it.'

'I think about things like that all the time. I can't help it, it's the way my brain works. It's worse at nighttime; I can't stop thinking about things. Anything really that happened during the day, usually, things that didn't make sense to me, I repeat it in my mind, over and over. I watched that film, "Groundhog Day," and it was like that, the same thoughts over and over. I can lie awake for hours. It's the same when I have to learn something that is new; it takes me a long time to understand what I need to do. It doesn't always make sense to me. I spend a lot of my time being confused, trying to work out what people mean because most of the time they don't really say what they mean.'

They approached a stall selling cheese. 'Oh, that stinks, it smells like dirty socks.'

'It tastes better than it smells. Do you like cheese?'

'I'm not a lover of cheese but brie is the chocolate of all cheese. It's excellent when melted on beans and toast.'

'I've never tried that. Let's see if there's some here.'

Adam scans the display and soon finds a slab. A cheerful woman wraps the cheese in cellophane and then cuts a small portion and offers it to Dylan. He hesitates before accepting it. The woman gestures for Dylan to eat, 'It nice, you like.'

Dylan looks at the cheese as if he has just picked it off the ground and then turns towards the woman. 'You didn't wash your hands. That's unhygienic. '

Adam smiles politely and pays her. She looks at Dylan with a puzzled frown as he walks off, turning the cheese in his hand and examining it. 'A fly could have landed on it.' Dylan says, with a tone of disgust in his voice.

'Give it to the cats, they won't mind.'

'You'll have to wash the cheese when we get home.'

'I will don't worry.'

The market is busy, it is almost lunchtime, and several tourist coaches have stopped, deploying an army of holidaying bargain hunters, who throng the stalls and narrow walkways. Adam can sense Dylan's anxiety and decides it's time to leave.

'You know that if you want, you can speak to me anytime about things that you might be struggling to understand.'

'I understand most things.'

'What I mean is, if you want to speak about your dad then that's alright.'

Dylan shrugs. 'Mum said that Dad made many wrong decisions and, because of that, he ended up in a lot of trouble.'

'He did, but I'm sure he regrets that now. What you need to remember is your dad still loves you and, if he could turn the clock back, what I mean by that is, if he could do things differently, he wouldn't have got involved with those bad men. You do understand that Dylan?'

'I balance my decision making with logic, I find that's the best way, I usually argue about lots of things because I normally think I'm right. Other people don't always think so, but you can't argue with logic. What Dad did was wrong, that's what mum said. Because of Dad and his friends, a lot of people's lives were ruined. He did bad things to people, and that's not a good way to live your life. So when I think about that, the logical part of my brain tells me he should go to jail… Now that the summer is nearly over, you will be going home soon.'

Adam smiles fondly at Dylan. 'I'm not sure what I'm going to do.'

They are now walking along the lane that leads to the house. Dylan has picked up a fallen branch and is waving it above his head.

'Whoosh, whoosh,' he says, enjoying the sound. He stops walking and looks at the ground. 'I've never told anyone this. At night, sometimes, I could hear mum and dad arguing; I use to hide my head under the pillow or put my earphones on and listen to Mozart.'

'I think things will be a lot better now.'

'If you married mum, you would be my dad.'

'That's not going to happen. What made you think that?'

'I saw you kissing her.'

'Oh, I see.'

'That's alright. That's what adults do when they like each other.' He says without hesitation.

'Yes, they do and I like your mum, she's special to me.'

'That's ok; If you like mum and she likes you, it makes sense for you to stay here instead of going back to your old job,' Dylan says, seriously.

It sounds so simple, Adam thinks. He ponders it for a second, and why shouldn't it be?

The lane gently curves; they are above the sea now and the trees on each side become thicker. Adam can see a yacht; from the distance between them, it looks stationary, but he knows it is not, for as the minute's pass, he can see its progress. He thinks it a pertinent analogy for his life; his feelings for Georgia are no longer obscured by the uncertainty of whether they would ever be reciprocated by Georgia, they have moved on, and he is calm, for he has examined his conscience, and they have done nothing he is ashamed of. He will follow his intuition.

They wander back to the house, both of them content; Adam smiling broadly, Dylan enthralled in his studious examination of the curves and angles of his branch.

Georgia is sitting on the wicker sofa on the patio, gazing out over the expanse of sea and sky. The morning air is soft and still. A small bird lands on the wall and is unperturbed by Georgia's presence.

'Here you are. I wondered where you'd got to.'

She turns and attempts a smile as Adam sits next to her. She pulls her shoulders straight and composes herself. He

can see she has been crying. Her eyes are vivid with tears
and her mouth trembles. In the last few days since the
diary's revelations, Georgia has been dismayed. She has
wondered over and over why her mother never told her
about her real father and her sister. Years lost, possibilities
abandoned. The truth of the matter is Georgia now feels
relief and regret; relief that she now knows, and regret for
what could have been.

Was her mother's reluctance born out of a fear that, if the
truth were told, it may have undermined their past, their
connection, and trust?

Georgia can now see the impossibility of it all. She must
have felt trapped. Georgia understands her mother's
reluctance, and she feels a growing sense of shame at how
she has judged her. Georgia's guilt is intense but equally,
her regret hurts.

'Did Dylan enjoy the market?' She meets his gaze
levelly.

'Yes, I think he did. We bought some cheese, but it
started to get busy. A few buses arrived. The village must
be getting popular, it's definitely part of the tourist trail
now.'

'That's good; the locals need all the money they can get.
It can be quite quiet in the winter.'

'What have you been up to?'

'Oh, I've just been thinking about things, a lot of things.'

'Like what?' He angles his head and looks at her closely.

'I've been trying to make sense of the past.' She rests her
hands in her lap. 'I remember when this wall was built.
Have you ever wondered why they built it like that,
stopping at one side of the tree trunk and starting again at
the other side so that the two olive trees have become part
of the structure of the wall? I remember Mum was adamant
the trees had to stay. She said they'd been there for
hundreds of years, standing on the edge of the precipice
through rain and storm, summer and winter, protecting us
from the drop into the sea and they would continue to do so.
I've just remembered, when I was a young girl I gave them
names.'

'What did you call them?' Adam asks, amused.

'The one on the left is Rita and the other one Kathryn.'

'Females.'

'Yes. Do you like their names?'

'I'm not too keen on Rita, but Kathryn makes up for it.'

'I always thought they were like a frame, it looks like a picture in between; see how their branches touch at the top.'

'And what a picture.'

'This is one of my favourite parts of the garden.' She touches the bracelet on her arm. 'Mum gave me this as a birthday present; we were sitting here actually. I had no idea she loved this spot until Theresa said yesterday. When I need to think and untangle my thoughts I come here, I've done that for years. At home in Edinburgh, I often walk along the Waters of Leith, but that doesn't compare to this, does it?'

'No, not exactly. It's certainly special.' Adam looks at the Ionian as it shimmers with a nacreous sheen.

'I feel like I've just stepped off a roller coaster, it's still hard to take it all in. So much has happened in such a short space of time, so much has changed. I've changed. I have a sister who doesn't know I exist; do you think she'd want to meet me?'

'After the last few days, anything is possible.'

'I was walking in the garden earlier and, by chance, I came across a spider making a web from one flower to another. I thought, what is the chance of that? Of all the flowers in this garden, I happened to come across this little spider. I watch it for some time; it worked continuously, never stopping. It's a wonder of nature how they can produce such intricate structures, they're really works of art. Do you know what popped into my head?'

'No. But you're going to tell me.'

'The story of Robert the Bruce or was it William Wallace? Whoever it was, it's not important, let's say it was William Wallace,'

Adam smiles. 'It was Robert the Bruce.'

'You know the story?'

'Yes, the spider in the cave.'

'That's right. He'd lost a battle with the English and was hiding in a cave when he saw a spider trying to climb the wall of the cave or something like that, but my point is, this spider kept falling to the ground but that didn't deter it, it kept on trying, again and again until it succeeded.'

'And what has Robert the Bruce's spider got to do with you?'

'I want to meet Pavlina. I'm not going to give up until I've done all I can to bring us together. I want to meet her Adam.'

Adam seems to hesitate for a moment. He lifts his hand and touches her face, and then he says seriously. 'Theresa needs to speak with Pavlina. Theresa has kept the truth from her; you have that in common at least.'

'We do. We have that connection.'

'Theresa did what she thought was best for her family. If she tells Pavlina the truth, there's no guarantee Pavlina will want to meet you. '

Georgia's mind wavers. There is a silence between them.

'I know, I know, but, she's my sister, and she has a right to know. I have to see things for what they are today as well as how they were in the past. '

There is a little silence. She studies the sea for a moment and gives Adam an affectionate squeeze.

'Look at the sea and sky,' Georgia says, brightly. She points between the two ancient olive trees.

'Where else have you seen nature look so striking? It amazes me each day; I'll never get tired of looking at it. We virtually have our own beach as well.' Georgia shakes her head. 'Why would I ever want to leave this place, it's part of who I am. Does that make sense? It does to me. I'm connected to this house, this island, I always have been. Even as a child, this was my special place; it always has been I think. I belong here.' She makes a sweeping gesture with her hand. 'I've just found out I'm actually half-Greek.' She smiles at the thought and takes Adam's hand. Georgia is filled with a sense of excitement and expectation. 'My whole life has been leading me to this point, this very place, this time. I can't go back and be the person I was; not now, not ever, not after all that has happened. I don't want to go back to my old life I left that in Edinburgh. I don't want to leave here, Adam. I'm not going back to Edinburgh.'

'Where does that leave us?'

She puts her hand to his face. 'Wherever you want it.'

'I love you, Georgia.' He feels an immense need for her, and an inward weightlessness, as if he is floating on an enormous bubble of exhilaration. Adam wraps his arms around Georgia and is intoxicated by the smell of her hair.

She lifts her eyes to his face and she knows no matter what happens, he will always be there for her. She thinks she knew it, the moment she met him.

Chapter 54

An Olive Branch

Georgia is propped up by an elbow, lying on her side and watching him sleep. The curls of hair on his chest rise and fall with his shallow breaths. Adam's eyelashes flicker, like an insect's wings, and she wonders if he is dreaming.

Georgia slides from the sheets and he stirs, moving onto his side.

Georgia takes a shower, cleans her teeth, and wraps a fresh towel around her. When she returns to the bedroom, Adam is awake.

'You're up early. Did you sleep all right?'

'Yes, I did. I'm just excited, that's all.' Georgia hears the elation in her voice. 'What do you think I should wear?'

'Something casual, not too dressy.'

'What if she is dressed up, she looks glamorous in the photograph. She probably dresses like that all the time. I'll wear a dress, I think.'

Adam props a pillow against the headrest and sits up, observing her.'

Georgia is looking at the photograph of her sister. Adam watches her excited face, and he feels happy for her.

'I feel so nervous. I don't think I'll be able to eat breakfast.'

'Have toast, at least.' Adam says.

'You're probably right. I don't want to feel sick.'

'Good. I'll make some toast once I get dressed.'

Georgia looks at the photograph again and feels great relief. Theresa was the go-between. She made it all possible. Georgia thinks of what it must have cost Theresa to tell Pavlina, after all these years, of the sister she did not know existed.

Fear had risen in Theresa like bile. Her vulnerability was a sacrifice she was willing to make. In baring the truth, there were no more secrets. She had felt the curse of their erosive effect on her mind and soul for decades. There could be no going back now.

Theresa arranged to meet Pavlina on one of her visits to Corfu. As an adult, Pavlina was wealthy in her own right. Although she inherited Stelios' estate, Pavlina studied interior design in London, returning to Athens, where her reputation grew as did her company amongst the city's business and social elite, decorating and furnishing their villas and holiday homes.

It was not unusual for Theresa and Pavlina to meet during her visits to Corfu. Over the years, when times were hard, Pavlina would give Theresa an envelope with money in it and she always bought gifts at Christmas and name days. Once, Pavlina paid for a private clinic in Athens for Theresa, who needed a cardiac bypass, and Pavlina was insistent she should pay for the best private care in Greece for her mother.

Theresa's secret had been suppressed for so long that, once shared, the outpouring of relief she experienced came as a surprise. She spoke of the detail, the twists, and turns and Pavlina listened without interrupting. Apart from her relief, Theresa was prepared for Pavlina to despise her. She paused to let the information sink in, but they sat in silence for a long time; to Theresa, it seemed an eternity.

Finally, Pavlina said, very deliberately, 'I want to meet Georgia, but I have questions I need answering.'

Theresa explained. Since Emily had kept the real identity of her father from Georgia, it had put Theresa in an unthinkable position. Even if she wanted to tell Pavlina she had a sister, how could she? Theresa would have risked Pavlina wanting to meet her sister; it would have been impossible. Over the years, she had many discussions with Emily on the matter and they decided, right or wrong, throughout the years, to let it lie.

That all changed the day Georgia read the diary, and Theresa knew it would only be a matter of time before Georgia discovered the truth about her past. Neither Emily nor Theresa could have foreseen such an outcome and, if they had, Theresa was sure they would have acted differently. And now there is compromise and acceptance. Theresa is no longer the guardian of the secret. It has grown a life of its own, and she has had no choice but to allow it to thrive and accept its unnerving consequences. And now, she wishes she could share this burden with Emily but she is alone, an old woman, facing the decisions of the past.

She has been offered an olive tree, but she doesn't know what the branches look like, not yet. That will depend on Georgia and Pavlina.

Chapter 55

From the Darkness and into their Light

Georgia waits patiently. She stands there looking at the sea and she thinks of the impending meeting ahead; she feels more vulnerable and uncertain than she has ever felt in her entire life. Georgia closes her eyes and wishes her mother was with her, to witness this meeting. She can see her mother's smile and hear the timbre of her voice, but then the image slips away. When she opens her eyes, Georgia feels optimism, a determination that, maybe today, the events of the past will eventually get put right. For decades, what was broken will today have the chance to begin a process of healing.

She walks to the small wall at the edge of the patio and sits between the two olive trees, looking out onto the garden and, further on, to the house.

She thinks of the time she found the diary in the attic and opened its first page, a moment that changed her life.

From the corner of her eye she can see the vegetable garden, now neatly fenced. It has a new addition to it, a small trough that stands just outside the gate and in it, Georgia places a handful of vegetables every other day so that Ellen's goats can feed. Ellen always waves a greeting and smiles at Georgia, whenever Georgia is in the garden; the formidable Elena and Georgia have abandoned their feud since Dylan's safe return.

It is hot and airless; Georgia opens the umbrella so that it shades the seats. She raises her hand to her hair and places a stray hair behind her ear. She is already adjusting to the knowledge she has a sister, her mind has accommodated that fact, but she feels unprepared for the reality of it.

Georgia had debated where they should meet. Here at the house, Theresa's house or somewhere neutral like Corfu Town? It was Theresa who suggested meeting at the village church and visiting Stelios' grave.

'Wouldn't that be perfect, his two daughters visiting him together for the first time?' And so it was agreed. She breathes deeply to calm herself; it is time.

Georgia is trembling as she nears the church doors. She rests her hand on the church wall and tries to gather herself, to compose a sense of conviction to see this through.

Inside, the church is cool, the pews empty. The altar is awash in gold-framed icons, "*windows into heaven*", as the Greek Orthodox Church refers to them. Around the church, candle stands sit in front of various icons and, as Georgia turns her head, she can see the figure of a woman, lighting a candle; she then bends, kisses the icon, and then makes the sign of the cross. Georgia stands very still. She hesitates, not wanting to interrupt this ritual. Georgia has seen it many times before in the churches she has visited but this time the act seems more poignant. It feels as if Georgia has interrupted an intimate and personal moment she is not meant to witness.

'Pavlina?'

She turns and they hold each other's gaze. Georgia's palms are damp and her mouth is dry.

'Georgia?'

'Yes.'

Pavlina's hair flows down her back, like her mother's and Georgia can see the resemblance. Just like the photograph, Pavlina is attractive in real life. An arresting face, she has Theresa's mouth, and shallow wrinkles around her eyes; there is no mistaking the likeness. Georgia feels self-conscious of her own looks and wonders what Pavlina thinks of her. Georgia has tied her hair back and now thinks of it as a mistake.

There is a hesitation in them both before they hug, awkwardly at first, before relaxing into their embrace. They hold on to each other, each unwilling to let the other go now they are together and, when they do, a tear rolls down Georgia's cheek, and Pavlina reaches out and brushes it away. Georgia regains her composure and fears it will not last. Pavlina hands her a lace-edged handkerchief.

'Thank you, I promised myself I wouldn't.'

'I might ask for it back.' Pavlina smiles, as her eyes brim with tears. 'You are just how I imagined.' Pavlina says.

'Am I?'

'Yes. Theresa said you looked like your mother. She showed me a photograph of her.'

'She did? I had no idea.'

'Yes. I asked. I was curious to know. Theresa said my father loved her very much.'

'Have you any memories of him?'

'Some, but not much. I was too young.'

'Yes, I suppose.' Georgia runs her palm over her dress. 'I wasn't sure what to wear today; somehow it seemed important, but not now.'

'You look lovely, you wear it well. I have a similar dress.'

'You remind me of Theresa when she was younger.'

'You have known her most of your life.'

'Yes, for as long as I can remember. She is part of my family.'

'I wish I knew your mother.'

'She knew about you. I don't know if she met you when you were younger, but obviously not as an adult.'

'No.'

'Are you married? Do you have children?' Georgia asks.

'A long time ago, but not now; no children, unfortunately. You have a son, Dylan.'

'Yes, he is fourteen.'

'I'd love to meet him.'

'Maybe you could come to the house… for dinner sometime.'

'I'd like that.' She says genuinely. 'Theresa told me about your husband, I'm sorry.' Pavlina touches Georgia's arm.

'It's ok… it had been over between us long before that.'

'We must have the same taste in husbands… maybe it's a sister thing.' They both laugh, where before there was a palpable tension in the air. This breaks the ice between them.

They both smile and begin to relax in each other's company.

'Tell me about yourself.' Pavlina asks. 'I want to know everything.'

'Everything?'

'The short version will do for now.'

They speak for a while, in the silence of the church amongst the yellow flicker of the candles, and the icons looking down on them. As Georgia talks, there is a stillness about Pavlina, and she listens intently as if she is a vessel and Georgia's words are pouring into her.

When Georgia is finished, they leave the church, and as they walk to the graveyard Georgia feels light-headed and covers her eyes from the sun's glare. She reaches into her bag and puts on sunglasses. Georgia looks at Pavlina. There is a shine along her dark hair, and her skin glows in the afternoon light. Pavlina walks with an elegant and straight posture, and Georgia notes Pavlina is at least two inches taller than she is, even in their flat shoes.

In the graveyard, they pass an old man tending to flowers. It is then that Georgia notices the flowers in Pavlina's hand.

'I didn't bring flowers,' she says sadly.

'These are from both of us. Don't worry, it's a habit of mine.'

When they come to the graveside, Pavlina holds Georgia's hand, and she brings it to the flowers and says, 'We'll both give the flowers to our father.'

Once the flowers are laid, Georgia holds Pavlina around the waist and they stand in silence with their own thoughts. Georgia thinks of the photographs Theresa gave her, and how happy her mother and Stelios were. She wonders what her mother would have thought about all of this and when Georgia thinks of the last few days she is astonished at how quickly events have progressed and how they are ending here, with the two of them standing together as sisters at their father's grave.

She has no memory of her father, just a few pictures. The images of them fill her mind and make her chest tighten, her heart quickens, and she draws in a quick breath; the burning sensation that fills her throat wants to escape. She struggles to keep it at bay.

The past has relinquished its hold on her. It had raised many questions, but with the answers, her uncertainty recedes. A new beginning awaits her, one to be shared with those she loves. And that is the meaning she takes from all of this; to live each moment as if it were her last with those that touch her life, the ones she loves, for they have taken her from the darkness and into their light.

The End

Get the FREE novella, Heartland, by Dougie McHale. Click on the link below.

https://www.subscribepage.com/heartland

A note from the author

Thank you for taking the time to read The Boy Who Hugs Trees. If you enjoyed it, please consider telling your friends or posting a short review. Just click this link http://amzn.to/2uemCnv scroll down to customer reviews and click on the button 'write a customer reveiw.' As an author, I love getting feedback from readers. Thank you for your kind consideration.

If you'd like to be first to know about any of my books, please visit me on my website and sign up for occasional updates about new releases and book promotions. I'd love to hear from you:

**Visit my website

http://www.dougiemchale.com

**Like me on Facebook

https://www.facebook.com/www.dougiemchale

**Follow me on Twitter

https://twitter.com/dougiemchale

The Girl In The Portrait

A novel by Dougie McHale

A story of the secrets we keep, and the power of forgiveness to heal even the most damaged souls.

London, 1905, The Quartet, a group of classical musicians are about to embark on a tour of Greece. When a celebrated artist paints The Quartet's portrait, no one foresees the drama that is to follow.

2016, in a small village on the coast of Fife, Mark tries to escape his past. When the woman he once loved, Abriana, unexpectedly contacts him, he accepts her offer to travel to Zakynthos and help her uncover the mystery of the heir to the portrait.

Abriana is a woman with a past she is determined to confront, at all costs. Forced to come to terms with the nature of love and betrayal, Mark discovers that the portrait's secret is about to play out its final episode.

**Buy From Amazon UK **Buy From: Amazon USA

The Homecoming

A novel by Dougie McHale

It only takes a second to change a life…

Louis Satriani, a successful architect, has a perfect life - or so he thinks, until he finds out his partner is having an affair. Distraught, he abandons his life and embarks on a journey that will take him through the landscapes of Greece and into a family's hidden past…

Maria Nasiakos, a young attractive tour guide, living on the Greek island of Zakynthos, feels that life is passing her by. When she meets Louis, a decision is made that will change both their lives forever…

Forced to confront past love and betrayal, Louis has to choose between his heart and head. As he unravels the truth about the extraordinary past of Maria's mother, can their love survive life changing events and the unfolding of a secret that can only be resolved by a homecoming?

** Buy From: Amazon UK ** Amazon USA

Excerpt from The Homecoming

Prologue

1941

The sky is lacquered in milky clouds and a watery sun. They amble along a farm track bordered by hedgerows, birdsong accompanies their progress. He frantically flaps his hand around his head, irritated by the continuous drone.

'The bees are attracted to your brylcream.' She grins. She pulls her hand along a grass stem and rubs the dislodged seeds between her fingers.

'We're going to France soon.'

'When are you going?' A slight panic rises in her voice.

'In a few days; the lads are saying that it'll be over in six months.'

'Six months is still a long time,' she says with a tremor of anxiety.

'It will go by quickly enough. Before you know it, I'll be back home. We were told yesterday. Our basic training is over now, and once our leave is finished, we're off to France.'

Her heart begins to pound. He burns with excitement.

'I've never been to France. Ayr is the furthest I've been from home. I went there on holiday one summer when I was still at school. It rained every day.' He laughs.

She looks at him seriously. 'This won't be a holiday. You're going to war. This isn't a game you're playing.'

'I've been well trained. It's not as if we don't know what we're doing,' he says, offended by her accusation.

'I'm sorry,' she placates. 'It's just that my mind's been occupied lately. I was going to wait awhile longer before I told you, but it seems I don't have the luxury of time now.'

'Tell me what?' He frowns, still recoiling from her rebuke.

She takes a deep breath, reaches out and takes his hand.

'I'm pregnant. I've already been to see the doctor.'

His eyes widen. 'You're having a baby. You're having a baby,' he repeats.

'That's what it means.' She smiles.

He pulls her towards him. 'Have you told your mum and dad?' There is a slight panic in his voice.

She shakes her head. 'No, not yet. I'm dreading it?' She feels her heart sink.

'They'll have to be told. But you can't do it on your own. I'll be there with you. We'll need to do it soon.'

'It's all happening too quickly. I haven't even got used to the idea myself. A baby... me.'

He holds her face in his hands. 'You'll make a wonderful mum and when I get back from this war, we'll get married and be a family.'

'You'd better come back to me Robert Williams.'

He kisses her forehead. 'All the wars in the world won't keep me from you.'

***

A determined concentration crosses the doctor's face as he stares with intent at the protruding mound of matted hair that glistens between the girl's trembling legs. He has rolled the sleeves of his white shirt above the elbow, yet speckles of blood stain the fabric, like paint flicked from a brush.

'One more push lass that should do it,' he encourages through tobacco-stained teeth. It is the deliverance of a prayer, not a fact.

Flickering candles illuminate the blackness of another power cut in a soft light that splays a dance of elongated shadows across the wall. Ice cold air seeps through the window frame and floats over the small room. The doctor feels it on the back of his neck like breath whispered against his skin. Her skin, coated in sweat is flushed, apple red, in contrast to the white nightdress crumpled and creased across her thighs.

Huddled in murmured prayer, two tenebrous figures lurk in the corner. Irritated, the doctor looks over his shoulder.

'Get me a towel,' he barks and adds impatiently.

'Quickly.'

The contractions seem endless, the involuntary waves that move inside her are a constant and painful reminder that the life within is eager to escape its confines.

When it is over, she is delicately placed on her mother's chest.

From the shadows, they move, and like thieves snatch the baby from her.

'The necklace,' she pleads.

'Don't worry my dear I'll see to it.' The doctor's words are soft, apologetic and heavy with shame.

Edinburgh 2002

Two Seconds to Steal a Lifetime.

Louis ran through sheets of rain, regretting his decision not to have hailed one of the ubiquitous black taxis that patrolled Edinburgh's George Street, now conspicuous by their absence.

His fingers, wet and numb, clenched the collar of his coat. He cursed his attempt to stem the flow of irritant droplets staining his shirt in damp dark patches and moulding the cold material uncomfortably to his chest.

Escaping the constant deluge, he finally entered the warm hallway with an involuntary shiver. Rainwater dripped from him, forming globular beads on the floor. A sudden stillness settled around him, he felt tired and quickly removed his drenched jacket with a welcome relief.

Louis had enjoyed a few drinks with work colleagues in a city bar, and now his taste buds stirred for more. In the kitchen, he plucked a beer from the refrigerator. He savoured the cold sensation as it caressed his throat and wondered why the first drink from a bottle was always the best.

It took a few moments for the contours and shapes of accustomed objects to gradually unfold, emerging from the darkness, as the refrigerator's thrum washed over him, reminding him, as it always did, of the purring of a contented cat.

He placed the half-drained bottle on a work surface and slid his feet from the confines of his shoes, a release that enabled him to curl and stretch his chilled toes. He considered making something to eat. Emma would be asleep, and the satisfying appeal of sliding beneath the sheets, and feeling the warmth of her body against his skin, pulled him towards the bedroom. The door stood ajar. Revelling in anticipation he peered through the dull light. Gently, he pushed the door which protested with a tired creak.

The crisp white sheet provocatively rose, like a solitary hill, shrouding the bed, and sparing his eyes, however, the emanating sounds were not as conducing. The sheet slid from entwined bodies, exposing their nakedness. Louis felt himself drowning as if rushing water had engulfed his lungs, stealing his words of reprisal with involuntary gulps for air. He stared at them incomprehensively paralysed.

Emma lifted her head. 'Oh shit, Louis… I'm sorry.'

The words hang in the air, taunting him. Instinctively she covered herself and her shame. His world suddenly stopped upon its axis. This kind of thing did not happen to him, to Emma, and then a profound rage grasped him, multiplying in his mind, electrifying every nerve and sense, urging him to tear the sheet from her.

He moved into the room, a demented animal, and his life of intricacy and detail, the life he identified as his own was ripped from him, it ceased to exist. Two seconds to steal a lifetime.

About the author

In a past life, Dougie has been a dockyard worker, student, musician, and songwriter, playing in several bands, performing live and recording music. Dougie lives in Dunfermline, Fife, with his wife, teenage daughter, older son and golden retriever.

The Boy Who Hugs Trees is his second novel, inspired by a love of all things Greek, her islands, people, landscapes, sea, light, and ambience all of which are important themes and symbols in his writing.

Printed in Great Britain
by Amazon

26348234R00175